S

Book 1 of P

By Michael Sliter

Dear Nils,

Enjoy this book
with a cup of tea
Some fish and
chips!

Mike

For Madeline, my little dragyn

Contents

Map

ARDIA

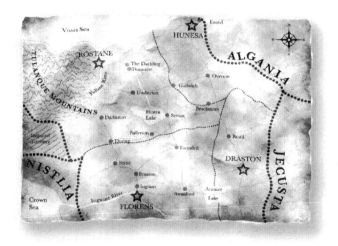

Legend

Duchy Capital

☆

Duchy Border

....

Country Border

●●●●●●●●●●●

Chapter 1

Fenrir took a last long pull of the cheap stout and shoved his pewter mug across the bar with some reluctance. He'd probably had five or six pints of the horrendous stuff over the past couple of hours, but he deserved a bit of fortification.

It was stressful work, after all, taking a man's finger.

The former guardsman slapped down a few yets and left the dingy little tavern without a word. In a town as small as Umberton, Fenrir couldn't escape without notice, though; the wandering eyes of the locals followed him out the door. A traveler–especially a big man draped in relatively fine, dark clothing–was inevitably an object of curiosity to the local bumpkinry. But, it didn't matter. After this evening, he would be out of this piss-poor place. And, a few days on, he would be back in the comforting walls of Rostane, his home, and arguably the greatest city in Ardia.

Fenrir strode further out into the inky darkness of the evening, moving stiffly along the hard-packed dirt road. His right knee was even tighter than usual, and he grimaced as the twenty-year-old ache loosened, one painful step at a time. The lingering winter chill certainly didn't help matters, as the soreness was always worse in the cold.

He spat the bitter taste of beer onto the ground and cursed at the squalor of this place. Umberton was barely more than a village—a gathering of a few hundred loggers, laborers, and the odd artisans. During the day, the place was surprisingly colorful. In fact, the town practically glittered with crimson, most of the building facades highlighting the only resource that allowed this place to even be a speck on a map: Arbutus wood. The Arbutus tree only grew in this region, something about the soil making it flourish. The Yetranians said that this region had formerly been ashlands, earth devastated during a battle of the gods in times long past, with the bodies of the dead giving the land a strange, sanguine fertility. Superstitious nonsense, of course, like most Yetranian religious prattle. Regardless, products made from the twisted, blood-hued tree were incredibly desirable among the rich and notable. They sold for small fortunes in the Ardia's major cities and countries beyond, though apparently none of that trickled back to Umberton itself.

In Fenrir's experience, the people who did the hardest labor rarely saw the best rewards.

He pulled his collar tighter around his neck and began to pick his way down the road more quickly, which was a more difficult task than it seemed. Unlike Rostane, which in the evening shined nearly as bright as day thanks to modern gas lamps and cleverly-placed mirrors, Umberton was almost completely dark now, the waning moons obscured by meandering clouds. Lamps and torches lit the entrances to the few red-faced taverns, but the scant light was swallowed by the night before illuminating the main throughway in any meaningful sense.

This was fine from a practical standpoint. Fenrir didn't exactly want to announce his presence to any wandering Umbertonians. Nonetheless, the darkness did pose a few problems—namely, the mounds of donkey and horse shit, as well as the occasional pothole that littered the well-used road—so Fenrir wound his way down the street carefully, avoiding these obstacles as best he could. If it hadn't been dark, Fenrir knew he would look completely ridiculous, a broad, muscular man mincing his steps and shuffling around even the smallest of impediments. However, necessity was necessity. Tripping and twisting his already weak knee would make this job immeasurably more difficult. Even worse would be falling in the waste ditch, an eight-foot deep crevasse of putridity running along the south side of the road. The god of stench embodied in a layer of runoff, night soil, assorted trash, and Ultner knew what else. Umberton was a shithole, literally and figuratively.

7

After a quarter hour-long awkward dance down the center of Umberton, Fenrir ducked into a side lane, moving toward the large, two-story house that he had scouted out earlier in the day. The light shining through the glass-paned windows–a lavish luxury in a place like this–showed that his date for the evening was, in fact, awaiting his courtship.

Fenrir allowed himself a moment's rest, leaning down to tighten the straps on the leather support brace he wore on his knee. A friend of his, a physician, had designed and created it especially for Fenrir. It was, in many ways, one of the most important tools of Fenrir's trade. Sending a silent thanks to Martis Aieres (who would undoubtedly disapprove of his current task), Fenrir took a quick, fiery sip from his silver flask and continued toward the house.

As he approached the front door, Fenrir paused, sucked at his teeth, and swallowed. He considered himself neither a coward nor a brave man. Just a practical man who did what was needed, when it was needed. Of course, what was needed did not always align with, say, the law. But this was a world where men needed to do the occasional unsavory thing to keep ahead, and Fenrir was willing to do that thing. So, here he was.

He took a deep breath and forced himself to release it slowly. After a pregnant moment, Fenrir stepped onto the wooden patio of the house and, abruptly, felt his consciousness ripped from his body in a dizzying maelstrom of flashing colors. When the disorienting experience faded, as it always did, Fenrir could see himself from a distance—as if he were hovering around his body, a spirit attached by an ethereal, binding leash. He was able to observe and think and ruminate, but unable to control his body's physical actions.

It was confusing as Pandemonium, whenever this fission occurred. Phantom-Fenrir, watching his Body-Fenrir do the hard work while his consciousness simply observed from afar. Fenrir had never been able to discern a pattern in the timing of these manifestations. It had happened for the first time when he was about fifteen. He had been fighting with his brothers, which was a fairly routine occurrence. Yet, somehow, that day must have been different because, abruptly, Fenrir had seen the quarrel from above, and been watching as blood flowed as never before in a fraternal conflict. It had been terrifying, with his mind straining and screaming from above while his body struggled below.

But that had been decades ago. Now, his Phantom emerged as a matter of course. He'd never known it to happen to anyone else, though it wasn't as if he brought up the oddity in polite conversation. Anything hinting at the unknown or the arcane in the inflexibly superstitious, Yetranian-heavy Ardia was a quick path to a knife in the dark.

Besides, this particular ability wasn't worth bragging about. It was fucking useless.

Phantom-Fenrir saw Body-Fenrir standing before the rich Arbutus wood door of his target's two-story home. He thought that he cut a rather intimidating figure in his tar-black shirt and dark trousers, a deep brown cloak wrapped about his frame. Standing six feet tall, and with the broad chest and the sinewy arms of a man who had spent his entire life training with weapons, Fenrir could understand why he was perfectly-suited to his current line of work. Well, near perfectly. His past failures weren't worth considering in this moment.

He saw himself reach beneath his shirt and expose the heptagram medallion hanging around his neck. The sharp, seven-sided star—the symbol of The House, his current employer—was nearly impossible to handle without cutting oneself. Fenrir supposed such cuts were intended to be symbolic of opposing the powerful underground organization, but he tended not to overthink it. Leave philosophizing to the Scholars and Savants, he

9

figured. Leave the appendage gathering to him and the other enforcers.

Body-Fenrir tried the doorknob, finding the door unlocked and unbarred—a strangely fortuitous start to the venture. Fenrir's consciousness skipped ahead, fluttering through the doorway and along the ceiling like an impossibly fast spider. He saw himself enter the house and walk across the greeting room, tracking dirt and various excrements onto a decorative carpet. Apparently, he had stepped in some animal dung without realizing, or smelling, it. Phantom-Fenrir could see that his body was tense, and that his hand was resting on the hilt of the wickedly curved knife that was strapped to his belt. The first floor was barren; Fenrir did not see the quarry he was seeking, and so his body proceeded to the stairs leading to the second level. From Phantom-Fenrir's disembodied view, he thought that, if his body was attempting stealth, it was doing a hideously bad job. The floor was creaking, the buckles on his boots were jingling, and he occasionally bumped into furniture. Apparently, spending a few hours at a tavern was not the greatest of ideas when one's stealth needed to be more on par with that of a fox than an ox.

Regardless, the stairway was the only exit from the second story, so even if the occupant had fair warning, there would be no escape. Body-Fenrir stomped up the stairs, clearly abandoning any pretense of covertness. The stairs emptied into a large, brightly-lit chamber that constituted the entirety of the second floor. On one end of the room was a sleeping area comprised of one large bed that was flanked by two decoratively-carved end tables. Above the bed was a painting representing a scene that was commonly displayed in the heavily religious Ardia. A slender, bare-chested woman, her silvery-white hair covering the most desirable bits, was perched atop a rock, arms held high and apparently cleaving the crimson firmament, parting the skies and allowing pure light to sneak through. Men and women knelt nearby, cowering below the rock, giving obvious obeisance to the goddess, Yetra. Typical Yetranian dross.

On the other end of the chamber was an office area made up of a wide and solid wooden desk, bookshelves, and several ropey plants. Everything was made of Arbutus, hinting at the barely-restrained wealth of the owner. Atop the desk was a bronze Scales of Justice statue, the universal symbol of office of an adjudicator in Ardia.

Phantom-Fenrir could see himself approaching the desk. The man sitting behind it, who was obviously aware of Fenrir's presence, continued to pointedly ignore him, bending over a blue leather-bound book.

Body-Fenrir paused two feet back from the desk, arms crossed. He waited another moment. When the man turned a page in his book, Body-Fenrir pointedly cleared his throat.

"I knew that one of you filth would be here eventually," the man said, exhaustion weighting down his voice. Still, though, he did not look up.

"Filth? Filth is a term that should be reserved for men who do not fulfil their obligations, Adjudicator Frommis," Fenrir answered, his deep monotone filling the second story like the knoll of a funeral bell. "Filth is a term for men who take yets for services not rendered."

Martin Frommis slowly raised his head then, glaring at Fenrir with icy hatred. He was an older man, silver hair trimmed short and revealing a balding pate. Despite a slight hunch to his shoulders, though, he still appeared to be sound and wiry in the manner of a twisted, but strong, Arbutus tree. Frommis' eyes were still, too—unafraid. Fenrir supposed that the man had seen worse than a House enforcer. Years of adjudicating in a great city would give one perspective, after all… a bird's eye view into Pandemonium.

"You know I didn't have a choice. You *filth* offered coin. Coin you knew I needed to cover my daughter's dowry, so she could be married without the embarrassment of her father's tumble into poverty. My investments, everything I had saved, all lost thanks to a greedy, thieving banker." Frommis scrubbed at his lined forehead with one hand. "But, the evidence levelled against Pontz was too strong. Had I adjudicated in his favor, there would have been a riot; I would have been torn to shreds!"

Frommis continued to meet Fenrir's dispassionate gaze, a beta wolf challenging the pack leader.

"I don't know why you are trying to convince me." Body-Fenrir unfolded his arms, rolling his shoulders. Loosening his neck with a sharp pop. Frommis flinched at the sound. "Besides, you took the money, no? And here you are, living in the most expensive house in this shit town, rubbing in the fact that you took our money without fulfilling your promise. Tell me, did you even try?"

"I had no chance. Pontz was a clear murderer. He was caught covered in blood near the scene, laughing and jesting. He disemboweled the victim, you know. A young, pregnant woman! You people knew this was the situation. I tried to explain it!" Frommis continued to finger the oversized leather-bound book in front of him, his voice rising as he spoke.

"It was my understanding that you were paid to make that evidence disappear, to make the witnesses change or doubt their testimony. To find other witnesses to discredit this evidence. Whatever needed to be done. But, no matter. The House has decided to render the punishment, and I have no authority to override the words of my superiors," Fenrir noted with a careless shrug.

"But..."

"You waste your words, adjudicator."

Phantom-Fenrir, from his floating vantage, could see his body stepping forward. Could see himself reaching for Frommis' wrist, almost as if time had slowed. He could also see Frommis grasping for something under his book. His phantom self screamed a warning. Useless, he knew.

As Frommis began to extract the hidden dagger, Phantom-Fenrir thankfully saw his body anticipate the move. Before the dagger had even cleared the book, Fenrir snatched up the Scales of Justice statue and crushed Frommis' hand against the solid wood of the Arbutus table. Frommis screamed, dropping his weapon, and clutched the injured hand to his chest as he fell heavily back into his seat. Judging from the audible snapping he'd heard, the Scales had broken at least a couple of bones.

Fenrir couldn't decide if that was terribly fitting, or terribly ironic.

"Enough. You've had your payment. And look, I can return your money. I can give you more coin!" wheezed Frommis, breathing heavily, his face a mask of pain.

"You know it doesn't work that way, Frommis. The House always leaves its mark. Now, left or right?"

Phantom-Fenrir could hear his emotionless voice filling the chamber. By Ultner, he could be intimidating.

"Please, no… Please, please," whimpered Frommis, his earlier confidence as shattered as his hand. "You don't want to do this."

"Left. Or. Right?" Fenrir asked stoically, skirting the desk to take his place next to Frommis.

"Left, in the name of the Goddess! Left!" Frommis managed through his clenched teeth. The unbroken hand. This man either revelled in pain or he wasn't thinking clearly.

"Left it is."

Phantom-Fenrir saw himself step behind Frommis, pull out a knotted rag, and shove it into the man's slack mouth. Tying it snugly behind Frommis' head, Fenrir pulled out his curved, serrated knife with one hand and grabbed Frommis' left wrist with the other. Having had multiple tiny bones in his other hand broken, Frommis must have already been in true agony. Maybe too much pain to truly realize what was happening, as he barely resisted. Fenrir could see himself pushing Frommis' left hand flat against the desk, forcing the man's body forward. He wrapped the adjudicator's little finger into the palm then; he did not want to do any ancillary damage.

Fenrir rested his knife on the man's ring finger and began to apply pressure, to saw. A hush permeated the room, the sort of quiet that exists in the space between when a vase tumbles from a table and when it shatters on the floor. Or, just before a ship careens into a jagged collection of rocks during a storm.

Just then, in that gap of quiet, a voice called up from downstairs.

"Father? Father, are you home? The welcome room is a mess!"

Chapter 2

"Father? Are you upstairs? Seamus and I are here. Sorry we're so late!"

All at once, Fenrir's consciousness slammed into his body, hurtling through space in the course of a disorienting moment. His eyes burned as if they were infected, and he blinked confusedly at Frommis, trying to get his bearings. His knife had just bit into the skin of the adjudicator's ring finger, the clean, red line not yet bleeding. Fenrir drew the weapon back, and the serrated knife shook slightly in his hands, as if being held by an epileptic geezer.

Fenrir took a deep, settling breath, eyes darting between his victim and the stairway. How in the name of Yetra's tits had he forgotten to lock the door? This bastard adjudicator lived alone and rarely had visitors, but Fenrir still should have taken basic precautions. This was not going to end well.

"Martin? Is everything okay?" A deeper voice called from below. Seamus, evidently.

"Father? Are you proper? We are coming upstairs," shouted the high-pitched voice of the girl.

Frommis, the voice of his daughter sinking into his pain-addled mind, lost the vague look he'd had in his eyes and started to struggle to his feet. In response, Fenrir dropped Frommis' wrist and grabbed the broken hand, applying pressure, shutting down any escape attempts—pain is an excellent deterrent. As the retired adjudicator writhed in pain, his shouts muffled by the gag, Fenrir leaned in close and held up his knife in a steadying hand.

"Be still now, adjudicator, or this knife will find a home in your daughter's chest," he hissed. Frommis quieted abruptly with a whimper, the agony in his hand or Fenrir's empty threat finally bringing blessed silence.

Fenrir—enforcers in general--never killed on these jobs, per strict orders from the superiors in The House. Which was fine; he wasn't exactly a practiced, willing killer. In his former life, he'd been a guardsman in Rostane, tasked with the protection of the Plateau, the great fortress that rose above the city like a blocky, indifferent father. Counterintuitively, guard duty at the Plateau was one of the safest jobs in Rostane. There hadn't been a real war for decades, and blunted, half-edged swords were all that were used for drills or tourneys. No assassin would ever attempt those walls, so there'd been no need for Fenrir to be any sort of a killer.

So, he could fight his way out, but the knife wasn't an option lest he cause undue harm. He'd already fucked this up enough by being caught mid-mutilation. He'd rather not risk more ire from The House.

The windows were open; he could jump to the street and lose himself in the darkness. Fenrir ruled out the option nearly as soon as it occurred to him, though; with his knee, he would almost certainly just end up broken and thrashing in the street like a crippled dog, struck by a passing cart. His better bet was rushing by Frommis' daughter and son-in-law—Seamus sounded like the name of some scrawny farmer anyway—using the ancient art of surprise to his advantage. H could lose himself in the darkness and make his way back to *The Crooked Tree* where his horse was already saddled. He'd have to be careful since it was dark and the horse could easily break a leg, but better his horse's leg than his own.

But, he still needed the trophy for his superiors. To come back empty-handed, especially after raising this ruckus, would be dangerous or even fatal.

Frommis renewed his struggle, reflexively pulling back as Fenrir released his broken hand. Fenrir struck him a quick but forceful backhanded blow in the face to further disorient him, and then he again grabbed his left hand—the intact hand—and laid it flat against the Arbutus desk. Frommis was barely responsive, staring a dead man's stare and breathing wetly through his bloodied nose. Fenrir again leveled his blade against the ring finger, the bloody line from earlier as good as a sign saying "cut here." He began to saw, this time being less careful of the other fingers.

"Father! Father, what's happening? Seamus, come quickly! There is a man attacking father!" shouted Frommis' daughter, who had just topped the stairs into the upper chamber. Fenrir pushed his full weight into his knife just as Frommis jerked away from him, the enforcer's blade cutting all the way through the ring finger and nearly severing the middle finger, as well. Frommis was lost in pain now, staring at his mangled hand as Fenrir yanked at the ring finger, which had still been attached by a string of bloody skin. He shoved the finger into an inner pocket and re-sheathed his knife. The whole thing was a mess; Fenrir's hands were slick with blood and his fine clothes–dark though they were– were speckled with red. But, nothing to do about that now. He was much more concerned with getting out of this house and out of this gods-forsaken town.

Frommis' daughter—a doughy girl who had the most unfortunate features of her father—was still standing at the top of the stairs, stunned, as Fenrir began toward her. As he approached, a man, presumably Seamus, came up the last step. Seamus was a big man. By Ultner's cock, he was a very, *very* big man.

"Shit!" muttered Fenrir, noticing the telltale burns of a blacksmith's trade lacing the man's muscled forearms. Why couldn't this woman have married a nice, skinny farmer? Or a delicate wood carver? Or anyone other than this cursed giant? There was no going back now, though, and Fenrir lowered his shoulder as he closed the remaining distance to the blacksmith as quickly as possible. He crashed into the huge man, feeling like he had run into a plow horse. Luckily, he had enough momentum to knock the blacksmith back a foot or two, which was all that was needed. Fenrir and the surprised Seamus both crashed down the stairs, arms and legs flailing. Fenrir tried to stay on top of the man as they hit the landing on the first floor, and he was mostly successful, slamming into the giant's chest but then bouncing forward and clobbering his own head against the wall.

A high-pitched wailing filled Fenrir's ears. He first thought the noisome sound was his pounding head, but realized quickly that it was actually Frommis' daughter, shrieking like a mountain goat. Fenrir supposed he couldn't blame her.

He staggered unevenly to his feet, amazed his knee was intact but knowing that he needed to get out of the house. Fast. Looking back, he saw the giant lying at an awkward angle, unmoving. Definitely hurt, potentially dead. Shit. That could mean more trouble for him back in Rostane.

He threw caution aside and ran out the door and down the lane, back toward the main road—through the dung and the muck, praying he'd avoid any major divots or potholes. He could still hear the incessant howling of Frommis' daughter and now he could see lights bursting to life in nearby houses. And some additional shouting voices in the no-so-distant distance. Shit. Fenrir continued his sprint through the darkness and suddenly found himself falling into open air. The sensation lasted only a split second before he hit some foul-smelling water and waste. He had overshot the main road and fallen eight feet down, right into the sewage ditch.

It was abhorrent. The slime had splashed into his mouth, mixing with the blood from where he'd bitten his tongue in the fall. The awfulness of it filled every sense he had—could one "hear" disgustingness? It seemed so, when crud was wedged in one's ears.

He gagged and started vomiting, which made his head ache even more, but he also managed to get back to his feet, and was standing almost knee-deep in the vileness when he heard a gaggle of voices. He crouched low with the sound of them, trying to force down the impulse to again be violently sick.

"Head toward the adjudicator's house and figure out what's going on. It sounded like a goat was dying over there! We'll stay here and wait for Questa in case anyone is hurt," commanded a deep, male voice.

Listening from below, Fenrir had a sudden, perverse need to laugh hysterically–the girl really *had* sounded like a goat.

The footsteps moved off, presumably toward Frommis' house. Fenrir inched up the incline by fractions and peaked into the road. He could just make out what looked to be three men standing on the main road, looking toward the location of his terrible mishap. Now he'd never be able to get back to the inn and get his horse in time; once the townsfolk figured out what had happened, all of Umberton would be up in arms. Plus, he could see the dim light of lanterns in the distance, coming from the direction of the inn. His horse–his father's, rather–would have to be left behind. No loss there, at least. Darian de Trenton had horses to spare, and knowing that the old bastard would never get this stolen horse back brought Fenrir some mild pleasure.

The only escape route, then, was the one in which Fenrir was already mired, so he started to move slowly through the sewage ditch, trying to avoid slipping and splashing. Trying to ignore the unnamed substances rubbing against his legs and working their way into his boots, between his toes and under his nails.

He had successfully traversed about thirty yards when he slipped and went down, hard, to his good knee. Remaining crouched in the slop water, he could only hope that no one had heard his grunt and splash. Luckily, no call of alarm arose. The droning of cicadas and chirps of other night crawlers seemed to have created enough of an auditory cover.

Another twenty yards, and Fenrir could hear agitated shouting from behind him. A lot of shouting, with the words "Frommis," "fingers," "blood," and "Seamus" echoing through the night like the accusations of the damned. And meanwhile, he continued to move through the ditch toward the edge of town, a bit more quickly and a bit less quietly. Between the insect symphony and the outraged townsfolk, it seemed unlikely anyone would hear him. He needed to get some distance before Frommis' daughter was able to collect herself and explain what had happened, before they mobilized the militia or sent out a pitchfork mob.

Frommis' house, thankfully, was close to the fringes of the town, and the sewage ditch was becoming shallower. There were only a couple more houses on the opposite side of the main road before Fenrir would be out of town and safely cloaked by the night. From there, it would be easy to avoid capture until the morning—and by then, he should be well on his way back to Rostane. A three-or-four day walk, as long as he didn't take any detours.

As he finally climbed out of the ditch and snuck a glance over his shoulder, though, Fenrir could see many more lights in the distance—both lanterns and torches—some of them getting smaller, and some... getting bigger. A group was heading down the road right toward him. Apparently, it was time for him to take a detour into the long grass and subsequent Arbutus forests to the north. By Yetra's delicious tits, it wouldn't be a comfortable journey, but it was a necessary one.

Fenrir ran off, tendrils of shit-soaked hair striking his face like a dozen severed fingers.

Having been quite literally caked in shit and fleeing a torch-bearing mob, necessities like food and water didn't seem particularly important when Fenrir left Umberton. But now, reeking to the high Harmony, Fenrir found himself still stumbling through the forest hours later, the composite toll of the day's events having left him an exhausted, ravenous, stinking shell of humanity. To top it off, traveling cross-country through a forest at night had been exacting a price on his knee, which was aching more than his head at this point. And his head was no minor nuisance, either. In addition to the new lump on his skull, his hair was matted with a good deal of dried blood. It formed a rather macabre plaster when combined with the various bodily fluids that had also bathed his scalp.

Worse than the aches and pains, though, was the fact that he'd lost his little silver flask somewhere during his flight. Maybe it lay on the landing, near Seamus' body. Or, maybe it floated and bobbed about in the crevasse of filth that facilitated his escape. Either way, he'd had the thing for near five years, a gift from a lover. Sentimental value aside, it had been full of a Sestrian rum sharper than Ultner's pointed cock. And, Fenrir could have used a little prick right about now.

The only real upside to his situation was that it was starting to rain. The waste, blood, and excrement that had formed a pasty shell on his body were beginning to run off in rivulets. It would do little to combat the stench—*that* had sunk in too deep into his clothes and probably into his very pores—but it went a long way toward making Fenrir feel human again. He tried to also catch some rain in his mouth to wash away the awful, lingering taste, but he was largely unsuccessful.

Forests had the tendency to all look similar—trees and shrubs, sticks and rocks. Luckily, Fenrir had absorbed a great many seemingly useless bits of knowledge while standing guard in the Enlightenment, the Plateau's library. A visiting Savant had spent weeks educating wealthy merchants on the beauty of lunar navigation, how to use the twin moons to pinpoint directionality while traveling. The smaller blue Ummis and the larger white Phanos could be triangulated with the Crimson Star to pinpoint one's location. Fenrir didn't understand all of details, but in early spring, the positioning of the three—just visible through budding branches—put him traveling northwest.

As it turns out, being punished with Enlightenment guard duty had some benefits, after all. Considering the captain had punished him for drinking on the job, Fenrir supposed he could thank alcohol for bestowing him with this accidental knowledge. If only he had his godsdamned flask…

A cold, gray light was beginning to filter in from behind the clouds, heralding the coming of a miserable dawn. With it, Fenrir felt a sudden urge to sit for a while. Finding a relatively wide, straight tree, he collapsed with a deflating grunt. Then he winced as he straightened his bad knee, leaning his head tenderly against the lumpy bark behind him.

Unfortunately, resting forced Fenrir's tired mind to reflect on the mistakes of the last day. To say that this whole job had not gone as planned was perhaps the understatement of the year. Frommis had been documented as living alone and spending his evenings working late into the night, rarely having visitors. Fenrir was supposed to have been able to walk in, subdue the man, bind and gag him, and take the finger before casually strolling back to his horse and setting up camp a few miles down the road. Based on the plan, no one would be expected to find Frommis for a few days. Fenrir would have been back in Rostane by then.

Instead, he'd been attacked by his target and caused more injury than was necessary, breaking one of the adjudicator's hands and maybe even severing an extra finger from the other. The House was notorious for their calling card—removal of the ring finger for an initial offense. In that way, targets of The House were always clearly marked, and *everyone* knew what that mark meant. The four-fingered (as they were often called) had wronged someone important, had made some serious mistake. This person should be avoided, as they might either err again or continue to draw the wrong kind of attention. Being four-fingered could cost a man his career, a woman her social status. A low-born, four-fingered man might end up stabbed or dead, as it was notoriously bad luck to be in proximity with such a person.

There had even been stories of working-class men—laborers, porters, losing ring fingers as part of their dangerous work, and then intentionally having a second finger removed to avoid being mistaken as four-fingered.

Thinking of the mission's basic goal, Fenrir checked his inner pocket, fishing out Frommis' ring finger (luckily retained in his flight), letting the rain wash over the appendage to clean off the blood and the filth. It wasn't a clean cut; it was jagged and diagonal, just above the knuckle. Fenrir hadn't noticed that there was actually a ring still embracing the finger itself—a shining white gold ring adorned by a brilliant blue sapphire. Yetra's golden nipples, he wanted to pawn this ring, but somehow, his benefactor would know. And with him having bungled this job, he needed to keep the remainder of his expedition transparent and above-board. The valuable ring might even soothe sore feelings.

In his two years working for The House, this wasn't the first job that that he had botched. The other time, there'd been a woman, a servant at the Plateau, who was the target. The conventional understanding that The House only targeted people who had directly wronged them was not always true. Sometimes, The House—or someone contracting with The House—sent messages, with innocent people getting caught up in the mix. This servant, Emma Dran, had already been known to Fenrir. In fact, she'd been quite *intimately* known to him (a bit of a sore point with his now-ex wife). They had been lovers for years—at least, they had been before his disgrace at the Plateau, before his job had been unfairly stripped from him. Before Fenrir had taken up with The House.

Emma had been his first target of this nature, his previous work with The House having been primarily based around protection duty or an occasional shakedown for coin. Of course, when he'd been given his assignment, he hadn't known his mark was Emma. He'd just been given a vague description, a date, and a location. It was supposed to have been easy: take a finger from a serving girl who lives in a small room in the servants' quarters of the Plateau. The servants' quarters were not in the fortress itself. Rather, they were in the area behind the Plateau, directly accessible by a large wooden lift as well as the lower gate, which was set aside for servants' quarters, barracks, staging grounds, storage, and sundry other less glamorous purposes. All of the many services required to maintain the population and protection for a fortress housing at least three thousand souls, as well as a constant stream of visiting dignitaries and supplicants. Little Town, it was nicknamed.

Fenrir had had no problem accessing Little Town or the servants' quarters that night. There'd been almost no need for stealth, which was perfect, as Fenrir was without a clandestine nature. The yearly Yetranian Ascension celebration had been hosted at the Plateau that night, so only a few servants—those assigned to clean up after the great banquet—had been occupying the quarters. And even had anyone heard any noise from his target, none would have intervened. As it turned out, scandalous nobles frequented the servants' quarters and were often none-too-gentle with the women. Or, occasionally, the men.

The servants' quarters were endless hallways of near-identical rooms, differentiated only by combinations of letters and numbers. Navigation was easy, and Fenrir had found his target's room with no trouble. It may have been a trick of his memory, but the whole place was awash with the faint, familiar scent of citrus, zest of lemons and oranges. He had paused and leaned against the

24

stone doorway, pulling back the curtain just a bit. He remembered seeing a mass of red curls on the bed—the beautiful hair of his once-lover Emma. She was nearly ten years younger than him, and beautiful beyond belief. Emma was the personal handmaiden of one Lady Escamilla Breen, a powerful woman in Ardia who owned huge tracts of land, but was formally without title. Whenever 'Lady' Escamilla frequented the fortress, Emma was always at her side. Outside of this, Emma served among the general staff of the Plateau. Many nobles maintained staff in this way, as it reduced cost from their own coffers.

In all likelihood, one of Escamilla's male counterparts—irritated by her success despite her commoner blood—had contracted with The House to teach her a lesson. But, rather than strike at Escamilla directly (unlikely anyhow unless The House held their own grudge against the powerful lady), they'd decided to attack at her omnipresent handmaiden, expecting that a four-fingered servant would bring Escamilla shame.

Fenrir had watched Emma sleep for a long moment, recounting the nights that they had spent in each other's arms. In a room just like this, too, as Fenrir could hardly have brought Emma home to his wife. Gods, he'd loved this woman before him. Much more than the ill-tempered shrew he'd married to appease his father.

Fenrir had approached the sleeping Emma, grabbing a gag from an interior pocket. He had brushed back her hair, just so that he was able to make out her features in the dim light. He had stroked her cheek—Emma was ever a deep sleeper—fighting the urge to kiss her supple lips, to take her as he had so many times before. To leave with her, run from his shame at the Plateau, from his new life as an enforcer. The foolish thoughts of a younger man with hopes, dreams, and prospects.

Instead, his gentle touch shifted into a rough grab, forcing her mouth open and shoving in the gag. Emma had awaken then, desperately scrambling and flailing her limbs. Fenrir had climbed on top of her, using his weight to hold her down, managing to pin one of her arms with his knee. He had reached for his knife, planning on simply overpowering her and taking the finger. But just then, she had looked directly at his face and paused, ceasing her struggles. She had locked onto his eyes for a long moment, and he had simply restrained her, returning the look. Dear Yetra, he had actually started to tear up, so beautiful were her emerald eyes, so red were her curls. So... soft... were their memories together.

His heptagram had been dangling an inch from her face.

All at once, he had shoved her hand against a wooden end table, trying to isolate her ring finger and bringing down the heavy knife with all the force he could muster. As she'd screamed through the gag, he had seen his mistake—in his haste, he had severed three fingers and the upper part of Emma's hand. He'd released her hand as she screamed through her gag. Screamed and cried, her eyes squeezed shut as she writhed in pain. Then, she had opened her eyes long enough to look at the bloodied remains of her hand, just before mercifully losing consciousness.

Fenrir had taken her bedsheet, cut it into strips, and bound Emma's mutilated appendage as tightly as he could, trying to reduce the blood loss. He had sat on her bed at her side for several long minutes, his hand on the side of her face. Remembering. And then he had scooped up her ring finger, wrapping it in some cloth, and left the servants' quarters and Little Town, delivering the prize to his masters. They knew of his failure, of course, and he forfeited his pay and nearly his life. But, as always, he managed his way through the danger.

While recalling his failed exploits, Fenrir must have drifted off to sleep. He woke sometime in the late afternoon, every part of his body aching. Muscles long underused felt as if they were on fire as he dragged himself to his feet, and several joints creaked and popped in a rather alarming manner. It had stopped raining at some point during his unintended slumber, as the sun was now shining merrily through the newly-budding trees.

The cool temperature of early spring was, unfortunately, not conducive to drying his cloak and clothes. He was still damp, still smelling as sour as week-old trash.

With the sun well above the horizon, Fenrir was able to orient himself (although he still felt relatively dizzy from his uncomfortable slumber and aching skull). Luckily, he had been traveling in roughly the right direction, and he must have covered a good deal of ground. He didn't see a single Arbutus tree, and the oaks and pines had started to thin out. Fenrir knew this area: he should soon join up with the Hunesa Road, or one of the numerous, small tributary roads that would take him back to the Rostane Highway. With luck, he would be back in Rostane sometime in the next few days. In the meantime, he was bound to stumble across one of the dozens of villages and towns that dotted this region. Somewhere to find a meal and a change of clothes. He was going to burn these vile rags at his first opportunity.

The sun to his left, Fenrir set back out for home with a slight limp.

Chapter 3

The inn was surprisingly busy for this time of the evening, with every seat taken and even a few patrons resting—and drinking— on the floor. The Duckling and the Boat Inn was always a popular stopover for folks traveling between Hunesa and Rostane via the southern path, catering to those who preferred the road less traveled. The Hunesa Road, the more direct route between the two cities, tended to become quite congested in the early spring as a result of trade traffic. This in mind, many people were opting for the longer and bumpier, but significantly less crowded, path connecting the major cities… the road on which the Duckling fortuitously sat.

This translated to great business for the inn, which was famous for its duck eggs, a delicacy sourced from Dunmore Lake just to the south. It also translated to very sore feet for Merigold Hinter as she bobbed and weaved through the crowd, expertly balancing empty crockery and platters on extended arms. Having been on her feet all day, Meri was really starting to feel the fatigue. Despite the fact that she'd been serving food from breakfast until dinner, she had not had a chance to eat a single bite herself. And, dear Yetra, the Duckling was *hot*! Her long, nearly-white blonde hair, gathered low in a loose ponytail, was sticky with sweat, and errant pieces were clinging to her neck and ears. Her face—pale with a small nose, thin lips, and blue eyes that she thought were too far apart—was abnormally flushed with exertion and heat when she happened to glance in a mirror.

"Meri, get these over to the white table by the fireplace! Two men, two women," hollered Ragen from the kitchen window, raising his voice to be heard over the din of the crowd. Ragen was Merigold's father—as well as the owner, repairman, brewer, launderer, and cook at the Duckling. He had always had a lot of trouble delegating, and instead tended to take on the brunt of the work himself. Too much work, in Meri's opinion. He was in his late forties, quite fit from years of labor, but Meri occasionally saw him looking pale and breathing heavily, sometimes even when he wasn't straining himself. She often counseled him to retire—or at least take it easy—but of course he wouldn't listen.

A rugged man, probably a hunter, staggered into Meri as she was reaching for the platter, and she nearly lost her balance and tumbled into the group. Luckily, another man had caught her gently and placed her back on her feet.

"Sorry, sorry," the hunter mumbled, bowing his head to Meri and walking back toward a group of like-dressed men.

"Thank you, Farmer Murphy!" Merigold said, smiling brightly at the lanky fellow who'd saved her a few bruises.

"Of course, my dear," said Murphy, looking askance at Ragen before returning her smile. Ragen's face, of course, grinned right back, but Meri understood Murphy's hesitance. Ragen was fiercely protective of her.

A road inn could be a hard place for a woman to work, and particularly a woman with features as delicate as Merigold's. However, Meri rarely experienced the typical plight of a bar maiden; men generally left her alone. No pinching, no insults, and rarely even disrespect. Meri recalled once, when she was only sixteen, a traveler had smacked her behind, snagging her by the ponytail as he did so, calling her a *very* dirty name. Ragen had leaped through the kitchen window, knocking aside food and other patrons, a furious bull seeing only blood. He had rushed up, grabbed the traveler's shoulders, and fiercely punched him square in the nose. The man's face had disappeared into a spray of blood as he fell out of his chair. The man's companions—two rough-looking men—had both stood up and flanked her father. Ragen was fit, but he was not a tall man, and both men had been noticeably taller and bulkier. Nonetheless, Ragen had been in a scarcely-controlled rage. As the first man swung a fist at him, Ragen had simply absorbed the punch into the top of his skull

29

while his left arm caught the man right under the jaw, knocking him back into his chair. Ragen had turned, face red, eyes blazing with a single purpose… and found the third man already restrained by Meri's Uncle Emmet and another inn patron. It had taken obvious effort for Ragen to regain control of himself. His muscles had been tense as carbon steel, his teeth gritted, and his knuckles bleeding. Merigold had felt, for the first time, fear while looking at her father.

In the six years since then, Meri had experienced no problems with men. The Duckling saw travelers from all over the country— even from the neighboring Algania and Jecusta—and yet, somehow, they knew about the hands-off policy. Word must have spread quickly and internationally. Even on a busy night like tonight, no one thought to touch her. And that included Saren, a forager and mender from Dunmore who she fancied. Saren was here with some of his friends and, aside from one kiss months before, they had always been at arm's length.

Shaking off the fog of reminiscence, Meri grabbed the tray from Ragen, who gave her a weary smile in return. Four bowls of stew and a plate of seasoned duck eggs. No beer. She balanced the tray on one arm—dear Yetra, it was heavy! Or, more accurately, Meri was near exhausted.

Luckily, there was a cure for that. As Meri wove through the crowd, she *drew* from the patrons. Touching a man's hand here, a woman's arm there, she was able to draw a bit of energy and somewhat rejuvenate herself. This was always a tricky game, as it took effort to draw. She had to put in ten eggs to get a dozen. And she also had to be careful to draw just a bit from each person. Otherwise, they might notice. But, she *was* very good at the game after so many years of practice.

The experience was as refreshing as an icy drink of water in midsummer, as delectable as a bite of Florence Marsh's apple pie after a long service at the chapel, and as comforting as Ragen's hand on hers when she was sick. Drawing, simply put, was amazing. Feeling inestimably better, Meri made her way to the white table and dropped off the plate of food, her eyes barely taking note of the group. One of the men, though, trapped her with his strange voice.

"Thank you kindly, girl. I've heard tell of your duck eggs and could not pass through this region without sampling the delicacy," said the man, a smile evident in his voice. Meri stopped and appraised him, his accent piquing her interest. He seemed to be emphasizing the wrong syllables in many of his words, speaking very deliberately and yet also incorrectly. From his olive skin, it was clear that he was a foreigner, that he was not accustomed to speaking Ardian. Sestrian, maybe?

"Of course, good sir," said Meri, returning his smile kindly. The man was handsome in an unconventional way, she supposed. He was clean-shaven with a broad jaw and a strong nose. He had an evident cleft chin; the cleft was so long that it could have been a scar, in fact, but Meri thought it was natural. He was young, maybe even younger than she was. "I am happy that you decided to stop by our humble inn."

"My lady, it is certainly my pleasure," he responded, eyes gleaming with pleasure.

The man seemed to legitimately be having an excellent time. He whispered something to a lovely woman next to him, a pale brunette with boy-cut hair, who barked a strident laugh at his comment. The woman had such delicate features that, with her short hair, she had the appearance of a storybook pixie. Meri's eyes lingered on this beautiful woman for a long moment before turning back to the cleft-chinned man.

"If I might be so bold, good sir, from where do you hail? Your accent is very unique, and I am very interested in the world outside of Dunmore," she offered, touching the man's arm to get

31

his attention. The man drew back from her touch, though, the smile leaving his eyes if not his face.

"Oh, my dear. I have been traveling so long that I can hardly remember where I began. Algania, the Green Peninsula, Rafón, even places beyond the Crown Seas," he said, eying her warily. One of his companions, an unobtrusive man with a small scar splitting his eyebrow, nudged him. "If you would excuse us, my lady, we would like to partake in our fine food before it grows cold."

"Of course! I apologize for interrupting—I just hope that you enjoy your meal. Please let me know if you need anything more," said Merigold, not knowing what she'd done to upset the man or his companion. Perhaps, wherever he came from, you didn't ask questions about origins. Or, maybe she'd just misread the whole situation.

As she backed away through the crowd, she thought the unobtrusive man—his features average in all regards—gave her an appraising look. And, had he winked at her? Strange people. Regardless, she quickly forgot about the group as she collected empty dishes and rushed around the restaurant, still feeling renewed from her earlier drawing.

A few hours later, to Merigold's relief, the crowd had finally started to thin out. Several parties had retreated to their rooms for the evening and just a few stragglers were still enjoying crocks of beer. Ragen had been brewing his own beer of late, and there were a few folk from Dunmore and the surrounding communities who hung around until the keg was emptied every night. With their being regulars, Ragen tended to give them a discount, or even allowed for bartering. He was always very willing to trade,

32

though Meri often enough insisted that he only take yets. Too often, she felt like he was on the short end of some of these deals.

With only regulars in the Duckling at this point—Saren unfortunately not being among them—Meri finally had a chance to sit down and have some leftovers: stew and a small handful of duck eggs, which Meri actually refused to eat. She loved the little ducklings from Dunmore Lake. The lake, itself, was more of a swampy wetland, the perfect environment to attract thousands upon thousands of ducks every year. She always fed the ducklings bits of bread and other crumbs, and she felt so guilty that all of the eggs harvested could have been adorable little ducklings. Half the town made their living foraging duck eggs, though, and there were strict regulations against over-farming the nests. If a nest had ten eggs, a gatherer could take no more than five. Afterward, they had to leave a little red flag near the nest, indicating that it had already been farmed for the season. Meri knew that some gatherers over-farmed and would bury the nests, and she hated those people. Wiping out a family of adorable, fuzzy (if occasionally ornery) birds for just a few extra yets was intolerable. Unforgivable, so far as she was concerned.

As she was resting and eating in the kitchen, Ragen came by to sit near her. He seemed as healthy as a man in his twenties, displaying no hint of the weakness that Meri had seen more often of late, although his expression did look a bit more serious than usual.

"Long day today, my little flower," he said, rubbing at his eyes with the back of his hand. "You've been on your feet for most of it—how are you feeling?"

"I feel good, Papa! You know me—I can stand for days, if needed," said Merigold, smiling at Ragen. And she was mostly telling the truth. She was down to the dregs of what she had borrowed from the patrons, but the thick stew was filling her with warmth and energy.

"You are a bundle of energy, just like when you were little," said Ragen, his face creased into a fond smile. Her father's smile was rare and special, always seeming like a gift. It brought her a deeper warmth than either drawing from patrons or the stew.

"I wish I had half your energy, Papa. Though I do wish you would spend a few days away from the inn. Uncle Emmet can handle things. Maybe we could go together, see Rostane? I so want to see the Plateau." Small chance, for either Ragen taking some time off or her ever seeing the capital of the duchy, but Meri simply had to try. Perhaps she would wear him down one day.

"No, I could never do that with spring travel season just finding its stride. Now. Chapter of Errance, opening line of section eight?" Ragen queried, an eyebrow raised.

"Let's see… 'It is a poor man, indeed, who relishes idleness. Diligent hands ease the burden of others, and is that not truly Harmony?' Is that right?" Merigold could almost recite the entire *Book of Amorum*, the Yetranian holy text, but Errance was a dense read.

"Close enough, my flower."

"Still, you mustn't overdo it, Papa. Taking care of yourself isn't the same as idleness."

"You remind me of your mother when you talk like that." There was a sorrowful wisp of a smile on Ragen's face now, memories bright in his eyes although it had been nearly eight years since her mother had passed into Harmony.

When Merigold had been fourteen, she and her mother had fallen gravely ill. Her mother had passed away from the illness while Meri lay in a fever dream for months. Ragen had tended to her as if he were battling Ultner, himself. The folks of Dunmore often said that Ragen had beaten death in those days. They also said darker things—that Ragen had had a crazed look in his eyes, that he'd been willing to do anything to bring Meri back to life.

That he'd made a deal with dark forces. But, Meri had only heard whispers from time to time. Ragen was likely enough to beat senseless any man who voiced such accusations aloud.

Meri didn't actually remember anything from the time of her illness, however. Really, she only had impressions of all that had come before it—her childhood, her friends, even her mother. It filled her with guilt that she could scarcely recall the woman who'd birthed her, aside from some vague recollections of blonde hair, blue eyes, and a feeling of comfort. After Meri had recovered, she'd had to reassemble her life, and Ragen had been there for her, every step of the way. Rather than resenting Meri for surviving while Lilth—her mother—had passed on, Ragen loved her that much more for it. Clung to her, even. Maybe a little too hard.

"I wish I remembered Mother," Meri said. She heard a small movement, and then found herself embraced by her father. She snuggled in close, a sudden catch in her throat. Her father smelled of food, woodsmoke, and sweat. The smells of home.

"Meri, I know you worry about me," said Ragen, pulling back after a long minute and looking down at his hands. "I worry about you, too. More than you can know. I know that it can be hard here, at times, at the Duckling. I see you looking down the road, wondering what is out there. Talking to patrons, longing for stories of their travels. I tell you, my flower, things are good here. So many people do not have a safe place, a meal, their health."

"Papa…"

"You are safe, here, Meri. This is home, no matter what. It will always be here for you, as will I. Remember that, even if…" he drifted off, still not meeting her eyes.

Meri didn't know what was going on with Ragen this night. He was rarely this sentimental, and rarely this… forthcoming about his emotions. He was often so busy that they would go for days without saying more than a few words outside of "take this to the blue table," "it's your night to mop," and "be sure to pray before bed." She was comfortable with that. She'd never been much for talking. She liked to ask questions and let other people speak, to learn without having to really offer much in return. It seemed easier that way.

"Papa, of course this is my home! I love being here with you, working at the Duckling, seeing all of my friends from Dunmore and all of the interesting people who come by! I wouldn't trade it for the world," said Merigold gently, her most convincing voice ever at the ready. In reality, of course, she ached to see the world. Just being a stay-over in other people's lives wasn't enough for her. She loved seeing the different styles of clothes, all of the different colors of skins. Hearing the different languages and accents. Smelling the unique perfumes and scents over the reek of the road.

"Okay, my little flower. Just remember that I... Oh, looks like we have a late guest. Welcome, sir, to The Duckling and The Boat! You seem chilled—would you like a seat by the fire?" asked Ragen, noticing the man through the kitchen window. He rose from the table, leaving Meri with her cooling stew. Meri sat for another moment, took a final bite, and then followed Ragen back into the common room.

When Merigold saw the man, however, she paused for a moment. Ragen was showing him to the white table, the one nearest the fireplace. The man, limping slightly, was dressed in close-fitting, rough-spun clothes, the durable type worn by most farmers. They didn't seem to fit him, and not just because they were tight. The man had greasy brown-blonde hair hanging down to his jawline, maybe with a hint of gray at the temples. He was also a bit unshaven, with more obvious gray stemming from his chin and jawline. But, despite his dirty appearance, he was fairly handsome. This was something she would think of afterward, though. For now, she simply got a strange, almost visceral feeling

36

from him. Something from his eyes, maybe. Or the hunch of his shoulders. A feeling of… violence? Of regret?

Ragen, having gotten the man settled, gestured Meri over and placed his hand on her shoulder. He met the road-weary guest's eyes. "Meri here will wait on you this evening. We've put out the kitchen fire for tonight, but I believe we have some leftover venison stew that should still be warm. We also have bread, baked fresh this morning, and a handful of our famous spiced duck eggs."

Meri approached then, the unusual feeling she got from the stranger starting to subside. The man smiled at her—a charming smile, with teeth much whiter than his clothing would have hinted at. Most farmers, in her experience, had awful teeth.

"Greetings, good sir. As my father said, I'll be helping you this evening. Would you like any of the food that he mentioned? Or would you like to try some ale or whiskey? We might have some of my father's home brew left, if the locals over there haven't drained it," said Meri, gesturing at an increasingly boisterous group of Dunmorians she had known for years. "We also have beer imported from Hunesa and Draston. And maybe a bit from Algania, too."

"I'd love nothing more than a local ale and some of those famous eggs. In Rostane, we hear of your delicacy all the time. At the Plateau, in fact, I recall the eggs being imported from this very inn," said the man, his wide grin persisting despite his obvious weariness.

The Plateau? Odd for a man in farmer's clothes to know anything about the great fortress in the heart of Rostane. "Yes, I remember… My father went to take them himself, leaving me and my Uncle Emmet in charge here."

Meri recollected the time very well; it had been three or so years ago. She had begged and cajoled and bribed and cried to get

Ragen to take her along. She'd wanted so badly to see the fabled fortress, standing high and overlooking one of the biggest cities in Ardia—housing over two hundred thousand souls! She'd wanted to see the marketplaces, the docks, watch a play, devour some food that wasn't cooked by her or her father. But, Ragen hadn't budged. It had been a small victory she'd won, even getting him to allow her to even work those days with Uncle Emmet. He had originally planned to close down the inn entirely while traveling with some *hired* help.

"I would love to hear more about the Plateau, if I might be so bold. Let me get you an ale and get you some food, and I will return shortly," said Meri, giving him a curtsy. Sometimes, Ragen wouldn't mind if she sat and spoke with the customers— especially when the business was slow. He said it built customer loyalty, making them want to come back to the Duckling even if the road was a little bit longer. He was an excellent businessman in that way. He was always thinking ahead.

She left the man by the fire and went back to the kitchen. Ragen wasn't around. She guessed he had gone to compost the trash or get some extra wood from the shed. He was never gone for long, not until Uncle Emmet arrived for his midnight to mid-morning shift. She busied herself around the kitchen, filling a platter with the leftover stew (still surprisingly warm), some fresh rye bread, and the few remaining duck eggs. She found a bit of Ragen's homebrew left at the bottom of the keg then and filled up a crock.

As she picked up the platter and stepped toward the common room, a sudden dizziness fogged Meri's head and turned her legs to jelly, as if she had just spun around a dozen times and ran three miles. She collapsed into a chair—nearly losing the food and drink—dropping her head in her hands and waiting for the weakness to pass. This sometimes happened when she drew from patrons too much during a long day—she tended to crash once she wasn't able to draw more. It was a very particular type of fatigue.

Meri almost felt hungry now, but not in a way that could be sated with food. There was certainly an emptiness, though; her experience told her that she would feel better after she rested for a moment, and back to normal by morning.

Moments passed, as did the worst of the faintness.

Leaning back, Meri pulled back the hair that had come loose around her face, straightened it with her fingers, and re-bound her ponytail. She tweaked her blue sapphire earrings, small blue studs that seemed to shimmer constantly, at least as Meri saw them. They were a keepsake from her mother, and Meri never went without them. She had so few reminders of her mother in her life, and since her memory was so cloudy from the fever dream, she treasured her sapphire studs above all else.

Reminding herself that she only had to hold it together for an hour or so longer, and thinking of her bed upstairs (there was no way she was walking back to Dunmore tonight!), Meri again grabbed the platter she'd prepared for the traveler, leaving the kitchen. The man was sitting at the edge of his seat at the white table, his hands held up against the heat of the fire. She noticed that he was a muscular man with a broad chest and arms that strained at the tight fabric of his poorly-made shirt. Maybe it was just his rather imposing appearance that had given her that uncomfortable feeling earlier. Now, hunched in front of the fire, the man actually dripped with vulnerability—a street dog having finally found shelter for the night.

She set down the platter on the white table, startling him with the sound.

"Thanks, girl. I'm Fenrir. Fenrir de Trenton," he said expectantly. Meri had never heard the name before, but his tone suggested he felt it was important enough to merit recognition. Although he was dressed like a farmer and smelled worse than a sty, she could tell well enough that his clothes didn't accurately reflect his status. Something about the way that he spoke, the way that he held himself, suggested he was more than a simple farmer.

"It is lovely to meet you, good sir."

"Fenrir," he corrected.

"Fenrir, then. You can call me Merigold."

"Well, Merigold," he said with a wink. "Sit with me. Let me tell you of the Plateau and Rostane while I enjoy this delicious-smelling food. These eggs are as delectable as I remember."

Between bites, Fenrir began to tell her of the Plateau. And he painted quite the picture, as eloquent as a traveling bard. Meri could see herself standing at a window of the great fortress, wearing one of the colorful silk dresses typical of a noble lady. She was looking out over the city, seeing the red-brick roofs of residences, shops, and warehouses, smoke drifting lazily from chimneys. To one side, she could see the graceful Tulanque Mountains, impossibly high peaks cutting the clouds. To the other, the busy Fullane River was choked with boats and ships, moving between the docks and the sea, bringing in and sending out the many goods—textiles, beers, steel, precious metals—that were the lifeblood of Rostane.

Then, Meri could see herself at a ball in the expansive chambers of the Plateau, eating delicacies from around Ardia and beyond. She passed on the local duck eggs, of course, as she spoke with dignitaries from around the continent, speaking of politics and plays and music. She even saw herself dancing, the arms of a well-dressed, lithe nobleman... maybe a baron or a viscount... wrapped about her slim waist. People from all over watched her as she simply stared into the eyes of this beautiful, strong-jawed, well-groomed man. Interestingly, he looked like Saren—just a cleaner version. And Viscount Saren (she decided he was a viscount) couldn't look away from her. Despite all of the important courtiers and dignitaries in the room, the viscount only cared about Lady Merigold.

Meri was still listening to Fenrir, his tale of being the heroic, honorable guardsman floating at the fringes of her own fantasy. Something about fighting off assassins, protecting the old Duke Penton. Assassins didn't play much of a role in her own Plateau, a place where few folk could pass by Lady Merigold without bowing deeply and smiling at her attention. Sure, there was an armored guardsman here or there, but they were more decorative in nature. No, her Plateau was grand and beautiful and only filled with people who she wanted to see. In fact, it was filled with people who wanted to see her. She still responded to Fenrir with the appropriate social niceties, "yeses" and "Oh, tell me mores," but she also continued to drift dreamily through her own version of Rostane and the Plateau. And she loved it.

Soon, though, Meri realized she was actually drifting off to sleep. The weariness from the long day, the fatigue from drawing too much, and the hypnotizing voice of Fenrir were causing her eyelids to lower languorously, her shoulders to relax. Yet, she wanted to hear more. She wanted to hear of the city itself, of the markets and the plays. She wanted to see herself as Lady Merigold, strolling with her escort through Rostane, with crowds straining to see her over the heads of her retinue. She wanted to browse through the stalls and the shops, examining beautiful oddities from around the world.

As Fenrir spoke, his arm rested on the table just inches from hers. In fact, his hand was much closer to hers than she remembered. Curious. She shifted in her seat, touching his hand with the tips of her fingers, almost as if on accident. And she drew just a little bit from him—enough to keep her going for a few more minutes. Fenrir didn't appear to notice. Lost in her vision of Rostane, Meri drew some more... more than she'd intended. More than she realized. Enough to keep her fantasy going longer.

A sudden vivid image of tore into Meri's skull. Amidst fierce rain and illuminated by lightening, she was shattering someone's skull, with a... belaying pin? Blood sprayed into her eyes.

"What in the name of Ultner's cock?" exclaimed Fenrir in surprise, leaping away from her and knocking over the bench in doing so. He snatched at Merigold, his strong grip on her wrist, hurting her. She was too stunned to react. The pain in her wrist was Lady Merigold's. She had fallen while stepping out of her carriage, landing hard on her wrist. Was there blood on her hands? She felt suddenly terrified, weary, and even sad. Luckily, her retinue was there, helping her back to her feet.

"What did you do to me, you little bitch?"

Lady Merigold heard this hissed at her from the crowd of Rostanians. Wait! Through heavily lidded eyes, she saw a face, older and handsome, inches from hers. Meri wasn't in the market. She was in the common room. In the Duckling. She was staring into the blue eyes of a man she had only met an hour or two before, remembering his name was Fenrir. And he was hurting her.

Meri was about to say something just as a fist slammed into the back of Fenrir's head.

42

Chapter 4

Three days more found Fenrir approaching the southern gates of Rostane amidst a great deal of traffic and the setting of the sun. And he felt like shit.

After the innkeeper had hit him, he'd been carted a few miles down the road, in the wrong direction no less, and dumped in a ditch. This was a typical punishment for traveling drunks in small towns that either didn't have any holding cells or that just didn't want to bother detaining an itinerant inebriate. A peasant or farmer would cart the drunk halfway home and drop them on the side of the road. Surprisingly, those who'd taken him off hadn't robbed Fenrir of the little remaining money (or the human finger) that he'd been carrying, and his heptagram was still secreted in his boot. In fact, they had left him with a rather fresh loaf of wheat bread, which had been a surprising kindness.

He had awoken near morning and vomited up everything that he had eaten the night before. Actually, he must have become violently ill at some point earlier, because his peasant clothes, stolen from a clothing line on his journey from Umberton, were stained and reeking of rotten eggs. Weak as a malnourished dog, Fenrir had tried to cover some ground with the rising sun at his back, but he'd soon become sick again and had to pause until several minutes of dry-heaving had passed. And, by the gods, there'd been the sun to deal with. The sun had felt like it was melting his eyes, so bright it had been. Apparently, falling down the stairs and bashing one's skull, followed by having that same spot beaten in by a surprisingly strong innkeeper, was not conducive to a day of walking.

Fenrir had ended up having to crawl off the road and lay in a shady grove of apple trees for a time, trying to regain some semblance of health. He'd drifted in and out of sleep, not really noticing the passage of time, simply rolling to one side to relieve himself. He'd tried to eat some of the bread, as well as an immature, sour apple, but not been able to hold even that down. Fenrir had passed the next two days in a haze, lying amidst piss and vomit, staying out of sight of any passersby.

By the second evening, he'd been sitting up with his back against a tree, his shirt balled up behind his head to cushion the increasingly-swollen lump on his skull. With the sun thankfully hidden by the distant Tulanques, he'd finally been able to take in his surroundings and puzzle out his location. Luckily, thanks to guard duty in the atrium at the Plateau (where he had done little more than stare at a map of Ardia for hours on end), even a concussed Fenrir had the wherewithal to pinpoint his present location. As it had turned out, his lunar navigation—and daytime ambling—was not as precise as he had hoped; he had ended up near the tiny foraging village of Dunmore. Too far east. Planning on stopping at that gods-damned inn for a bite, Fenrir had instead found himself beaten and lugged toward Hunesa down a minor road, only recognizable to him now because of these apple orchards.

That evening, Fenrir had managed a few miles back toward Rostane, walking slowly to reduce his dizziness and nausea. He'd passed The Duckling and the Boat again, and briefly considered putting in another appearance. For a bed or revenge, he wasn't sure. Either way, given that just moving in a straight line had been enough of a challenge, he'd opted to trudge on, putting the inn about a mile behind him before falling asleep in the brush.

With the dawning of the next morning, Fenrir had found himself to be both still alive and actually able to tolerate the sun. He'd managed another mile or two, finally reaching the Hunesa Road. This time of the year, the road was busy, and he'd been able to convince a trader (with a couple of his remaining yets) to take him toward Rostane in the back of his cart. After a few hours of trundling through well-irrigated, rolling farmland, freshly plowed and smelling like cow shit, the trader had reached the Rostane Highway and decided to set up shop at the crossroads. He was selling a variety of aged cheeses and hard breads, and likely hoping to entice hungry travelers on their way in to, or out of, Rostane. Plus, if he managed to sell his entire stock outside of the city, he would be able to avoid the rather stringent gate tax.

After thanking the cheese trader, Fenrir had quickly found a clothing vendor. Many people had had the same idea as the helpful trader, and the crossroads had thus become a crowded, impromptu market. Fenrir had spent the bulk of his remaining yets on a new white, woolen shirt and black trousers, something better made than his tight, vomit-soaked peasant rags. Then, among the milling shoppers and traders, he had managed to find someone selling a nice, light broth to go with his remaining bread, bringing his money pouch down to one final yet, a bit of string, and a ball of lint. His queasy stomach had quieted a bit with his flavorless meal, though, and Fenrir had thus mustered enough energy to walk the last stretch to Rostane.

Now, Fenrir was approaching the southern gates—exhausted, nauseous, aching, and generally feeling like old trash. Not to mention nervous. At this point, his benefactor at The House would have been expecting him for days. And, given the type of organization The House was, his benefactor would likely already know about the better portion of his misadventures. By the gods, how had this happened? The first part, taking the finger from Frommis, probably killing a giant blacksmith, and inciting a mob in the town, was bad enough. But, getting lost in the woods and subsequent farmland (which he partially blamed on a likely concussion), being knocked unconscious by an innkeeper, and being discarded in a ditch—all that was an absolute embarrassment to The House. He would have loved to sic the proverbial dogs of this organization on that innkeeper, but then he would have had to admit what had happened, and that was something he could never do.

Frankly, Fenrir wasn't even sure what had led to his ignominious beating. He had been in the middle of flirting with that cute country bumpkin, a little beauty with blonde hair and blue eyes—her brand of beauty common enough in Ardia. Her rear, however, was uncommonly rare. Merigold, or Daffodil, or something like that. As was typical, he'd had her enthralled in his stories of Rostane and the Plateau. These country girls; they were so easy. He'd been able to tell that this girl was particularly engaged with the dancing and pageantry of the nobles, so he had focused on that. It had seemed to be going quite well, and he had been fairly sure he would be sharing her room, hopefully, for free. She wouldn't have been his first innkeeper's daughter. Then, she had touched him.

At first, Fenrir had felt a little flutter. That alone had been somewhat unusual for him. She was certainly not the first woman to reach out and touch him, and the place that she'd touched him was rather innocent, after all. But, she was young and beautiful and her touch was soft, almost accidental. As she had continued to rest her fingertips on his hand, he had felt... a wrongness. Like she was stealing something essential from him. He'd felt a pull—a gentle tug, really—and felt himself slipping away, bit by bit. It was possible that he'd just been exhausted, or that it had been a trick of his injury-addled mind, but he didn't think so. His reaction had been visceral and immediate, with him jumping up and grabbing the girl's hand. Moments later, he had found himself face-down against the table, his head exploding in pain and his eyes cloudy. He had managed to roll over, noting this his assailant was the innkeeper, before he'd lost consciousness.

Whatever had happened with that Merigold girl (definitely her name, he thought now), Fenrir was unlikely to ever find out. Assuming he survived his benefactor's inquisition, and kept his job and his skin, he'd never be going back to that inn. He'd hopefully never see that little chit again, or her surprisingly sturdy father. Fenrir had always followed the old adage "grudges are like whores; hold on too tightly and you'll catch an elbow to the nose." And, like whores, grudges were easier to forget when they were miles away.

Fenrir had finally reached the southern gate of Rostane, its imposing thirty-foot tall stone walls filling his field of vision, with only a few buildings visible behind the fortifications. In close proximity to the Tulanques, Rostane was a city of granite and marble, built to be permanent and imposing, if not visually appealing. The cobble streets were straight and well-planned, and the buildings blocky and practical like the great fortress that rose above the city, a towering island in a sea of beige, white, and burnt red. The Plateau was visible from anywhere in the city, so high did it rise above the houses and shops, the warehouses and manufactories. It was build atop the ruins of an ancient pyramidal structure, moss-and-ivy-covered ruins from a time long past. Few even realized this; they simply accepted the massive structure as the floating patriarch of the city, giving little thought to the foundation.

Those who were unfamiliar with the city might have found the entire sight to be beautiful. There was beauty in strength, after all.

But, like most of those who were raised in the city, Fenrir noticed none of this.

Above the gates rose two slender turrets, these being manned by guardsman who appeared imposing to unaware travelers. Fenrir knew better. Wall duty was typically reserved for new recruits, men who could barely swing a sword or a spear. Sure, in their armor and their green and gold wolf-emblazoned tabards, they had a dangerous look about them. But, they were likely numb with boredom and exhausted from standing all day in their heavy equipment, sun cooking them like turkeys in the oven. A child could probably knock them over with a wooden sword.

This was the main ingress into the city and, it being late afternoon, the line of foot traffic attempting entrance into the city was growing shorter. The guardsmen at the gate itself tended to be veterans, with some having actually seen battle. Never in Rostane itself, of course, but either in quelling minor tax-related rebellions or, more likely, border skirmishes with the mountain-dwelling Wasmer to the west. But Wasmer had been quiet for at least fifteen years, a tentative peace having been informally negotiated, with the veterans of the incursions being integrated back into regular service.

These veterans were exactly what was needed where money was involved, and a great deal of money was collected by duty officials at the southern gate. Trade being the major driver of commerce in Rostane, tariffs were imposed on nearly every imported good—hence the informal market square at the crossroads just a few miles south. Periodically, Little Duke Penton would sally forth some soldiers to break up the crossroads market, as he saw this as high thievery from Rostane and, as a result, from his own coffers. But, ultimately, it would always re-form like a boil on his ass.

"Name and reason for visit?" asked a bored, stocky guardsman, not bothering to look up from his register.

"De Trenton, to fuck your mother in her wrinkly asshole," replied Fenrir, grinning broadly.

"Well, you'd better bring a gallon of vinegar, because she'll need some cleaning first. Fen, I'd ask how you are doing, but it's pretty obvious. You look like a partially-drowned weasel who took a nap in shit," replied the guardsman, a hint of a wry smile curling one side of his mouth, wrinkles creasing his eyes. Silas was a few years Fenrir's senior, and starting to go gray.

"I've had better weeks, Silas. I'd rather not talk about it. What news?" asked Fenrir. Silas waved for another city guard to tend his post, and the two stepped inside the city gates, moving into the shadow of the wall to allow traffic to move by unimpeded.

"About me or this rat nest of a city?"

48

"To learn about the rat or the nest? How about one then the other?"

Silas barked a laugh. "Well, I've actually *got* some news for a change. You know I'm tired of this city guard shit. It's better than fighting the Wasmer, but I'm too old to be dealing with angry little merchants all day. I put in to retire, last month, and my papers were denied," said Silas, taking a swig from a small canteen. Fenrir felt a sudden, aching thirst, though he knew the canteen held only water.

"Denied? Can they do that?"

"The legal men say they can in the case that there is a 'deemed threat' to the duchy. They told me that there's evidence that the Wasmer are stirring, breaking the peace, raiding some villages. Saying that the hairy bastards are stealing some of the commoners from the border towns to the south and the west. So, no resignations are being taken." Silas smirked. "It smells like bullshit to me."

"So, you're stuck gathering tariffs until the day you die?"

"No, that's what I was going to tell you. I threatened to get my own legal counsel, and the little duke's men caved almost immediately, gifting me a promotion! I'm to be made a Knight of the Wolf! Sworn in next week, a whole noble ceremony and shit." Silas had a wide, goofy grin on his face now. The Wolf Knights— the elite personal guards of Duke Samuel Penton III, the ruler of Rostane and liege lord to the dozens of counts and barons in the duchy. Penton III had been dubbed the little duke by his detractors, which consisted of—albeit quietly—most of the people in the city. Penton II had been a great man, working tirelessly for the betterment of Rostane and the unification of Ardia, while his son did little but for the betterment of himself. Fenrir knew father and son personally, though neither had ever spoken to him; a suit of armor in the corner of an audience chamber does little to merit attention. Regardless, the "little" moniker was accurate; Penton III would never be the man his father had been before his death.

Frankly, the little duke was a pompous shit.

"Wolf Knight, eh? Protecting the little duke will be better than this?" asked Fenrir with a raised eyebrow, gesturing at the shuffling mass of traders and travelers.

"Eh, it couldn't be worse. But, I will work fewer hours and the pay will be much better. With what I'll be able to put away, I'll finally be able to open a herbology shop when I truly do retire." Silas had always taken an interest in plants and medicine. A strange hobby for a soldier.

"Well, congrats, my friend," Fenrir said, slapping Silas on the shoulder.

"Thanks. It'll be just in time, too, to protect some of Ardia's finest noble slugs. By the way, have you heard that little Penty is sending out invitations, trying to institute another Ardian Council? The first one since... well... you know."

Fenrir groaned at the unwelcome reminder. Silas had been one of the guards in the room at the time of Fenrir's topple from grace, at the previous Ardian Council, three years ago. He wasn't likely to live that down, even if he lasted another hundred years.

"A council, huh?" Fenrir worked to keep his face neutral.

"As you would expect, Penton seeks to make himself king, although we all know that he's a quarter the man that his father was. Word is that few of the big players are interested. Every duke—and the duchess, even—sees himself as having the best claim. They say that Draston and Hunesa are sending second and third sons, or even just minor vassals. Nothing of import could possibly be accomplished there."

"So, why bother, then? Why would Penton spend the money necessary to host all of those sweating, silk-clothed pigs? Is he so deluded that he actually believes he could be king?" Fenrir realized he was speaking too loudly. Though most disliked Penton, it was to be kept to a whisper. Not all guards were as lax as Silas.

Silas glanced over his shoulder, ushering Fenrir deeper into the shadow of the wall, out of earshot of any passersby.

"So?" Fenrir prompted, quieter now.

"We city guard have a theory, though there may not be much to it... You know, my story—unable to retire, being promoted— isn't much different from a lot of other veterans coming up on their twenty-fifth year. We're stuck in the military on a technicality, some obscure law that no one has invoked in recent memory. As always, blame the Wasmer, right? But, there's more."

"More?" Fenrir scratched at his head wound. The thing was throbbing again, so much so that he could hear the blood pounding in his skull, a severe hangover without having to pay for the liquor.

"There's been a spike in military recruitment, officers traveling from village to town, offering an easy life as soldiers. More than a typical spring bolstering, and it's doing more than just replacing those who retire. No one *can* retire, after all. So, Rostane is finding itself with a larger military than usual. Bigger than each of the other three duchies of Ardia."

"So you're thinking..." Even with a headache, the pieces weren't hard to assemble into a coherent picture.

Silas again looked around furtively, his face paler than usual. "Yeah. War. If Penton doesn't get what he wants through politics, maybe he'll go to war to take it."

There was something in Silas' expression. Did Fenrir see fear, there? From the man who had protected him, outnumbered and with his knuckles bloodied, from other recruits back in training? Back when Fenrir had been little more than a stupid kid, running away from his problems?

"What of Florens? Surely Malless must have some idea of these machinations." Duke Henrik Malless of the southern-most duchy was Penton's primary rival, his domain being equal to Rostane in population and wealth, though not military power. Florens was focused on trade and culture, art and science. There hadn't been a war for seventy years, after all, and there was little reason to maintain an army aside from dissuading bordering countries from aggression. Jecusta and Algania were never the friendliest of neighbors.

"Like I said, these are just rumors among the city guard, and really just the veterans. They might be false. We veterans of the Wasmer incursions are jumpy, after all. And besides, it's said that Duke Malless himself may be coming to the Ardian Council, though probably only to gloat. He seems to be gaining popularity across Ardia... improving roads and bridges, opening schools and universities in cities across his duchy. Lowering tariffs to encourage trade. Even in the last week, a huge mercantile retinue from Florens set up shop in the warehouse district. Apparently, they're driving some Rostanian merchants out of business, and little Penty is none-too-pleased. Though, you don't have to worry—your family fortune is safe."

"So, Malless might be oblivious of any threat if he's coming to Rostane," said Fenrir, ignoring that last bit. "Or, your suspicions are misplaced."

"Just so. Like I said, we are a jumpy lot. Anyway, Fen, it's been good to see you, but I really need to get back. Tariffs need collecting, you know." Silas patted the sword at his side. The thing was probably rusted into its scabbard by now.

"Yeah, yeah." The discussion of war should have been more distracting, but Fenrir wasn't a soldier anymore. And, besides, he still needed to report back to The House; with his luck, he might not survive to see any war, even if it were to happen. "I'll see you soon."

Fenrir began to blend back into the crowd, his mind already pushing thoughts of the little duke into the periphery.

"Oh, Fen," said Silas, grabbing his arm and speaking quietly before he could leave. "There is one thing that might ignite your interest. Ever hear of Martin Frommis? He's a recently retired adjudicator, formerly of Rostane, now living in Umberton. That little town with those crooked red trees? Well, apparently, he was hit by The House, but things went poorly. He was messed up pretty badly, might lose more than just a finger. And, his son-in-law isn't doing so well, either. They think there's something wrong with his head. You, or your friends, know anything about this?" Silas asked, looking at Fenrir askance. It wasn't exactly a well-kept secret among his circle that Fenrir had taken up with The House. Of course, the organization guarded its secrets well, but enforcers like Fenrir found it nearly impossible to keep their identities safe, and The House did little to help with the endeavor. Fear of retaliation was about the only thing that kept Fenrir safe.

Fenrir shook his head wryly. "I'm sure I have no idea, Silas. It's a shame. Though I'd imagine Frommis must have done something to deserve it." Like condemning the murderer of a young woman, and refusing to destroy the evidence or bully witnesses.

"Well, just be aware, Fen. I hear that the nobles are out for blood about this. Apparently, Frommis was well-respected, even among those ass-licking, blood-sucking slugs." The nobles, of course, never liked when a message from The House was too extreme. There was some solace in the fact that the organization always took a finger before taking a life.

"Thanks for the warning, friend."

Friend, indeed. Even though Fenrir's current choice of occupation ran in direct opposition to Silas', the man still protected him. Fenrir needed to treat Silas to a beer in the near future, assuming his wife would let them go out. For whatever reason, that shriveled old witch didn't care for Fenrir. Must be a bad judge of character.

As much as Fenrir would have preferred to slink to his boarding house and sleep off his various injuries, he knew that it was in his best interest to seek out his benefactor and get the inevitable out of the way. At least, if they killed him now, it would halt the terrible pain that was again building in his skull. So thinking, Fenrir wove his way toward the warehouse district, and toward the current headquarters of The House.

The sun had just set behind the jagged Tulanques, streaking the sky with dark blues and oranges. Yet Rostane was just as alive at dusk as during the day. Torch-bearers were lighting bright oil lamps on all of the major roads of the city. With intelligently-placed mirrors reflecting the light, it seemed to be practically always daytime. This also created the illusion that the city was safe for people to wander and explore, which Fenrir knew firsthand was not true. The House was not the only illicit power in the city, though it was the most influential and organized.

Nonetheless, the stone-cobbled streets were packed with people going about their business, carousing, or otherwise moving about with or without a purpose. On every street corner was a tavern or inn, filling the streets with the smells of food, the sounds of laughter, and the occasional fistfight. Packs of city guards maintained order, patrolling the most populous areas, their glinting spears and measured pace providing feeling of security and protection. Any traveler would think that Rostane was a pleasant, modern, thriving city… at least on the surface.

Fenrir, however, was going below the surface. Just as a solid structure could be undermined by termites, Rostane had its own lurking parasites. Fenrir happened to be one of those—a cognizant bloodsucker. Dodging a fat man and squeezing between a couple of food carts, he started into an unlit alleyway (affectionately named Vagabond Stretch), taking a shortcut toward the warehouse district. This alley, as with most alleys in Rostane, hid what the regular people and nobles pretended to ignore. He passed piles of refuse and rotting trash, stepping over bundles of rags that contained remnants of humanity, people who either failed themselves or been failed by society. Sometimes, these guttersnipes would simply sit in filthy run-off instead of moving a few feet to a dry patch, so resigned were they to their suffering.

Occasionally, the destitute reached out for him, imploring Fenrir to part with some of his money. Some invoked Yetra's name, attempting to guilt Fenrir into sharing. *Yetra bless you.* To be honest, it did almost work at times; this day, he even got to the point where he had his fist wrapped around a small yet—his last one—and was about to toss it to a ragged boy who couldn't have been more than twelve. But, instead, he clung to his coin tighter, feeling the edges digging into his hand.

The elaborate drainage and waste system in Rostane only applied to the main streets, and as a result, many alleyways were heaped with human fecal matter and other unknown substances. The smell brought back unbidden memories of slogging through the waste ditch in Umberton, with unnamed stuffs smeared on his hair, face, and clothes. With his stomach still queasy at the thought of it, Fenrir quickened his pace, avoiding the poor wretches lining the lane and trying to keep his boots from absorbing yet more waste matter.

Looking down, focused on quick-stepping around moist trash and feces, Fenrir almost collided with someone standing, wide-legged, in the middle of the alley. He came up just short, ungracefully skidding to a stop an arm's length away. The man blocking his path was tall, taller than Fenrir by at least a head, and certainly heavier. He carried a good deal of weight distributed across his body, looking for all the world like a strongman who had been overindulging for the last five—or ten—years. Fenrir sighed, knowing instantly that the situation meant trouble. He sighed again when he heard motion behind him... likely another street tough who'd been camouflaged in the rags of a derelict. The man in front of him had a wide, toothy grin.

"Greetings, brother. I hope you've enjoyed your stroll through our territory. The fee for passing through is whatever money you've got in your pockets," said the big man with surprising articulacy, his stomach jiggling a bit as he chuckled.

"Sorry, *brother*. I haven't any money, but I do have an object for trade," said Fenrir, reaching into his boot and pulling out the heptagram, placing it around his neck. Most street toughs wouldn't be willing to tangle with The House, not if they valued their lives. His medallion was essentially a free pass with criminals in the city. Or, at least, it had been in the past.

Toothy's smile widened. "I don't think I'd accept that for trade. Looks fairly worthless. Maybe I'll take one of your fingers instead."

Fenrir heard something move behind him just as he dove between the wide-legged stance of Toothy. He twisted as he hit the ground, landing face-up and lashing upward with his leg. Caught completely off-guard, Toothy took the brunt of Fenrir's foot square in the grapes. As Fenrir scrambled backwards and regained his feet, the big man went hard to the ground, making a splash in the filth. Now visible, Fenrir saw that the second man— wait—woman was wielding a knife. With Toothy down, the

56

woman—wait—girl was less certain as she approached Fenrir, but she vaulted the body of her larger companion with relative agility. She couldn't have been more than fourteen years old, with hair short like a boy's, but her feminine features were undeniable even beneath a layer of grime.

Fenrir didn't wait for the girl to collect her courage and attack. Instead, he struck first, hitting the side of her blade with the flat of his hand and kicking her, also right between the legs. Though women might lack a certain small (or large) part that made this move particularly incapacitating for men, kicking them hard enough anywhere was usually enough to bring them down. Such was the case with this one. Feeling a certain guilt as he disarmed the fallen girl, Fenrir reminded himself that she likely would have gutted him, had he not moved more quickly than she. He approached Toothy next, kneeling next to the big man's body, which was still curled in a fetal position.

"Well, *brother*, that was a mistake," said Fenrir as he crouched, cuffing the man in the ear with an open palm. The man just groaned, almost whimpered in fact, his hand still firmly fixed between his legs. "Or should I say, sister?" Fenrir hit the man again, feeling more means spirited than usual. It had to be the exhaustion, or the head wound, or just anger from being attacked in his own city. By the gods, one of the only advantages of his position in The House (aside from the decent pay) was immunity from the low-lives of Rostane. Apparently, that wasn't to be the case today.

"Uhhhh. Please... leave... uhhh... Morgyn... alone," groaned the man, still unable to move. Morgyn. Must be the little chit that he'd disabled with a well-placed kick to the muff. Maybe this man's daughter? It wasn't like a street tough to care about another without some familial bond.

Fenrir grunted as he straightened, his blasted knee sore from the squatting, anger and aggression fading like the whimpers of the man lying before him. The girl Morgyn was still nearby, having brought herself up to one knee with her short, dark hair disheveled. Tough little kid. She was glancing around for her knife. Fenrir saw it and kicked it away, sending it down the alleyway. The girl slumped, defeated.

Fenrir appraised her for a long moment, his exhausted, cracked mind wandering to a different place, a different time. A place he never was, and a time that never happened. But, in his mind's eye, he saw a different girl there, kneeling in the muck. A girl with blond hair, eyes the color of the sky. Eyes full of accusation. Full of hate.

He reached into his pocket and clasped his last yet, squeezing it with an strange mix of emotions. He brought it to his face, examined the stamped visage of Yetra on the square piece of copper, and tossed it onto the ground in front of the girl.

Without looking back, Fenrir continued his walk to the end of the alley, shaking his head either to clear the fog or in regret. He wasn't sure.

Apparently, Fenrir was doomed to spend the short remainder of his life covered in filth. His new shirt—less than a few hours old—was already ruined. And with his boarding house on the west side of the city and the warehouses on the east, he couldn't change now. Even had clothing shops or carts still been open, his last yet had gone to that guttersnipe, Morgyn. Not that he could have found anything decent for a single square yet.

Fenrir pondered his options briefly and decided to just discard his shirt entirely. It was a chilly evening, but he didn't want to approach his benefactor while he was so obviously smeared in filth (he couldn't help the state of his breeches, but at least they were of a darker color. And the smell... well, he was stuck with that). Luckily, this was the warehouse district and, even with only the stars and the moons for light, porters were continuing their work, shirtless and heavily muscled from years of such labor. Fenrir actually fit nicely into this setting. Even with a few years of questionable health practices behind him, he'd still maintained much of his bulk. Never the trim, lithe swordsman, he had a heavy musculature, particularly in the shoulders. And that had played at least a small role in his newest nickname.

"It's the Bull!" called a young man from nearby, leaving behind a small crowd of people. "The Bull has returned from his rampage! Not that I'm surprised. You always hear a bull coming."

"Garrett," replied Fenrir flatly. He'd never liked the little tattooed bastard. Too cocky.

"Well, Bull, I see you finally made it back. And quite a finger you cut," laughed Garrett, apparently quite proud of his little wit. "Tennyson was looking for you earlier. He's probably still lurking about. Oh, and he didn't look pleased. Granted, he never looks pleased, but...." Again, the kid chuckled.

Fenrir shouldered by Garrett without responding. Garrett was one of those kids who thought he knew everything, and could do anything. Truthfully, he was quite skilled at his job, being an enforcer like Fenrir. Much more effective than Fenrir, too, to be honest—the kid could slip in, extract a finger, and leave before anyone knew he was there. Fenrir's nickname stemmed as much from his shoulders as his technique: break down a door, knock people about, and eventually get what he needed with a lot of ancillary damage. And a lot of noise. Just a lot of smashing, really. Of course, that had only happened a couple of times, but no one ever talked about his successful extractions. Regardless, though, the nickname had followed Fenrir and, after his most recent incident, it was even more likely to stick.

Closing the distance to the current headquarters of The House, or at least the only headquarters that he knew about, Fenrir slowed down a bit. The warehouse was like any other, being a tall, gray-bricked building, supported by a wooden frame and topped with a red-bricked roof. There were no noticeable windows, although Fenrir knew that thin slots of stone could be removed and quickly converted to arrow slits in the case of a raid. The door—which was surrounded by slightly sinister-looking men and one particularly heavyset whore (Jenni; she was essentially a mattress for low-ranking members, coming very cheap) was recessed a couple of feet. In the event of an emergency, the residents could lower a heavy portcullis made of fine steel, likely impaling anyone below in the process. The place really was a miniature fortress.

Fenrir tried to swallow his nerves and clear his mind as he approached the thick door, realizing that the last two doors he'd entered—Frommis' house and the inn's—had boded quite ill for him. Trouble travels in threes, the saying went, and Fenrir could only hope that the third manifestation of trouble wasn't behind this door.

"Oh, it's a Bull! Back fr'm mudder thingz and getsa finger," said one of the mildly-sinister men, slurring his words from obvious inebriation and staggering to rest on a railing. Fenrir didn't bother to try and understand the weasel-faced man who, incidentally, was often called Weasel within the confines of this organization.

"Hey, sweetness. You interested in some love later tonight? I have a slot before the rising of the second moon," offered Jenni, propositioning him with her most seductive voice. He could see unmentionable stains on her dark blue dress.

"Not tonight, Jenni. Got business inside. Tomorrow night," promised Fenrir, with absolutely no intention of following through.

"I'll be looking forward to it, sweetness," she said, licking her lips. He shuddered a bit as he pushed past the group, entering the warehouse. He may have had some bad luck with women, lately, but wasn't ready to take that plunge.

Though the outside of the warehouse resembled any other in Rostane, the inside was a different story entirely. He walked into a tavern, complete with a polished oak bar and full kitchen that filled the space with the delightful aroma of the famous Rostanian clam chowders and stews. The fishy odor turned Fenrir's stomach today, however. The walls were decorated with beautiful landscape paintings of the Tulanques and the Fullane River, all nailed to the wall, and instruments of war, all of these being replicas but, nonetheless, still anchored to the wall as a precaution. It was busy, too, as crowded as any normal tavern. The House had a great number of moving parts, from errand-runners to protectors and enforcers, servants and spies, merchants, leaders, and unknowns. The latter group was simply a label that Fenrir had made up to describe members who had no discernable talents or purpose, and yet still seemed to have a relatively high standing. Fenrir assumed that they were rich, men and women who bought their influence in the house with cold, hard yets.

Many people insisted on donning masks whenever they were at this location, being afraid of potential blackmail due to their association with The House. As a result, the tavern reminded Fenrir of a freaky, interspecies menagerie, with birds, wolves, mice, and some grotesque monsters milling about, drinking and eating together. Fenrir never bothered with a mask. He wasn't important enough to merit notice. Anyhow, too many folks already knew about his involvement. Fenrir *had* thought that he had some modicum of protection just by being a member, but perhaps that wasn't the case.

He scanned the jungle for Tennyson and didn't see him in the common room. His benefactor always wore a distinct silver mask of Ultner, so he was hard to miss. Knowing that he was likely in the offices upstairs, Fenrir started heading in that direction, ignoring a few calls of "The Bull is here," and "Have a beer, Fen!" Though he had an aching thirst for a tall one, carousing was not on his mind at the moment.

A protector stood at the bottom of the stairs, leaning against the rail with his arms folded. Fenrir didn't know this man personally, but he had seen him in passing. Another big man like himself, but six inches taller. A man who had the casual bearing of a warrior but the obviously fuzzy face of a Wasmer. Not many of them in Rostane; Wasmer weren't exactly welcomed with open arms, nor did many Wasmer decide to enter the gates.

"I'm here to see Tennyson," Fenrir nodded to the protector.

"You be the Bull? I believe he be expecting you. Proceed upstairs," said the Wasmer, his mouth moving just a bit differently than a human's—a byproduct of its accommodating the extra canine teeth. This one had obviously filed them down, though, to more closely resemble a human. The practice was scorned by the traditionalists in the Wasmer society, but was more and more adopted by young Wasmer as the years went by. Of course, he wouldn't pass as a human unless he shaved his forehead and cheeks also, and lost that particular Wasmer way of speaking. The muscles of his mouth had not caught up with the teeth-filing job, either, and his diction wasn't exactly impeccable.

"Thanks, friend." Fenrir took a step forward. The Wasmer put a hand on his shoulder.

"He do not be happy, today. Take care. Maybe your choice of shirtless will lighten his mood." Fenrir barked a laugh. A Wasmer with a sense of humor. His humor immediately dissipated at the thought of confronting an already unhappy Tennyson.

Fenrir headed up the stairs resignedly, pausing at Tennyson's office door to knock five times in a specific pattern. He heard shuffling in the room then, followed by the scraping of several deadbolts being unlocked. A cautious man, Tennyson was. A dangerous man.

Ultner—at least the visage of Ultner—opened the door. The silver mask was frightening, a demon wearing a twisted smile, his face covered in spikes and horns, boils and sores. The portrayal of the god of death and the champion of Pandemonium, wearing black robes and all. The reflected lamplight rendered the spectacle even more menacing.

"The Bull. Fenrir de Trenton, third son of the merchant king, Darian de Trenton, the first merchant to revolutionize cold storage for the transport of slaughtered animals and seafood. Last surviving son of the merchant king, Darian de Trenton, still without his father's favor. What the fuck am I going to do with you?" questioned Tennyson, his voice always higher than Fenrir would expect to echo from the face of death. It obviously wasn't his real voice. The man really took pains to protect his identity.

"I'd consider a commendation and a promotion," said Fenrir, all bluster as he pulled Frommis' finger from his pocket, the valuable ring still attached. "I have a feeling that no one in Umberton will consider crossing The House in the near future." He tossed Frommis' moon-pale finger onto the table.

"I see things differently. I see a town that's furious due to the excess injury of one of its most respected citizens. I see a volunteer militia recruiting heavily because one of their lieutenants—and their blacksmith—is all but brain-dead. I see representatives from that town and surrounding villages demanding that Rostane cracks down on The House, which is theorized to be out of control. I see nobles in Rostane, thought to be allies of The House, behaving in ways counter to our interests. And I see—and smell—my enforcer, the Bull, a man who can't sneak into a dark room full of deaf children. A man who bungles half of his jobs."

"Well, there are always different perspectives," shrugged Fenrir, his voice holding a bit of a quaver. "And I only bungle about a tenth of them." Had he truly hoped for a laugh from the demon in front of him?

"Any fraction is too much, de Trenton." Tennyson scooped up the desiccated finger, ring and all, and turned to a small, discrete wooden box on a nondescript shelf. With little ceremony, he creaked open the lid and tossed in the finger. Fenrir wondered if that box was full of fingers in various state of rot. What does one do with dozens of ring fingers collected over the course of years?

Tennyson turned back to Fenrir, twisting with the grace of a dancer, considering his enforcer from behind his mask. Fenrir shifted under the silver scrutiny. "Do you know why recruited you, brought you into The House? It wasn't because of your bar room brawling skills, although those are relatively impressive."

Fenrir remembered the time after his dismissal from the Plateau, adapting to his drastic change in circumstance, his relatively simple, predictable life torn to shreds. He remembered the shame and the listlessness, hiding the truth of what happened from his friends and acquaintances, trying to reestablish a new life for himself. After his wife finalized the divorce after a years-long separation, Fenrir worked odd jobs to get a bit of coin that was unerringly transmuted into alcohol. For a time, he'd run protection for one of the rowdier taverns—The Shaved Goat—and often had to break up fistfights. It was a job that he surprisingly excelled at, finding an outlet for his frustration following his attrition from the guard. He'd routinely broken arms, wrists, and legs. Unfortunately, he'd often caused too much damage to the patrons and the tavern, and lost the job soon after he'd gotten it. The night he'd been fired for literally knocking teeth from the mouth of a wealthy merchant (who had no place in a shithole like The Goat), there'd been a note and heptagram sitting on the bed in his boarding house. The note had simply had a date, time, and location.

Fenrir had gone to his first meeting with Tennyson two days later.

"No, I chose you because you know the Plateau. You know the people, you know their routines. You know the pathways, and you know the guards and the patrols. I thought you had some real potential there, to slip into the Plateau and... enforce. However, after your first job, I realized that this wouldn't be the case. You would never be more than a middling enforcer. Now, I realize that you aren't even as good as middling."

"Tennyson, I—" Fenrir began, an explanation heavy on his lips.

"You what? Can you really argue that you have the skills of even Garrett, that boy who has half your years and experience? Can you convince me that your blunder has not just cost The House a great deal of money? More importantly, favors?" asked Tennyson, moving forward like a snake, his voice becoming quieter, more sibilant. Bright eyes flashing from behind Ultner's face. Fenrir felt exposed.

"I-"

"I know you fancy yourself as having a bit of a silver tongue, especially with the ladies. But, I'm no duck egg-eating country bumpkin. I'm not susceptible to your charm."

Fenrir took a step back. Obviously, Tennyson knew more than he'd expected. Or, he'd just happened upon the most coincidental reference of the century.

"So, the question is, what will I do with you?" His hands were under his robe now, perhaps gripping the dual daggers that he was reputed to wield with deadly effect. No one had ever seen it happen but, in observing Tennyson's stance and posture, Fenrir didn't doubt his capacity for murder.

"Tennyson, I made a mistake. A few mistakes. Pandemonium, a lot of mistakes. But I am loyal to The House. You cannot doubt my loyalty." He was sweating now, his bare chest glistening under his partially-graying body hair.

"I do not doubt your loyalty; just your competence." Tennyson seemed ready to spring forward, an adder coiled for attack.

"I proved it earlier today. In fact, I have information for you!" Even to himself, Fenrir's voice held desperation.

"Let's see what you have, and I will tell you if it is valuable." Tennyson still held his hands under his robe, but he was now standing back on his heels.

"Once I came into town, I took the shortest path to come see you. I went through that alley off of the Grand Parkway: Vagabond Stretch. Between the Parkway and Penton Street. Two people assaulted me, a muscle-bound warrior with big teeth and a lithe girl with short hair, maybe eighteen years old. I revealed my heptagram, and they laughed. *Laughed* at me, at the heptagram!" said Fenrir, exaggerating his plight for Tennyson's benefit, but being careful not to overdo it. Obviously, this was a man who could uncover the truth.

"They threatened to take my finger, and that was when I bested both of them, weaponless."

"And did they make mention for whom they were working?" Tennyson walked back to his desk and sat down, then writing something down in the huge, black-bound book that was omnipresent on his desk.

"No. I would have assumed that they were ignorant to The House, even foreign to Rostane, except for that last bit about my finger."

"Interesting. Did you dispatch them? Capture one?"

"Incapacitate them, yes. Kill them, no."

Tennyson sighed heavily, delicately setting down his pen and leveling a demon's stare at Fenrir. "You are poorly suited to this line of work, Bull. Fenrir. De Trenton. You think you should leave our enemies alive *without* even securing one for interrogation? You have the brains of a disease-addled donkey."

"Maybe so," Fenrir said glumly. It hadn't even occurred to him to fling the girl over his shoulder and bring her for proof. And killing the pair as they lay incapacitated in the muck? He didn't need that on his conscience.

"*Maybe so.*" Tennyson echoed his words mockingly. "I do not understand you, de Trenton. You are more than willing to maim. How many bones have you broken from those undeserving? How many fingers have you severed from good men? It doesn't seem to bother you. You are like a dumb dog—I can point and say 'fetch,' and you'll bring me a boney stump, wagging your tail and begging for a scratch behind the ears."

"I'm former military," mumbled Fenrir, glancing at Tennyson askance. That's what he'd been taught—do what he was told to do. After twenty years of being told to fetch, chasing the stick was second nature.

Tennyson ignored the interruption. "Like the dog, you are single-minded and unable to act outside the confines of expectations. This little attack of yours, in Vagabond Stretch, was an opportunity for you. To show that you can be more than a simple errand boy. More than a dog. But, like the job itself, you've somehow burrowed below your potential. You've fallen short."

The silence hung in the room like the axe of a headsman. The moment stretched on past the breaking point; Tennyson might have been asleep behind his mask. Fenrir cleared his throat, trying to work some moisture into his sticky mouth.

"So, what next?" Fenrir asked. If Tennyson was going to finish him off, rambling excuses weren't going to help.

"This was your last job as an enforcer for The House," said Tennyson, voice as glacial as the ice fields of the Domain.

With lightning speed, the man again twisted to his feet and plunged his hand into the interior folds of his robe. Something glinted in the light as Tennyson flung his hand out, hurling the object at Fenrir as Fenrir swung his arm up in an ineffectual block. A sharp, cold sting blossomed on his chest, and he grasped at the wound. But… it was just a sting. His arterial lifeblood wasn't flowing through his fingers, and his heart continued to beat. The iron payment chit, having bounced off his chest, was still spinning on the floor.

Fenrir looked like a fool as he scrambled after the heavy metal disc and scooped it up. Tennyson watched silently, arms folded.

"This was your last job as an enforcer, but The House will require more from you. For now, take some time off. Clean up and buy some new clothes. You look and smell like literal shit." Mockery echoed from behind the silver mask as Tennyson ushered Fenrir out, shutting the door right on Fenrir's nose. The clicks of a half-dozen locks were a friendly goodbye.

Fenrir clenched shut his eyes as a draining relief flooded his body. Obedient dog or not, he'd survived yet another failure. Fenrir reached up to rub the spot where the heavy chit had impacted his chest, just over his heart. His skin was still tingling with the vague memory of fear.

Chapter 5

Merigold couldn't stop thinking about that man, Fenrir. Even a week later, with spring traffic at the Duckling heavier than she could ever recall, he still loomed heavy in her thoughts. Certainly not because of his looks—he'd been handsome, but almost old enough to be her father. Rather, Meri felt guilty, remorseful. What she'd done, what she'd caused. It was unforgivable.

As she walked from the Duckling to Dunmore, Meri continued to ruminate. Dear Yetra, she'd been so engrossed in his story that evening. She'dd been able to see everything that Fenrir had described... the tall stone walls, graceful balustrades, the ballroom. She'd heard the voices of the nobles, felt the touch of Viscount Saren as they danced. She'd even smelled the exotic scents from foods and perfumes from over the seas! It had been almost as if she'd been living inside a dream, so strong had been her imaginings.

Then, she had drawn from him. Just a little at first, like she so often did, just for a bit of strength, to keep the dream unfolding. And for a second, her visions of the Plateau had been even stronger. Then she'd drawn even more, almost on reflex, taking from Fenrir a surfeit of power. More than she had drawn ever before. Not on purpose, though...

Meri could not deny that she'd felt a rush, both of energy and of details, about the Plateau. She almost hadn't been able to separate reality from the visions, and hadn't even noticed that Fenrir was hurting her at first. Then he had cussed at her, somehow knowing that Meri had stolen something from him. Although she hadn't been able to perceive his hand digging into her wrist, she'd thought she could *feel* him, his emotions. He'd been scared, terrified even. And mournful.

And, there was that brief vision of blood on her hands as she crushed someone's skull with a belaying pin, the crimson splatter infiltrating every other part of her vision.

Ragen, seeing Fenrir seize her, had immediately launched himself at the man, striking him from behind. After Fenrir had gone down, Meri had pleaded with her father, saying that the man had meant her no harm, that it was her own fault, that she had incited him. Ragen wouldn't hear it, though, and had loaded Fenrir's semi-conscious body into Farmer Denny's cart. At least she'd managed to secret a loaf of bread into Fenrir's shirt when no one had been looking, as well as to convince Farmer Denny to put Fenrir somewhere he wouldn't be robbed. The poor man. He hadn't been at all intimidating like Meri had thought upon first seeing him. He'd instead been strong and eloquent and... sad.

Over the next few days, Meri had felt like she was hollowly going through the motions of her life. Chopping wood, cleaning guest rooms, serving food and beer. She would still smile and laugh as her job required, but she didn't feel any joy. Even meeting new people—a dark-skinned man from Rafón, a noble woman from Rostane accompanied by her entire retinue, a impossibly tall man who traveled with a giant, shaggy dog that he'd tied out front like a horse, and a band of traveling mercenaries based out of Hunesa—none of these experiences had elevated her mood. If she started to feel a glimmer of positivity or optimism, her eyes would be drawn to the fading bruise on her wrist. And again, she would feel an emptiness. Even praying to Yetra for guidance and strength did not help.

Those who harm others, by design or misfortune, dip their feet in Pandemonium and are filled with a potent poison. Longorius, *The Book of Amorum*. Meri felt this poisoning her body and soul. The guilt of it was making her sick.

Merigold didn't dare draw from any of the Duckling's patrons now. She'd even sworn to herself that she would never draw

70

again. She didn't know what had happened with Fenrir—how she had drawn so much, how she had lost control. But she didn't want that to happen again, and didn't want anyone else to be hurt. Consequently, Meri was exhausted. She could barely remain standing by the end of the dinner rush. Her face became pale and drawn by the end of a long day. She had little appetite and had begun to lose weight. She ended each night trying to hide how worn and unstable she had become, lest Ragen become worried.

This day, a week after her encounter with Fenrir, Meri was supposed to head back to the village. Despite her efforts to hide her weakness, Ragen had finally noticed the changes in her and *ordered* her to take the next few days off. Meri would normally have seethed at such a demand, particularly as her father never took his own advice, but she had grown so weak that she didn't argue. Much.

So, Meri found herself walking the three miles or so between the Duckling and Dunmore, planning on spending her time at the village house that Ragen owned but rarely visited. Her father was a major figure to the people of Dunmore, working to pass laws and mediate disputes, helping the town with small public works, giving unerringly of himself. He had a house built in the village to show his commitment to Dunmore, though he nearly always made the walk back to the inn no matter the time of night. Meri would spend a few days resting here, in this empty, unused house. It was not an alluring option, but little seemed alluring to Meri right now.

Though, Meri did have to admit to herself that it felt good to walk, to be outdoors, and to be away from people. The inn could be so confining and restrictive, a cage with doors and windows. But now, traveling alone for even a short spurt, she could close her eyes and imagine she was bound to faraway places, lands of unparalleled beauty. Lands where she was more than a bar maiden near a crossroads.

Granted, this fantasy was difficult to maintain, what with her aching feet, the biting insects, and the smell of manure emanating heavily from the surrounding fields. It was even more difficult to be imaginative at all, given her mood.

As Meri approached the footbridge, she finally saw something that bolstered her spirits for more than a moment, and even the brownish-yellow contusion ringing her wrist could not drag her down. Saren stood there, leaning lazily against the railing and chatting with Chad, one of the younger boys in town. As she approached the bridge, Meri had to work at concealing her creeping smile. She cursed herself for wearing an old blouse, one that was covered with the various food and dirt stains of her occupation.

Those who are faithful shall be forgiven in the face of transgressions. Yearen. He probably wasn't referring to clothing options, but citing verses always gave Meri some solace regardless of true relevance.

Saren was such a handsome man. He had short, deep brown hair and a strong jaw sporting a well-groomed beard. His nose was a little uneven, having been broken at some point last year. Though he was wearing a loose yellow shirt and dark breeches right now, Meri had seen him shirtless, wading in the lake and foraging, with his lean, well-muscled chest and flat stomach glistening with water and sweat. He was a year younger than Meri, but that meant very little in a small village like Dunmore. And besides this, both were well past their majority.

Meri licked her lips and decided to be bold.

She hitched up her skirt, showing off just a bit more leg. She felt about as graceful and subtle as the ducks flapping and quacking beneath the bridge, but her best friend, Sandra, had said that Meri had to be more obvious, more assertive. More aggressive. Sandra was very popular with men, even occasionally spending nights with travelers at the Duckling. Probably as a result of this, Ragen would always frown when Sandra's name came up, and he willfully avoided the girl. Regardless, Meri was determined to take Sandra's advice. She had nothing to lose at this point, and potentially a lot to gain.

As Meri stepped onto the footbridge—a very simple affair of wooden planks that stretched over a shallow portion of wetlands—Chad looked up, grinned, and immediately ran off, leaving her and Saren alone. It was the first time they had been alone together since they shared that kiss those months ago, when she'd gotten cold feet and run off. Meri remembered the gentleness of his lips, the smoothness of his face (he hadn't had the beard last year), and the strength in his arms. The taste and smell of ale in his mouth. He had pulled her close, just outside of the inn, kissing her deeply. It had somehow been both soft and firm, seeking yet commanding. Though she had kissed him back, she'd quickly grown too nervous and had run back into the Duckling, saying something about needing to get the fire burning or the tables cleaned or something. It was a regret, and she had enough conversations with Sandra to know that she wanted more than just a kiss.

"Oh, Saren! How nice to see you!" Meri smiled wide, holding her hands in front of her in what she imagined to be a very feminine way.

"Hi there, Merigold. Away from the inn today?" offered Saren, presenting his own dog's smile. "It's been a while since I've seen you outside of the Duckling."

"Yes, in fact, I am taking a vacation from the inn. My father hired six new girls from town to help cover the extra spring traffic this year," said Meri, barely noticing that Saren's smile had withered at the mention of her father. "So, I'll be spending a week or so at our house in Dunmore."

"That's great, Merigold. So you'll have some time to yourself, then?" he inquired. She nodded, her heart beating rapidly. "Well, maybe we will bump into each other while you're in Dunmore."

"I certainly hope so, Saren," she said coquettishly, trying to emulate Sandra's voice. Being just a bit breathless when saying his name, drawing out the 'ess' sound. The move seemed lost on Saren; Sandra did say men could be as thick as sodden-brained plow horses.

"Well, I'm off to help Farmer Denny mend his plow. The man is constantly breaking that thing. You would think he'd know how to avoid rocks by now." Saren nodded politely to her. "It was good seeing you, Meri. I hope to see you again very soon," he said, still with that wide, charming smile. He nodded again, pushed off the railing, and walked past her, heading toward the Duckling

Meri held her breath for a moment, feeling a lump in her stomach the size of a full clutch of duck eggs. She felt like she was standing on a precipice, about to pitch forward into a fifty-foot drop. But…

"How about tonight, Saren?"

He stopped, not turning around. He appeared… he appeared tense, she thought. His shoulders were slightly hunched, and his fists were clenched. What had she done? Had she upset him? Why wasn't he saying anything? It felt like hours, days even, had passed. Dear Yetra, her cheeks were already flushed—this was a mistake. She was going to have to run away, jump on some random farmer's cart, and move to Rostane or Hunesa, and become a bar wench or beggar. At the very least, she would never leave her room again. Finally, Saren broke the silence.

"Not tonight. I'll be staying with Farmer Denny and his family. Tomorrow night… I'll find you," he said over his shoulder, continuing his walk away from town.

Meri remained frozen on the bridge, her heart hammering thickly in her ears as she watched him go. In no more than a few minutes, he was lost from sight, rounding a bend in the road, leaving her to doubt that she had been so brave, so bold. But she had been, and she fell to her knees at the thought of it, not sure whether to laugh or cry.

In the moment, Merigold didn't think at all about the fading bruise encircling her wrist.

Arriving at their village house, Meri realized that she and Ragen hadn't spent a night there in near two months. Luckily, in exchange for a hefty discount on Ragen's homebrew, the nearest neighbors spent time maintaining the small property, keeping the weeds cut back and the yard free of branches, mending the fence and porch when needed and so on. Despite Ragen being the wealthiest man in Dunmore, the village house was relatively modest, keeping with the theme of the other residents. Ragen did not want to show off his wealth, and he preferred to reinvest his earnings into the Duckling anyway. He was also more than generous in paying for the duck eggs, the lifeblood of the town. He would even purchase them when the supply outweighed the demand. Meri had never quite understood why he did that. He would always end up throwing them away before long, so that it seemed like such a waste.

Meri unlocked and entered the house to immediately collapse onto a dusty chair, exhausted from both the walk itself and her turbulent emotions. Finally, she would have some time alone with Saren! She promised herself she wouldn't be scared this time, wouldn't let nerves overtake her. Well, she might be nervous, but she certainly wouldn't run away. Not this time. She would show him the very best of her, and he would realize just how perfect they were for one another. He would see her sweetness and her charm and know that she was the one for him. After tomorrow night, Saren would propose to her, Merigold Hinter, who would soon be the wife of the man she had loved since childhood. As much of it as she could remember, anyway.

She'd often dreamed of her wedding day. The entire town would be there, all of her friends and family, in their worship-day best. She would wear the white dress that was her mother's—Meri knew Ragen had stored it in the inn's attic—and a crown of her namesake flowers, yellow and orange petals woven into her hair. Taneo Marsh would lead the ceremony, of course, and would read her favorite verse from Phillipa, her chapter mostly focused on love and joining.

Love is divine. Love is Harmony. Let Harmony root within the hearts of these before us, and let their vines become so entangled that it is unclear where one ends and the other begins. For true love has no beginning or end—it is eternal. Let these before us be joined by Harmony for all time.

She and Saren would kiss then, of course, with a gentle, enviable embrace. Afterwards, her father would host a reception, a festival in the village green. Sheri and Liza Pilt would play their flutes, and the town would dance, Saren and Meri in the center of it all. Kev Andem would sing songs of spirited songs of love in his deep baritone. They would break bread together as a community, as a family, and her Ragen would give a speech, laced with love, but releasing her into the care of Saren. It would be a perfect day. The best day of her life.

Meri smiled a soft smile at the thought—it was girl's dream, but one that could become reality if her date went well. First things first, though. Meri had to get ready. She was actually pleased that Saren had delayed until tomorrow. It would give her a chance to see to a new outfit. She saw her long-abandoned knitting basket then, but realized that she would never finish her blue shawl in time for her evening with Saren. She could go back to the Duckling and get one of her nice dresses from her wardrobe, but she didn't want to risk running into Ragen. And with no peddlers currently in town, Merigold had only one option.

Meri pounded on Sandra's door for a third time, knuckles smarting from the heavy blows. Her friend tended to sleep until late in the day and, given the position of the sun, Meri was pretty confident that Sandra would still be at home. Her older friend's home was smaller than Ragen and hers, a whitewashed wooden cabin consisting of little more than two rooms and a closet. Sandra's parents, bakers both, had left for Hunesa years ago in the pursuit of profits, leaving Sandra to her life in the small village, gifting her their land and the isolated house on the eastern edges of town. It was part of a ploy to find the wild girl a husband—an enticing plot of land and well-built, cozy home for the cost of taming Sandra. The plan, of course, had failed.

Sandra, bleary-eyed and with her hair askew, finally answered the door. She blinked in the light of the sun and squinted at Meri for a moment, as if trying to divine her name.

"Merigold! Izzat you?" Sandra asked, sounding a bit disoriented.

"Of course, Sandy! Rise and shine!" said Meri in an intentionally high-pitched voice. Sandra flinched and motioned for Meri to enter.

Despite her rarely being home, Sandra's house was a cluttered mess. Expensive clothes were strewn about, dishes lay discarded on nearly every surface, and there was an odd odor in the room.

Meri couldn't place it, but it smelled thick, maybe old oil, perfume, and liquor. Almost automatically, Meri began picking up clothes as Sandra slumped back onto her couch, sighing like a sunset.

"What do you need, Merigold? I don't feel too well today," said Sandra, closing her eyes and pressing her fingertips to her brows. Even in her disheveled state, Sandra was undeniably a beautiful woman. With waist-length strawberry blonde hair, an hourglass figure, and a symmetrical face with large, luminous green eyes, it was no surprise that she was so popular with men. Meri, even, constantly felt her gaze drawn to Sandra, to her near-perfect features that might have been molded after Inessa, the pagan goddess of desire that the girls in town whispered about. Though men like Saren were strong and charming, they lacked the simple grace of women, the perfection of form, and a certain... softness that Meri found so inviting. But, whenever she found her eyes lingering on Sandra's—or another woman's—lips or hips or hands, Meri looked hurriedly away. The Yetranian faith warned against such thoughts and behaviors, and Merigold was nothing if not devout.

Love is the catalyst for procreation. All else is touched by Pandemonium. Longorius. His chapter was full of warnings.

Her devotion had always been there. As long as she remembered, Merigold had attended each Yetranian service in Dunmore and celebrated every religious holiday. She had memorized nearly every passage in *The Book of Amorum*, and held her faith close to her heart, just as Ragen and Taneo Marsh had taught her. Merigold had even tried to spread the joy of Yetra through her actions, just as the Book advised, and adhere to the tenants of the faith as well as she could.

Although, she often fell short. Occasional white lies, infrequent manipulations, and very rare extended glances at

78

women. And, the fact that she was finally willing to bed a man before being married.

"I just wanted to see how you were doing," said Meri sweetly. Sandra groaned, sensing the ruse. "Actually... I could use two things. Some clothes, and some advice. So... I... Earlier today, at the bridge..."

"Spit it out, little sister." Though not truly related to Meri, Sandra was about five years older and had self-styled herself as the older sibling in their friendship.

"I... that is... I asked Saren to meet me tomorrow night. Ragen won't be around." The last part was a hushed, conspiratory whisper.

Sandra sat straight up, clenched shut her eyes, and flopped right back down with a dizzy groan.

"So, little Meri is finally going to become a *big girl*," she drawled, a sly smile crossing her tired face.

"Sandy, it's not like that! It's... well, it *is* like that! And I'm not sure what to do. I thought, well, that you might give me some advice." Meri flopped to the chair opposite Sandra and began playing her fingers through her hair.

Sandra pushed herself into a seated position, and with more success this time. She leveled a glare at Meri, her eyes sparkling emerald ponds. "So, you came to the local whore for advice?"

Whore. Meri had heard that word whispered around Dunmore and the inn, particularly from other village women, about Sandra. Sandra bitterly resented the term, and said those others were simply jealous that she drew the eyes of their brothers, sons, and husbands. "Absolutely not! But, you have so many stories, and I thought you could help. And, who else would I talk to? My father?"

"You know I'm kidding you, little sis. But, I'm surprised, though." Sandra fumbled around with some matches, lighting a sweet lavender candle. The usually-calming scent filled Meri's nostrils, though it did little to massage her taut nerves. "You've been talking about Saren for a year, now. More than a year, maybe. And, you've always talked about marriage first. What makes you suddenly so bold?"

"I... I'm not sure. Maybe, I felt like I needed to *do* something for a change. Instead of continuing to wait. I'm sick of waiting, Sandy." Meri continued to fiddle with the ends of her hair, tugging on the platinum locks. She didn't look up.

"And what would your Taneo say about this? What would your Yetra say about this?"

"He is not *my* Taneo, and she is not *my* Yetra. Taneo Marsh belongs to the Dunford, to the people. And Yetra belongs to us all." Sandra theatrically rolled her eyes and stuck out her tongue. She wouldn't soon be a convert. "But, I've thought about this. *The Book* speaks a great deal about love, about laying with a man. The act is sacred, and it is meant to bring new life into this world, to spread Harmony. *The Book* says nothing about marriage; I think that's something added later, more of a tradition than a Yetranian law. And... I think I love Saren, and that he can grow to love me. I think we can have something special."

"You love him?" Sandra's tone was flat.

"Well... I might. And Phillipa writes 'The only risks worth taking are those for love.' So I need to take that risk. You've hear what they've said about Saren and his friends—they aren't interested in the cow unless they are sure they like the milk." She'd heard rumors about Saren, that he was quite willing to bed women in Dunmore and some of the small, nearby communities. Farmers daughters, that kind of thing. She'd seen no hard proof, but the whispers... Most men, Meri thought, seemed to treat

Yetranian guidelines on sex and marriage as more loose suggestions than rules.

"And, you expect your... *milk* might convince him to buy Merigold, the mooing cow?" Sandra raised an eyebrow.

Meri shook her head. "No. Or yes. But, I think that Saren and I have a deeper connection than you expect, than he might have with other girls. And, I think we just need a night together to continue to build our bond. Like Phillipa says...."

"'The only risks worth taking are those for love'," mocked Sandra. She stretched languorously, shifting and reclining into her couch like a dog seeking just the right spot for a nap. "Your little book can justify anything if you look closely enough. But, use whatever justification you need, little sis, to finally get yourself speared."

"It's not like that, Sandy. It's more than just... lust," said Merigold, not sure whether she was being honest with herself. Why was she so keen on making love with Saren? Because she truly expected that Saren would end up her husband? Because she loved, or could love, this handsome forager and mender? Because she wanted some distraction from her guilt about that Fenrir? Or, was there some other reason, hidden from even Meri, that pushed her toward this man?

Sandra smiled a knowing smile. "Whatever you say, flower girl. Now, relax and let me tell you a little bit about how a man works."

Sandra began teaching then, starting with how to kiss a man. How to gently brush his lips and then pull away. How to kiss his neck and move to his ear and whisper something dirty.

"Something like 'I can't wait to feel your sword inside me.' You try, little sis."

"Um… 'I want to feel, uh, your sword, uh…'" attempted Meri, turning as red as the innards of a cherry pie.

"That's great—you are really getting it," said Sandra sardonically. "Either way, let's continue. With your cute little body, you can say gibberish and still make a man pop out of his trousers." Meri felt like her head would pop with so much blood having rushed to her face.

Sandra continued, discussing how to remove a man's shirt without interrupting the kissing. How to step back and remove her own blouse, in full sight of that man. How it made them go crazy. How to start handling him with his trousers still on, making him want it so badly. Then, lying back on whatever surface was nearby—a bed, a counter, a barrel—and beckoning him. Letting him remove your garments. Forcing his head into your flower (but be sure to scrub first! Sandra had a great recipe consisting of ungle flowers and vinegar). "Then, once he's done you a favor," Sandra said, "since his cock likely won't be able to do the job on its own, unlace his trousers. Let him enter you, but draw backwards so he'll have to move slowly."

"But, Sandy. Does it hurt… the first time?" asked Meri, starting to feel a touch of excitement about the whole ordeal—a very physical excitement, truth be told. The arousal mingled with her anxiety until the two swirled together like a summer storm.

"Gods, I can barely remember. I was so young," said Sandy, becoming a bit withdrawn, face shadowed. "But yes, I believe it hurts. And let him know it hurts! Men revel in that pain, knowing that they are the first to despoil you."

"Not despoil! I told you, Sandy, it's more than that. He will come to love me."

"Love and fucking are not as related as you think," Sandra said, her face as serious as stone. "Now, even though he is inside you, on top of you, don't give him control…"

82

Sandra continued to discuss how a woman could use her legs and buttocks to maintain control, to push him out and guide him in. How she could, and should, flip him onto his back and lower herself upon him, just a little at a time, just onto the tip of his cock at first. Then, how to crash down upon him, taking the entire thing. How to lean back and pull back her hair, putting her body on display as she moved up and down on top of him. And, when he seemed like he would climax, how to remain completely still for a minute or more, buying more time, making him last. Then, when he finally would finish, Sandra said it would be like the rush of a waterfall.

Meri couldn't help her excitement at this point in the conversation, her lips parted and her eyes wide. Locking with Sandra's green eyes for a long, breathless moment. Then she glanced away, letting her hair fall over her face.

Love is the catalyst for procreation. All else is touched...

"So, two things. You will need some promade and axsil extract. It will keep you from bearing a child. And you Yetranians do *not* want to get pregnant before marriage. Say whatever you will about love and creating new life through Harmony, or whatever they are feeding you in that chapel. But, you end up unmarried and pregnant, you'll see how quickly they turn their backs on you."

"Sandy, I can't..." Meri began.

"And second, keep a little olive oil on hand just in case you grow nervous." Sandra barreled right over her concerns. "Just rub a little bit down below before the action begins. But be subtle—no man likes to know that he fails to make a woman wet."

Sandra, seemingly completely recovered from her earlier malaise, walked into her second room after she finished offering this last bit of advice. In a matter of minutes, she returned with a small burlap bag containing two small vials—one of the extract and one of olive oil. And, over her shoulder, she had a simple, dark blue dress.

"Here, little sis. This will get you through the night. And this dress will set off your eyes, making them appear to glow. You will do fine. I just know you will! I'm very proud of you, little sister. Or should I say, little woman," Sandra laughed at her own joke as she cupped Meri's chin in her hand for just a moment before pushing her toward the door.

"Now, if you'd excuse me, little sis, I have my own date to prepare for."

Chapter 6

Following his encounter with Tennyson, Fenrir slept for two straight days. Evidently, the adrenaline from having his life threatened, first by a street-tough and some little girl, and then by Ultner himself, had combined with his head injury to create a perfect storm which simply shut down Fenrir's mind and body. He awoke confused and dehydrated, uncertain if the last several days had been real or a dream. A vivid and dangerous dream, to be sure—full of muck, fingers, and small, short-haired urchins stabbing him in the stomach. Based on the wholeness of his midsection, the odds were at least slim that the latter event had occurred.

Stumbling out of his boarding room, Fenrir made his way down to the nearest spigot and took a deep drink of water. Rostane was famous for its water system, where great water barrels stood atop many major, local buildings. Urchins (and even some industrious, impoverished adults and the occasional Wasmer) carried water from the local wells and the Fullane River to the tops of these buildings all day, keeping the barrels filled in exchange for a meager living. The water was then forced out of numerous spigots and outdoor public showers around the city, allowing people to easily access the liquid for their various purposes. In this way, Little Duke Penton could give lip service to helping the poor and homeless, both in allowing them easy access to water and in providing jobs. Of course, it had been his father, Samuel II, who'd actually invested in these public works.

A current beneficiary of the system, Fenrir drank his fill and soon felt better, noticing that even the ache in his knee was beginning to lessen. The contusion on the back of his head was far less sensitive to the touch, too, and he could actually bear sunlight without any pain. To capitalize on his recovery from injury, and to help him feel human again, Fenrir thoroughly washed himself, first buying a bar of beeswax soap from an ironically unclean vendor. Fenrir's purse was full of coin. He realized he must have cashed in his payment chit before returning to his room and commencing his temporary coma.

Fenrir chuckled at the thought. Even scared shitless and suffering from a bruised brain, securing his hard-earned cash was at the top of his damaged mind.

Once he'd washed, he found that evening was approaching, and a gnawing emptiness in his stomach sharply reminded him that he had last eaten at the crossroads market two and a half days before, so Fenrir set off to find a meal and a beverage a bit stronger than water.

Fenrir listlessly ambled toward the Gathering, a cluster of inns and taverns decent enough to offer a good meal and drink, but rough enough that he could afford to be a frequent visitor. He hadn't the motivation to move any faster than a stroll. It may have been the malnutrition or the lingering effects of his head wound, but Fenrir was in a stupor, as if he were wading through the wetlands again as a young recruit, knee deep in muck and barely mustering the strength to press forward. His mind, too, was distant and disjointed, and seemingly unable to peel away from his recent demotion within The House.

Truth be told, Fenrir had never particularly relished the job, working as an enforcer. He might be willing to break bones and detach digits, but Tennyson was wrong—he didn't do so happily. Some enforcers would beg from more work, desiring an outlet for their sickest desires. Aaron the Slicer, for instance, relished causing fear and pain, taking the finger one tiny slice at a time. The Demon—Fenrir didn't know his real name—'convinced' people to slice off their own finger, typically using various threats against their loved ones or more delicate parts of the body. "Your cock or your finger," was said to be his preferred ultimatum. Maybe there were some cocks mixed in with Tennyson's box of fingers.

No, Fenrir didn't relish the work, but he was willing to do it. The most staggering regret about this was all about status. After being disgraced from the Plateau's guard, Fenrir at least had some semblance of status, of respect, working for The House, and there was not a single damned job that paid better. With only a few contracts a year, he'd been able to pay his rent, stay well-fed, and keep himself at least relatively drunk most evenings. There'd even been money left over for other obligations. Soft, warm, feminine obligations.

Now he no longer had that guarantee, and he didn't know what The House would want from him. From Tennyson's tone, Fenrir needed to lie low for a few days. As always, they would contact him when he was needed. Just what he would be needed for, he had no idea—nor did he know how lucrative his new role would be. He would obviously not be taking any more fingers, and he certainly wouldn't be getting a promotion to eliminator: essentially the same job, though the conclusion was a dead body. The real trick there was to eliminate with very little visible harm, aside from the missing finger taken previously by an enforcer. A real art, it was.

Though his future was relatively unknown, Fenrir at least retained some modicum of control in his life. He still had a purse full of coin and the ability to get truly, and obliviously, drunk.

Arriving at one of his favorite spots, Yetra's Embrace (surprisingly, not a religious establishment, but actually the name of one of Fenrir's favorite sexual positions), Fenrir got a table and ordered some ham, fried potatoes, and a local stout ale. And more ham. Gods, he was starving. Lisa, the bar maiden, winked at him. She was generally too old for his tastes—about his age—but nonetheless, he still gave her his patented charming grin. Any port in a storm, and, in his experience, Lisa's port was still pretty cozy.

He quaffed his first stout in one long pull and called for a second. By the time his food came, Fenrir was finishing up his third and starting to feel the effects. A week sober, coupled with an extremely hollow stomach, must have affected his tolerance. He started digging into his ham and potatoes, barely stopping to chew or breathe.

The Embrace was not particularly busy this evening, so Fenrir was able to subvert Lisa from her tasks and sit with her, regaling her with his latest partially-fabricated story. It was based in truth, but Fenrir knew that the exaggerations were always more believable.

"That's right, sweet Lisa. The innkeeper simply attacked me for talking with his daughter! I was being a polite traveler, telling a small-town girl about the wonders of Rostane, when I was suddenly struck from behind. Luckily, I rolled forward as he struck, and it was only a glancing blow," he said, partially mimicking a dive forward. Taking a sip from his sixth tall drink for the evening, Fenrir started thinking that Lisa was looking like a better and better option. He was supposed to be lying low, after all, and what better place to hide than another person's bed?

All at once, Fenrir felt his consciousness ripped from his body, hurtling toward the ceiling in spray of colors and sounds. The fucking Phantom, at a time like this. Phantom-Fenrir, in the typical dissociated way, could see himself animatedly speaking to Lisa, a woman of average height and build with raven-black hair tied in pigtails. Despite her age, she was actually rather pretty, and only had a few wrinkles at the corners of her eyes and lips. Fenrir, next looking at himself, and seeing a week's worth of beard that was as much gray as brown, with his body showing a bit more paunch on the sides than he would like, realized that he might have to start realigning his expectations regarding women. Although, listening to himself, he appreciated that he still had a knack for weaving a story.

Behind his corporeal body, though, Phantom Fenrir noted that there was a dark-hooded figure approaching. The evening was a bit chilly, but the skies were clear and there was no hint of rain. In Fenrir's experience, an obscured head typically meant trouble. And that perception of trouble was reinforced by the flash of metal that he spotted at the figure's wrist.

He could see this person approaching him while his body continued to talk, laugh, and sip at his beer. Phantom-Fenrir willed his body to react, to move, to recognize the danger. He tried to move his legs, his arms, or even to turn his neck to notice this figure. To mobilize his body in some way, to *protect* himself. But there was no response. Body-Fenrir continued to carouse and flirt, and nothing Phantom-Fenrir tried could prompt his body to defend itself.

Ultimately, it was luck that saved Fenrir's life. His body told a story of obvious heroism, fighting off multiple inn patrons (mostly skilled swordsmen) with the discarded leg of an old barstool, and meanwhile the figure closed the distance. Just as his assailant struck, knife arching toward the right side of his target's neck, Body-Fenrir knocked over his beer while pantomiming the battle. As the beer splashed all over Lisa and pooled on the ground, Fenrir lost his balance and flailed his arms. The small knife of the hooded figure, rather than plunging into Body-Fenrir's neck and severing an artery, sank halfway into his bulky shoulder.

Phantom-Fenrir could see his body pitch out of his seat and land on the ground, staring for a moment at the knife in his shoulder before roaring and jumping to his feet. Though not trained in this particular skill in the military, he was quite familiar with reacting to a sudden attack in a bar while halfway into his cups. The would-be assassin let out a curse and darted toward the door. Fenrir grabbed a bar stool with his good arm and flung it at the man, hitting him squarely in the back. As the man lost his feet, Body-Fenrir started forward toward his assailant. Phantom-Fenrir tried to call out a warning, but it was again ineffectual—his corporeal self immediately slipped in the spilled beer, going down hard. Right on the knife sticking out of his shoulder.

The phantom and body were suddenly rejoined in a confusing blur, and Fenrir felt as if his entire arm had been dipped in tar and set alight. He tried to ignore the pain and push himself back up and toward the door anyway, but his attacker had already recovered and was nowhere to be seen. Confused patrons were milling about, deer in shock as one of their own was taken down by a predator. Rather than making a failed attempt at pursuit, Fenrir slumped back into a seat and attempted to pull out the knife, which had been lodged two or three inches deep into the meat of his shoulder.

Luckily, he was The Bull. If he'd been a smaller man, something important might have been severed. But, by Ultner's deviated asshole, did it hurt!

Thankfully, Lisa was very gentle with him that night. After cleaning his puncture wound with grain alcohol, she (urged by the owner of Yetra's Embrace, who would rather not involve the city guard) egressed him to her room, sewing him up with the deftness of someone who had mended clothes her whole life. Fenrir continued to sip on the strong alcohol he'd been given, granting him fortitude as the needle entered and exited his flesh repeatedly, catgut binding his skin together. Then, very gently, Lisa mounted him, moving slowly to avoid jarring his wound and further distracting him from his pain.

Between the wound and the liquor, the aching fun lasted quite a long time.

In the morning, despite the new agony from the stabbing and the more familiar throbbing of hangover, Fenrir left before Lisa began to stir, quietly dressing in his breeches and bloodstained shirt. He needed to do some reconnaissance, and try to figure out who was targeting him. This wasn't a random attack—from his phantasmic vantage, Fenrir could see the hooded man move, unerringly, toward him.

The list of people who would desire his death would be long, as long as the number of fingers he'd collected. But, his membership with The House should have protected him from retaliation. *Had* protected him from retaliation for the past two years. Which could mean that The House's stock was falling in the city—those street toughs who attacked him evidenced that theory. Or, it could mean that The House, itself, resolved to scrub him from their roster in a very permanent way. That Tennyson decided not to stain his floorboards with Fenrir's blood and thought a delayed, public hit would be best. If that was the case, Fenrir would have to run, leaving Rostane behind. Leaving the country behind. Even then, he might not be safe. Fenrir had no idea how widespread the organization really was.

It wasn't a long walk back to his boarding house, where he'd have a chance to put on some less blood-spattered clothes. At this rate, he would need a new wardrobe. Fenrir held his right arm gingerly, pinning it to his chest with his left arm to relieve the pressure on the wound. He couldn't catch a godsdamned break. He'd probably need to have an actual physician check out his wound and perhaps get him in a sling for a couple of weeks. With luck, he could find Martis, his physician friend who lived near the Plateau.

Lost in thought and pain, Fenrir paid no mind to a group of three men waiting at the entrance of his boarding house. As he fumbled with his key, though, one of the men roughly grabbed his good arm.

"Fenrir de Trenton, I need you to come with me," said the man in a measured, precise voice.

Fenrir twisted out of the man's grip and turned rapidly, clenching his teeth as his wound strained at the stitches. The three men were wearing well-made silk clothing, their shirts each dyed a brilliant blue and bearing a small, three-masted ship emblazoned on the breast. The color and insignia denoted their loyalty. To his father, Darian de Trenton.

"Siggy, I don't have time for this shit right now. Tell my father that I'll be by tomorrow," said Fenrir, assuming he'd be halfway to Hunesa by then.

"It's *Sigmund*, you little shit. And I'm afraid this isn't optional," said Sigmund Fitra with a smug smile. Sigmund was a little older than Fenrir, and one of his childhood... acquaintances. Fenrir hated the man. Actually, hate was an understatement. Fenrir loathed him with an unmatched passion. If Sigmund were being tied to an oil-soaked stake by an unruly mob and was crying to Fenrir for help, Fenrir would provide the match. And kindling. And maybe dance about the bonfire a bit for good measure.

Fenrir knew he could take Sigmund in a fair fight. The little slug was all skin and bones. Probably the reason that he'd brought the muscle in the form of Frye and Frayne Masterly, two other childhood acquaintances whom Fenrir hated a bit less. They were too dumb to hate. But, given their presence, Fenrir had little choice but to comply. Frye and Frayne were twins, each the size of a walrus and about as handsome. He'd once seen Frye wrestle a small horse to the ground on a dare, and Frayne was at least as capable.

"Fine, I'll see the old man. Let me change my shirt and I'll be right down," Fenrir said with his best disarming grin.

"You think I'm simple? You are coming with me now, clothing be damned. When Principal de Trenton 'requests' someone's presence, they come immediately. No matter how slovenly they look." Sigmund theatrically examined Fenrir with a curled lip.

Fenrir shrugged painfully. It was a shame that Sigmund wasn't as dumb as he looked.

"You're the boss, *Siggy.* Lead on.*"

Sigmund clenched his fists and took a step forward, as did Frye and Frayne, too dense to do anything but mimic their leader. With an obvious effort then, Sigmund regained control, his pinched face twisting into a sinister smile.

By the gods, Fenrir wanted to smash that fucking twisted face. Actually, he once had, which accounted for Sigmund's slightly crooked nose. One of the best days of his teenage years.

The group of four wove their way through the western district of Spring Market where merchants were just starting to set up their wares. The highest-quality meat and produce was always sold in the Spring Market, meaning that it was clogged with farmers and their carts attempting to reach their rented stalls. The butchers and fishmongers tended to have storefronts, offering a variety of local chicken, fish, beef, veal, and duck. Many of these butcher shops were clients of the de Trenton merchant empire, utilizing the specialized cooling system invented by Fenrir's father. Everywhere, there was a reminder of his father.

As the group walked through one of the food markets, Fenrir abruptly stopped at a stall and ordered some kabobs, a Sestrian favorite that was becoming increasingly popular in Rostane. Lamb on a stick, the perfect street food. Frye, Frayne, and Sigmund were taken off-guard and walked a few extra steps before anyone noticed the sheep who had strayed from the flock. Sigmund reversed first, storming angrily back to Fenrir just as he turned around holding four kabobs. Sigmund glowered as Fenrir handed a kabob each to Frye and Frayne. Fenrir made as if to hand one to

Sigmund, as well, but instead fumbled the kabob with his injured arm, flicking Sigmund's silk shirt with bits of juice before the stick of meat tumbled to the ground.

"My apologies, Siggy. Injury and all," said Fenrir, his voice oozing sincerity.

Sigmund drew close, hissing into Fenrir's ear. "You will pay for that, you little shit-mouthed, wannabe criminal. You'll be getting yours soon enough. All I need to do is watch and wait. It's almost too easy, watching you dig your own grave."

Frye and Frayne flanked Sigmund, with Frye tossing aside his food and trying to look menacing while Frayne tore the meat off of his own stick with his teeth, licking his fingers as the juice coated his skin.

"Well, shall we see my father?"

The de Trenton estate was more of a stronghold—an armed compound—than a typical wealthy merchant's domain. In the northeast quadrant of the city, relatively isolated from the warehouse district by design, the walled compound had its own private guard: the Blue Adders, trained by masters of war from around Saiwen and Ingrem, the southern and northern continents. The Adders were certainly better trained than the city guard, Fenrir knew for a fact. These warriors—resplendent in the signature vivid blue of the de Trenton family—stood watch at the closed gates and vigilantly patrolled the walls in trios at uneven, unpredictable intervals, vicious, prowling cats of prey. Unlike the guards along the walls of Rostane, these men and women showed no sign of boredom or negligence. And for good reasons. Six times in the last four years had infiltrators been caught, all of them attempting to extract the secrets contained within the compound. Such intruders were dealt with harshly, typically killed by the Adders in "self-defense." One body part at a time.

There were over two-dozen separate buildings in the compound, including the surprisingly austere, but intimidatingly large, living quarters, workers' and servants' quarters, the extensive barracks (the Adder's Nest), and a private stable (from which Fenrir had openly purloined a horse just a couple of weeks ago for his trip to Umberton). Set back from the storage facilities and warehouses was the crown jewel of the de Trenton estate. And it was an ugly fucking jewel. The laboratory was little more than a gigantic, reddish-gray, rectangular prism. A huge, windowless building with five-foot thick walls, a massive water barrel on the west side of the roof, and a steady flow of steam emitting from dozens thick tubes protruding from the roof, countless horns from the head of a demon. The steam—visible from any vantage in the city—gave the laboratory its sinister nickname... the Furnace.

If the Furnace's appearance was not auspicious enough, there were forty Blue Adders standing guard along the perimeter, changing shifts every hour to ensure attentiveness. There were a dozen more soldiers standing atop the roof; not a desirable shift, given the heat that sprayed from the steam pipes. Fenrir had always though that his father might as well have written "Secrets Inside" in big black letters on the side of the building. Not that it really mattered; that building was more impenetrable than the Plateau.

Sigmund, Frye, and Frayne led Fenrir not toward the living quarters, nor toward the Furnace, but rather toward the shipping depot. Near the second, much wider entrance to the compound, the shipping depot was always hectic—if an extremely organized type of hectic—during daytime hours. Wagons and carts lined up for attention, with one trader, wagoner, or teamster allowed per vehicle. Each agent pulled up to one of five loading areas, handed the lead porters an order, and the order was filled quickly and efficiently by a team of talented porters. The whole area was even kept clean by an industrious group of boys (typically children of the porters or servants) who were tasked with gathering up the animal droppings and putting them all in large, mobile receptacles. Fenrir understood that the shit was sometimes used by the chemists and researchers, but had never wanted to know exactly how.

Sigmund led the group into a back entrance of the depot, nodding to a pair of Blue Adders as they went, both of them females. Fenrir grinned and winked at the ladies. One ignored him completely, while the second—a vaguely-familiar Sestrian with a long, dark braid—narrowed her eyes and hissed at him. He must have been losing his touch.

The inside of the depot was its own brand of organized chaos, an anthill, with porters running to and fro, shifting a variety of boxes, crates, and barrels to the loading docks to address the day's orders. Meanwhile, the depot was constantly resupplied from the other warehouses which, in turn, were always being filled with imported goods from around Rostane and beyond. Spices, meats, and even furs—the business had grown so much that Fenrir barely recognized some of the products. For instance, there was a pile of coats that must have been made out of some sort of lizard. A giant, man-sized lizard. Fenrir made a mental note to figure out where those coats came from, and then make a concerted effort to never go within a hundred miles of the place.

The fifth loading dock was the most heavily-staffed and heavily-guarded, as it was where the specialty product was concentrated. The creation upon which the de Trenton fortune had been built. In specialized chests, lined with triple-thick wool insulation, was burning ice. Blocks of a steaming, pinkish substance, created with chemistry and—for all Fenrir knew— probably magic. The substance had the ability to pull the skin right off of a man, but within those chests, meats, beers, wines, and so on would keep chilled for up to two weeks. This had revolutionized trade, and well-guarded de Trenton laboratories had been built in most major cities in Ardia, not to mention those that had appeared in major shipping ports in Sestra, Rafón, and Algania. Competitors from all over the known world had attempted to duplicate—or steal—the burning ice recipe. But, the Blue Adders prevented that.

Fenrir reflected on the darker side of the de Trenton empire as they moved through it. Stories of a researcher in Hunesa turning up missing, his laboratory being destroyed with a small explosion. Rival merchants suddenly giving up their life's work, moving to other countries. Even a former chemist from the de Trenton lab finding himself without a tongue (but also with a huge pile of yets that had allowed him to move to a small island off the coast of Sestra). Nothing was ever linked back to Darian, but Fenrir had more than just suspicions.

Up a set of stairs, a pair of Blue Adders. A long hallway down, another pair of Blue Adders. And then Fenrir found himself face-to-face with his father, Darian de Trenton. Darian was a man in his early sixties, resembling a leather whip. The man, tall, tanned, and sinewy, seemed to emanate a feeling of barely-restrained force, a trebuchet inhibited by a single pin. His eyes—a deep blue, almost black—seemed to absorb everything around him. And, when that gaze locked upon an unfortunate target, it seemed to strip a man of his defenses, peeling back skin, muscle, and flesh to see the soul beneath. As Darian sat behind his modest desk, hands steepled, Fenrir found himself under this fierce scrutiny for a solid minute—which felt like an hour.

"Principal, we have retrieved the man Fenrir de Trenton. Please note that he did not come willingly, and he needed to be persuaded," said Sigmund, keeping a carefully-professional tone.

"Sigmund, thank you for *your* service and loyalty, as always. You are dismissed," noted Darian, his voice gravelly from years spent near caustic chemicals.

"Principal, I had thought…"

"Dismissed. Now."

Sigmund gave a small, deferential bow, turning toward the door. Quite accidentally bumping Fenrir in his injured should while leaving the room. Meanwhile, Darian continued to dissect Fenrir with his razor stare, whilst Fenrir felt increasingly uncomfortable.

"Father, it has been some time," started Fenrir, unable to bear the scrutiny any longer. He knew better than to speak first—one of the primary rules of negotiating—but it was difficult not to break under his father's examination. Every discussion with this man was a negotiation.

"Fenrir," said Darian with a nod. Not "son." Never "son."

"I hope the day finds you well, Father. You look as healthy as always." The thought of Darian being unhealthy was almost laughable. Fenrir hadn't ever seen him sick, and any injury was shrugged off. When Fenrir was a boy, before Darian had fully established his mercantile empire, he still recalled seeing his father's hand impaled by a piece of glass during a small explosion in the chemistry lab. Darian had walked out of the laboratory, pulled the glass out with some pliers, wrapped his injury in a cloth, and gone immediately back to work. The man was as immovable as the Tulanques.

"The same cannot be said of you, boy," Darian grated. *Boy*. Fenrir could almost pretend that was a term of mild familial endearment, although he was relatively sure that Darian called everyone 'boy.'

"My apologies, Father. I lacked the opportunity to change my clothes. Your summons came so quickly. I had a small accident, but I assure you it is nothing to worry about," Fenrir said, falling into the familiar formality of having both worked for his father and served for a decade and a half in providing protection for nobles. Fenrir shivered now, though, having the distinct feeling that Darian knew exactly what had happened. His father had a larger network than even Little Duke Penton. By Ultner, his stretch might even rival The House.

"What do you require of me, Father?" Might as well get to the point. Somehow, this meeting was less desirable than that he'd had with Tennyson.

"Tell me, boy. What have you been up to over the last year or so?" asked Darian, knowing damn well what Fenrir had been up to, if Sigmund's earlier comment had been any indication.

"I've mostly been working, on and off. Primarily running protection duty for caravans operating between Florens and Hunesa. Merchants are always looking for men with military experience," explained Fenrir. This wasn't precisely a lie. In the last two years, he had protected exactly one caravan each to Florens and Hunesa. In both cases, he'd spent his money upon arrival, getting drunk and brawling in Florens, and getting really drunk and whoring in Hunesa. Either way, a long walk home.

Darian rose from his seat—a simple, well-made wooden chair—leveling his gaze at Fenrir. His father had about an inch on him, but it might as well have been a foot.

"You lie, boy. And, I am not surprised by this. You always lie," said Darian, not raising his voice. Still, Fenrir felt his malice. "No, you've been off doing work for your new *friends*, the parasites that infest this city. In fact, I understand you recently had a run-in with Martin Frommis, a long-standing friend of this family."

99

There was no point in hiding it. "Yes, I bumped into the man," said Fenrir.

"*Bumped* into him?" Darian raised an appraising eyebrow.

"With a knife."

Darian stepped closer to Fenrir, standing an arm's length away. Fenrir could smell the omnipresent mint on Darian's breath. To Fenrir, it was the odor of rotten meat. "Some honesty, at last. It must be a hard thing, a personal thing, to hurt a man in the way you do. I wonder how it's changed you. Has it changed you, boy?"

Fenrir had no idea what Darian was after here. Whatever it was, Fenrir wanted to give him the opposite.

Fenrir grinned his most irritating grin. "I am the same man that I have always been, Father."

Darian studied Fenrir's face while Fenrir labored to maintain his smile. His father's eyes, sharp as twin knives, cut into him, searching for something. Fenrir's heart pounded hollowly in his rib cage while his stomach twisted and roiled, as if he'd drank a gallon of sour milk. His eyes stung as he struggled to meet Darian's glare without blinking, still maintaining Ultner's smile.

After an eternity, Darian shook his head, apparently not finding what he was looking for. "I shouldn't be surprised. You are nothing more than a common criminal, an unsightly stain on our civil society. You know, boy, I once thought you could be something great. I once thought you could even step into my shoes, one day, and run all of this. You were always clever, smart. Able to see beyond the immediate problem. Able to sway people to your side, even when you were obviously wrong."

"Like I said, I'm the same man I've always been," said Fenrir.

"Unchanged." Darian spat the word like the fiercest insult. "Unaltered. At one point, I expected more from you. That you would quit that military foolishness and take your place in the family business. Ever since your brothers died…"

"They were *not* my brothers," growled Fenrir, briefly overcoming his dread of his father, the Bull replacing the compliant son.

Darian stepped forward with a speed that belied his age, slapping Fenrir across the jaw. "You will not interrupt me, boy! My sons, they were. And, whether you shared a mother or not, they were your brothers. After they died, your place was here, learning the business. But you stayed in the military, continuing to underachieve at an amazing rate. What was it? Fifteen years with only a single promotion? A promotion that I arranged! Certainly nothing you earned."

Fenrir's cheek stung and he shrank in the face of his father's anger. He felt, again, like he was a child, being berated for shirking his duties. For showing any sort of weakness. For coming home with a mangled leg after being nearly beaten to death by Sigmund, Ethan, and Aiden. But, he wasn't a child anymore. By the gods, he would not be treated like this. The Bull continued to buck.

"And nothing I wanted! It is beyond you to understand that people can be satisfied with what they have, satisfied with their lives. I did your bidding. I married that shrew Bethany, gave you a granddaughter."

"I didn't want a granddaughter! I wanted a son who is worth a damn, and I wanted a line of strong heirs for this empire that I have built. This should be a legacy to span generations, to last hundreds of years! But you, Fenrir, couldn't be bothered to inconvenience your life by honoring me, your godsdamned father. The man who gave you life." His rage was popping, boiling pitch, threatening to burn Fenrir. But, Fenrir was beyond caring, lost in his own fury at being struck, at the frustration of the past days.

"Yes, you gave me life and nothing else! You've never treated me as a son. The third born, spawn of the second wife." Fenrir's fists were clenched at his side.

"I loved Astora, you ungrateful sloth!" snarled Darian, twisting back as if to strike Fenrir again.

But, Fenrir persisted. By the gods, he had nothing to lose at this point, given that he was likely to be killed by someone or another in the near future. He stepped forward. "I'm certain you did, the way that you ignored her. The way you let your *heirs* demean and humiliate her for her Domain looks, her Domain ways. My mother, the only true person in my life, brought to the brink by your negligence and the abuse of your children."

Darian struck at Fenrir again, but Fenrir was ready this time, blocking the blow with his forearm. Then, suddenly, he was on one knee, clenching shut his eyes and grimacing in pain, his father's hand digging into the puncture in his shoulder, tearing apart the stitches.

In barely more than a hiss, his father said, "I called you here, today, to see if there was anything left of the man you could be, to see if you were worth salvaging. To see if any honor remained with you. To see if, maybe, your hard life had made you a harder man. A better man. Instead I find a shell, little more than a vile little criminal, taking up with the savages in The House. I thought I might be able to find my blood somewhere within you, find a true heir. But, no."

Fenrir grasped at Darian's wrist as he continued to dig his fingers into the wound. Darian batted aside the attempt.

"From this day forward, you are no longer my son. You are no longer my heir. You are no longer a de Trenton. If I find you using my name, you will be severely punished. If you enter any of

102

my holdings, you will be killed on sight. I would kill you now if I thought you knew any of the family secrets. Your sloth is saving your life, but I am never to see you again."

Darian released Fenrir with a shove. He landed hard on the ground, twisting his weak knee in the process. Darian's hands were dripping with the blood of his former son. Now, just the blood of a man on the street, so far as he was concerned. Fenrir, clutching his widened, bleeding wound, staggered to his feet. He stared at the man who he'd once considered his father, expecting to feel anger. Or sadness. Or even remorse. But all he felt was the pain of his wound and the desire to inflict pain, any kind of pain, upon the man in front of him.

"Sleep well, *Darian*. With the blood of your son, and his mother, on your hands," Fenrir said through gritted teeth as he turned and limped out the door.

Chapter 7

Merigold was ready.

She scrutinized herself once more in her full-length mirror, a birthday gift from her father when she'd reached her majority, years ago. Sandra's dress was gorgeous. A simple, dark blue sleeveless affair with a moderately-low neckline (lower than Meri was used to, but still respectable), the hemline falling just above her knees. The dress must have hung off of Sandra's willowy frame, but it was nearly a perfect fit for Meri. She tied a small, white ribbon around her waist, and found an old, but still mostly white, shawl to drape over her bare shoulders.

Meri had even taken the time to braid her hair in a special way. Most often, she wore her hair in a loose ponytail, which was quick and kept the hair out of her face while she waited tables. Today, she wove her hair into three separate braids and then further wove these together. The result was a tight cascade of icy blonde hair that flowed over her shoulder. It took two hours, but Meri was very pleased with the result. It perfectly complemented her sapphire studs.

She tinged her lips red with a salve she had made from berries and wax secreted away from her father. He never liked for her to alter her appearance, saying that she was perfect as she was. Of course, he didn't have to look into the mirror and see how thin her lips were!

Merigold also spent the time to make sure that she was groomed and cleaned… everywhere. Just like Sandra had suggested.

Now, she just waited. Dear Yetra, why hadn't she picked a place to meet Saren? He'd said that he would find her tonight. Where would he look? Would he come to her house? Would he be looking in the town square, or at the small tavern by the chapel? Should she head to the bridge? The sun was already going down, which, to her, seemed to suggest the evening had arrived. Meri wanted to leave the house and check other possible locations, but was afraid that she would miss him if he came to her home.

So, Meri continued to sit. And stand. And sit again. And pace. She started knitting her blue shawl for a few minutes, but then found that she was making too many mistakes and gave up the attempt. She'd have to spend twice as much time fixing all the dropped stitches the next day. She started tidying up the already spotless house next, dusting clean shelves, rearranging knick-knacks. Meri even moved a rug from the welcome room into her bedroom, just because.

She even leafed through *The Book of Amorum*, the only reading material in the house. But, she was briefly overwhelmed with guilt in response—Yetra would not approve of her plans for the evening. The goddess was said to have been completely chaste before her Ascension.

Yetra raised her hand, cleaving the crimson firmament in twain, freeing the world from the scourge of Pandemonium, bathing the earth in Harmony. Her purity and her need gifted her with the requisite power. Prenen.

Merigold did not understand how she could be simultaneously dreading and eager for her meeting tonight with Saren. Part of her wanted to toss aside this fancy dress, stuff herself back into her bar clothes, and head back to the inn and work nonstop. To do what she was used to, what was normal, what was safe. The other part of her wanted to toss aside the dress the second Saren arrived, taking him into her, finally discovering what love really was. To do the things that Sandra spoke of. To show Saren that she was all he wanted, all he needed. Standing at the window, she felt her legs shaking with fear and anticipation as she focused on the path leading to her house, awaiting Saren, the man she loved.

The sun had set now. There was no more light to see by, and Meri was sitting in the rocking chair, assuming that her planned evening wasn't going to happen. By now, the dinner rush would have ended at the Duckling, and she'd normally have been either cleaning up the kitchen or running errands to the various rooms of the inn, delivering pillows, sheets, and additional food or beer. Ragen would be tending to the regulars, and the more robust and thirsty travelers, handing out ales, food, and stories. Dear Yetra, she missed the inn! That was where she belonged, working with her father, attending to travelers from around the world. Doing the...

A knock at the door. A knock!

Merigold jumped from the chair to her feet, stumbling as the rocker righted itself and bumped the back of her knees. Her heart was pounding, and she stood for a moment trying to collect herself. She was ready. She was definitely ready.

Opening the door revealed Saren, looking freshly cut and trimmed, wearing a white shirt and brown pants, anchored by a set of suspenders. Sandra hadn't given Meri a strategy for suspenders! Merigold didn't know how those worked, so she would have to figure that extemporaneously.

"Hi, Saren. How are you this evening?" Meri asked, attempting to sound as if she hadn't been panicking for the last hour or two over his arrival.

"I'm doing fine, Merigold. You look lovely tonight," he answered, a smile playing across his mouth.

"This old thing? I just had it lying around the house. Speaking of, would you like to come in?" she asked, stepping back from the door to welcome him. Saren scrutinized the opening, but didn't cross the threshold.

"I thought we might go for a walk. Does that sound okay?"

Saren was always so considerate, asking rather than assuming.

"Of course! Lead the way!"

The two of them left Meri and Ragen's home, and began walking slowly toward the center of Dunmore. The sound of cicadas and hoppers created a comfortable silence that neither of the pair breached. Meri simply walked next to Saren, at his side, waiting for whatever would happen next.

The pair walked through the village. The square of the town was made up of a cluster of about fifty houses, a general store, a stone chapel, and a small tavern, all built in a similar fashion, using processed lumber from a nearby mill. Most houses were whitewashed, although a few folks had imported red or yellow paint from Rostane, and all were raised a couple feet from the ground in case of flooding—a not uncommon danger, this close to the lake. The chapel was the largest building in town, being the home to the bell tower. Since Dunmore lacked a smith, the iron bell had been imported at no small cost to the townsfolk, with Ragen footing most of the bill.

While walking, Meri and Saren only saw a few other townsfolk, most of them on their way to or from the tavern. Dunmore was a working town, and folk were typically in their homes by dark, with the intention of rising around sun-up. Meri did hear some giggles from the shadows behind the chapel, though, and she wondered who was necking back there. Could it have been Sandra, or was it one of the younger girls like Marissa or Penelo, finding someone to spend the cool spring evening with?

Meri and Saren approached a small trail that ran along Dunmore Lake—one that Meri was familiar with. Saren offered Meri his arm, and she was happy to hold on. His forearm was well-muscled, and provided immovable support as they continued down the trail, still not sharing many words. Saren had lit a small lantern that he had swinging from his waist. The cicadas, night crawlers, and hoppers continued to play a symphony, getting louder and louder to the point that Meri would practically have had to shout to be heard. She felt as if they were isolated, away from everything that she knew. About a mile from the village, that might as well have been a reality.

Meri suddenly stopped and pulled back from Saren's arm, turning and facing him.

"Is everything okay, Merigold?" Saren asked, some uncertainty evident in his voice.

"Yes, everything is wonderful," she said, parting her lips and meeting his in a passionate kiss. On her toes, Meri could feel Saren's beard, his lips, his tongue. She could feel his muscular body against hers as she continued to meet his lips. She could even feel him harden beneath his trousers. Meri almost pulled back at that, but persisted. She must show Saren that she could be the woman he needed, not just the innocent girl he'd grown up with.

She broke the kiss and whispered into his ear "I've wanted this for so long, Saren. As long as I've known you." It wasn't as dirty as what Sandra had suggested, but it was more honest.

Saren didn't say anything; he just kissed her fiercely for another moment. It was perfect. Just what she had always imagined. Until she was bitten by a mosquito. And another. Then, she became more aware of the strong taste (and smell) of beer and liquor in Saren's mouth. And a third mosquito bite! She pulled away and swatted at her leg.

"Come with me. I know a place," he said, taking Meri by the hand and leading her further into the woods.

They continued walking for nearly an hour, taking small paths that Meri did not know. Stepping over roots and ducking under branches, Meri was starting to get tired and sweaty. This was not quite the romantic setting she had envisioned. Her careful cleaning process was undoubtedly undone by now, and she had built up quite a collection of bug bites and small scrapes on her bare legs and arms. Having made the mistake of wearing sandals (she hadn't expected to be walking several miles in the dark), Meri was now sporting a stubbed toe and a rolled ankle. Saren no longer strictly supported her, but had her by the hand, pulling her along. He seemed completely unbothered by the walk and the intrusion of nature. Of course, he was wearing boots and was nearly completely covered by durable clothing, not to mention the fact that he was more accustomed to these paths and the outdoors in general.

Twice, she almost turned around, almost told Saren to lead her back home. But, she couldn't find the nerve.

Those journeys most fraught with peril tend to yield the richest rewards. Though the path didn't quite reach the level of being perilous, Yearen's aphorism would hopefully apply. That chapter had an aphorism that would apply to any situation.

They finally came to an almost undetectable clearing— something that Meri might have missed, had not Saren paused and turned—with a small cabin nestled under some willow trees. Hidden, really. Built in the old style of stacked and interlocking logs, it was old, moldy, and certainly abandoned. But, as Saren opened the door, Meri realized that it must still be in use. From the light of Phanos leaking into the windows, Meri could see that it was relatively clean on the inside, although it smelled of dampness, and unlit candles were scattered throughout the interior. There was a small kitchen area, apparently stocked with food and water. And there was a thin mattress sitting in the corner, covered in a grimy-looking, white-and-green knit quilt, similar to the ones they had at the inn, although much dirtier. Saren went around the room, lighting one candle from his lantern and then using that to light others in succession.

"What is this place?" asked Meri, stalling a bit as Saren walked toward her, setting his last candle on a simple wooden stand next to the bed. Flickering lights illuminated the single room now, and Meri was almost certain she saw a rat skitter behind a cabinet.

"It's an old trapper's cabin," said Saren, obviously not wanting to elaborate.

"Really? Tell me more!" The bed, that thin, uneven straw mattress, did not look particularly inviting. And, because of the heavy moisture and increasingly-evident smell of mildew, Meri was worried that it would be full of bugs, as well.

With a sigh, Saren went on. "Before Dunmore was primarily a fishing and foraging village, the area attracted a lot of fur trappers who made a living off of the beavers and muskrats in the wetlands. Since the egg trade has become the major source of income in Dunmore, there are fewer trappers around, and, if you know where to look, some of these cabins."

"Really? Wow, how did you find it?" asked Meri, knowing the history of Dunmore's trade probably better than Saren. Her father's business touched essentially every part of the economy for Dunmore and most of the surrounding villages. She'd heard of these cabins, hidden in the woods and wetlands primarily so that these trappers could avoid paying taxes.

"We went out exploring and found it." Again, he showed no desire to elaborate.

"Who was with you? When did you…" Saren silenced her with a kiss, pulling at her shawl and tossing it aside. Dear Yetra, she was covered in sweat from the walk, and she was feeling simply disgusting. Saren must be tasting the sweat off of her upper lip! In the same way, she continued to taste whatever booze he had sucked down before coming to see her.

His hands were on her bare shoulders now, and he started walking her sideways toward the bed, his mouth still intertwined with hers. Now his hands were on her hips, her behind. She almost fell, her ankle hurting, but he held her up, hands continuing to explore her body, becoming more and more rough, grabbing and grasping.

Suddenly, Meri found herself falling onto the thin mattress, hitting her hip hard against the wooden bedframe and letting out a yelp. Saren stood above her, working on the buttons of his shirt. Meri realized that her legs were parted, and her dress was nearly hitched up to her waist! She struggled off of the bed, rolling over her bruised hip and regaining her feet. This was all wrong! A bug-infested, thin mattress in a moldy rat-nest of a cabin, miles from her home, her body covered in cuts, bites, and sticky perspiration. Her ankle and hip throbbing with pain, and a boy who was being rather inconsiderate.

Meri pulled down her dress just as Saren successfully unbuttoned and removed his shirt. As the candles illuminated his muscular and hairy chest, Meri nearly changed her mind again. But, this wasn't how she'd imagined her first night. It just wasn't right.

"Saren, I've waited for this night for so long. And... I... wanted it to be perfect. Look at me. I'm a mess. And look at this place! We can't do this tonight. It's just not right." Meri had finally found her voice, and realized she should have turned back when they were on the path, when she'd first snagged her ankle on that exposed root.

"Meri..." Saren said in a somewhat cajoling tone.

"I'm sorry, but this isn't going to work! We are going to have to do this another night" said Meri, doing her best to be assertive.

"Meri." This time, as an imperative.

"Please, take me home," Meri said, pushing past him. Her fairytale night was over. Sandra's picture of being with a man—with Saren—as vivid and... arousing as it had been... it couldn't happen tonight.

Suddenly, though, Meri was yanked backwards by her hair. Her painstaking efforts at creating a beautiful triple-braid saved her from losing a chunk of her scalp, but her head still stung all over. She would have fallen, too, had Saren not roughly caught her, spinning her around to face him. Squeezing her wrist with one hand, right on her fading bruise, his other hand was still clenching her triple-braid, pulling her head to one side.

"You little fucking tease," Saren hissed, meanness in his eyes. "Do you know how long I've waited for this? You led me on last year by the inn. And then you practically begged me to take you out tonight! I was going to say no, but I could tell you wanted it."

"Let go of me, Saren!" Meri demanded, struggling against his strength. "Do you know what Ragen would do to you…"

The back of Saren's hand came as a surprise, hitting Meri hard across the face. She saw starbursts, white and red, as tears came unbidden to her eyes.

"Ragen," he spat. "That dirty old shit. That fucking mad man. Do you even know what he did to me? Do you have any fucking idea? He saw us, last year, outside the inn. He saw you run away. And he attacked me, unprovoked, breaking my nose and wrist! Said if I ever come near you again, he would see me dead."

"I didn't know, Saren!" Meri said, trying to shake herself free of confusion, tears running down her cheeks. "He didn't mean it!"

"You two, always protecting each other." A tug at her hair, pulling her ear to her shoulder. More pain. "I was going to let it go, stay away from you, stay away from him. By the gods, I wanted vengeance, but no one would tangle with Ragen, the richest man in town. Ragen, the most *generous* man in town. Ragen, the whore-fucker."

Saren leaned in close, running his tongue along Meri's neck, from her collarbone to her ear. She shivered, recoiling at the venom in his voice as much as from his touch. "But, I have a different type of vengeance in mind now. You, Merigold."

Merigold was stunned, disconnected. One arm was pinned to her side, and the other struggled uselessly against Saren's iron grip on her hair. All she could to lessen the tearing pressure on her hair was move in exactly the direction that Saren wanted. He continued to roughly kiss her neck, biting here and there, likely leaving marks if not drawing blood.

"We wouldn't be here if you had just left me alone. Or, if you had just followed through. Or, if your father wasn't insane. But, now I'm going to make you mine whether you want it or not."

Merigold had a moment of clarity then, and struck Saren in the ear as hard as she could with her free hand. She instantly regretted it as he flung her to the ground by her hair and kicked her in the stomach. Meri tried to scream, but could do little more than squeak and cough.

"You little bitch!" shouted Saren, grasping his ear, unknowingly echoing Fenrir from a week ago, or a lifetime ago.

Meri reached out and grabbed Saren's leg, resolved to draw from him, to hurt him like she had Fenrir. To hurt him much worse. She managed to grab hold of his bare leg for a moment, and reached into herself like she had so often before, to draw energy from him, to pull whatever it was that she pulled. To take as much as she could.

This force, this power, this energy. She had always been able to see it clearly before, like a vessel, glistening with color, contained within another person. Different people had different types and amounts of energy to pull from, and she could sense that, as well. And she would typically just skim a bit off of the surface at a small cost to her own reservoir, but ultimately gaining energy, strength.

Now, Meri intended to draw as much as she could from Saren. But something was wrong! Something was blocking her. She couldn't see. She couldn't concentrate. She couldn't feel anything within Saren. It was like she was touching a barrel, or a broom, or something inanimate. And, even worse, she couldn't even feel anything within herself. Her head hurt too much, and her stomach burned as if she had swallowed a searing hot coal.

And her brief window of chance was over. Saren hauled Meri to her feet and bent her over the bed, her head hitting the bare mattress forcefully, causing her to bite her tongue. To taste blood. Saren tore her dress as he pulled it above her hips, her waist, bearing her flower to him, to the world. He had one of her arms twisted behind her back, jerking it upward to stop her struggling. Meri felt him ram himself into her without preamble, without warning. She flinched, choking back a sob, as he failed to penetrate her, and she heard him spit. He jammed his saliva-soaked hand roughly into her as she cried out with pain, tears renewed, running down her cheeks. And then Saren was in her, his manhood causing surprisingly less pain than his fingers, but the feelings of wrongness and the aches across the rest of her body more than made up for it.

The last sight Meri saw before clenching her eyes shut was her hand, clenched in a fist in front of her, and the fading yellow ring on her wrist, once again flaring with pain from Saren's harsh grip.

Chapter 8

By the gods, his shoulder was killing him! Being stabbed by an assassin and then having a man dig his fingers deep into the still-fresh wound, tearing stitches, stretching flesh, has that effect. When that man was your father, the pain should have been deeper. But Fenrir was still experiencing the physical pain far more acutely than anything emotional as he staggered toward the Plateau. He clearly needed to see a physician, and Martis Aieres was the only man he really trusted.

His life was starting to feel a bit too cyclical at this point: once again, he was lurching through the city, his shirt torn and soaked in blood down to his boots. This was becoming an increasingly bad habit. Most strangely, Fenrir was also feeling the pain in his knee rather acutely. He had heard that feeling pain in one area of the body was supposed to lessen pain in another part. That was why people would dig their nails into their own skin just after stubbing a toe, or poke themselves in the leg with a knife when experiencing a particularly rough hangover. That logic didn't seem to be applying itself to Fenrir, though, and he was a limping mess.

He had done a lot of walking and off-roading, lately. Certainly more than in previous years, since the time that he'd left the Plateau. Or been asked to leave the Plateau, rather. Even as a guardsman, he'd done some patrolling, but most of his job had been standing still. Straight and tall, by a door, a window, or atop a tower. In a library. Mind-numbingly boring most times, particularly during the day at the posts where the nobles and other inhabitants of the fortress frequented. But at night or in isolated posts, Fenrir and his fellows had been able to let down their literal guard. They'd dice or talk or joke, leaning against the wall or crouching, sitting back on their heels.

Truth be told, Fenrir had developed a knack for standing still with as little effort as possible. With the right fit, a man could simply occupy armor that was more or less a shell supporting itself. And with the right mindset, a man could completely lose himself for at least a few hours, either sleeping with his eyes open or floating contentedly in waking dreams. Fenrir would be the first to admit that he had little imagination, but every once in a while, he'd find his mind wandering, either on some grand military adventure or reliving some of his conquests, his extramarital exploits. Granted, he'd learned very early in his career that one did not want to think too deeply about such exploits in particular when one was wearing full ceremonial armor with a codpiece.

His actual military experiences were limited, though. When he'd originally run off and joined the Rostanian military at sixteen years of age, he'd been inducted as standard infantry. Despite his prosperous mercantile roots, or maybe because of them, he'd been placed with a true bastard of a sergeant, Winston Alus, a dirty peasant promoted beyond his level of competence. Apparently, being a hero in the border skirmishes with the Wasmer qualified a man to scream at the top of his lungs at new recruits, beating them into shape (sometimes quite literally). Fenrir had been a quick study back then and received far fewer beatings, physical and psychological, from this sergeant than had others in his squad. The others had not taken kindly to that.

Ultimately, Fenrir had washed out of the infantry because of his knee, about two years after he had started. The squad had taken many forced marches at double-time, and Fenrir had found himself unable to keep up. The pain had often been too much, and he would limp along gamely, throwing off the formation. The break in formation would result in reduced rations, extra drills, or additional duties, all of which were likely to draw the ire of his brethren, and the resulting abuse from his squad would weaken his knee further. Rather short-sighted, Fenrir had always thought.

The final blow came when they were marching to the border with Florens. Fenrir's knee gave out altogether and he was left behind by his squad, some of his comrades not even bothering to step around him. He ended up limping back to Rostane alone, with no food and no water, and meeting with Alus upon his return. The sergeant really was a complete bastard, but he'd been impressed enough with Fenrir's fortitude that he'd done one genuinely kind thing for him: he had passed Fenrir's name to Daren de Hosta, a Captain of the Guard at the Plateau. Alus and de Hosta had served together in some of those skirmishes with the Wasmer, although de Hosta, being of wealthy mercantile roots, had ended up with the cushier job at the Plateau. And thus, Fenrir had himself come to the Plateau.

Surprisingly, reflecting on the varied causes of his knee pain had distracted Fenrir somewhat as he staggered through the city. He'd taken off his shirt and applied as much pressure to his wound as he could muster, partially to staunch the steady flow of blood and partially to look less like a ruffian. As it was, he was getting suspicious looks from honest city folk and patrolling city guards. Luckily, his insight into the protection occupation in Rostane helped him once again. It was unlawful for a city guardsman to detain a citizen unless that person was disturbing the peace. As long as his shambling, bloody presence wasn't causing a fight or a riot, Fenrir was safe from molestation. Although, he did stick to side streets (but not alleys), just in case he came across a guard who was less rule-bound than others.

Martis Aieres lived in a quite well-to-do area in the shadow of the Plateau. Being a staff physician at the fortress, primarily working with nobles, Martis had amassed a fairly substantial fortune and had purchased a small castle of a house, complete with servants and one of the best cooks in all of Rostane. He didn't have an office in the city itself since most of his work was onsite at the Plateau or at the estates of nobles, so Fenrir found himself staggering down Vineyard Lane. The stately boulevard was named for the grape vines lining both its sides, creating a great deal of ambience and providing additional privacy for the wealthy residents of the area. Expansive gardens flanked the road and the magnificent decorative roofs of the homes—estates, really—and could be seen peaking over high stone garden walls. Import taxes went toward the planting and maintenance of these grape gardens, the so-called beautification taxes. Fenrir had heard many tirades from his father about these taxes, how they took money from honest merchants to make the lives of worthless nobles better. And as inevitably happens with children, even those dead-set on being nothing like their parents, some of these feelings had taken root and lingered within Fenrir, and he felt his customary resentment as he limped by the gnarled, twisting vines.

Fenrir's timing was impeccable. He arrived at the Aieres estate just as his strength was finally giving out. Leaning his good shoulder against the rough, mortared stone wall for support, he walked down a thin, enclosed lane to the main point of ingress, which was a huge, oaken gate. He gathered himself, pushed off the wall, and stood tall, grabbing the iron knocker—shaped like a lion—and bashing it against the heavy wood. A small viewing window opened in the door almost immediately, indicating that a steward must have been sitting just nearby.

"What business…" The sound of a throat clearing loudly. "Would a man of your, ahem, caliber, have at this location?"

"I'm here to see Martis."

"I'm certain that *Sir* Aieres, ahem, would have nothing to do with you." Fenrir had heard that Aieres had been knighted for service to the duchy. It had completely slipped his mind.

"Listen, I'm a friend," Fenrir managed, lurching forward against the door. "Fenrir de… If you don't let me… in… you will find yourself… without a job." He was gasping at this point. He'd lost more blood, and was in more pain than he'd before realized. Now that he was close to his destination, he couldn't push back the blinding ache much longer.

"Ahem. I will investigate your claims. I, ahem, kindly ask that you wait here."

"Wait, get back here, you… villainous… something." Exhaustion was taking hold, and Fenrir had little energy enough for keeping his feet, let alone for witty insults. This little pissant was going to pay, by the gods! Or, he'd worship this man for letting him in.

Leaning heavily against the door, shivering and trying to maintain his balance, Fenrir found his mind wandering back to this morning, to his father. They'd never had what anyone would claim was a good relationship. Fenrir was the third son, born of the second wife, the southerner, the nomadic witch, Astora.

His mother had been everything to him. He'd fit in so poorly with his family, with his so-called brothers, with the cutthroat mercantile business. His father had all but ignored him most of the time. Darian had traveled so frequently in those early days and, when he'd been in Rostane, he'd been actively involved in his experiments. The longer stretches that Darian had spent at home, he had spent primarily with Ethan and Aiden, educating them in economics and teaching them the ins and outs of the business. Showing them the secrets of the expanding de Trenton mercantile empire, and the burning ice. Fenrir had never been privy to those secrets, and honestly had never had much interest.

He and Astora had spent much of their time walking around the city together, touring the markets, milling about the various districts. They had particularly enjoyed sitting in a secluded spot by the Fullane, not far from the docks at the widest part of the river. Fenrir remembered holding back branches to help his mother work her way through the brush at the edge of a park, having to rediscover their special place every time. But, that had been how it remained their special place.

Astora would teach him of the far south traditions there, away from the bustle and casual cruelty so pervasive in the de Trenton

119

estate. He'd learned of the religious holidays that his mother celebrated, considered pagan rituals here in Yetranian-heavy Ardia. Fenrir had loved to hear about the dances and the songs of his mother's people, and he'd occasionally convince her to sing. Astora would rarely raise her voice above a soft murmur, almost as if it were sacrilege to voice the songs of her people so far away from home. And though Fenrir couldn't understand the Domain tongue, he could follow the rise and fall of her voice, feel the emotion in her melodies. Many of the songs were mournful dirges, the Domain being a harsh land, with the southern folk often falling to hunger, cold, and disease. However, many of the songs had filled Fenrir with hope—hope that his mother would be happy, finding joy here in a land so different from that of her birth. Hope that he would develop a relationship with his brothers, and that they would respect him, that they would stop hurting him. Hope that they would stop hurting Astora.

Fenrir was unevenly humming one of those songs now, distracting himself from the agony of his wounds, keeping himself on his feet. He remembered this song the best. Astora had told him that it was the song of her tribe, the Srota. Most of the tribes of the Domain were nomadic, following the herds of snow elk and seals. But the Srota were a fishing people, staying in their region regardless of ice or months of darkness. Astora told him that during the darkest and coldest part of the year, the endless night, the Srota would sing this song. To bring them hope that the sun would again rise, that the winter would end.

Even though the winter did end every year in the farthest reaches of the south, it had never ended for Astora in the much more temperate land of Ardia. After she'd ended her own life, Fenrir remembered singing this song quietly at her wake, over her body. He'd been the only one who gave a damn about Astora at the wake or anywhere in Rostane, most of the attendees being Darian's business partners and sycophants, bowing and scraping for extra attention, discounts, and for a slight edge. So it had been

Fenrir, mourning his mother alone, singing a song of hope when he felt no hope at all.

As he fell to his knees against Sir Martin Aieres' grand wooden door, Fenrir resolved that de Trenton would be replaced by his mother's surname. A name honored by the Srota, a name as old as the people of the Domain. *Kalabrot.* Translated to the Ardian: he who breaks the cold. The Coldbreaker. It was Fenrir's last thought before he finally succumbed, losing consciousness at the doorstep of his salvation.

Fenrir was standing on a tall hill overlooking a valley, a wide, rushing river in the distance. It must have been the winter, as what grass there was appeared to be either dead or dormant, and almost all visible trees were stripped of leaves, their bare branches creaking as the wind periodically gusted through the canopies. Interestingly, Fenrir had no impressions of cold. In fact, he couldn't move a muscle, but at least he wasn't hurting anymore. Even more strangely, he had the impression that he could see in all directions at once. Rather than being disorienting, the enhanced vision felt entirely natural.

In the distance, not too far from the river, he could see a tall, squat building with the appearance of an ashen stone cube, a grand staircase leading to the top. At the peak of this odd structure was what appeared to be a temple, crowned by a great fire burning in a golden bowl, its purplish smoke dissipating into the colorless sky.

Behind him—or in front of him, it was all the same—Fenrir could hear melodic voices, speaking to one another from the other side of the hill. All at once, a large group of men, clad in brownish robes and bearing spears and shields, crested the rise as they headed toward his position. Many wore unadorned hoods, and several others, not equipped with instruments of war, had helms resembling the plumage of some great, azure bird. The group, at least five hundred strong at this point, was still some ways off, but Fenrir could have sworn that most of the feather-capped warriors were women.

Now, another army approached from the river. Time seemed irrelevant on this hill; the first group was moving quite slowly to his position, while this second army seemed to advance with great speed. These were quaintly armored folks, some riding on large, grizzled animals that Fenrir had never seen before. These creatures were shorter than a horse, but twice as wide and long! Each bore several men, and some of these men wielded staves adorned with the skulls of animals. Foxes, wolves, great birds.

All at once, the armies collided, the first group awaiting the larger army with the strange mounts and antiquated leather armor. The musical voices of the defenders grew louder, and Fenrir recognized the sounds as belonging to a dialect of the Wasmer. Wasmer fighting what looked like humans, albeit humans of a sort that Fenrir had never seen. They were pale-skinned, their pupils nearly white, and though many of them had long hair, it was generally wild and unkempt. Others were bald, and they all fought with a singular ferocity Fenrir had never seen. It was if they had no cares aside from tearing the Wasmer to pieces. Some of these strange men even abandoned their weapons to throw themselves bodily at the Wasmer, impaling themselves on the spears, but not stopping their attack until life bled from their bodies.

Both armies flowed around Fenrir, not noticing him in the least. Slowly, the Wasmer were driven back by the superior numbers and the furious onslaught of the attacking army. Before long, one of the shaggy animals drew close. Fenrir could see now that the creature had an extra pair of legs supporting its middle section, and a special harness system creating a sort of saddle upon which road several warriors. One of the riders dismounted and approached Fenrir directly, not looking through him as did the others. The rider bore a stave with the skull of a large cat, and was wearing a cowl that covered her face. A second and third rider, the third being very slight in build, similarly dismounted and joined the first, wielding a goat stave and eagle stave, respectively. The cat-skull stave wielder pulled back her cowl and reached out to touch Fenrir, though he could not feel her hands on his body.

And then she ripped the very life out of him.

"As you can see, the wound was abluted and any severely damaged tissue was removed. The remainder was sutured using a long, curved military needle, as gouges this deep rarely occur outside the confines of battle. Or severe accidents with tools. Because of the blood loss, the patient has been unconscious for nearly a day and required a transfu… oh, the patient wakes. Please, leave us for now."

A calm, relaxing voice, like water babbling over shale. Fenrir struggled against the extreme weight of his eyelids. When he managed to get the gummy things open, he immediately grimaced and squinted against the bright light. As his vision adapted, a large, sterile room became more visible around him. The walls were white-washed and free of décor. There was a small wooden bench along one wall, and a chair right next to the bed that Fenrir was apparently occupying. Turning his head, he saw the distinctive braided beard—now mostly white—of Martis Aieres.

"So, you've decided to join us, Fen. You took quite the nap, there," Martis said, smiling, his good humor always bubbling to the surface. Surprising for a man in an occupation where he witnessed death on a weekly basis.

"Indeed. I've had a long day."

"It's been at least two days since that wound was inflicted upon you, a day and a half since the wound was exacerbated. You nearly bled out on my doorstop; terrified old Kanic half to death," said Martis, his strong hand resting on Fenrir's wrist. Martis was about ten years his senior, but had the finger dexterity of a juggler from one of those traveling shows.

"Kanic, huh? I vaguely remember some ass barring me entrance. I suppose I should thank the man, but I'd rather punch him." Fenrir's low chuckle transformed into a painful cough.

"Kanic does have that effect on people, but I could never hope for a better servant. Now, what brings you to me in this sorry state?" Sorry state, indeed. Fenrir's shoulder was burning, but not nearly as sharply as before. The knee continued to throb, too, and he could both hear and feel his heartbeat pounding thickly in his skull.

"Trouble."

Fenrir gave Martis a recap of the assassination attempt. He trusted few people as he trusted Martis. The physician had been his first friend when he'd joined the guard at the Plateau. Captain de Hosta had forced him to see Martis after receiving Sergeant Alus' recommendation, to see whether Fenrir's knee was permanently shattered. De Hosta would not take a crippled guardsman, no matter what Alus said.

Martis had met a very reluctant Fenrir. In fact, Fenrir had been a real prick, resisting the examination, unwilling to report pain in response to different tests. But Martis knew his business, and had nimbly examined Fenrir's knee with powerful fingers, twisting his knee to locate the pain, which was made evident by Fenrir's reluctant grunts and moans. Martis had soon managed to disarm Fenrir's hesitancy with his optimistic, kindly temperament, though, and been able to establish a diagnosis. After a small operation in which Martis removed a splinter of bone from his joint, and during which Fenrir had learned of the remarkable properties of a substance called ether, the two had become fast friends. Fenrir had never understood why this intelligent, charming man would want to befriend a relatively unlearned guardsman who'd run away from home, but it never seemed to matter.

"...and she stitched me up. I won't give you the lurid details that immediately followed, but I would categorize that day as slightly above average," finished Fenrir.

"Ah, I never understood your way with the ladies. I've always been of the monogamous sort, like the noble swan. But, even the swan occasionally wishes he were a wild turkey, especially when he observes you, gobbling about," said Martis, using his typical circuitous wit. "Now, your shoulder wound was much worse than a simple stabbing. It seemed like someone tried to stick a pestle in the mortar of your shoulder, so to speak."

"Not far off, Martis. Let's just say that my father and I had a falling out."

"Ah, the epic battle continues! The steely will of Principal Darian de Trenton versus the indomitable spirit of Fenrir de Trenton."

Fenrir appreciated that Martis didn't ask for details about the incident. But given his talents, Martis could probably guess what had happened based on the forensics of his wound. "It's no longer de Trenton. It's Fenrir Kalabrot."

"It was that bad, then?" Martis' lips were a straight line, as close a frown as the physician ever wore.

"Yes, it was that bad," said Fenrir, struggling into a seated position on his bed, assisted by Martis' guiding hands. Fenrir's head swam, but he remained upright.

"Kalabrot. If I am not mistaken, Coldbreaker? I've always thought that you had Domain blood, but I was never certain." Martis had likely been certain, Fenrir knew. Ethnography was a hobby of his.

"Yes, my mother…"

"No need to speak more, my friend. Might I recommend that you go with the translation? Coldbreaker is quite an intimidating name, something that might be helpful in your current line of work."

"By the gods, you know about that?" Fenrir felt his cheeks redden. He'd been working for The House for two years, and thought he had accepted his new role in the world. But, though Martis' expression had not changed, Fenrir felt a great press of guilt now, as if he were being smothered by the spotless, white sheets that covered his body.

"When a man is unconscious and even his boots are soaked in blood, it is customary to undress him. And, it is difficult to miss a heptagram sheathed in an inner boot pocket." The physician's smile twisted wryly.

"Martis, I…"

"Again, you have no need to speak more. I imagine there were few options left to you, after that day. You know, I've always thought that what happened at the Ardian Council was a true misfortune, and I am still at a loss to explain it. The bump on the head, of course, was an effect, not a cause, of the event. By the way, is that a habit? You've obviously been recently concussed, and the back of your head looks like you were dragged across gravel. What happened, and what symptoms have you experienced? The wound seems old."

"Well, uh, it's a long story…" stammered Fenrir, surprised to get a word in.

126

"Ah, forgive me. I tend to go off topic when it comes to the practice of medicine. But, yes, that day was a misfortune. A man must do what a man must do, though. I understand that, and I bare you no ill will for your current line of work. In fact, I am impressed that you have the fortitude to do what is necessary for the job. Perhaps the steely will lies not just with your father. On occasion, I've been occasionally forced into unsavory things, so I can relate to the dilemma," said Martis, his usual jovial expression having darkened with the words.

"Thank you, my friend." Fenrir guilt melted away from the warmth of his friend's empathy. And he was relieved that he wouldn't have to put words to his current predicament. Besides, Martis had figured out the whole scenario before Fenrir had even awoken. Seeing the heptagram, Martis would have known that Fenrir was employed by The House. And the only one who would likely attempt harm on a member of the underground organization would be The House itself.

Of course, now, in light of the events of the past couple of days, Fenrir wasn't so sure. The House was the most likely suspect, of course—Tennyson trying to erase him after the incident in Umberton. But, Tennyson had said that The House was not done with him. Unless that had been a veiled threat, there was the possibility that Fenrir hadn't been targeted by his own organization at all.

It very well could have been Darian de Trenton, his own father, who'd sent a hired killer. The man was heavily suspected to have murdered before, and Fenrir was certain those suspicions were based in truth. The disappearances and relocations of so many of Darian's competitors were too coincidental and, in Fenrir's experience, coincidences just didn't exist. In his case, Fenrir would not have been surprised if the assassin had been sent by his father as some twisted test. If Fenrir could survive the attack, Darian would consider him, once again, to be an heir, and

127

thus would have summoned him for that meeting. That was the way that his father worked, the twisted old fuck.

He had no hard evidence for this claim, though, and wouldn't have considered presenting evidence against his father regardless. The only detail that would have hinted at his father's involvement in the assassination attempt was that his father had known exactly where his shoulder wound was, jabbing his fingers into exactly the right place. But, it had also been obvious that Fenrir was wounded—he'd been covered in dried blood. And it was possible that Darian had seen the wound through the small tear in his shirt. Or, Darian had already known where to strike…

So, either his father, a powerful merchant king, or Tennyson, a leader of spies and murderers, were out to kill Fenrir. And, there was even the possibility that the attack had nothing to do with Darian or Tennyson. Perhaps some four-fingered fuck wanted revenge on the wielder of the knife. Regardless of who was after him, he had little choice but to get out of Rostane. That is, as soon as he was sufficiently recovered.

"So, what's the prognosis, Martis?"

"Well, there are a few things to consider. First, your shoulder wound. The knife wound did not do much in the way of real damage, but the exacerbation after the fact tore some muscle. You will need to keep your arm immobilized for at least two weeks while the muscles mend. Along those lines, you lost a great deal of blood, and I needed to do a transfusion," said Martis, gathering medical supplies into his omnipresent satchel.

"Who was the lucky donor?"

"One of my student assistants. A young lady volunteered, in fact. You have a way about you, Fen. Even comatose, apparently. Regardless, you will feel very weak for the next few days, so don't be surprised by that."

"I'll have to thank this young lady myself."

"Of course you will." Martis' tone was flat as a pond on a windless day. "Also, your head wound was not completely healed."

That accounted for those weird dreams, Fenrir thought. By the gods, Wasmer fighting rabid, pale humans, and giant, six-legged beast of burden. But, he might as well ask about something else that had been on his mind.

"Martis, have you ever heard of... how do I put this... people having out-of-body experiences?" asked Fenrir.

"Oh, certainly. Those who are briefly on Harmony's threshold have reported that they can see themselves from a great distance, as if they were hovering outside their own body," said Martis as he straightened the sheets around Fenrir's body like a fawning mother.

"No, not when they are dying. Like, a person floating above their body, watching their body performing actions, but unable to control it." Fenrir didn't add that he'd felt this a few times already, and that most often, he was in danger in some way. Yet, danger was not always a trigger—he had been in quite a few fights, taken a literal handful of fingers, without becoming disembodied. Without seeing through the eyes of his phantom.

"If you experienced this, Fenrir, and if we are not speaking from a theoretical perspective, I would expect that it is a symptom of the concussions and a twisting of your memory."

No, it was more than that.

"Never mind, Martis. It must be the concussions." Martis glanced up at him, meeting his eyes for a moment. Then, he shook his head and shouldered his satchel.

"With head injuries, it is important to keep hydrated. One of my attendants will ensure you are drinking plenty of water. And, oh, you appear to have done further damage to your knee."

That was a forgone conclusion. The joint felt like it must be the size of a jimpa melon, and even in his current state, he could tell the swelling was cutting off circulation to his lower leg. Thinking back, Fenrir realized that he must have slammed his knee into the ground during his father's vicious attack. And probably again when he'd fallen senseless at Martis' door.

"We will need to get the inflammation down, and I will then determine what can be done. Luckily, I have the perfect thing for such inflammation." Martis' eyes glinted in the pale light of the room. "Have you heard of burning ice?"

Fenrir groaned.

Martis encouraged Fenrir to spend his convalescence in his medical ward, unconcerned that Fenrir might draw attention from Tennyson or his father.

Apparently, the physician had opened a medical school in his own backyard, quite literally, and was bringing in talent from wherever he could find it. In speaking with various students and assistants, Fenrir learned that one was an herbalist's son from Hunesa. Another was a young wise woman, obviously Sestrian based on her mocha-colored skin. A third had once been a beggar from the very streets of Rostane. The medical school had its own entrance, too, and Fenrir's bloody journey through the front door of the estate had caused quite a stir.

Fenrir felt like a dissected animal, what with these assistants inspecting his wounds on a thrice-daily basis. One inserted sea urchin needles into his knee to relieve the pain and help with swelling. Another woman, named Aggy—a corpulent woman with an exaggerated beak of a nose, who'd given her blood for

Fenrir's transfusion—changed his shoulder bandages daily. And she often lingered at his side, tittering a surprisingly contagious laugh.

Fenrir felt like he was gaining strength rapidly as the days passed. At a week, he was able to bear his full weight on his leg. At three weeks, he was out of his sling and moving his arm in full circles. During this time, he didn't have any more strange dreams, which was quite a relief. That last dream had been so intense, so real. Especially the last part, where those oddly-dressed warriors with the eagle, goat, and cat staves had wrenched away his life. Fenrir had been convinced he was dying, and it had been no pleasant way to go. It had felt as if his blood was trying to tear through his skin, to evacuate his veins and arteries, but had no path to exit. The feeling of pure pressure had been immense. Fenrir felt agony far past the point at which he should have died. And then, suddenly, he'd been waking in a hospital bed, surrounded by medical students and Martis.

Luckily, the dreams really must have been a remnant of his head injury, and those symptoms were gone. Now, he was focused on regaining his strength and then getting out of Rostane, finding a new life as Fenrir Coldbreaker. Maybe he could find some place far enough away where he could join the military, finally taking on a small command. It was true he'd never wanted to move through the ranks at the Plateau. Partly because he was satisfied— good pay, little responsibility, and easy access to serving women—and partly because his father *had* wanted him to be promoted. But, somewhere far away from Rostane, he could see himself being the one giving orders for a change, and doing a better job than Sergeant Alus or Captain de Hosta. Maybe even becoming a Captain of the Guard himself.

That would be an interesting experience, he thought, and Fenrir may very well have been good at the job, but, on the thirty-ninth evening of his recuperation, he found a visitor waiting in his room. A visitor who ruined any ambitions that Fenrir might have had regarding a new life in a different country.

"You are a hard man to find." A surprisingly high-pitched voice filled the room like a knife scraping a plate.

Fenrir, having just walked into his room, whipped around and fell into a fighting stance, balanced on the balls of his feet, his hands positioned in front of him and ready to strike. Left arm in front to protect his injured shoulder. Tennyson stood behind the door, arms folded over his deep gray robe. Silver Ultner mask reflecting the soft candlelight illuminating the room. The demon-figure seemed to grin, as always.

"Fenrir, why so jumpy? We are friends, aren't we?"

Fenrir didn't relax his guard. "What do you want?"

"I'm certainly not here to hurt you. If I wanted you hurt, you'd be four-fingered. If I wanted you dead, well… draw your own conclusions." Fenrir could hear a hint of mockery in Tennyson's voice.

"Well, *someone* tried to kill me," said Fenrir, not quite ready to leave himself open for attack. Although, if Tennyson had a weapon, his fists would avail him little.

"I don't like having to repeat myself. I told you that The House wasn't done with you, despite how poorly you performed in Umberton. But that's ancient history, at this point. The nobles settled down, as they always do. A bribe here, a threat there. Balance has been achieved."

Fenrir sat down on the edge of his bed, still a bit uneasy, and gestured toward the bench on the other side of the room. Unexpectedly, Tennyson actually complied, sitting and crossing one leg over his other, leaning toward Fenrir. Very out of character of him.

"Big things are afoot in this city, in this country. Beyond, even. The House may be in balance with those that govern our fine city, but there are more scales to equalize. For instance, another power, attempting to rival our own organization, has arisen in Rostane. They are calling themselves *Recherche Oletta.* The Seekers of Oletta," Tennyson said expectantly, a freakish school teacher awaiting an answer. Like a good boy, Fenrir complied.

"Oh, um. Oletta. Isn't that one of the old gods? Maybe of life and nature? Mountains?" Fenrir was trying to think back to his post at the Enlightenment. He'd heard enough lectures about the old gods, rites, and rituals. "I believe that the Wasmer used to worship her, and she had some popularity among peasants, as well. Thousands of years ago?"

"Impressive memory for a dog." Fenrir felt the urge to growl at the man, but the irony wasn't lost on him. "Oletta, Goddess of Stone and Wisdom. Her name means wisdom, in fact, in old Auqinen. Your encounter in Vagabond Stretch was consistent with their activities—charging tolls, attempting to undermine The House wherever possible. That man, that girl. Do you recall whether they were adorned with a shiny black stone hanging around each of their necks?" Tennyson leaned forward.

Fenrir shook his head. "I don't believe that I saw anything like that, but the whole situation was quite hectic."

"It is no matter. *Recherche Oletta* is my concern at the moment. You will be involved in another balancing act. There are certain personages in the upper echelons in Ardia who are attempting to covertly consolidate power. If these personages were to achieve power, it would be at odds with our own interests."

"I thought we remained neutral in such political maneuverings, and our services went to the highest bidders," remarked Fenrir.

"How idealistic!" Tennyson barked a discordant laugh. "No, this would represent a drastic shift in Rostane. In all of Ardia, in fact. So, in this situation, we are not neutral."

Fenrir wasn't sure, but he could almost hear a tension in Tennyson's voice. "I am here to serve. I would like an opportunity to make up for my failures." Fenrir earnestly meant this, too. Whether or not The House had actually tried to off him or not, he would rather stay on the good side of such a dangerous organization.

"Good. You are on a protection detail of the highest importance. A certain person of power is in a position where she needs to be smuggled out of the Plateau. You are to facilitate this, and bring her to her estate. You are to act as her protector in all things and are not to act in any way counter to her wishes, except as necessary to preserve her life. Upon safe arrival, you will continue your post until contacted by one of my agents."

"I appreciate your trust in me, Tennyson. But, the details are a bit vague."

"In good time. I must go, for now, but you will be given instructions in the usual way." Meaning that someone would find him, no matter where he went. "I can't stress how important your task is to the survival of The House and the preservation of your own life. Again, I would not put you in this position unless forced. We are spread thin as a malnourished whore."

"Thanks again for your confidence," said Fenrir, his voice flat.

"Ah, Fenrir, don't be petulant. This type of work is more within your skill set. Although, I might suggest you brush up on your swordsmanship." Tennyson twisted to his feet and turned to leave. Fenrir blew out, the stress of every meeting with this man a palpable force in his body, almost distracting him from the ache in his shoulder. He touched at the healing wound, clenching his teeth at the memory.

"Tennyson," hazarded Fenrir.

"Yes?"

"I would beg a favor of The House."

A pause. A long pause. "I'm listening."

"Darian de Trenton. I'd like him to be taught a lesson."

Another pause. And then the sound of laughter flattened against the silver of his mask. Fenrir thought he heard real mirth. Tennyson turned back around, the fading chuckle emitting from Ultner's face. Truly disturbing.

"You can't have thought I would agree to that," Tennyson said through his laughter. "Alienating probably the most powerful merchant in Rostane—maybe Ardia. Your father. Because, what? You had a little fight with him? After I just told you how much is in the balance? I've overestimated your intelligence."

"Fine, then. Sigmund Fitra."

Tennyson seemed to consider Fenrir then, tilting his head slightly, the horns of his mask glinting in the candlelight. Fenrir felt anxious as Ultner's visage studied him, and he felt an urge to say something. But he held his tongue and simply stared back.

"Hmmm," Tennyson finally said. He regarded Fenrir for another moment and then, without another word, he flowed from the room like a shadow at twilight.

Chapter 9

The dripping sound was back. First, there was the *pook*, the sound of the molecules of liquid disengaging from the ceiling. Then, there was the higher pitched *kee*, as the liquid impacted with the existing puddle. The sound changed, over the hours, as that puddle grew wider, deeper. It was the one thing that could cut through Merigold's torpor. And she couldn't take it anymore.

Most of the time, it was so dark that Meri couldn't see her hand in front of her face. She occasionally lit her lantern to experience the sensation of sight, to remind herself that she still existed, that she was still alive. That her life wasn't the nightmare that it seemed to have become. But, she needed to conserve her fuel, never knowing when her captor might return to restock her supply. So Meri sat in darkness, occasionally standing and feeling her way around her prison. The walls consisted primarily of tightly-packed dirt, this periodically broken up by vertical wooden supports and horizontal planks designed to buttress the soil and clay. The ground itself was uneven, with water pooling in the minute valleys throughout the room, and particularly around the perimeter. When it rained—at least, Meri assumed the sound above her was rain—these pools would grow larger. When her skin of water ran out, these little pools formed the bulk of her hydration.

Food, on the other hand, was plentiful. Bags of dried, salted beef strips. Thin, gamey bits of meat that increased her thirst tenfold, with a taste that turned her stomach. Not to mention the effect the meat had on her bowels. Her chamber pot—a large, wooden bucket—was overflowing in one corner, but Meri's nose had become desensitized to the scent.

The first time Saren had come back, he'd been cautious, penitent. He'd said that he had drunk too much that night, that he'd lost control. He'd said he didn't know what to do, that he would be a dead man if Ragen, or anyone in Dunmore, found out

136

about what he'd done. Saren had said that Meri needed to stay here, in the cellar under the cabin, for just a couple of days while he sorted it all out.

He'd sounded so much like the old Saren, the boy she'd thought she loved. Sensitive, quiet, uncertain. And Meri had hit him in the head with a rock.

He'd beaten her mercilessly then, hitting her in the stomach, the breasts, the legs. He'd only left her face alone, as if beating her through her torn, dirty blue dress was somehow easier for him to bear. When she'd been lying on the hard, uneven cellar ground, unable to move, unable to resist, Saren had dragged her back up the ladder, into the cabin proper, and had his way with her once more. Meri had felt him penetrate her again, heralding tears that she'd thought had already been exhausted from the beating.

Afterward, Saren had dragged Meri back into the cellar. He'd cleaned the room of rocks and rubble, bits of wood, anything that could be used as a weapon. Leaving Meri lying in a small puddle of water, he had absconded the cellar and tossed down a water skin, several bags of dried meat, and a large bucket. Minutes later, he had climbed back down the ladder and laid the white and green blanket from the cabin bed over Meri's shivering, aching body, almost gently. He had left his lantern burning near Meri when he again left the cellar, taking the ladder with him.

As soon as she'd felt like she could stand after the assault, Meri had desperately searched her surroundings, trying to find a way out. She had checked all of the corners to see if Saren had missed anything that could be used for a weapon. She had tried scaling the walls to get to the cellar door. She couldn't get any traction, though, and, even if she could, Meri was almost certain that she had heard a key scraping on a metal lock, making her efforts meaningless. She had even tried to tunnel her way through the hard-packed dirt comprising the walls of her prison. After hours of trying, her fingers had been blistered, bleeding. Nails broken. And she'd only had a couple of inches to show for it before reaching a very hard clay.

Initially, Meri had prayed to Yetra, beseeching her goddess for strength. For salvation. For hope. But, the goddess had never answered, and soon Meri had stopped asking. After years of attending services, trying to emulate the values described in the scriptures of *The Book of Amorum*, she felt betrayed. Her faith was a big part of who she was, of who she wanted to be. But, if her goddess had abandoned her, who was she, really? What was left?

Yetra shall watch over all of those who live in Harmony, providing protection and guidance. Deontis. Deontis was a liar.

Now, days had passed. Weeks, even. Maybe months? Meri couldn't know for sure; time was only measured by how often Saren visited her. His visits were a sick, twisted charade that played out in the same predictable pattern of perversion each time. First, he would lower a rope that she would tie to the handle of her chamber pot. He would draw out the bucket, her mess sloshing over the edges. He would then come for her. He would take her upstairs and would speak to her like a friend, almost as he had when they'd been younger. But then, without warning, his eyes would grow hard, his face pinched with fury, his voice dripping disdain, and he'd drag her to the bed and rape her again. Meri learned quickly not to struggle, as it would only spark Saren's increasingly violent temper. Afterwards, he would act contrite and penitent, sometimes even apologizing. He would then direct her back to the cellar, refill her water jug, toss her a bag of food, and leave. Saren might have visited either thirteen or fourteen times in this way. Meri had lost count.

She had tried drawing power from Saren again when he came for her. But, as before, she couldn't feel anything within him—no vessel, no power. And she could not feel it within herself, either. Merigold felt empty, hollow, broken.

Hopeless.

She was sluggishly pacing around the cellar, fingers running over the walls. Her fingertips were calloused and insensitive to the rough surface by now. She took a wide path around the chamber bucket and resumed her walk of the perimeter, her fingers barely perceiving the coarse dirt, the splintery wood. She moved automatically, taking small steps to increase the time it took to circle the space. The hand not touching the wall fumbled with her sapphire studs, still intact on her ears. They did little to complement her new outfit; Sandra's beautiful blue dress had been abandoned, shredded and covered in filth. Saren had brought her some of his own clothes; they were far too large, all the more so as Meri continued to lose the little bit of fat that had occupied her body.

As Meri continued her plodding patrol along the wall, dragging her hand along the planks far above her head, she suddenly felt a sharp pain in her finger, the feeling briefly cutting through her stupor. She retracted her finger, putting it in her mouth and tasting blood. Marking the location in her head the best she could, Meri fumbled around for the lantern, which Saren had thankfully refilled after his last violation. With numbed fingers, she worked the flint to create light, and then she shuffled back to where she had cut herself.

Her eyes were unaccustomed to the brightness, but she fought through the sting and examined the walls through slitted eyes. Dirt and hard-grained wooden planks. She felt above her head, on a plank just at the tip of her reach. Nothing. As her pupils constricted and her vision cleared, she continued to search, not seeing or feeling anything. But, something must have cut her finger. Something sharp, and bigger than a splinter.

Meri slowly ran her hand back and forth, finally feeling a small stab again. She squinted in the low light. It was a thick, slightly-damaged nail head, barely protruding from the wood, connecting a vertical support to a horizontal plank. She felt a small thrill.

She tried to wedge her fingers under the nail, but it was too far above her head for her to get any leverage. Looking around, Meri only had one option—she upended her chamber bucket into the corner. The hope of potentially finding a weapon, a way out, had renewed both her energy and her senses. The stench generated from the stirring and spilling of her waste made her cough and heave, but Meri rallied and dragged the bucket along the ground, setting it on end below her possible salvation.

Meri worked at the nail for hours. At first, she felt no movement at all and despaired, sitting down on the bucket with her hands on her head. But then she continued to pull and jiggle and pry at the head until finally, miraculously, she felt some miniscule wobble. She felt another surge of hope and continued to work at the head, her injured finger continuing to bleed, and with new cuts opening on others. She finally thought to wrap her oversized sleeves around her fingers, absorbing the crimson and giving her more leverage.

At the end of the struggle, Meri had extracted the entire nail. It was nearly six inches long, and about half as thick as her little finger. To her, it was a gleaming sword, her one hope for escape and revenge.

She set her cell back into its usual formation as best she could—even attempting to scoop her waste back into the bucket so as not to arouse suspicions, and barely stifling her retching as she did so. She then used the nail to help her cut a strip from her bag of dried meat, and she wrapped that around the head of the nail to create a grip. She pictured her make-shift knife plunging into Saren's stomach again and again, defiling his body much as he had defiled hers. The thought of his blood washing over her hands brought an unconscious grin to her face.

And then, Merigold waited.

Maybe a half a day passed before Meri the heard noises above. The reluctant squeak of the cabin door as it opened. The ponderous scratching of the bed as it was dragged across the floor to reveal the cellar door. The dreadful thump of heavy boots. Of multiple pairs of boots. And, the echo of voices. Multiple voices.

"Yeah, she's down there." Saren's smooth speech carried through the cracks of the floor.

"Alright, I'm ready for this." Meri didn't recognize the voice, hushed as it was.

"I'm not so sure about this, Saren." She thought that one might be Chad, one of the boys from town. The mop-headed, smiling son of a scribe." This doesn't seem right."

"I told you. Ragen tried to kill me. Merigold tried to kill me. You've heard the rumors that they've made a pact with dark powers, back when she was sick. They're the reason that the fever ran through the village last year, and why the Michelsons' house burned down last month! You've seen Ragen running through town, threatening everybody, looking for his witch of a daughter. He even punched Alan, busted his face, for some imagined insult to his daughter. Both of them are a threat to us, to all of Dunmore. This is us fighting back." Merigold shivered. Saren spoke the conviction of a zealot, as if he actually believed his own fabricated story. That she was to blame for disease and disaster, pestilence and death, like a witch from the stories. That Ragen was violent and erratic, a menace. And that she somehow deserved her fate.

"Okay, okay. I know. Well, let's get to it," said the younger voice.

Meri gripped her makeshift knife in her left hand as tightly as she could, feeling the bite of the cloth as it pinched her fingers. And then she walked into the corner and deliberately released it with a sigh like a dying woman. There was nothing she could do against three men. Or, two men and one boy. She took in a deep breath and let it out slowly, closing her eyes. Trying to imagine for a moment that she was back at the inn, back in her warm room. Safe with Ragen watching over her. But the picture was vague, grainy, as if she were viewing the scene through frosted glass. She could barely remember Ragen's face.

The ladder was lowered into the cellar.

"Merigold, come up here. There are some people here to see you."

She climbed slowly, a woman condemned, trying to hold back tears. Trying to find the numbness that had been her shield. But, the brief promise of salvation from earlier seemed to have woken her from a dream. And the waking world promised to be a terrible place.

Saren leaned next to Chad and Paul, another forager from Dunmore. Chad was sixteen years old, wild brown hair partially covering his angular face. His father, Terrin, was a local scribe, making his living hand-copying *The Book of Amorum*. Chad, of course, assisted his father and likely knew the holy guide better than even most Taneos. In contrast, Paul was an older man with short-cut gray hair, a well-kempt beard, and yellowed teeth. Saren smirked at Meri as she scanned the faces of the men in the room. She probably couldn't hide the terror from her eyes, or the tremor from her limbs.

"Hi, Merigold. How are you today?" She said nothing.

"Merigold. I'm very happy to be here today," said Paul in his raspy voice, smiling a wide, ominous grin. He was as old as her father. She'd always felt a little uncomfortable around him, and now the burning coals in the pit of her stomach, the fiery fear, told her that her anxiety hadn't been enough.

"Well, there are some people here to help me with you today. If you wouldn't mind…"

Meri began to shake uncontrollably, as if she were suffering from a palsy. She forced herself to clench her teeth to keep from biting her tongue. Her weakness was so much that she nearly tumbled back down into the cellar. Perhaps that would be best, hitting her head, letting darkness take her. Letting it all end, forgotten by all except her maligned father.

The vision of the three men swam before her, and she clenched shut her eyes, wishing the thin eyelids had the ability to block out reality. How much more could one woman take? How could Yetra allow this to happen to her? To anyone? How could men such as these before her be allowed to exist? To thrive? Merigold felt a cold anger replacing the hot fear in her stomach. There was a wrongness to this, that such men should be allowed dominate her, control others. They were the ones who deserved to suffer, who deserved to be locked away from the world. But, the world was not just. Yetra was not just.

"Merigold." Saren's tone held a soft warning, as if he were admonishing a child for getting into mischief. "Merigold, you know what you need to do."

Her fists clenched at her side, as impotent as those of that admonished child. She longed to strike him, to make him pay. But, with a shuttering exhalation of breath, she relaxed her fists, mind focused on her instrument of vengeance discarded in the cellar below. She would endure. She *had* to endure.

143

Meri removed her oversized pants and went to the bucket of water in the corner to wash. It had become part of her routine. He never let her wash afterward—only before. She moved back to the bed then, sat down, and set her feet on the bed. She dared not look at the men for more than a second. Paul's hungry, wolfish look threated to shatter her fragile resolve.

Again, she tried to picture the Duckling. The common room, with its different colored tables, painted so that it was always easy to know which tables to serve and what payment to collect. The roaring fire by the white table. The friendly people, drinking their beer, eating their eggs and stew. Then, Saren was seated, there, at the blue table, along with Paul. The common room suddenly felt cold. Unclean.

But Ragen was there, too, protecting her. He hit Saren, just as he had that man who'd groped her when she was younger. Just like he had with Fenrir. He broke Paul's yellowed teeth as the man leered at her. Her father, her guardian.

Closing her eyes, Merigold could picture Ragen's face clearly, again, as the two men and one boy closed in on her.

Chapter 10

The so-called Great Hall felt like anything but. It was far smaller than one would have expected, and certainly more drab. There was little in terms of adornment and decor aside from a single, gigantic painting of Yetra's Ascension. But the lighting was so dim that none of the guests could make out the details of said painting. The guests themselves were rather drab, as well. Clothed like peasants, they sat at a long, wooden table, each facing the front of the room. Each had a servant standing slightly behind and to their left, as was dictated by protocol—almost as a joke. Spurning the conventions of protocol, however, were the armed guards who stood several feet back from each guest.

As if anyone had the illusion of actually being a guest, Emma Dran thought as she surveyed the not-so-great hall from her position at Lady Escamilla Breen's shoulder. She was dressed slightly better than her mistress, with her own simple, light orange dress at least having a splash of color. The clothing forced upon the "guests" was meant to embarrass and shame them, forcing them to feel as if they were as inconsequential as peasants. Coming from such stock herself, Emma had never thought there was anything humiliating about the men and women on which this country rested. The lower classes kept the country fed with their farming, kept rooms warm with their logging and forestry, and kept the country safe with their huge presence in the military. Nonetheless, the people forced into such mean garments as they wore now did not universally share Emma's views.

As always, Lady Escamilla seemed unaffected by the situation. She was actually the daughter of a failed merchant, not a noble by birth or by name. Unlike her father Garrick Breen, Escamilla had a knack for trading. Rumor had it that Escamilla had started with a bag of fruit in a small town near Florens, trading for more yets than it was worth. Then, she'd bought some figs from a down-on-his-luck traveling Sestrian, and sold those for triple what she'd paid to the kitchen of a noble house. She'd continued to provide various supposed delicacies to this noble house until she'd had enough money to have a substantial inventory and her own small warehouse (a shed, really). But, Escamilla always had her ear to the ground, and could always predict the market. Right before one of the more serious border incursions by the Wasmer, Escamilla had invested every ounce of her wealth in dried beef and hard-baked, long-lasting, and tasteless bread, making a fortune by selling these needed supplies to the military of Florens and Rostane. Before colorful scarves became all the rage among the notable in Draston, Escamilla had acquired an endless silkworm farm. She always knew, it seemed, what the world needed.

Eventually, Escamilla had begun investing in land, particularly land with often unrecognized potential. Her first purchase, a seemingly valueless plot of forest in Florens, actually contained some of the most productive sour apple orchards in Ardia. This had allowed Escamilla to generate wealth with minimal investment of her own time. And as her orchards had become more profitable (primarily because of the hard cider that was distilled from the sour apples, which no one wanted to eat raw), Escamilla had continued to buy up land from across the four duchies of Ardia. Emma was continuously surprised to hear how the nobility tended to mismanage their wealth and land, but Escamilla always seemed to know when a count needed to settle gambling debts or when a baron had lost a whole crop of wheat to pests. Before long, she'd owned land in all four duchies— Rostane, Florens, Hunesa, and Draston. Enough land that, if it were put together, she could almost have had her own duchy. As a result, she'd become widely known as Lady Escamilla. The woman who rivaled the dukes and the duchess.

Escamilla was now in her early sixties and, while no one would ever have said that she was an attractive woman (even when she'd been young), she did have a certain presence. An air of poise. Of power. She was skinny—nearly skeletal, in fact—her body and face being all hard angles and lines. Her hair had gone completely white decades earlier, whether due to stress or heredity, no one could say. What people could say was that, when captured by her eyes, they immediately felt sized-up, as if they were a product to be bought or sold. And Escamilla was very good at buying and selling.

And now, this powerful, self-made woman was prisoner in everything but name to Little Duke Penton. Emma shifted her gaze from her mistress to the man sitting before his "guests." Samuel Penton III was a disappointment when compared to his father, Samuel II, who had truly been a great man. His forethought, creativity, and sensitivity had revolutionized Rostane. Ardia, even. His public works included his creation of a water system that provided jobs for the poor, as well as an accessible water system available to the public, a reduction in taxes for the lower classes that allowed peasants to actually achieve success and increase their station, and a huge investment in ship-born trade that continued to stimulate the economy. He'd also implemented a beautification tax with the goal of making Rostane more appealing to travelers. However, this had been executed poorly, so that the enhancements only impacted already attractive upper-class areas.

It had been at Samuel II's behest that his peers—Dukes Malless and Proan, and Duchess Fraunt—and subordinates had met at the Ardian Council three years before, with the goal of putting treatises in place that would truly unite Ardia for the first time since King Thontos had been in power: uniting trade, military, and policies. Unfortunately, Samuel II had taken ill during that event, though it was common knowledge that there must have been some foul play involved. Following his death, Samuel Penton III, the Little Duke of Rostane, had come into power. The moniker "little" had nothing to do with his size or appearance, but rather the fact that he would always rest in the shadow of his father.

Emma's eyes were drawn to the little duke now. He was actually a very tall man, as nobles seemed to breed for imposing physical characteristics, if not intelligence and sense. He had an average build which appeared to be enhanced by his penchant for wearing armor whenever he was giving audience. Even now, he wore a breastplate that emulated the chiseled body of a strongman, as well as an opalescent-white cape emblazoned with the wolf of Rostane, peeling back his lips and bearing his fangs, flecks of spittle evident in his grin. Duke Samuel had a similar issue with spittle when he spoke, and particularly when he was angry. Like now.

"I am uncertain why you continue to resist my offer. The price of resistance is high, as you know. Just ask Baron Erlins," spat Duke Samuel, rising from his ornate chair.

As Theran Erlins had been tortured extensively in front of this group and was now presumed dead by the "guests," they were unlikely to have an opportunity to engage in such questioning. Erlins had been similarly imprisoned by Samuel II, and Emma considered him to be a brave fool. He'd thought to escape in the conventional way, with steel and muscle. To his credit, Erlins had killed three guardsmen before being brought down, bleeding from a serious wound in his leg. In an excruciating two hour-long session, his body and spirit had been utterly destroyed after that. Fingernails had been removed from both his hands with pliers, and his left hand entirely removed—one bone at a time. Whenever Erlins had lost consciousness, Savant Iolen, a Senior Scholar at The Enlightenment and the acting physician, would inject him with a potion that would keep him awake. Eventually, the stump of his hand had been cauterized with the flat side of a sword, heated to glowing in the hot coals of the fire, and Iolen had said that he would be unable to administer more potion without fatal consequences. So, the big man had been carted off, and was either imprisoned or dead by now.

Emma had been horrified during the entire session, growing more and more sickened at the sight of the torture, the blood. Her own hand had been mutilated years ago by a man she'd loved, and she only retained her thumb and index finger. Though she still had the ability to grasp and carry things, it always brought her a biting pain. Her mutilation had been an indirect attack on Lady Escamilla from one of her many jealous rivals, or so Emma assumed, and had just happened to be perpetrated by Fenrir, a man she had made love to many, many times. A man who'd professed his own love to her on numerous occasions, but who'd been entangled by his obligations to both his wife and his father. A man who'd violently maimed her hand as she'd locked eyes with him.

"What, nothing to say? All I expect is that you swear fealty to me, relinquish the control of your armies to Rostane, and provide a portion of your income to the Rostanian treasury. In return, you will be allowed to continue ruling your lands and be provided a royal advisor to guide you in matters of the state. Or, you share the fate of Erlins. It seems like an easy decision, not one meriting such impertinence," said the duke, now with the hint of a self-satisfied smile.

There were five guests in the room. Aside from Escamilla, there was Viscount Alexander Saford who ruled a large plot of land outside of Hunesa, Earl Michel Fraunt, the son and heir of Duchess Emily Fraunt of Draston, and Count Arn Sinder, who ruled a county within Rostane, itself. And, the crown jewel of Samuel's designs, Duke Henry Malless, ruler of Florens and the little duke's chief rival.

"Ah, little Samuel." Duke Malless' voice was hard, his smile tight. "With or without me, Florens would never capitulate to Rostane. If I swore fealty to you, they would simply appoint my son as duke and consider me dead. If you took Eric, then the next in line would step up. Right now, you are in a very uncomfortable situation. As soon as my true status at the Plateau is known, you

149

will have an army at your southern border. And with the treaties I have in place, Florens would have support from Jecusta and you would easily be outmanned." Unlike Erlins, Malless was not a fool. His calm, confident voice was exceptionally effective at controlling the room, and that quality always set the little duke into a rage.

But not now. Not today.

"What is that you said about Eric? If he were taken, the next in line would step up as duke? Your cousin, Regis Tawney?" Samuel gestured to the other man standing at the front of the room.

Lord Faris—Emma was uncertain of his first name—was the little duke's chief advisor. He supposedly hailed from Algania, and had taken a seat on the advisory council of Samuel III during the border incursions with the Wasmer. It was partially due to his efforts, both in strategy and diplomacy, that Rostane had been able to reach an uneasy peace with the fur-skinned folk. Now, he stood, his black and silver hair fixed in a loose ponytail, wearing a long, red cloak despite the heat in the room. At least, Emma felt the room was hot. Her palms were sweating.

Lord Faris retrieved a bulky bag from behind his chair and approached Henrik. He paused in front of the duke, looking into his eyes with an inscrutable gaze. And then he upended the bag, spilling onto the table a decapitated head which rolled toward Henrik. Henrik pulled back out of his chair and jumped to his feet, immediately feeling a spear point at his back.

"Let me adjust this," said Lord Faris in his deep, calming voice, reaching for the head, which had landed face down. With his righting of the head, Emma saw a white, pinched face that she did not recognize. But, Lord Malless did.

"You fucking bastard. Florens will see you dead," he whispered venomously, his voice carrying far in the unembellished stone chamber.

"Viscount Regis Tawny, third in line to the ducal seat of Florens," said Little Duke Penton. "Now in no condition to rule. So, if something unforeseen were to happen to young Eric Malless, the fourth in line would take the seat. That quivering blob of a man, Taean Tawny. Do you think that he could stand against me? What do you think he would have done if exposed to Erlins'... rehabilitation? Florens is lost one way or another."

"Eric will never stand for this." Henrik glared at Samuel, and Emma thought that there was a high probability that Henrik was going to rush him and be cut down. But, he was both too brave and too smart for that.

"With all due respect, your grace, Eric does not yet know of your fate. He has been receiving regular letters from you, detailing your continued negotiations with Rostane, sealed in wax with your insignia, the river otter." Lord Faris was all respect, even as he gave Henrik news of this treason. There was not a hint of sarcasm in his voice, nor mockery in his face. "Your grace, in a week, Eric will ride out for the traditional Awakening Celebration hunt in the Dentony region bordering Rostane. A regiment is being sent to the border, and will overtake Eric and his small group of nobles and soldiers."

Henrik slowly sank back into his chair, apparently beaten, a lion finally tamed.

"This is in your hands now, Henrik. What shall become of your beloved son, Eric? He is certainly a fine swordsman and will no doubt give a good accounting of himself. But, against the numbers we send, he is destined to fall. Then, you become expendable, as it will be much easier to deal with Tubby Taean than you," said Penton, his glee barely restrained.

"Your grace, I will have an answer for you tomorrow," responded Henrik in a hushed, hollow voice that carried none of his usual confidence or authority. Emma was stunned that he appeared to be giving in. She'd thought his backbone was steel,

151

unable to bend, break, or even chip. This cousin, Regis, to whom belonged the disembodied head, must have meant a lot to him. And, the threat to his son, even more.

"Of course, my dear Henrik. However, you must be quick, as the orders for the incursion have already been sent. My fastest messengers are only as fast as their horses." The little duke appeared satisfied in his apparent victory over Duke Malless, despite having had to utilize appalling methods. Malless must have known something like this was coming. They all had; the past two or three weeks had been full of heavy implications and threats. Once Erlins had met his fate, they'd known what the little duke was capable of. It had only been a matter of time until one of them was targeted. Henrik represented both the biggest threat and the biggest potential profit to the little duke's cause. He was the obvious first target.

And by that logic, Emma believed that Lady Escamilla, being so wealthy and owning so much land, was the obvious second choice.

"And you, Lady Escamilla. What do I have to offer you, a woman playing at being a noble?"

"I imagine that I would not recognize any heads that you dumped in front of me, your grace," said Escamilla with her typical aplomb. Emma was ever impressed by her mistress, and sought to emulate her whenever possible.

"Ah, yes. The *Lady* Escamilla," said Duke Penton, leaning back in his padded chair. "She has touched so many lives and yet holds no close confidants. No children; likely barren. Faris, any word on family?"

"Your grace, we have been unable to locate any relatives of the Lady Escamilla," said Lord Faris matter-of-factly. Emma was not sure whether to like or loathe the man.

"That is a shame. Family opens people up for… discussions. I am aware that you have no current heir to your holdings."

"My affairs, your grace, are my affairs. I will mind them as I so choose," said Escamilla.

"Of course, of course. I would never think to pry into your affairs. Most nobles and competitors have already tried to do the same, and have had little luck. My mean resources could not unveil anything that has not already been found."

"I attempt to keep a low profile, your grace." Escamilla nodded respectfully.

"And yet, here we are. I know that you have standing forces guarding your operations across all of Ardia. They are to be mine. I know that you generate a great deal of revenue from your products. A portion of that is to be mine."

"Your grace, you are unable to compel me."

Emma wished she were Escamilla. So calm under pressure. She would have been physically sick, were she in Escamilla's chair.

"Actually, compelling you is quite easy. With no successor and heir in place, upon your death, your wealth and holdings would be absorbed by the duchy. Certainly, your loyal people would disperse, and that would not benefit me. And certainly, some of that wealth would be distributed to Florens, Draston, and Hunesa. But, given that those duchies are to be mine soon enough, I am not concerned with that. No, eliminating you, my Lady Escamilla, is the easiest option, if you are unable to bargain." The little duke again smiled, appearing to believe he had again defeated his opponent. Emma had a strong desire to gouge him in the eyes. Even her disabled hand would be enough for that.

"Your grace, you are welcome to take that chance. However, hypothetically, a lady of my standing likely has a number of contingency plans in place. Perhaps, if such a lady were to disappear under unusual circumstances, such plans might be released. Perhaps there are official, legal documents available, in the hands of a number of reputable barristers and bankers, naming an heir. Or, perhaps my wealth and holdings are willed to the Duchess Emily Fraunt, or perhaps Lord Unael of Jecusta. Even your *mean resources* tell you that we have a close, political relationship," Escamilla said, hands still folded on the table in front of her.

The little duke's eyes seemed to bulge at her calm, measured words, and one of his hands was clenched in a fist, his flesh clearly turning white even in the poor illumination of the Great Hall.

"So, your grace, you are welcome to take your chances. But, were I a betting woman, I would not wager on you achieving your desired outcome."

From her post behind Lady Escamilla, Emma wanted to laugh. Her lady had obviously won this round, just as she had gotten the better of so many men in the past.

Duke Penton looked as if he had been stung by a dozen hornets, so red was his face. He started to speak, but cut himself off. He glanced askance at Lord Faris, and the move was not lost on Emma. Faris who addressed Escamilla next, his own face as stoic as stone.

"My Lady Escamilla, you are dismissed for today. Your handmaiden and guard will direct you back to your quarters. You will be summoned again soon. Until then, please take your leisure."

Emma was immeasurably relieved when she and Lady Escamilla finally returned to their shared quarters. Emma threw herself onto the single bed in the austere room and let out a long breath. She felt drained by the stress of the day's audience, both physically and emotionally. All day, she had felt a rising tension, and now she felt like a piping hot tea kettle that was finally able to release some of its pent up steam. This kettle, however, had never been in a fire so hot.

"My dear, are you alright?" asked Escamilla, genuine concern clear in her tone. Though she was the one who'd recently been threatened with death, she was still the embodiment of tranquility, more concerned with the taut nerves of her handmaiden than her own.

Emma sat up on the bed. "Of course, milady. I simply find myself to be fatigued after the events of today."

"You can dispense with the formality, Emma. We are alone and the door is thick. The fact that it is meant to contain us works to our advantage in that it grants us at least a modicum of privacy."

"Sorry, Camilla. Old habits, you know," smiled Emma. Escamilla returned the affection with her own grin, somewhat softening her otherwise sharp features. She patted Emma's hand comfortingly, her thumb resting for just a moment along the scarred emptiness of Emma's missing fingers.

Emma had worked for Lady Escamilla for nearly ten years now, just as her mother had before she'd succumbed to a terrible and deadly stomach flux that had run rampant through Little Town years ago. Experienced servants had been painfully hard to come by afterward, and nobles had been terrified that their every little wish would no longer be met—or, at least not to their standards. There had been a frantic rush to fill empty slots caused by the death of so many servants, and Emma had been one of those hired. She'd been known to the steward of Lady Escamilla's household, as she'd often helped her mother with her work, and because she'd had at least modest experience, she had immediately stepped into her mother's role with Lady Escamilla. Thus, the steward had been freed up for the unenviable task of hiring, training, and supervising the less experienced lot that had flooded the Plateau.

For a time, Emma had simply served as Lady Escamilla's personal handmaiden whenever she'd visited the ducal seat of Rostane. But as months passed, Escamilla had begun to give Emma rather unusual tasks. *Find out what, and how much, Lady Wister ate for dinner. Retrieve a codpiece from the armory. Determine why Earl Paron was feuding with Baron Holstrom.* Then, she'd been asked to name residents and visitors to the Plateau based on descriptions or sketches, a task she'd struggled with given the sheer number of people residing in and visiting the fortress, and one which was further complicated by all of the shifting titles—Count Esterly of Simaw was also the Baron of Rente, until his son had married and become the new Baron. Little by little, over a period of several years, Emma had become Lady Escamilla's spy.

"Camilla," Emma said, hesitantly, and not for the first time. "I am so sorry that you are imprisoned here. I should have…"

"You could not have foreseen this. The little duke masks his plans well. If only he were as good a ruler as a plotter, we would not be in our current predicament." Escamilla was all composure and reassurance. The strength of this woman!

"Still, I was the one that lost track of Malless. I just assumed that he had left the Plateau. If I had kept track…"

Camilla interrupted again. "I don't expect your powers to be limitless. You are still confined by your duties at the Plateau. While you are relatively invisible to my supposed peers, Steward John holds you accountable. Trust me, my dear. Were you to blame here, I would have already had words with you."

Once, several years ago, Escamilla had asked Emma to determine what deal Earl Cochran had been attempting to make with Baron Erlins. No matter how she'd tried, though, Emma had been unable to overhear any relevant conversations, or find any revealing documents in either office or chambers. But, instead of telling Lady Escamilla that she'd failed, she'd made up something about a trade agreement. The conversation that ensued upon Escamilla's rather quick discovery of Emma's attempted deception had left Emma shaking and weeping, though Escamilla had not even raised her voice. Since then, Emma had told no lies. A hard woman, indeed.

"Camilla, what are we going to do? I don't want to see you sharing the fate of Erlins or that Regis, though Regis might have been better off." Emma shivered at the thought of the baron's torture.

"I have told you before. A smart woman always studies her opponent first and moves second. If I had decided to leave the Plateau two weeks ago, when I was 'invited' to stay in this chamber, then I might have missed learning Erlin's fate, or what Malless' ultimate decision will be. I might have missed that Eric Malless is in danger, or that the little duke looks to Faris when his emotions get the better of him. I have been in no real danger at this point because, as I made clear, the little duke still needs me." Escamilla joined Emma on the bed, resting her head on the simple oaken headboard.

"I understand, Camilla. But haven't we studied enough? I don't want either of our heads to end up in a sack!" Emma felt some pride at avoiding a quaver in her voice.

"Well, between you and me, I really couldn't have left any earlier, because it takes time to make these kind of arrangements," said Escamilla, a hint of humor in her voice. "Just as I don't believe that your power is unlimited, you have to know that I am also not a magician, waving my hand and affecting a dramatic escape."

The two women shared a laugh at the comment, and for a moment, Emma could almost forget that their lives were in danger. Emma rested her head on Escamilla's boney shoulder, and Escamilla rested her head on Emma's own. The gesture was small, but it brought Emma some comfort. It was a brief respite, though, as Escamilla pulled away and reached from something secreted in her brassiere.

"Now, my dear, please go fetch our dinner from the kitchen. And, if you wouldn't mind… Yarvey." Escamilla placed a tiny thimble-like object into Emma's hand, and Emma immediately secreted it in her sleeve. As Escamilla's spy, Emma was ever passing notes through a complex network of servants, residents, and visitors, and could never have kept track of the causes and effects of these notes.

Emma rose from the bed and cross the room, knocking on the door three times. One of the two guards answered. Alex Poe was his name, and he wasn't a bad sort. Emma had little respect for the guardsman of this fortress, finding that they were gambling, womanizing slobs. Or cold-blooded murderers and maimers. Or both. Even so, Alex had always been polite to her, and he practically beamed upon seeing her face. She wondered how he felt, holding two women captive and witnessing the calculated power-mongering that came from Duke Samuel II. But she knew, from her association with Fenrir, that guardsman were little more than dancing bears seen in traveling shows, obeying commands and sitting quietly otherwise.

"Miss Emma. Are we headed to the kitchen? I will lead the way." He turned smartly on his heel and began a measured march down the hall, Emma hurrying to keep up.

She should have felt flattered that she merited her own personal guard, though she knew that it was simply an effort by the duke to keep his plot disguised for a little longer. Even the guardsmen assigned to watch Escamilla, and Malless and the rest, were kept confined, forced to sleep in a cluster of connected chambers and forbidden from leaving the interior portion of the fortress. As far as Emma could tell, it was an effective policy. The rest of the world appeared oblivious to the fact that several important figures in Ardia had not been seen for some time now.

Emma had suggested to Escamilla that they ask Alex for help—he seemed like a decent man, someone who might chafe at holding the nobles against their will. But Alex had been in the room that day, witnessing Erlins' torture. Escamilla had said that, if the guards hadn't changed their course after that, they were either cowed by fear or had evil in their hearts. Looking into Alex's brown eyes, Emma had hoped it was the former.

Winding through the maze-like servants' passages, Emma accompanied Alex to the secondary kitchens and approached the rear ordering window. One had to still feed the prisoners; as far as the secondary kitchen staff and the rest of the Plateau knew, they were providing meals for nobles who were secreted away from the public eye, discussing matters of national security. Alex was just out of sight, but Emma could sense that he was still close enough for listening.

"Ah, Emma. Is it time for Lady Breen's supper?" asked the serving boy named Yarvey. Emma gave him a quick little smile, and he blushed bright red.

"Yes, and if you could give her a double portion, that would be lovely. My lady is famished."

The boy ran off as Emma leaned against the counter, replaying the events of the day in her head. The duke was becoming increasingly violent, it seemed, and she was scared for both herself and Camilla. The duke was three years younger than Emma, and had occasionally treated her poorly when their paths would cross back when Samuel II had still been in power. He would grab and pinch her, and had boorishly propositioned her on multiple occasions. Luckily, she had been able to duck his advances. There were always much more willing women for him, many of them far above Emma's station.

Her musings were interrupted when Yarvey returned with a tray, laden with roasted chicken breast, some spiced potatoes, and a pile of seasoned mustard greens. As she reached for the tray, she brushed his hand, releasing the small thimble she'd carried into the space between his fingers. This message would begin a journey that Emma didn't fully understand. The thimble-object was covered with tiny buttons and, from what Emma understood, the buttons could be pushed to create specific patterns. Yarvey would pass the thimble to whomever the first portion of the pattern indicated. That person would examine a different row of depressions and pass it on to yet another part of this clandestine network. Eventually, the note would reach the correct person, who would utilize a tiny, pin-like key to access the message, which could likely contain no more than a sentence or two. It was unclear whether any individual within the chain knew all of the patterns, although it seemed likely to Emma that there must be someone orchestrating the entire scheme. Who that person could be, though, was beyond her ken.

Emma carried the tray back to her mistress' room, refusing Alex's offer to carry it for her. Rather than use her maimed hand and risk dropping the tray, she held the tray firmly on one arm, balancing it on her wrist. It was a skill she had mastered relatively quickly following her injury, in order to stay useful to Lady Escamilla. Emma knew that Escamilla would have kept her on regardless, but Emma did not like to feel as if she were a charity case.

Bidding Alex good evening, Emma re-entered the chamber, finding Escamilla standing, apparently considering a vase of indigo flowers. That vase contained the only color in the room, and Emma had had to work hard to convince the folks from the kitchen to provide her with flowers. She felt proud that she had been able to secure something that provided a bit of cheer for the otherwise drab room. Escamilla always seemed so patient and enduring, and yet Emma could sense a subtle sadness about her. So subtle that, if Emma hadn't spent so much time with the woman over the past decade, she would easily have missed it.

Escamilla started at the loud click which echoed through the small chamber as Alex closed the door behind Emma. She turned and gave Emma a thin, forced smile.

"Please, my dear, please join an old woman for dinner."

"I don't see any old woman, but I would be happy to join you, Camilla." That drew a slightly more authentic smile.

The two tucked in to their meal, both able to eat despite the stress of their current predicament. Or perhaps because of it. Emma thought that she could have eaten another quarter chicken, so hungry she was. In practically no time, the heaping, doubled-sized meal was gone, and both women leaned back in their chairs feeling content.

"I wish I could serve you tea. I know it has only been two weeks, but I miss sharing our chamomile together before bed," sighed Emma.

"Typically, I would agree with you, my dear. However, I would rather not be drowsy this evening. We are leaving the Plateau. Tonight."

Escamilla and Emma collected their things, sparse though they were, slipping them into a pillowcase in place of a satchel. Emma had little choice but to continue wearing her orange dress, her only other option being stained with flecks of blood from Erlin's torture. Samuel had tossed dismembered bits of fingers at the guests as he'd given a speech about the idiocy of opposing him. Emma shivered at the recollection. She packed the stained dress in case of emergency, but couldn't bring herself to don the gruesome garment.

Lady Escamilla was clad in oversized peasant clothes—a rough-spun cotton blouse and pants—as that was all that had been provided for her. Even in such ill-fitting and unflattering garments, she held herself in a way that made her seem every inch a noble, even if that would never be true. She was truly splendid, no matter what she wore.

Emma wheedled gently in an attempt to determine how, precisely, they were going to be exiting the Plateau, but Escamilla was tight-lipped. All she would do was continue to stress the need to "be ready." As eager as Emma was to escape her imprisonment, she was also terrified. How would they get out of here? What if they were caught? Even if they got out of the Plateau, how would they get out of the city? She couldn't bear the thought that she might end up in the torturer's chair, made an example of to keep the others in line. She had lost fingers before, after all, and the idea of enduring that pain again turned her stomach into writhing snakes. She twisted a lock of her long, curly red hair about her finger, finding comfort, as she always did, in the softness of the hair on her skin.

Their meager belongings packed, the two women sat on the edge of the bed and continued to wait. There was no window and no way to accurately mark the passage of time, but Emma roughly estimated that it must have been well past high moons. She briefly rose and began to pace, but Escamilla bid her to sit once more, to conserve her strength for what lay ahead. A statement which only made Emma more apprehensive.

When it seemed that Emma could wait no more, when the tension in the room had her every nerve as taut as a clothesline, there was a noise at the door. Both women bolted to their feet, Escamilla uncharacteristically showing her nerves through her jumpiness. There was a fumbling at the lock and then the door creaked open slowly, cautiously.

A guardsman walked into the room, wearing the typical armor and ornament of the Rostanian military. He was a big man, broad at the shoulders and with arms like those of a blacksmith. The low profile of his barbute, coupled with the low light of the room, masked his features.

"My Lady Escamilla? I am here to escort you to safety." That voice…

"Sir, remove your helm. I would see those with whom I do business. And certainly those who risk their lives for me."

Slowly, the man removed his covering. He had a beard, equal parts brown, blonde, and gray. His head, glistening wetly with sweat, was shaved bald. Recently shaved bald, it seemed, as there was a small stream of blood trickling down behind his ear, the drops failing to coagulate as they mixed with his heavy perspiration. With these changes in appearance, Emma almost didn't recognize him.

But, his every feature was etched into her memory, and a scant disguise couldn't hide him.

She stormed across the room, snatching up the vase of indigo flowers as she went. Eyes blazing, Emma swung the vase with all of her strength at Fenrir's head.

Chapter 11

Fenrir's eyes widened at the sight of the vase careening toward his head, but he reacted in an instant. He batted it aside with the back of his leather-bound hand, knocking it clear out of Emma's grip and into the open air.

"Shit!" he cursed quietly, watching it tumble through the air, already regretting his decision to take on this ill-conceived, dangerous mission—he pushed past Emma, knowing that he would never reach the vase before it crashed into the ground and caused a commotion that could bring guards running. By the gods, did he need yet another reminder that stealth was not his bent?

But there was no shattering of glass, no stomping of boots from guards converging on the room to investigate. There was merely a small thud and an "oomph" as Lady Escamilla dove forward, catching the vase an inch from the hard stone floor. She rose stiffly then, set the vase down, and slapped Emma across the face.

"What are you doing, you spoiled, stupid child? Are you trying to get us killed? I thought you were smarter than that, Emma!" Escamilla hissed through clenched teeth, her rage barely contained.

Emma appeared contrite in the face of Escamilla's anger, but she didn't cower.

"My Lady Escamilla, I would like you to meet Fenrir de Trenton, former guardsman of the Plateau. Although he appears to be grayer and balder. And fatter. Oh, and I almost forgot: he is also the man who mutilated me." Emma was herself furious, her face red from anger as much as from the aftermath of the slap.

Fenrir shifted his feet awkwardly as Escamilla scrutinized him. He felt surprisingly exposed in the face of this severe older woman, and the livid scorn from his former lover (not to mention

164

his first victim) wasn't helping. The silence stretched out uncomfortably, but Fenrir was accustomed to standing for long periods of time, gaze carefully unfocused. And, by Ultner, just wearing this steel and leather armor, etched with the Rostanian wolf, he felt as if he had never left his job. He felt more secure, more confident. Even his reflexes were faster, judging from his blocking of that vase.

Escamilla was the first to break the silence, letting slip a wry chuckle. Fenrir wasn't sure whether to feel relieved or worried.

"Oh, the games the gods play with us. I was there, de Trenton, to witness your fall. Both figuratively and literally."

"It's not de Trenton. Fenrir Coldbreaker now, at your service." Fenrir bent his head deferentially as he shared the news of his reformation. Emma snorted derisively at the new name, earning a glare from Escamilla.

"Well, Sir *Coldbreaker*..." Escamilla rubbed at her hip, probably bruised from her swandive. His new name sounded ridiculous coming from the lady's mouth. Perhaps Fenrir shouldn't make life-changing decisions while bleeding out on the doorstep of a friend's house in the future.

"I'm assuming you have a plan to lead us safely out of this graceful fortress."

"Indeed, my lady. There are stipulations, however. First, you must keep your *help* under control." Emma bristled like a furious dog. Fenrir shouldn't have said that, but he didn't know how to react to Emma. When he'd found out that his charge was Lady Escamilla, he'd hoped that Emma would not be involved. That Emma had been dismissed after their... incident, although that probably would have led to her being destitute. No one would hire a four-fingered pariah, let alone a two-fingered cripple. In the several days that Fenrir had had to prepare for this assignment, he had simply blocked out the fact that he might see Emma. It had allowed him to avoid thinking about how he felt about her and about what had happened. How he felt about himself.

"Second, you must stay absolutely quiet. It seems, my lady, that *you* recognize that necessity." There he went again, poking the beast. Emma was visibly fuming by this point. "Finally, you are to follow my orders exactly. If I say 'jump,' you will jump as if the floor were on fire. If I say 'run,' you run as if Ultner's cock is aimed at your backsides."

"Of course, Sir Coldbreaker," said Lady Escamilla, with a slightly raised eyebrow, but otherwise no sarcasm. "Now, what is the plan?"

The two women followed Fenrir silently through the servants' passages. The Plateau was built with royalty—or at least nobility—in mind, and the builder had clearly adhered to the adage that "servants should neither be seen nor heard." As a result, thin servant passages honeycombed the fortress proper, allowing servants to scurry through these narrow passages much like rats. The passages were certainly as narrow as rodent burrows, too, and Fenrir had to turn his shoulders as he walked to keep his pauldrons from scraping discordantly on the stone. As he swung his arms about, navigating the twists and turns, his lantern cast shadows—demons running along the wall, following them like Ultner's own entourage. They certainly cut quite a scene: an armored guard practically performing acrobatics to maneuver his bulk at every turn, a straight-backed noblewoman clad in the gold and green livery of palace servants, and a sullen servant trailing slightly behind, clenching her crippled hand. Fenrir would have been amused by the whole situation if it hadn't been for the very real possibility of their being killed, or worse.

166

Surefooted, Fenrir continued to guide Escamilla and Emma through the maze, having navigated these passages many times before. In fact, he had spent a good deal of time in the more private, less-traveled servants' passages, entertaining the servants themselves. Once with Emma, come to think of it, although he was actively working to repress that thought. Instead, he focused on the path. Presumably, the little duke had blockaded this area of the Plateau completely, with guards paired off at each possible entrance aside from the kitchen, but the duke did not know the secret ways and shortcuts. Fenrir didn't even know some of these ways, but Tennyson's scouts had provided him with enough detail to get him where he needed to be. It turned out that, though the fortress was very difficult to enter unseen, it was actually relatively easy for one to stay concealed once they were inside the heavily-guarded gates.

"What did you do to Alex and Kincaid?" Emma demanded abruptly.

"Who? And keep your voice down!" Fenrir hissed.

"Our guards. Kincaid is a bucket-headed, small-cocked fool like you, but Alex is kind and gentle. Very *unlike* you."

Fenrir didn't flinch at her jab, either about his manhood or his virtue, but he responded through clenched teeth. "It is better if you do not know." Fenrir certainly didn't know. He'd simply been told that there would be no guard at the door that night, and there had been no guard. He had approached the hallway cautiously, having arrived through the conveniently unprotected servants' passages. His hand on the short sword sheathed at his hip, steeling himself for the possibility that he might have to ambush and kill a man or two. Thankfully, as Tennyson's contact had promised, no one had been there, though he'd heard voices just down the hall. Whether due to bribery, threats, or poison, he did not know, and frankly, he didn't care. The House was utilizing a lot of resources on this mission, and he just hoped to the gods that that meant his chances of success were good.

In retrospect, he shouldn't have been here in the Plateau, surrounded by danger. He should have ran, left Rostane, far before Tennyson caught wind of his location. But, instead, he lingered with Martis, leisurely recovering while surrounded by fawning medical students. He ate rich food—broasted duck, corn soufflé, and buttered vegetables and so on—and enjoyed hot steams and baths. He just took time to walk around Martis' stunning gardens, beginning to bloom as spring truly vanquished the last traces of the cold. He and the physician engaged in meaningless, trite conversations about nothing, joking and laughing as Fenrir told stories of being a guard, or Martis spoke of particularly irritating patients. In short, Fenrir felt, for the first time in years, safe.

But it was a false safety. A lull in the shit-storm that had become his life, of late. He should have run. Should have left.

Lost in thought, Fenrir nearly missed the echo of excited voices up ahead. Fenrir stopped abruptly and held up his hand, halting the trailing women in their tracks.

"Follow my lead and act like servants. My Lady Escamilla, keep your eyes lowered and your head down. Yes, like that, and hunch your shoulders a little. You are too well-known within the Plateau, and we don't want anyone recognizing you. Emma, keep between me and the wall if you can. That hair will give us away in a second." As would her hand. "We only have a few hours until anyone knows that you two are missing, and we want to be as far away as possible by then."

Fenrir resumed his march down the hallway, correcting his posture, placing his feet with purpose and making it no secret that an armed and armored guardsman was walking down the corridor. Over his own clang and clamor, he could no longer discern whether voices were still present, but this was a rare moment when subtlety would not be his friend. Once again, he was part of the guard of the Plateau. The elite guard, even, as the armor provided by Tennyson's agent was from one of the duke's own, the Knights of the Wolf. And, a Wolf Knight would do little to mask his approach in a servants' tunnel.

Fenrir's mind flitted to his friend Silas, who would be a Wolf Knight by now. He hoped he wouldn't become tangled in all of this.

As he rounded a curve, praying that his charges were still behind him and appropriately following his instructions, Fenrir noticed three servants clustered together, apparently chattering or gossiping, so enthralled with whatever they were talking about that they didn't notice Fenrir's obvious approach. They were so oblivious, in fact, that he could only assume they were sharing some particularly juicy gossip. Fenrir stopped about twenty feet shy of them, loudly clearing his throat, and enjoyed watching the members of the trio jump simultaneously. One, a chubby and grubby woman with mousey hair and shallow-set eyes, looked for all the world like an odd, sickly lizard. He recognized her. Lopen. That was her name. The other two, he did not know. They were younger. And all three had guilt stamped on their faces.

"Our apologies, m'lord, for impeding you." Ah, the delicate pleasantries of servants, deference to their betters beaten into them by the castle stewards. How Fenrir missed it. "The news 'as just been so shocking. Please forgive us." All three bent their heads to him, one of the younger ones visibly quaking.

He had forgotten how good it felt to instill such fear.

Fenrir should have known better, but he had to ask. "What news, Lopen?" The lizard-looking woman started, surprised that he knew her name. She squinted at him. Shit. He was terrible at subterfuge.

"*The* news. About 'is grace, Duke Malless." He heard a gasp behind him. Lizard Lopen glanced around him, noticing Emma and Escamilla for the first time. Fenrir shifted and puffed out, attempting to block more of the corridor.

"I've not been on duty. Enlighten me."

"M'lord, 'e jumped! That is, 'is grace threw 'isself from a balcony way up in the Plateau, and 'e fell down into Yetra Lane just before sunset. The news is all over the fortress. The city, even. 'Is grace, Duke Eric, is to be successor in Florens. Only nineteen years of age, poor boy."

Fenrir had seen Henrik Malless many times. He particularly recalled him taking charge during that godsdamned unfortunate day in the council chamber, his last day as a guardsman. In Fenrir's experience, silently observing the leaders of Ardia from his place as a well-paid, steel-cased ornament, few of the nobles were worth a damn. They tended to be all style—questionable, garish style—and rarely substance. Intrigue without real intelligence. They had scant knowledge of their own holdings and business affairs, delegating these duties to an army of administrators and secretaries, the people who truly ran Ardia. Instead, the nobles seemed to care about little but their constant social maneuvering and bickering, currying favor here, belittling a social enemy there. The type of petty politics that Fenrir also saw in the people who dealt with his father.

Malless, however, had not fit into that standard noble mold. He'd been strong, assertive, and resourceful. The sword he'd often worn at court hadn't just been for show. While not entirely undefeated in tournament combat—a more delicate type of swordplay that the Rostanian guards practiced—he'd been the victor more often than not. Fenrir had actually felt respect for the man, and he felt a pang at learning of Malless' fate. And he was also surprised that Malless would have pitched himself from a balcony, into the streets, where he would be found by commoners.

Seemed entirely unlike the man. But, he shrugged off the emotions he felt quickly, focusing on the task at hand.

"Distressing news, indeed. Well then, long live his grace, Duke Eric Malless. Now, if you would excuse me, we have business elsewhere."

"Of course, m'lord."

The gaggle of servants pressed against the wall so that Fenrir, Emma, and Escamilla could squeeze pass. Fenrir did not look back, but he hoped that the ladies, Escamilla in particular, still followed his directives. The last thing that they needed was for rumors to be flying about that Lady Escamilla, dressed in the livery of a servant, was not in her chamber, but sneaking through the walls of the Plateau.

Within moments, the group of escapees was out of sight and back on their way.

"Malless. I can't believe it. He was alive and hale only this afternoon. Why would he have killed himself like that?" asked Emma, addressing Escamilla.

"Malless is not a man who would give his life in vain. Especially not in such a tasteless manner. Given the circumstances, I would expect that he managed to organize an escape attempt, much as we did. And, I would gather that it went awry, with Malless ending up somehow near a balcony," said Escamilla.

"But he wouldn't have just jumped. He must have been forced out."

"Emma, you must think! The little duke wanted Malless' capture to be a secret. What would happen if Malless were killed secretly?" Escamilla's tone was similar to that of a Savant quizzing a student at the Enlightenment.

"Well, news of his succession would be delayed. Maybe for weeks. Months."

"Yes. There. Then what?"

"And then Penton could capture or kill Eric, leaving Taean next in line."

"So…?" Escamilla continued to push Emma, and Fenrir listened intently, willing his armor to squeak less.

"So, Malless must have realized that he was trapped and had no escape. That the only way to save Florens and his son was to ensure that his body be found in a very public way. That the news would travel faster than Penton's fastest runners, as news often does."

"Excellent, Emma. You are making up for your churlish behavior earlier. You must always think of all possible angles, of all possible motives. Your life may depend upon it. All of our lives might depend on it."

Fenrir half turned, glancing back. "My lady, I would hate to interrupt this lesson, but we are nearing our destination. I would counsel silence."

"As you say, Sir Coldbreaker." Again, no hint of sarcasm from Escamilla, although Emma glared daggers at him with a fury that matched her curly red locks.

Eventually, after what seemed like half the night, they reached the bottom of a very narrow, very steep, and very long spiral staircase. Fenrir, his bulky body confined by even bulkier armor, almost fell a time or two. But, they eventually reached the lowest level of the Plateau and approached the western armory, their ultimate destination.

For a moment, Emma's curiosity overcame her long-standing disgust for Fenrir. "Once we reach the armory, then what? There are only two exits from the Plateau: the front ramp and the rear lift. You'd better not get all killed." Her hands were on her hips, fiery curls spilling over her shoulders. Gods, Fenrir remembered her standing like that, only wearing far fewer clothes.

"If I wished you harm, Emma, I would have simply left you in your cell. In fact, my employer gave me no directives regarding *you*. I could still leave you here," Fenrir hissed at the red-haired, red-tempered woman. He'd always been good with the ladies.

Emma stepped forward, her eyes flashing. Escamilla placed a restraining hand on her shoulder, digging in her fingernails. Emma took a visible, deep breath, exhaling slowly. "Okay. What comes next?"

"We are meeting another associate who will lead us the rest of the way." Fenrir actually didn't know who they were meeting, or how, exactly, they were getting out of the Plateau. Evidently, Tennyson had been worried about what might happen if Fenrir were captured, that he might give away some secrets of The House. Or, he just plain didn't trust Fenrir. Regardless, Fenrir still attempted to radiate confidence to Escamilla and, particularly, to Emma. For some senseless reason, it was important to him that he appear poised in her eyes.

As if that would justify what he had done to her.

Thinking of that, Fenrir glanced down at the gnarled remains of her hand. A hand that had once caressed him, tickled him, dug its nails into his back. Now, despite her subconscious efforts to conceal it, her hand was obviously little more than a mangled appendage, looking for all the world like a lobster claw, even opening and closing slowly as she spoke. Fenrir recalled that

Emma had always had that nervous habit, clenching and unclenching her hands at her sides when anxious. Steward John had used to become furious that Emma was unable to stand completely still, appearing both relaxed and alert as a servant should. Her hands were always in motion.

"We are going to be entering the armory through a door known only to a select few. We should avoid the guard, as they will be on the other side of a locked gate. However, let me move out first and ensure that the way is clear." Confident. Assured.

While the ladies remained in the shadows, Fenrir continued his cautious walk down the hallway, coming to a stop and turning to face what appeared to be a blank, mortared-stone wall. He listened, ear to the stone, for several long moments. Hearing nothing, he placed his forearm and shoulder against the wall and pushed. He continued to strain, digging his boots into the ground. Nothing. He stepped back then, considered the wall, and moved over two paces. He once again braced himself against the wall and pushed. Nothing. Harder.

And then he was tumbling into the armory, his own armor clanging as he ricocheted between the ground and the false panel as the mechanism released all at once. So much for stealth. As usual. He drew his sword and held it in front of him, though he could see nothing but the dim light from his lantern, still back in the servant passage. He listened and waited. He let his eyes adjust to the low light and could make out that he was standing directly within the armory, surrounded by racks of spears and swords in various states of repair, from the flawless to rusty relics. He had apparently knocked aside a stand of halberds, which had unfortunately been placed in front of his passage, adding to the metallic symphony that he had produced. Bad luck.

Seeing and hearing nothing for several minutes, Fenrir reached back through the wall and beckoned the women into the armory. He retrieved his lantern and handed it to Emma, watching her fumble it since he had accidentally proffered the light to her crippled claw-hand. Another good move on his part.

The western armory was a massive, multi-room compound, primarily housing weapons and shields, as opposed to the eastern armory, which was larger and contained suits of armor. Fenrir, Emma, and Escamilla were in a smaller room adjoining the main armory hallway. Fenrir pushed the false panel back into place, set aright the fallen weapons stand, retrieved the lantern from Emma, and led the group toward the hallway with no real goal in mind. Someone was to meet them in the armory, and that person obviously knew that they had arrived. Unless he was deaf, of course.

Fenrir walked carefully down the hall, keeping the light of the lantern focused in front of him as well as he could, glancing into each room as he passed. Weapons, shields, and more weapons. He didn't see anyone, and was becoming anxious that his contact had already been caught, killed, or just never made it into the Plateau. Without this person, they'd be screwed deeper than a sixteen year-old virgin at the Ascension Festival.

"Whatcha doin'?" A small voice asked from behind the group. Fenrir spun around, roughly pushing past the women to place himself between them and the unknown lurker. He held his sword out in front of him, shifting himself into a light, balanced stance, his weak knee positioned behind him. He adapted his vision to the shifting of the dim lantern light, which fell upon a small figure that seemed very out of context.

It was a small girl, little more than five feet tall, wearing rough-spun, loose-fitting burlap clothes like a beggar. Her hair was short and brown, and Fenrir could only tell it was a girl because of her feminine facial features—delicate chin, luminous brown eyes, and plump cheeks. And suddenly he realized he had met her before. He saw her eyes widen in mutual recognition, despite the fact that his features were largely concealed by his helm.

"Morgyn, was it?" Fenrir asked, hesitantly.

"Was it?" The girl, looking right at him, blatantly rubbing her crotch with her left hand as a subtle reminder of that day on Vagabond Way.

"What are you doing here?" Fenrir had a sinking feeling that he knew. He sheathed his sword.

Morgyn reached under her shirt and pulled out a heptagram, this one identical to the one that Fenrir had left with Martis. What was she doing working for The House? He didn't know the entire roster, but last he'd heard, this girl was possibly in the employ of *Recherche Oletta*, the organization rivaling his own. The girl glared at him.

"I'm getting you out of here." By the gods, his fate would hinge on this little girl, a girl whose bruised crotch ensured her loathing of him. Now, he'd be journeying with two women who detested him and a third who would likely sell him if it suited her interests. Fenrir had heard all about how ruthlessly mercenary Lady Escamilla could be.

"It's not safe for a little kid like you to be running around. You'd better just tell me where to go and run along."

"You'd never make it. And, besides, I only get my money once you are out of here." She smirked at the word "money."

"Seems I've little choice in the matter, then. We need to keep moving. But, I want you to stay behind me." Fenrir leveled a long, disdainful look at the girl. "It will be safer that way."

Suddenly, Morgyn wasn't standing before him, and his lantern illuminated just a bare stone floor. He turned, trying to locate the girl but seeing nothing. There was a loud bang and a flash of pain as something collided with the left side of his helmet. As he turned, he felt another blow against the back of his knee (luckily, the good one) and his leg buckled. Before a third blow could land, Fenrir—over his surprise and thoroughly enraged—let out a grunt and swung his arms backward, connecting solidly with Morgyn's chest as she tried to continue dancing around him in the dark. The girl lost her balance and fell to the ground, and Fenrir knelt on her and restrained her arms, forcing a small iron baton out of her hand.

"Get off that girl, you beast!" shouted Emma, pulling at his arm.

"The little bitch attacked me!" Fenrir hissed back. "And keep your godsdamned voice down, woman!" Emma covered her mouth. Gods, he hoped that no one had heard the commotion. He peeled off his helm, now dented at his temple. "What is your problem, you little fucking rat?"

"I don't need you to keep me safe!" Morgyn spat at him, baring her teeth.

Fenrir grunted, pushing himself up. After a moment, he offered a hand to the girl, who considered it for a moment before twisting to her feet without his help. Fenrir shrugged.

"Okay, lead us…" Fenrir stopped and strained his ears. He heard voices—a lot of voices. The sound of metal scraping on metal, perhaps a set of keys. Someone must have heard his helmet getting clobbered, or the shouting of the women. Fucking women.

"Oh cocks!" cursed Emma quietly. Escamilla even let out a small sigh, betraying her own anxiety.

"It's about time we get out of here. Morgyn, lead the way. And quickly," said Fenrir, taking charge of the situation, though his heart was pounding. He was surprised it wasn't ringing against his breastplate, announcing their exact location. "And take these. We might need them." He grabbed a couple of spears from a nearby weapon stand and doled them out to Emma and Escamilla, the former holding hers awkwardly in her good hand and her claw. Escamilla, as always, seemed perfectly at ease—even holding a weapon.

"Oh, this would be better." Fenrir corrected himself swiftly, taking the spear and handing Emma a slender curved sword, this time making sure to slip it to her good hand. He wrapped a leather sword belt around her hourglass form then, his hands lingering for a moment on her hips. Damn, but the memories. He quickly buckled a scabbard in place, and she sheathed the sword without any real grace. "Now, let's get moving. And quickly!"

Morgyn led Fenrir, Emma, and Escamilla down the main chamber hallway before abruptly turning to the right, into an adjoining chamber, a room that was adorned with a variety of shields. Though it was hard to see clearly by lantern light, Fenrir could identify several different crests on very different types of shields, including the Rostanian wolf, the Florens river otter, the noble horse of Algania, and the scorpion of Northern Sestra. There were many more that he did not recognize.

Morgyn moved into a corner of the room and crouched, fumbling for something under her rough shirt. Fenrir gestured for the other women to go on ahead of him to Morgyn, and he again drew his sword and faced the door, continuing to listen as he heard a loud, metallic creaking. The armory door. His palms were sweaty beneath his leather gloves, and he adjusted his grip on the sword before blowing out the lantern.

This whole thing had been a terrible fucking idea. He should have run.

"Hurry, girl!" Fenrir wheezed from his overactive lungs, glancing back at the women.

In the brief interim, Morgyn had procured a key and was working on unlocking a small trap door. Emma stood uncertainly nearby, sword now drawn and held out awkwardly in front of her.

Escamilla, on the other hand, had her feet staggered, and was holding the spear with both hands as if she were an infantryman. Fenrir hoped her fighting form was as good as her stance, because the footsteps and voices were getting closer.

"Get over here! Down—now!" said Morgyn, gesturing at the opened trap door. Escamilla didn't hesitate, running over and descending into the opening, gripping her spear awkwardly in front of her as she climbed downward. Emma hesitated at the threshold for a moment until Morgyn furiously gestured at her. She shoved the sword into the scabbard and descended next. Fenrir moved carefully backwards, sword still held at ready, until he reached their egress. He, too, sheathed his sword.

"Give me the key and get down there, girl."

"No." Her eyes flashed.

"Give it to me. I'm not going to argue."

The girl gave Fenrir another hard look, but handed him the key, which he almost lost in his gloved hand. She nimbly flung her legs over the edge, easily gripping the rungs, and was out of sight immediately. Light was visible from the main chamber, and Fenrir could now clearly make out voices.

"Spread out and check the rooms. Jermaine swore he heard voices earlier, and that banging didn't sound like no rats." This from a commanding voice, probably whichever sergeant had drawn the short straw for the night shift at a typically meaningless post.

Moving as quietly as possible, Fenrir lowered his armored body into the hole, trying to avoid scraping the walls. It was a tight fit, but he managed to descend a couple of rungs without much noise. He carefully gripped the trap door and began to lower it then, a small squeak coming from rarely-used hinges. He flinched and paused for a moment.

"All clear! Nothing here. Checking the next chamber on the right."

Shit. Fenrir guided the trap door home with a loud, metallic whine.

"What was that? Over here!"

Light slitted down into the hole just as Fenrir moved the door the final inch. He reached up, feeling around for the keyhole in the darkness.

"In the corner!" Heavy feet pounded toward the trapdoor.

Fenrir tried to focus on his dusty battle training, on what he learned during those early war games. Recruiters were pitted against recruits fighting with blunted weapons in battle lines. Despite the twenty intervening years, Fenrir remember the need to be disciplined, steady, in the face of a charge. No panicking. He moved the key calmly, systematically, until he found the hole. Fenrir drove the key home and turned it to the right, locking them in just as there was a tug on the door.

"Someone was here! Someone is down in the ruins! Call for the keys—we need to get down there!"

Fenrir let out a trembling sigh as he lowered himself into the darkness, entering the ruins upon which the Plateau was built.

Chapter 12

Emma reached the bottom of the ladder, her legs shaking as if she'd just run around the entire perimeter of the city. But it wasn't exertion that had her so unsteady. If they were caught, she and Escamilla would almost certainly be used as an example to the rest of the little duke's guests. Based on her experience with Penton's desire for women, she was petrified of what tortures he might contrive beyond crudely lopping off limbs and letting blood. All that was standing between them and a veritable army was that prick Fenrir and some little beggar girl. The girl had spirit and an amusing violent streak (at least, watching Fenrir get blindsided had been entertaining), but she'd be little use against any number of armored guards.

"Come over here, dear. Get behind me," whispered Escamilla out of the darkness. Emma felt her way over to her friend and employer, giving her a deep embrace. Escamilla stroked her hair for a moment, and then nudged her away.

"Tell me what you saw up there," demanded Escamilla quietly.

"Is this really the time?" Emma asked. Why would Escamilla persist with these lessons, even now?

"Now is exactly the time. Tell me what you saw."

"Well, that small girl, Morgyn, she knew Fenrir from before; maybe was mad at him. She was upset, and wanted to hurt him. She is fast, and she used the darkness to her advantage, moving in the shadows and striking at him. I'd love to take a shot myself," Emma added in a mutter.

"Exactly," said Escamilla.

"What?"

"You saw yourself, Emma. You saw a girl let her emotions get the better of her at a very critical moment. If that girl had contained herself, her emotions, would we be fleeing right now? Would there be armed guards at our heels?"

There was a pounding noise from above, and Emma heard shouts, though too muffled to make out the words.

"No, we would be down here without imminent threat of capture and torture. Now, can we please get moving?" asked Emma with a sigh.

"Not without our escorts. Shall we wander about down here, in the dark, until we starve to death? Or are consumed by whatever creatures frequent these shadowy places?"

There was a sudden click then, and a light flared into view a scant few feet away. Emma jumped while Escamilla shifted swiftly into a fighting pose. Once their eyes adapted, they saw it was Morgyn holding the lantern, having descended the ladder almost silently. The roughly-clad girl stood still, studying both of them, her eyes darting back and forth like she was a predatory animal. Emma felt like she was being sized up—and found wanting.

With a loud bang, Fenrir dismounted the ladder next, skipping the last few rungs and plopping heavily to the ground. He wiped his sweaty, bald head and scratched at his heavily-bearded face. So different from what Emma remembered. He'd once taken pride in his appearance, and he'd had lovely brown-blonde hair that he'd kept trimmed just below his brow. There'd never been more than a stubble on his face, and that only at the end of the day. With this new look, Fenrir appeared… barbaric. Dangerous. Frightening. But, she wouldn't give him the satisfaction of seeing her afraid. She drew herself tall, standing at the edge of the light and folding her arms, giving him as fixed and neutral a look as she could manage.

"Coldbreaker, where exactly are we?" she asked, carefully concealing both her contempt and her fear of the man.

182

Fenrir cleared his throat. "Well, the Plateau was not built upon a natural formation, as many think. Rather, it was built on the ruins of a much older structure, which has since been covered in moss, ivy, and dirt. I am willing to bet we are standing within those ruins," said Fenrir, his diction quite rehearsed. Emma was very familiar with Fenrir's tactics of repeating stories, rumors, and information overheard from others, claiming it as his own. Nobles, dignitaries, administrators, officials... they were all very open around guardsmen, sometimes forgetting that there was someone contained within the six feet of metal casing standing nearby. Often, Emma hadn't minded that Fenrir would parrot this information. In fact, she would encourage it. Much of what she'd learned about various people within the Plateau—and inevitably shared with Escamilla—had come from Fenrir's rather loose lips. Now, though, hearing his rehearsed, matter-of-fact, and slightly condescending tone, she felt a renewed urge to bash his head in with a vase.

Thankfully, Morgyn interjected. "We oughta get moving. It won't be long until they get a key and start searching down here. Only a couple of folks above have a key at all, at least, so we should have a head start."

"Lead the way, young one," said Escamilla, resting the shaft of her spear on her shoulder. Fenrir opened his mouth for a moment, sighed, and assumed a place as the rear guard. He must have decided that pursuit from behind was the most likely peril to the group.

The group walked down a wide hallway, the lantern light revealing walls made of large blocks of rough-hewn stone that stood in rather stark contrast to the uniform, mortared-stone bricks comprising the fortress above. The Plateau was at least two hundred years old, but this hallway, this place, was far older. Emma felt as though the air was harder to breathe; it felt stale and sour and thick. Dead, even, as if whomever used to occupy this ruin had all exhaled in unison just before they'd expired.

"What was this place before the Plateau was built atop it?" Emma asked to no one in particular.

"I heard it was a temple to one of the pagan gods, not sure which," said Morgyn, speaking quickly. "I've looked around a bit, but haven't been able to find anything good."

"How do you know about this place, young one?" asked Escamilla.

"That's not your business," the girl said offhandedly. Emma was shocked at her impertinence, and was sure that Lady Escamilla would not stand for it.

"Of course, my dear. I do not mean to pry. I am just interested in old places."

"I've been to a lot of old places," Morgyn said with a hint of a brag. "This place is nothing compared to the Farinx ruins in the Tulanque Mountains. Those are massive, and I've found good stuff there!"

"What kind of stuff, young one?" asked Escamilla.

"Oh, this and that. I found an old spear, made all of metal. It was worth fifty yets! There was a little old statue of a man riding a weird beast, too. It was carved from wood, but the wood didn't rot. I got ten yets for that."

As they walked, Morgyn continued to regale Escamilla with descriptions of her findings and exactly what each had been worth. Emma soon became bored, even as Morgyn became more animated in the telling. At least her lively chatter brightened these dreary hallways and temporarily chased away whatever ghosts were probably lurking around. Even the lantern seemed to shine brighter.

But what would happen once they got out of this place? Would there be war? She suspected that Eric Malless would not accept that his father had thrown himself from the palace and, with the impetuousness of youth, he'd likely put Florens at odds with Rostane. Rostane's military would have Florens outmanned, but if Henrik Malless hadn't been bluffing, they had Jecustan allies to call upon. The resulting war would likely draw in the other duchies, and potentially other nations.

Escamilla had her own unofficial standing army. On the surface, she merely kept a small force to guard each of her many holdings. But, were those forces to be combined, she would have a trained army of several thousand, enough to noticeably bolster the forces of Eric Malless or whomever else Escamilla decided to throw in with. The result would be a war-torn and divided Ardia, potentially leaving the country ripe for conquest from Algania, Jecusta, or even a sea-borne invasion from Sestra or Rafón. The Wasmer, too, might renew their attacks from the mountains.

As Emma reflected on the various costs of war, she wondered about her own fate. Frankly, she was terrified of pain. She'd heard people say that pain itself wasn't as bad as the fear of it. Those people had never lost a chunk of their hand. Surprisingly, she had barely felt the pain of her dismemberment at first. It hadn't been until she'd seen the damage, the blood sheeting down her arm and across the bed and nightstand, that the gut-wrenching pain had hit her all at once. Words were inadequate to describe the searing torment. Not to mention the persistent, sharp ache over the following weeks and months, even after Escamilla had brought in a surgeon, a man called Martis, to salvage as much of her appendage as possible.

Emma was resolved to take her own life before being captured and used as a demonstration like Erlins. She would not be tortured!

Morgyn continued to chat and lead them through a confusing crisscross of hallways, all perpendicular to one another. Every so often, the stone walls were broken by an opening into much larger chambers that Emma could not discern in the darkness. People might have lived in these great chambers, or perhaps some strange religious ceremonies were held within. Morgyn had said this was a temple to the pagan gods, and it certainly seemed plausible. This place had the dour atmosphere and unnecessary scale of religious constructions.

Emma was not a devout Yetranian, nor was Escamilla, but she'd attended services before. Primarily to gather information. A surprising amount of business was conducted during and after such services, and Emma had been able to reconnoiter a good deal of intelligence by simply attending them. She'd occasionally listened to the sermons and diatribes from the Taneos, as well, and they spoke a pleasant message of peace and equality, of something they called Harmony. But, then she would see a Taneo throw a boiling cup of tea at a servant or stumble out of a whore house in the warehouse district. While this did leave such men open for extortion, it stunk of hypocrisy and filled Emma with disgust.

But, even that hypocrisy might be better than whatever had happened in these ruins. She had heard that many of the old religions—particularly those of the Wasmer folk—practiced ritual sacrifices of animals and humans. This was, of course, after the sacrifice had been "made clean" through systematic and ceremonial torture. It was said that such a ritual would allow for the priest to absorb the soul of a sacrifice, absolving them of sin and making them one with whatever god was being honored at the time. Emma shuddered at the thought, that she may had been working atop a sacrificial altar for almost a decade.

Morgyn continued to lead the ragtag group through the maze with surety. They came to a narrow, steep ramp that brought them down another level. As they descended, Emma could feel the press of earth, or the Plateau rather, weighing down on her. She began to feel panicky and drew several audible, deep breaths in an effort to calm herself. Fenrir—who'd somehow ended up next to her—slowed down and snuck her a glance. A renewed flash of anger washed away the panic when she caught it, and she threw him what she hoped was a withering glare in return. He shrugged, shook his bald head, and continued forward.

"Hsssst!" This from Fenrir a few minutes later, getting the attention of Morgyn and Escamilla, quieting their chatter. "Hear that? Guardsmen."

Emma listened; Fenrir was right. She could hear the hint of voices, and an occasional obscured, barked order. They seemed a long way off, but even with the echoes, it was clear that, somehow, the guards had gotten ahead of them. Oh, cocks.

"They must have mobilized some other forces and come down a different entrance," said Fenrir, looking back the way they'd come.

"Brilliant deduction," said Emma, her hands busy as always. "What do we do?"

"Who knows how many entrances there are into this place," said Escamilla in a considering and calm tone. "These ruins have been locked up for years. I've heard whispers of them, and y sources told me that only the little duke and captains of the watch have keys."

"And me," smirked Morgyn, holding up the key that she had retrieved from Fenrir.

Where had this little beggar—or rather her superiors—gotten a key to this place that few even knew existed?

"Yes, and you, young one. But, these soldiers do not know the paths of this place. *We* have a guide." Escamilla quickly smiled at Morgyn, and Emma felt a surprising surge of jealousy. *Silly.*

"Which way, girl? We'd better keep moving," said Fenrir, gruffly.

Morgyn appeared indecisive for a moment, stepping a few feet down each path at the nearby intersection and listening intently.

"Follow me," she then said with conviction. Emma couldn't tell if it was feigned or real, but they had little choice but to follow.

They walked for about fifteen minutes, leaving the sounds of the pursuit behind. Whenever Morgyn came to an intersection, she would stop and walk a few feet down each hall, listening and even sniffing the air, a squirrel searching for a buried nut. Then, she would make a decision, and the rest would follow. Emma did not know how the girl kept her bearings in here, with few landmarks of any distinction, but they did seem to be moving steadily forward and downward, away from their hunters.

They descended another steep ramp, one that opened into a large chamber, the scant light of their lantern being quickly consumed by the inky darkness. Emma felt as if she were stranded amidst nothingness instead of encapsulated deep in a tomb of stone. It offered a different kind of fear, making her feel alone, insignificant. She edged closer to Fenrir, just to be near something solid. He didn't notice. Maybe he was having his own existential thoughts.

Morgyn halted suddenly, as still as a ceremonial guard.

"Young one, what is the matter?"

"I… um…" she stuttered. "I'm not sure where we are." Fenrir groaned, and Emma felt a stab of fear. The thought of being trapped here, in this blackness, was untenable. So thick was the darkness that their small, austere chamber above seemed like a safer option—even being imprisoned by a madman might be preferable.

"I knew this shit was a mistake," Emma heard Fenrir mutter. She had almost forgotten that this was all just a job for him. Something to pad his pockets with money. He'd just as soon cut off Escamilla's hand for a few Yets as rescue them from this place.

"Hold a moment!" Morgyn set down the lantern and ran off into the darkness, silent as one of the ghosts that prowled these halls. The girl must be touched in the head, Emma thought, running into the abyss that surrounded them.

She was gone for several long minutes, leaving Emma to fidget with her fingers. Fenrir was pacing back and forth, hand on the hilt of his sword while he muttered curses. Escamilla stood, her feet spread to the width of her shoulders, leaning on her spear as if it were a cane. Exhaustion painted her face in wrinkled grays. Emma often forgot that Escamilla was somewhere in her sixth decade, so powerful and poised she was. But, tonight, she'd dove to catch a vase, taken a circuitous route through the burrows of the Plateau, run from the pursuers nipping at her heels, and, earlier in the day, she'd been threatened with death. That would take its toll on a very young woman, let alone a woman in the last quarter of her life.

Emma wanted to comfort Escamilla, but knew that would be taken poorly. The older woman would be angry that her exhaustion was evident, if anything.

Morgyn reappeared, seemingly enthusiastic. She bounded into the circle of light, their little oasis in the desert of blackness.

"I found something!" she said.

"What did you find, young one?" asked Escamilla.

"A person! I ran off that way, and there was a dim light," she said, and pointed back the way she'd come from. "I saw him through a door with a window. There was a man in there, looking like he was in pain. He looked hurt! Come look!"

"No. We need to get out of here. If the guard suspects that these ruins are a back entrance into the Plateau, this place will be swarming with them for the foreseeable future. And then the ruins will be blocked off, utterly and completely. We need to move," said Fenrir firmly.

"Let us take a look. A few minutes shouldn't harm us, and we could potentially have assistance in our efforts to escape. We must take help where we can find it," said Escamilla, again standing upright, strong and confident. And appearing younger once more. Fenrir gave an exasperated sigh.

"I'd leave you if I had an idea of how to get out this fucking place." Not *quite* under his breath. "Alrighty, girl. Lead the way. Again."

After a few minutes, Emma could see a dim light shining through a small, square opening—a barred window in a door. Fenrir pushed past the group and peered into the tiny portal for a long moment. Emma heard a despairing moan coming from beyond the door. Fenrir turned back to the group, gesturing for them to come in close.

"There is a man in there, chained by his neck. I can't see his face, but he appears to be missing a hand," he murmured.

"Erlins," Emma and Escamilla whispered in unison, Emma as a question and Escamilla as a statement of fact.

"We need to get in there," said Escamilla.

"Give me a moment," said Morgyn, procuring a set of lock picks from a boot. She soundlessly worked at the lock, with only the occasional soft click betraying her presence.

"We don't know who else might be in there," said Fenrir. "We could be walking into an ambush. We should leave this person and find our way out. Now."

"How could you leave a person, any person, trapped in this darkness? What if that were you, down here, *Coldbreaker*? Are you such a cock-sucking cretin…" Emma hissed furiously until she was interrupted.

"Got it!" whispered Morgyn, following the distinct metallic snap and slip of a lock being popped. Fenrir released another frustrated sigh.

"At least let me go first," he said, drawing his sword. This time, Morgyn didn't argue.

Fenrir opened the door with a loud creak. The door had been recently replaced, as the wood was relatively fresh even though the hinges had begun to rust. He entered cautiously, sword held out in front of him, head swiveling left and then right. As soon as he cleared the doorway, Escamilla followed, her own spear levelled in front of her. Morgyn went in, as well, now bearing their source of light and holding her short iron baton at the ready in her other hand.

Emma found herself standing alone in the darkness. She hastily drew her curved sword from her belt, held it in front of her with shaky hands, and followed.

The room was relatively small, perhaps a dozen or so paces wide and long. Immediately next to the door, there was a chair and a desk covered in books, as well as two gas lamps left burning low. On the far end of the room were several shackles bolted to the wall. Two of them restrained naked men by their necks, with just enough slack that the men were both seated, slumped on the ground. Aside from the prisoners, the room appeared uninhabited, though the stench could have easily filled the great chamber nearby. Fenrir surveyed the room, shook his head, and drove his sword into his sheathe with a ring.

"Hurry up!" said Fenrir impatiently, taking a place by the door, standing easily at guard. A natural at indolence.

"Morgyn, check that man over there," ordered Escamilla, pointing to the motionless man deeper into the room. Morgyn did

191

not question the order, but walked cautiously toward him, iron baton at the ready, while Emma and Escamilla approached the one-handed man.

It was, as both had surmised, Baron Erlins. The man, known among the courtiers for his physically-imposing appearance, seemed to have folded in upon himself, diminished far more than even ten days of imprisonment could have accounted for. Chained by the neck, he sagged back against the wall, head hanging forward. The stump at the end of his arm—now a blackened mass of dried blood, burned tissue, and singed bone—was resting unsupported on the rough, damp stone floor. Based on the vile stench, Emma could only imagine what was saturating the stones around him. He let out an occasional groan, still unaware of their presence. Emma's heart ached for the poor man. Brave fool or not, he didn't deserve to be treated this way. No one did.

Escamilla moved forward and crouched just in front of the motionless body.

"Erlins. Baron Erlins," Escamilla said firmly. He didn't respond, so she reached out and shook his shoulder. He flinched back from her touch and slapped her hand aside, legs pushing himself back into the wall. He averted his eyes, looking down and away, his greasy, stringy hair covering his face as he cowered.

"No! No more... No," he moaned, and Emma could hear the weary anguish in his voice. The sound of a man who was resigned to his fate.

"Erlins. This is Lady Escamilla Breen. We are here to help you. We will leave this place together."

"No! No, please not again," he mumbled.

"Erlins! Theran! Look at me." Escamilla shifted her body so that she was now facing him, but he adverted his gaze to the other side. "Look at me!" Escamilla grabbed his chin and forced his head upward, brushing his hair out of his face. His eyes were wild, rimmed in red and darting left and right, his face covered in deep scratches. Escamilla gazed into his eyes, apparently trying to calm him with sheer force of will. Remarkably, it worked.

"Es... Escamilla? Escamilla Breen? This can't be. You can't be here," he stuttered, voice low and cracking.

"I can be anywhere I wish. And I *am* here."

"You can't be her. You're..." He coughed. "You're a serving woman." Emma was surprised that he was coherent enough to recognize that Escamilla's outfit was out of place. Strange, the details people focused on when they were under duress. Emma remembered, quite strongly, how long Fenrir's hair had been that night. How it had covered his eyes as he'd restrained her, and how she'd wanted to brush it off his face so that she could see him without obstruction. Of all the things to recall...

"Clothes do not make a person. I assure you that I am Lady Escamilla Breen. Now, are you enjoying your current accommodations or would you like to leave?"

"Will you hurry this up?" growled Fenrir. "Usually, when lamps are left burning, the occupants do not plan on being gone for long."

"Please... Escamilla. Help me," he said as a sob wracked his broken body. Erlins had often contradicted Escamilla in court, and Emma had thought her mistress resented this man. And yet, here she was, willing to risk her own life to free him from his tormentors.

"I... can't take anymore. They hurt me, so badly. Dark eyes, red eyes. They were stealing my soul. Gods, no!" The man sounded fevered.

Morgyn ran over to Emma and Escamilla at that moment. "The other man. He's dead." She sounded rather callous about it, Emma thought. Emma herself had only ever seen one dead body up close. Her mother's. With her mother having died of a stomach flux, it had been a very unpleasant death. Emma had been repulsed by the reek of it all. The blood, the vomit, the feces. And she'd felt intensely guilty for not wanting to linger at her mother's side, for just leaving her body outside for the corpse collectors to gather. But that had been the way of it during the outbreak.

"Morgyn, can you use your tools to free this man?" Escamilla asked, gesturing toward Erlins. Morgyn crouched, silent as always, and examined the collar.

"Give me a few minutes."

Emma watched the girl work for a moment and then walked over to the desk, glancing at Fenrir. He was standing attentively a few steps away, flanking the doorway. He must have closed the door, and his hand was again resting on the hilt of his sword, absently fingering the silver pommel. Emma was glad to see him betraying his nerves. She hoped he choked on his fear.

She examined the books on the desk. Most of them were in languages that she did not recognize, but there were two that were in the Ardian tongue. *The Complete Histories of Sardonia* (a country Emma had never heard of) and *Expanding the Nerring* (a word she did not recognize). She flipped through the *Histories* book for a moment, but found little of interest.

Shifting the books around, she found a set of keys on a ring.

She spun about, holding them aloft. "Escamilla! Keys!"

"Well done, dear! Quickly now," Escamilla said, waving Emma forward. Emma inwardly smiled as she pushed Morgyn aside, knelt down, and inserted one key, then another, and then another until she heard the click of the lock being freed. She pulled the collar apart and lifted it from Erlins' neck and shoulders as gently as she could, touching his skin and feeling that he was somehow both clammy with perspiration and somehow

194

unnaturally hot. Only then did she realize she was kneeling in his watery leavings, and she jumped to her feet.

"Erlins, can you stand?"

Erlins struggled to his feet, with Emma supporting him, grabbing his intact arm and heaving him upward. He immediately slipped from her grip, falling forward to his hand and knees, nearly hitting his head on the floor.

"Get up, Theran. Or are you going to let them come back for you? To continue hurting you? Maybe they'll take the other hand next, or maybe they will peel off your skin, one square inch at a time. Do you want that?" Escamilla demanded of the man.

With a great moan of exertion, he pushed himself back to his feet. He was breathing heavily, as though he had just shifted the very world. Emma thought that his eyes contained a madness, but a madness tinged with resolve. He took several staggering steps toward the door, but again, he began to fall.

He would have hit the ground, too, had Fenrir not darted forward to catch the diminished Erlins.

"Let's keep moving," said Fenrir gruffly, hefting Erlins over his shoulder before heading toward the door.

Chapter 13

With Morgyn again at the forefront, the group continued through the ruins. They found another exit from the great, dark chamber and proceeded on their journey, coming across yet another ramp to continue their descent. Emma was completely disoriented, but continued to push down her fear, knowing that her struggles were not nearly as bad as Erlins'.

She watched Erlins as his naked form dangled from Fenrir's broad shoulders, swaying limply with each step. He moaned and mumbled to himself, occasionally shouting "no" and "his eyes, his eyes!" He was still being tormented in his mind, even as they carried him away from his tormentors.

Fenrir, despite being burdened by fifty or sixty pounds of armor, continued to carry Erlins as if he were little more than a sack of flour. Four times now, he had set Erlins down and then shifted him to his opposite shoulder, Erlins being entirely non-responsive during these brief rests. Escamilla tried to talk to him, to learn what had happened since he'd been tortured in front of Duke Penton's guests, but the man would say nothing. Soon, Escamilla gave up, and everyone focused on their forward momentum.

Once, they heard some shouting voices in the distance. Sound was so distorted here, though, that they were unable to determine whether the guard was ahead of or behind them, above or below them.

After another hour, the entire party was growing noticeably weary. Fenrir was beginning to limp on his weak knee (Emma recalled that he'd often complained of his knee, it having been the reason she'd been on top more often than not). Escamilla was using her spear much more like a walking stick, leaning heavily for longer and longer bouts. Watching, Emma was worried for her lady, but didn't dare offer her arm in support. Morgyn, however, was tireless, the restless energy of youth coupled with the responsibility of being the guide propelling her forward like an eager dog.

"Perhaps we should rest," said Emma. "My feet are beginning to burn, and I'm not even carrying another man." She hated to use Fenrir's burden as an excuse, to even hint that she might give a damn about the man's feelings, but she wanted Escamilla to rest and regain her energy. And she wasn't lying about her feet. She expected that her blisters had formed their own blisters by now.

Surprisingly, no one objected. Fenrir set Erlins down more gently than she would have expected, and then he, himself, slumped heavily to the floor, armor ringing dully with the impact. Escamilla followed suit, albeit with much more dignity. Emma tried to do the same, though she was clumsy as a drunkard in comparison. Morgyn simply leaned against the wall. The group shared several minutes of silence then, and Emma found herself drifting off to sleep. She started at Fenrir's deep voice.

"We are running low on fuel," he remarked to no one in particular. The statement was greeted with further silence for a long moment. And then, Morgyn snuffed out the lantern. Utter darkness instantly blanketed them like a stifling woolen cloak.

Emma tried to slow her now rapid breathing, recalling that anything down here was likely long dead, and that the darkness held no monsters. That she had it better than Erlins, who continued to moan like an alleyway dog begging for a scrap of meat.

"No!" Erlins again shouted. "No more." Emma jumped at the sound of his agony, and felt as if she would cry. She heard someone shift and move over to Erlins, though. Escamilla? Morgyn? Not Fenrir—there was no creak of armor. She heard Erlins' frantic breathing begin to slow.

"We are on the right level," said Morgyn, suddenly and softly. It almost felt wrong for any of them to breach the deep silence of this place. They were alien to this ruin. They did not belong. "We just need to find the exit. We're close."

The feeling of hope was almost too much for Emma. She wanted to both dance and curl up in a ball. They were so close. But Emma had caught the fact that Morgyn hadn't sounded absolutely certain. These ruins—they were so large. The Plateau above catered to thousands, and yet it was only half the size of the ruins upon which it sat, maybe even less than half. They were looking for a single exit from this place and wandering around nearly blindly while doing so. What were the chances that they would find it?

"We should keep moving." Not Fenrir. Erlins? She heard some shifting and heavy breathing. "I can walk."

"Welcome back, Theran Erlins," said Escamilla. "I agree. We should get going. We want to leave this place while it is still dark. This is only the start of our journey."

"Aye, Lady. I... must thank you." His words were strained. Whether because gratitude was unfamiliar to him or because of the pain, Emma was uncertain.

"We will discuss the terms of your gratitude later. For now, we must be going."

Morgyn again lit the lantern, the rekindled light showing Erlins standing unevenly, cradling the stump of his wrist with his other hand. Emma wondered whether the man was missed yet. Whether his captors were looking for him. Erlins began walking, slowly, and Morgyn darted in front of him to lead the way. Again, they were on the move, though their pace was slower, hindered by both Erlins' lumbering gait and their collective fatigue.

After maybe a quarter of an hour, with Morgyn leading them seemingly at random, Erlins stopped without warning. He was bringing up the rear, barely within the light of the lantern, and the group almost left him behind. They would have if he hadn't begun speaking.

"No. No, please, no. Not now! They are coming for me," he said with a whimper, sounding as if the madness was again taking control.

"Theran, we need to continue," said Escamilla. "Unless you want them to catch you, you had better resume walking."

"No, it's already too late," Erlins said in a hushed whisper. "They know we are here. Blessed Yetra, no…"

Goosebumps took hold of Emma's flesh at his words. They livened her fears of being trapped, alone, in this temple abandoned to the old gods. Being stalked and hunted by whatever lived down here. She tried to convince herself that he was simply feverish and rambling, but his words held such terror, such conviction, that she knew he was not.

As if on cue, there was a howl in the distance, echoing through the abandoned chambers and hallways, ricocheting off the stone. Not like a wolf would howl. Wolves had intent and would seek to communicate with their pack, to coordinate their hunt. No, this was an uninhibited scream. Of pure aggression, pure hate, pure hunger. Emma covered her ears and closed her eyes tightly, feeling her legs shake at the discordant, soulless sound.

Fenrir ran back toward Erlins, grabbing the stunned man by his good arm and yanking him back toward the group where Escamilla was white-knuckled, gripping her spear, and Morgyn was crouching and hugging her knees.

"Girl, get up and lead us out of here. I don't know what is out there, but I'd rather not run into it," Fenrir said in a hushed, hoarse voice. "How close are we?"

"I think we're close. I don't know this place, but I know directions. And we are moving toward the exit," Morgyn said, her voice a whisper.

"Go, as fast as we can. Stay together, hands on weapons. Help Erlins. I will take rear guard." Fenrir's voice was shaking.

Another scream tore through the air as the group resumed moving at a stumbling jog, Morgyn leading with the lantern and Escamilla flanking her, spear at the ready. Emma was next to Erlins, ready to help him if he stumbled. Looking over at him, she thought that it seemed his fever was refocused as a mad energy. He was moving at a quickened but awkward pace, mouth turned in a grimace, brows narrowed and with his eyes squinting at the light in front of him. It was as if that light was the only thing keeping the man sane, pulling him forward in a fit of blind intensity.

"Almost there!" shouted Morgyn from up ahead, her voice drowned out by several screams released in unison so that the strength seemed suddenly to be melting right out of Emma's legs. She managed to continue, pure self-preservation and instinct managing to combat the vacuum of terror a little bit longer.

"Stop! I need to unlock it. The locks are complex and I will need some time," said Morgyn. They were in a hallway, just like the rest, but Morgyn had stopped at some steel rungs that must have been recently installed, as rubble still littered the floor.

"For the love of Yetra, hurry!" said Emma, feeling panic set in.

"Morgyn, get up there," Fenrir ordered weakly. "Erlins, start climbing behind her. Emma and Escamilla, keep your weapons drawn, but stay behind me. With luck, we'll be out of here in time."

Morgyn left her lantern on the ground and flew nimbly up the ladder while Erlins slowly attempted the rungs, hampered by his weakness and missing appendage. Fenrir drew his sword, holding

200

it at his side, resting the point on the ground. Emma knew, from speaking with him, that a novice would hold his sword at ready long before a battle. A veteran would conserve his strength. Emma drew her own curved sword and tried to emulate Fenrir's easy stance. But, her dread seemed to force her sword up, her arms already shaking. Escamilla was flushed in the dim lantern light, though she held her spear steady.

With a great piercing shriek, something pale and humanoid sprinted into the light, straight for Fenrir. He braced himself, his sword instantly up in the ready position, held two-handed in front of him. The creature launched itself at him, impaling its body upon his sword and pulling Fenrir to the ground with the momentum of its charge. Emma could see the creature continuing to flail its limbs at Fenrir, despite having been completely run through—the blade going in one side of the thing's stomach and out the other. Emma lurched forward to help, but immediately stepped back as two other creatures ran into their circle of light, each naked thing taller than Fenrir. One was little more than a white streak as it launched itself at Escamilla, only somewhat slowed as it jumped over Fenrir, who was still struggling with his own opponent. Escamilla lunged forward with her spear, targeting the man-like creature.

Emma had no time to focus on Escamilla, however, as the third creature approached. This one was not as madly heedless as the other two. It approached her warily, and was holding a large plank of wood for a weapon. It was also not as pale as the others, some color tinging its bare skin, and it was clearly male. The creature wasn't exactly emaciated, but was thin in a powerful, sinewy way.

She couldn't make out its face. It was entirely covered with long, stringy hair and the lighting was too low. She thought she caught a glimpse of a limpid, unfocused eye for a moment, but she couldn't be sure. The creature was breathing loudly, and she could almost feel the dampness of its breath. She heard more screams echoing in the distance just as the creature closed in on her, swinging the plank wildly in her direction.

Emma stumbled backwards, her sword moving into a parrying position. The plank connected with the curved blade, launching it out of her hands as the force swung her around and knocked her to the ground.

Sobbing, she scuttled away, dimly aware of the sounds of the struggle nearby. Escamilla was calling something out and Fenrir was roaring in his deep voice. More creatures had arrived. She heard the heavy breathing coming closer and closer to her as she cast blindly about for her sword. She felt the cold metal blade of the weapon just as it was pulled away from her, slicing into her flesh.

"Dear Yetra, protect me," Emma whispered a prayer to the goddess she didn't believe in even as she raised her arm to ward off the inevitable blow from the creature that held the plank above its head in a two-handed grip.

Emma felt a heavy weight hit her body then, and warm liquid run over her face. She didn't feel pain as she had expected. It just felt like she was being smothered. Breath was harder to come by, and she felt herself drifting away, lost in the darkness that permeated these ruins.

All at once, the weight was pulled from her.

"Emma, get up! I can't hold this up forever," shouted Escamilla, dragging the headless corpse of the creature off of her. Emma scrambled to her feet.

"What is happening?" Emma asked, confusion evident in her voice as she attempted to wipe blood off of her face. She merely smeared it over her skin. "Did you do this?"

"Look for yourself."

There were several bleached corpses surrounding them, as well as two that were less pale, like her own fallen attacker. One had a broken spear protruding from its chest. Fenrir was chopping away at another fallen creature, blood splattering against the walls and against his armor. Erlins, wielding Emma's short, curved blade with his remaining hand—now dripping with crimson—was battling two creatures. As one lunged, Erlins danced smoothly aside and cut deep into its side, a spray of blood blanketing the wall. The other, seeing an opening, tried to bash Erlins in the back with a chunk of debris. Erlins sensed the intention and spun around low, slicing at the creature's leg as it missed him with the rock. In a graceful move, he twisted back to slit the creature's throat before turning yet again to the first opponent who'd continued coming at him, despite the visible organs sliding out of its body. Erlins lunged forward, the tip of his sword burying itself into the creature's eye.

"By Ultner," Emma murmured, stunned and surveying Erlins, naked and covered in gore, his damp hair waving back and forth as he swiveled his head, hunting for another opponent. There was a clear madness in his eyes as they glinted in the lantern light.

"It's open. Hurry up here!" shouted Morgyn from above them. More shrieks came from nearby. Emma didn't hesitate, climbing the rungs hand over hand as quickly as possible, hindered very little by her mutilated appendage. She could almost taste freedom and safety, and it tasted wonderful.

The shaft grew narrower, and it was clear that she was no longer in a part of the ruins, but rather in a tunnel dug specifically to access this place. Who knew who had been entering and exiting the Plateau through this ingress, but she was thankful it was here. She pulled herself up into a dimly lit... butcher shop? Warehouse? There was meat hanging and draining from the ceiling, the room kept quite chilly by a strange substance that emitted a slow, pink steam. Morgyn was crouched by the opening that she had just exited, anxious and shivering.

There were noises and muffled shouts coming from below as Escamilla crested the opening, grunting as she pulled her body out. She was obviously spent, but she didn't linger on her knees. She immediately stood, twisted, and watched the opening.

A few minutes—or what felt like a few hours—passed, with Morgyn, Escamilla, and Emma standing in cold silence in the meat locker as sounds of fighting and screaming continued to travel up the shaft.

"We need to go back for them," said Emma, wondering why she said it.

"And do what? A little girl, an old woman, and a cripple against whatever demons are down there?" Escamilla asked harshly. Emma flinched at the 'cripple' remark. Escamilla sighed.

"Apologies, dear. It has been a long night." Escamilla gave her a small smile.

Cocks, it had been the longest fucking night of Emma's life. "Camilla, you are bleeding!" Both of them were covered in blood, but Emma had suddenly seen that Escamilla had fresh blood pulsing from a wound on her left forearm, soaking her servant's shirt. Emma next noticed another wound on her right upper arm.

"It's nothing, dear. Those things take their time in dying." Stoic, as always.

Emma searched the room, finding some stained but clean rags in a corner. She tore open Escamilla's sleeve, examining the wound on her forearm. It had the appearance of a bite, with two distinct rows of shredded flesh—teeth marks—marring the woman's wrinkled skin. More howling from below, and the clank of metal.

"Camilla, did it bite you?"

"It appears so. I thought it dead once I ran it through, but it got ahold of me." The effort Escamilla was putting forth in order to remain in control must have been immense. Her voice was even more measured than usual, and her fists were clenched at her sides. Emma began silently dressing both wounds just as Fenrir pulled himself out of the hole, his armor dented and awash in blood. There was no way to tell whether it was his or the creatures'.

"Close the door! Now!" he shouted to Morgyn as he shakily rose, drawing his dented sword.

"What about Erlins?" asked Morgyn and Emma simultaneously.

"He's lost. Now close the door! And lock it!"

Morgyn did just that, slamming shut the heavy iron trap door and reengaging the complex system of locks using several different keys. Fenrir stood, dented sword still drawn, until the last lock was engaged. Then, he limped over to a wall and slumped to the ground, dropping his sword next to him. He was obviously spent.

"Did you see Erlins fall?" Escamilla asked, walking over to Fenrir.

"No. As you left, more of those things came at us. I fought them off, trying to break away to the ladder. But it was as if a madness had taken Erlins. He fought like a Ultner-sworn demon. I'd never seen such swordsmanship." His tired face showed a weary awe.

They heard a pounding on the metal trapdoor then, and a muffled shrieking from below. Apparently, the creatures could climb ladders. Emma was almost too exhausted to be distressed by this.

"We had a short break and I shouted to Erlins to climb, but the man was lost. More of the creatures were coming, and he rushed off with his sword into the Ultner-cursed darkness." Fenrir sighed, vainly wiping blood from his forehead.

"Why didn't you go after him?" asked Emma, with more venom was probably merited.

"Woman, look at me. I've little strength left. My sword is notched, my armor dented." He met Emma's eyes. "And Erlins was not part of my assignment."

"You callous bastard," Emma spat. The man was a greedy hound, caring only about how to pad his pocket. She knew, firsthand, that he'd probably spend his earning from this job on whores and hard liquor. How had she once found his tolerance to strong alcohol to be charming?

"Enough," said Escamilla, voice lacking her usual strength. "As regretful as Erlins' loss is, this night is not yet over. Sir Coldbreaker, Morgyn, what is next?"

"Frankly, I didn't expect to make it this far," grumbled Fenrir. "Regardless, there is a small boat waiting to take us upriver and out of the city. We'll need to clean ourselves up a bit and move quietly."

Fenrir began peeling off his dented and damaged armor, leaving himself wearing only his white wool undershirt and black breeches. Emma had miraculously retained the pillowcase tied to her belt throughout the journey. It contained a change of clothes for both her and Escamilla. She had packed her orange dress after Fenrir had provided servant's clothes. She offered this to Escamilla, who declined and instead took the more serviceable peasant clothes.

As the group made ready, the women changing their clothes behind a wall of hanging meat, Morgyn asked the question that was foremost in Emma's mind.

"What was down there? What happened?" Her eyes were still wide, reminding Emma that she really was a child.

"They were demons," said Emma. "Monsters. They attacked us. Wanted to kill us."

"They weren't demons," said Fenrir, his voice restrained. So unlike him. "No, Emma. They weren't demons or monsters. Those creatures... they were people."

Chapter 14

It was only a matter of time.

Merigold sat in the cold, damp darkness, again impervious to the scent of her own filth. Had it been a month? Two months? A year? She had completely lost track of time while living in this perpetual blackness. Saren had stopped bringing fuel, and the lantern sat uselessly in the corner. Merigold continued to eat. In fact, she had been forcing more of the dried, salty jerky into her body in order to build up her strength. One could not expect to enact vengeance on one's tormentors when weak from food deprivation.

At the very least, since the first day that Saren had brought his friends, Merigold had been eating and drinking better. The visits, always Saren and Paul now, had become more frequent and Merigold rarely ran out of water before having her skin refilled, and she always had ample meat. She felt as if her strength was returning. Her body had stopped rejecting the horrid-tasting meat and she'd even taken to exercising—pushing her body off the floor with her arms again and again, sitting up to strengthen her stomach muscles, and remaining in a squatting position against the wall for as long as she could.

When she was alone, Merigold rarely set down her makeshift dagger. The rough strips of cloth had become a second skin to her. She knew every bump of the handle, every imperfection in the nail itself. And she knew exactly how she would use it.

When Saren next came alone, she would follow the typical pattern. She would be docile, avoid eye contact, and do what he said. She would go through her cleaning ritual, setting her pants carefully by the bed, the dagger secreted in the pocket, but within easy reach of the bug-infested mattress. Merigold would lay on the bed, on her back, part her legs, and allow Saren to violate her without resistance. After Saren spent himself inside of her, he tended to lay on top of her for several moments, his head resting against her neck, breathing heavily while he absentmindedly stroked her now knotted hair. Merigold planned on snaking her hand into her nearby pants in those moments, and grabbing the dagger and driving it into his neck—right underneath his chin. She had lain on the ground in her cell and practiced this stabbing motion again and again. And she knew she could catch him right in the jugular vein.

But Merigold would not let him die easily. She would push him aside and give him a dirty rag—the one that he'd made her clean herself with—to staunch the flow of blood. Then, she would drive the nail under his kneecaps, first his left and then his right. Ragen had once told her that the most painful injuries were in the knees, and she wanted Saren to suffer. And, oh, how she would make him suffer. Given that Saren had been torturing her with his manhood for weeks, or months now, Merigold would spear his berries also, one by one. And, she planned on piercing his twig, right down the middle. All while he bled out of his neck. All while she stared into his sick, soulless eyes.

But, Saren had not yet returned alone. Each time he had been back, Paul had been with him, his long, graying hair slapping her face as he grunted and heaved, driving himself into her. His rough, calloused hands grabbing her hard enough to leave bruises—bruises that she could feel, but not see, once confined to her lightless cell. Saliva dripping from his rotten-breathed mouth, hitting her in the eye. Sometimes, the men would take her one at a time, with Saren going first while Paul leaned against the wall, watching, his hand clearly stroking himself under his pants. Other times, they would take her simultaneously. Dear Yetra, she had thought about biting down, grinding her teeth, and tearing off a cock when this happened. But, she needed to be patient if she were to be afforded her vengeance. And, by now, she had the patience of Ultner.

Yetra, Ultner. The other pagan gods. So often had she prayed to Yetra in the weekly services and before bed, asking for Ragen to be healthy, for Saren to be safe, for Sandra to finally find love. Never selfish, always thinking of others, just as Taneo Marsh preached. Just like Yetra's living example, knowing she was to pray for others, never for herself. Those who prayed for selfish, greedy, and self-serving reasons would eventually be punished. Taneo Marsh said that they would not be punished by Yetra herself—you couldn't expect a lightning bolt to strike someone from the sky, but rather, a balance—Harmony—was maintained in the world through this praying, and avarice would tip the scales. Eventually, something would occur to even the scales.

Early on, Merigold had wondered what she had done wrong to deserve this horrendous punishment. To be imprisoned in the reeking darkness. To be raped, again and again, by a man she'd thought she loved. And another man who had always made her skin crawl. Had it been her lustful thoughts about Saren? Or even her immoral thoughts about Sandra from time to time?

Sandra. Sandra was someone who she tried not to think about. Her big sister, the girl who'd taught her more about the world, and herself, than Ragen ever had. The woman who Saren said was a whore. Not like the village women said, as an barbed insult meant to wound, but that Sandra would part her legs for money. For travelers. For men in town. For Saren. And... even for her father.

"You're a good fuck, you little witch. Nice and tight. Nice and wet. But I do wish you would move a bit more," Saren had said last time, slapping her across the face as he violated her. "Now, your little friend Sandra. *She* doesn't need to be told to move. She does everything she can to please a man. But I guess you get what you pay for, and she cost me a month's wages."

Her eyes must have widened at that, despite her efforts to show no emotion during these visits. He'd laughed, slowing his thrusts a little bit.

"Paul, can you believe it? She didn't know! The little witch didn't know that her best friend's a whore! Not only are you evil, you're also dumb. Why do you think she spends so many nights at the inn with strangers? By Yetra, your godsdamned father has even fucked her!"

Merigold hoped it wasn't true, Sandra selling her body. But dear Yetra, it made too much sense. Sandra was always going on dates with men in town, and even with travelers at the Duckling. Older men, men her age—she was always with someone different. She had told Merigold that she didn't want to be fettered by any one man, that marriage was for folk who didn't like to have fun. And have fun, she did. She often told Merigold of her exploits, about what different men would do to her. Meri would blush and avert her eyes, but continue to listen behind a shield of hair. She'd used to wish men would do those things to her, and that Sandra would... well, no. Not that. Never that.

But Sandra being with Ragen? That had to be a lie—just Saren trying to hurt her. Meri had no doubts.

Creeeak. Clunk.

The telltale sound of the door unlocking and opening to the cabin. Merigold immediately woke from a light, troubled sleep and twisted to her feet, her hand already clutching her dagger. Her salvation. She listened as footsteps moved hurriedly across the cabin toward the mattress. *One* set of footsteps. No additional voices. Saren had finally come back. Alone.

Merigold felt a bright flash of hope, but she forced herself to smoother the feeling. She couldn't allow Saren to see any hint of her intent in her eyes. She had to feel, and look, as empty as

211

always. Just the little witch whore, locked in a cellar, coming out to play once every few days. She squeezed the cloth handle of the dagger tightly, settled the weapon into her pocket, and released the handle. As always, she felt helpless without the rough fibers of the cotton-wrapped nail in her hand.

The scraping of the bed being dragged. The jingle of the chains. The *clink* of her cell being unlocked. The brightness of the candlelight as the cellar door opened, her constricted pupils burning.

But no rope for her bucket. Just the ladder?

"Merigold. Get up here, you little witch. Now!" shouted Saren from above. There was an odd tone in his voice. She couldn't identify it, but she was afraid. Meri patted her pocket to check for her weapon before slowly climbing the ladder, attempting to embody the empty shell that Saren expected.

Saren stood several feet back from the cellar opening, his arms at his sides and his fists clenched. He was dressed in short pants and a short sleeved, button-down red and white shirt. Summer must be setting in. Merigold recalled that her last evening out, with Saren, had been a bit chilly, though she had been sweating from the long walk.

Wait, though… his shirt wasn't red and white. It was streaked with something crimson, with what looked like blood! Was Saren bleeding? His face showed no trace of physical pain, and although it was streaked with tears, it seemed unlikely that so much blood was his. She almost asked him what was wrong, but caught herself.

"What have you done, you fucking witch?" he asked, his voice full of menace. "Answer me!"

"I… I don't know what you mean," Merigold stuttered, her voice hoarse from disuse. She took a small step forward, moving away from the cellar hole. He jumped backward, raising his fists.

212

"Stay back! You know what I am talking about!"

"Saren," she said his name. He flinched. "Saren, I truly don't. Please believe me." Her eyes were downcast, her hair across her face, but she could just barely see him from beneath her lashes. She stayed still, watching and waiting for an opportunity.

"The fuck, you don't. They're dead, Meri. Everyone is dead!" He gave a shuddering sob and wiped tears from his face. "And you killed them, you fucking witch! You killed them!"

Saren hurtled forward and slapped her to the ground. She fell heavily, twisting from the force of the slap, her knees hitting the floor and aching more than her face. Meri wanted to shout 'I'm not a witch!' to remind him that he himself had started those rumors about her. That there was no evidence of witchery. But she restrained herself, remaining outwardly calm, empty. Obedient. And she climbed back to her feet.

"I've been here, Saren. Down below," she mumbled, averting her eyes once more. She had realized over the past weeks that the man was like an animal: he took a direct stare as a challenge. But even looking away did not help Merigold this time. He punched her in the eye, closed-fisted, and she nearly pitched backward into the cellar hole. Dear Yetra, the pain! He had never hit her that hard, and she couldn't open her eye, her head feeling as if it had been crushed with a keg.

"The fuck, you have. I've seen your witchery. Dead plants, mangled corpses. My parents…" he moaned again, covering his face with both his hands. She regarded him covertly with her good eye while reaching into her pocket, her hand wrapping around her weapon. It was evident that Saren was mad with grief and rage, and she did not intend to be killed without making him hurt. Making him bleed.

Saren straightened, eyes still leaking tears, but with his face strengthened with resolve. "Dunmore has had enough of you. I've

213

had enough of you. I don't know how you did what you did, but I'd rather you die than continue to fuck a murdering witch."

He lunged, arms out and with his hand reaching for her neck. Merigold dodged to the right, simultaneously pulling out her little knife dagger and swinging it at him. She struck only air, Saren barreling right past her, evidently not expecting any resistance. Instead, he hit her leg, losing his balance and tumbling forward. Right into the cellar opening, where he fell more than ten feet to the hard-packed clay ground.

Meri rushed to the edge, looking down. The man was already struggling to his feet, though slowly, obviously in pain. Meri acted quickly, grabbing the ladder and heaving it upward with all of her strength. She cleared several feet and then felt a great force connect with the ladder from below, so that it jerked down toward Saren. She was pulled down to one knee, but narrowly avoided being thrown completely off balance.

No! Instead of continuing to pull, Meri shoved the ladder down as hard as she could, heard a grunt, and then hoisted upward with everything she had left. The ladder ripped free of Saren's grip and—praise Yetra!—she managed to pull it clear from the cellar, staggering backward several feet in doing so.

"You fucking witch! Merigold! You fucking witch!"

Meri moved slowly back to the opening and lowered her gaze toward Saren, seeing his handsome, hideous face in the low light.

"Drop that ladder or I'll kill you. I will make you suffer." He limped a little to the side, still staring up at her. It was almost as if he actually expected her to drop the ladder to him.

Meri was still holding her dagger, the rough cloth digging into her hand. So many times, she had pictured driving it into his neck, watching the blood spurt out of his arteries. Hacking at his knees. Piercing his manhood. Listening to him scream while she watched the blood drain from his vile, despicable body.

214

For a long moment, Meri felt a strong urge to allow Saren out of the cellar so that she could exact her vengeance. Thoughts of his pain were all that had kept her going during her captivity, all that had kept her sane as he and his friends abused her. But, perhaps leaving Saren here, in the dark, was better retribution than a painful but short death at her hands. He could experience the pure hopelessness that she had, knowing that there was no way out. Maybe she would return to feed and water him occasionally, prolonging his time in the cellar. Or, maybe she wouldn't.

Besides, there were still Paul and Chad to deal with...

"You bitch! Listen to me! You don't know what you're doing!"

Merigold ignored him. She had nothing to say to the man. Instead, she slammed shut the cellar door, locked the chains and removed the key, and pushed the bed back over the ingress. Saren's shouts grew dimmer and dimmer as she worked, muffled by the heavy, wooden planks and the bed. He was barely audible, just an echo of a nightmare.

No one had ever heard Merigold's cries for help.

She opened the door to the outside, and the sun touched her skin for the first time in so very, very long. Birds were chirping, bugs were buzzing, and the wind was rustling through the deep, varied greens of the trees and bushes. Everything was unchanged. Everything was different.

Meri took an uncertain step into the world, legs shaking, tears running unbidden from her squinting eyes. A beam of light worked its way through the foliage, warming her face, and she shrank back. She gave a great, gulping sob then and dropped to the ground just outside the door of the cabin, curling up and hugging her knees, her filthy hair covering her face. Dear Yetra, she was free.

Dear, dear Yetra.

Chapter 15

It was nearing dusk by the time Merigold found the lakeside path approaching Dunmore. Her home. She must have spent several hours on the ground outside of the cabin, feeling a tirade of competing emotions, but she had eventually begun the slow walk back. She'd been uncertain of the path; Saren had led her to this place in the night, and so much had happened since then. But she knew the sun, and even through the foliage and the clouds, she was able to navigate south until she reached the lake. She'd to pause often and rest, though, so unused to the exertion of walking outside of her cellar.

At first, it had been one foot in front of the other, stepping over occasional roots and ducking under occasional branches, avoiding sharp sticks and stones on her toughened, but still bare, feet. Her mind was overwhelmed with the immensity of her escape, the vastness of nature. She felt so… exposed… and she had to resist the temptation to curl back up. Return to the dark. She could hardly believe that she'd used to think her world too small, too confined. She hadn't known what it meant to be truly confined.

She patted her nail-knife at times, finding comfort in the hard, cold metal and the rough handle. There was scant comfort in thoughts of coming home.

Saren had denounced her as a witch. Paul and Chad believed him, and had gone so far as to violate her alongside Saren. Had others in town accepted these rumors, or was this just how Saren had convinced his friends to… enjoy her along with him? Meri had heard whispers about Ragen making deals with dark powers, and some people even refused to patronize his establishment or do business with him because of them. Some would instead hawk their wares at the intersection of Dunmore's unnamed path and Hunesa Road, while others would travel to other villages, or even Rostane and Hunesa. Ragen never spoke of these people but, through her own subtle interrogations, Meri had found out well

216

enough that they went to such pains because they didn't trust her father.

Even Ragen's generosity and openhandedness didn't protect him from rumors in this superstitious little village. Merigold, who was quiet and introspective—and far less giving than her father—would have no hope of shaking off the reputation of being a witch. And, dear Yetra, who knew what would happen to her as a result? Meri had heard from some Rostanians that, in a small town called Umberton, someone had burned down the house of a woman thought to be a witch. They had blockaded the poor woman in the house first to be sure that she'd burn. Meri had been sickened just to hear of the barbarism.

Yetranian teachings explicitly forbade the use of dark magicks—the power of Pandemonium on earth—and all Dunmorians were devout and literal churchgoers. People who used magic were thought to steal the souls of others. Steal the soul of the world, even. Such people were to be persecuted and driven away. Killed, even. *The Book of Amorum* did not explicitly say this, of course. But it could be inferred from the parables contained within, and Taneos made no bones about interpreting the verses to their flock. Many of these parables involved violence, particularly as a method for destroying magic and restoring Harmony.

Meri herself had been devout, attending services every week, listening to the words of Taneo Marsh and the messages of his teaching. And, she was afraid of dark magicks just like everyone else. But, maybe her exposure to all of the different folks from different parts of the world at the Duckling had made her more open-minded, and she always found that instigating violence upon those with different beliefs, or upon those who sinned, was contrary to the messages of Harmony preached so often by Taneo Marsh.

But that was no matter. Meri had been devout, but somewhere across the course of her torturous imprisonment, she had stopped praying to Yetra for help. Oh, she'd still called out Yetra's name, but she had come to realize that it was now a near meaningless exclamation rather than a prayer. There was nothing that she could have done to merit the kind of punishment she had experienced. Yetranian teachings said that a balance would be maintained, and evil would beget evil. But Meri's abuse had been a violation of both her body and her spirit. Nothing that she had ever done, or ever would do, could warrant such treatment. Meri swore to herself that she would never again attend a Yetranian service, assuming the village would welcome her—the witch— back at all.

Faith will be rewarded. A simple statement by Deontis. But, he was wrong. The whole damn book was wrong. Merigold vowed to wipe it from her memory.

The dimming, carrot-orange glow of the setting sun was such that Merigold wouldn't have noticed the blood except that she slipped on the unexpected wetness and went down on her sore knees and one hand. She stayed down for a moment, hanging her head and building up her resolve to continue on, until she noticed that her hand was thickly caked with sticky, deep red mud. She stared at her hand blankly for a moment before realizing, with a start, that it was not merely dirt on her hand. She jumped to her feet and frantically examined the ground, seeing a mostly-dried, brownish-red stain, rehydrated and made slippery by her sweaty feet, knees, and palm.

Merigold remembered that Saren was streaked with blood, and had said something about his parents being dead. She hadn't thought much about it, being focused more on staying alive in the face of his rage and, after that, the overwhelming reality of her escape. But here, this was blood! And on the path, the eastern outskirts of the town. Saren's parents lived clear on the other side of Dunmore. What had happened here?

218

Merigold felt a sudden desperation accompanied by a familiar sick feeling in her stomach, a shaking in her legs. She increased her pace toward Dunmore, ignoring the sharp edges of nature that cut into her bare feet.

She started noticing odd sights.

She had traveled this path before, and was familiar with the surroundings. On her left was one of her favorite trees—an old, great weeping willow. It was very climbable, and she recalled scaling it with Sandra, back before she had moved nearly full-time to the inn. They had shared some laughs, and Sandra had told her some of her naughty stories.

Now, the tree stood dead. But not in a way that trees usually appeared dead. This wasn't a situation where a tree had slowly decayed, its leaves and branches falling to the ground over time while the trunk still stood strong and true. Rather, the leaves on the willow were mostly still attached but were now a dusty-looking gray, as if they were turning to ash. The bark, peeling off the trunk in thick, heavy clumps, also showed a graying tinge, and the trunk was beginning to uproot, falling toward the water.

Merigold hastened to cover the final distance to Dunmore, fear lending strength to her liquid limbs. She rounded the last bend into the clearing that designated the edges of the village, trying to steel herself for what might be ahead.

Nothing could have prepared her for what she saw.

Dunmore, to her, was a beautiful place. The rows of raised, whitewashed houses, with a splash of color here and there. The bigger chapel, crowned with the enormous iron bell that Ragen had funded as a service to the town. The flowerbeds and well-trimmed hedges, maintained lovingly all down the main row of the town by the mayor's wife, Florence Marsh. And, most of all, the people. The simple, hardworking people of Dunmore.

This time of the day, with the sun just descending behind the trees, mothers would be calling for their children to take their evening meal. Men would be returning from their labors, shouting out to each other with ribald jokes. Some would be heading to the tavern while others headed home with their families. The sound of yelling, laughter, and labor would normally be filling the air.

There was no sound now. Merigold next realized that she should have heard the town a long way off, even before she'd come across the blood. Instead, it was silent. And the scene now before her was one of absolute devastation.

The greenery of the town was ravaged. Florence Marsh's hard work was now a pile of grayish ash, blowing into the air and filling the vista with a strange, pallid fog. Even the grass, in places, was black and gray, with the ruin tending to occur in a circular pattern, like pox on a child.

But the bodies. The bodies were what drew Merigold's eyes as she brought her hands up to cover her face.

There were corpses scattered throughout Dunmore. They were tossed across the path, on the decks of the houses, on the steps into the chapel. As Meri approached the square, she struggled to regain that empty, dissociated feeling that she had mastered during her imprisonment. The sight in front of her was so absurd, so grotesque, the blurred emptiness took her before long. And in her self-imposed stupor, she noticed that the corpses were very different in appearance.

Some bodies appeared untouched, as if the person had decided to take a nap in the village green. Merigold recognized some of these. Mrs. Polen, fallen on her own porch, wearing her favorite red skirt, the one embroidered with flowers. Florence Marsh, lying bent over a dead hedge, shears lying discarded on the ground nearby. And Lynns West, a little girl of seven years' age. A running, singing child, worried about nothing aside from making her parents happy and keeping her dog well-fed. She lay curled up right near the middle of the green, apparently untouched, but gone nonetheless.

Other bodies were so mangled and mutilated that they were unrecognizable to Meri. They appeared to have been torn apart by an animal, ripped by sharp teeth and rent by claws. Walking slowly toward the center of town, Meri noticed one corpse on her path where the face was shredded, and she could see bits of flesh and other matter strewn about. Merigold couldn't escape into herself deeply enough to block out this sight, and she vomited what little was left in her stomach, acidic bile burning her throat and mouth. She knelt near an intact bush, heaving until nothing was left inside of her, leaving her feeling even weaker than before. So much death. So many friends and acquaintances, gone.

Sandra! Merigold jumped to her feet and took off toward Sandra's house at a shambling run, avoiding circular patches of dead greenery and giving bodies—shredded or not—a wide berth. She checked each for a mass of silky strawberry-blonde hair, but thankfully didn't see any. Her own filthy hair slapped against her face as she pounded across the ashen grass.

She barely noticed, as she ran, a very dead rat lying in the middle of her path. Meri skirted the corpse and didn't give it a second thought.

She reached Sandra's house then, gasping from the exertion. She had rushed to get there, but now she paused on the threshold of the small cabin, afraid of what she might find. She wiped a stray tear away and opened the door.

The house was more disarrayed than usual. Clothing was tossed about, but that was normal. More surprising was the broken couch and the smashed bottles of liquor. There had been a fight here. Meri scanned frantically for any trace of Sandra. There was a small amount of blood on some broken glass on the ground, and a crimson handprint nearby. Meri knelt and held her own hand up to it and realized that the print was far too large to be Sandra's.

She sat on the unmade bed, simultaneously relieved that she hadn't found Sandra's body and also frightened of what might have happened. Sandra had fought back, that was clear from the blood on the broken bits of bottle and the bloodied handprint. But, had she escaped? Had she been taken? Merigold didn't care whether her surrogate big sister was a prostitute or not—she just wanted her to be safe.

Exhausted from her ordeal, Merigold laid back on the bed, unable to fully process what had happened. She needed to get to the Duckling as soon as possible, but her limbs weren't cooperating. There was nothing left. With hardly a struggle, Merigold unintentionally fell asleep on the bed of her best friend, the surrounding smell of expensive perfume mingling with a hint of copper.

Clang! Clang! Clang!

Merigold sat straight up in the bed, her heart beating wildly as she took deep, gulping breaths. Was that the town bell? Where was she? The cellar ground felt so soft right now, so inviting...

Wait. She wasn't in the cellar. She was at Sandra's house, sleeping in her bed. The bell was ringing, just as it would to announce the weekly Yetranian service. Merigold felt disoriented—was this whole thing just a dream? Saren, the cabin in the woods, the death in Dunmore... Had all this really happened?

Merigold reached over and lit a candle on the nightstand. She noticed her hands—nails broken, skin rough and dry. She was still clothed in Saren's filthy cast-offs, and she could smell herself over the lingering scent of perfume in Sandra's home. The house was as mess. And her eye socket was throbbing, tender from where Saren's fist connected with her face. No, she realized, it had all happened.

But the bell. The bell was ringing. Someone must still be alive in Dunmore.

Merigold tossed her filthy clothes aside, discarding them in the corner of the room. There was a jug of water that she used to wash herself quickly, using a rag, trying to forget that this was hauntingly close to her cleaning ritual back in the cabin. She rifled through some piles of clothing on the floor until she found a dress that fit her relatively well, a modest teal affair. Lastly, she hastily raked her hair into some semblance of order, untangling several strands from around the sapphire studs she had managed to retain throughout her captivity.

It was amazing how much a nap, a wash, and new clothes could change a person. She almost felt like herself again, if even for just a moment. But, she would need to face reality. Leave this house and see who was left alive. Get to the Duckling. Find Sandra and hope that Ragen was okay.

Merigold opened the door into the much cooler evening air and stepped out into the night. Dunmore was illuminated by the twin full moons—the smaller blue Ummis and the larger, but less visible, white Phanos. The blue and white light filtered through the ashy mist that still hung in the village like a thin blanket, lending the evening a dreamlike trait. If only this were a dream...

Merigold licked her lips and began hesitantly toward the Yetranian chapel and the hopeful chime of the iron bell.

Chapter 16

Hafgan Iwan glanced up impatiently at the twin moons, the white Gwyna and the blue Glasas—at least as they were known to his people. He had not yet learned what the humans called the moons, but now made a mental note to expand his vocabulary.

The Wasmer saw the full moons occurring simultaneously in the sky as a good omen, and Hafgan badly hoped that the prophetic nature of the sky would hold true tonight. Not that he had much faith. This plan smacked of desperation; a last ditch effort to retain some measure of control, to secure a powerful ally. But it was not Hafgan's prerogative to make decisions and determine strategy. He was to follow orders. At least for now.

So, here he was, leaning on his spear, concealed from sight while wedged between two bushes, waiting. If things had gone well, he would have been in bed by now, which led him to think that things must have gone poorly. He rubbed his eyes and slapped his fuzzy cheeks to keep himself awake. He needed to shave again. The curse of the Wasmer. If he wanted to blend in, he had to shave at least twice a day, including his forehead and under his eyes. And, even then...

There was a noise, nearby. Someone big was pushing through the brush, whispering angrily at his companions. Hafgan knew it must be the Bull, judging from the breaking of a thousand twigs. He'd met the man a single time before this, when the Bull had been wanting to see Tennyson after a botched job. Hafgan had only exchanged a couple of words with the big man, but the Bull had seemed to be on the verge of violence, as if he were touched by Traisen, the Wasmer god of war and vengeance. He'd had that look in his eye, it being one that Hafgan had seen many times back when he'd been living with his own people in the Tulanques. The look of a man who was lost, but had little desire to be found.

"Are we almost there? It will be light out soon," observed a rich, feminine voice, carrying clearly through the evening.

"Will you stop, Emma? We'll be there when we get there." This from a gruff, hushed voice that Hafgan definitely recognized as the Bull's. Hafgan decided to make himself known.

"You be... are there," Hafgan said, correcting himself mid-sentence. He stepped out of the bushes, into the light of the moon, and then immediately hopped back as the Bull's dented sword lashed out toward him. Hafgan spun his spear rapidly, staff and blade a near-invisible blur. He leapt to the side, halted the spin with his grip just below the blade, and bluntly cracked the Bull's sword hand with immense force. As the sword fell from the big man's grip, Hafgan next hit the weapon with his spear, knocking it into the brush. The big man grasped his hand for a moment and then assumed an unarmed fighting stance. He had spirit, this one. He'd certainly have been successful in the warrior caste, were he Wasmer and born to it.

"Bull! Stop, now, or you be having a full belly of spear," Hafgan barked, knowing that his Ardian was slipping with the adrenaline of the moment. He leveled his spear at the Bull as three figures emerged behind him. Three women, one middling in years, one young, and one in between the two in age. The entire group evinced fatigue in every motion and gesture—even the man leading them. The Bull straightened, squinting his eyes at Hafgan.

"Wait, you're that Wasmer? The one I saw outside Tennyson's?"

"Indeed."

"Why didn't you say so? I think you broke my godsdamned hand," said the Bull, shoving his injured hand into his opposite armpit.

"Apologies."

225

"It's been a long night, here. We've got some injured…" he gestured to the older woman. Must be the Lady Escamilla, the prize of this gambit. "…and some left behind. I'd like to finish the night in safety."

"You be… are safe now," said Hafgan, flinching at his obvious grammatical mistake; the second time he'd made the same one, too. He worked on pronunciation, and his grammar suffered. And vice versa. "We are having two of the Lady Escamilla's men ahead, in a boat. I will guide you."

Hafgan began walking along the waterfront, assuming that the bedraggled group was following him. The moons' shine reflected against the water, providing more than adequate light for even the humans to see as they walked. The boat was only a couple hundred yards ahead, and it was as clear as day to Hafgan's eyes, anchored a few feet from the bank in the vastly-wide Fullane River. Wasmer in this region of the world, who spent a good deal of time underground in the cave towns and cities of the Tulanques, had developed excellent vision in low light. Since living among the humans, Hafgan had been working to adapt his eyes to bright light and was beginning to be able to see a goodly distance during the day, but he would start to develop a headache over time, so he preferred to stay indoors or work at night as much as was possible.

Hafgan would not be accompanying this group on the next leg of their journey, whether they knew it or not. Rather, he had a very specific role to play. He glanced back to see whether the young girl was still following. She was trailing the group, smiling and asking Escamilla some inane question. Good, she hadn't darted off quite yet. That one wouldn't. She would want her payment, first.

Reaching the boat—which was anchored near the land, but nowhere near the actual docks of Rostane—Hafgan called out, "How are the tides this evening?"

"Low and cold," a voice replied.

"Then we'd had best be off," Hafgan finished the pass phrase, again flinching at his mistake with the contraction. Luckily, Escamilla's men weren't sticklers for grammar, and he heard heavy scraping as the men shifted the wooden plank into place, letting it fall loudly to the ground.

One of Escamilla's men, an older man with a very long brindle mustache, disembarked and headed straight to Escamilla, taking a knee and bowing his head when he reached her.

"My Lady Escamilla," he said, his voice quavering.

"Get up, Tilner Pick," she said. Hafgan could make out a slight smile on her face, likely one that would be hidden from human vision in the dark night.

He stood up, took a hesitant step toward her, and then they joined in an embrace for just a moment. Escamilla flinched at his touch, much as she'd gone toward it.

"My lady, you are hurt!"

"It's nothing. We need to be moving along, Tilner. Someone is certainly aware of our departure, and I do not know whether we will be pursued."

Hafgan was impressed with her diction. He hoped that, one day, he would have the language acuity of a noble. Escamilla had not been born noble, he knew, which gave Hafgan hope. However, she'd also not been born Wasmer. The Bull started boarding the boat, giving Hafgan a brief nod. Hafgan grabbed his arm before he was out of reach.

"Tennyson is having a message for you, Bull. You are to continue with Lady Escamilla and not leave her side. There are many that cannot be trusted, even those close to us. Await a message at your destination."

Fenrir groaned. "I guess it was too much to hope that I'd be off the hook once we were out of the Plateau. You wouldn't believe the night I've had. Yetra's magical clit, I don't believe the night I've had."

The big man did, indeed, appear drained, standing slightly slumped and obviously favoring his right leg. But still had a fighter's gleam in his eyes. Fenrir leaned toward Hafgan, briefly resting a hand on his shoulder. Hafgan wasn't used to being touched; he fought the urge to pull away.

"Take care of yourself, Wasmer. I'd recommend a change in occupation." He smiled wearily and limped slowly up the boarding plank.

Truth was, this *was* Hafgan's change in career. He'd been an apprentice to the *Dyn Doethas* of the *Carreg Da*, learning to lead the Wasmer people in both faith and battle. After what he'd lived through, of course, battle seemed to be the much more lucrative career choice. Besides, he had plenty of battle prowess, whereas his faith was lacking.

Lady Escamilla and Tilner boarded next, seemingly deep in conversation. Hafgan heard something about Brockmore, one of Escamilla's eastern holdings in Hunesa. Another woman followed, this one a red-haired woman that he hadn't expected to see. Escamilla was the only target for this particular mission. Regardless, as she walked by, she gave Hafgan a small smile, highlighting the dimples that humans found so charming. Unusual behavior from a human, smiling at a Wasmer. He smiled in return, his shaved-down fangs helping his mouth's shape resemble the softer smile of a human instead of the fiercer, more intimidating grin of a Wasmer. She raised her eyebrows and hastened aboard the boat. Apparently, Hafgan had not yet entirely mastered the human smile.

The guttersnipe, Morgyn, did not board, but instead fell into place next to Hafgan, surveying the boat. Specifically, her gaze was fixed on Lady Escamilla, her face inscrutable. Tennyson had put a lot in the hands of this little one, particularly given her dubious history. But, as always, Hafgan simply followed orders.

"Goodbye, young one. You were a fantastic guide!" Escamilla called, leaning over the rail as her men loaded the boarding plank back onto the small boat. Morgyn said nothing, but smiled and waved.

When the boat was out of sight—at least, when it was for the girl—she turned to him.

"Well, you've got my payment? I'll be expecting a bonus. You have no idea what we encountered." Her eyes were cold, her voice hard. It was as if the innocent, smiling girl that he'd seen was a shell, one that had broken as soon as her party left and birthed a tough little street-savvy ruffian.

Hafgan stared down at the girl, crossing his arms. Stared *way* down at her. She couldn't have been more than five feet tall, while Hafgan was a few inches over six feet. "I not be... am not authorized to provide a bonus. You will having to take that up with Tennyson." He'd caught at least one of his own verb conjugation issues as he spoke, but wasn't worried about impressing this one.

"Alright, give me what you owe me, and I'll talk to him tomorrow."

There was no give in this girl. Hafgan fished in one of his pockets and handed the girl a payment chit, to be cashed at one of the banks run by The House.

"I was supposed to be paid yets directly!" she'd raised her voice and narrowed her eyes.

Hafgan had half a mind to toss her into the river. "I cannot help you. Talk to Tennyson." Likely, Tennyson had provided the chit as some insurance that she would return, either to him or at least to the moneychanger, where he could have her abducted if need be. Hafgan would have done the same, were he a leader.

The girl exhaled a dramatic sigh and started off, pushing quietly back through the brush, retracing her steps. Making far less noise than the Bull. But, the Bull was made for destruction, while this little one was made for shadows.

Hafgan let her get a nice head start, waiting until she nearly reached the edge of his vision, and then set off after her. The nice thing about being a Wasmer was that it was exceedingly easy to trail humans at night. Whereas the girl might be able to see twenty or thirty feet ahead, Hafgan could see more than a hundred, with movement being exaggerated by his brain, drawing his eyes. This was another adaptation to living in the mountains. When one hunted underground or above ground at night, being able to see motion was a competitive advantage. And, given their low birth rate compared to humans, the Wasmer needed all of the advantages they could get.

He followed the girl along the waterfront, a cool breeze helping attenuate the heat that was stifling Hafgan beneath his tight-fitting brown robe and leggings. Wasmer were not made for summer. As he walked, keeping the girl in sight, he reached into his pack and pulled out a razor and some sweet-smelling jasmine lubricant, beginning to shave as he walked. He'd mastered this skill during his time in Rostane, finding it to be essential in masking his appearance—particularly in public places. Given that he was unsure of his destination, he wanted to remain as inconspicuous as possible. When he finished, wiping the cream and excess hair clean away with a cloth, he also pulled off his dark robe and swapped it for a light green one. Morgyn would be unlikely to recognize him. At a glance, he appeared nearly human. That was, until he opened his mouth.

The girl stopped suddenly at a warehouse front, and seemed to peer at the stone facade for a moment, hands around her eyes as if she were straining to read something. She stepped back then, shook her head, and ducked down an alley leading away from the waterfront and into a transitional neighborhood, a combination of fortress-like storehouses and low-priced housing. Slums, really, brimming with the cast-offs of Rostane. The poorer laborers, the servant caste, the dock workers, and so on. A rougher population than the city would lay claim to. Hafgan would typically have hesitated before spending time in the area, but now was not the time for hesitation.

He jogged to the warehouse and took a quick look at the facade that the girl had eyed for a moment. Nothing there—no sign, no words. Curious. Hafgan shrugged as he continued his pursuit, catching sight of the girl as she walked easily down the dirty road.

This girl, Morgyn. She'd been trouble ever since Tennyson had brought her into the fold a couple of years before. The man often focused on recruiting agents from among the less affluent population in Rostane, though, and Morgyn fit that mold exactly. She was a dirty little ragamuffin that most people wouldn't give a second glance. In fact, that was how she'd been conscripted into The House. The girl had tried to pickpocket a high-ranking member of the covert organization in the marketplace, and she would have escaped with a pouch of yets in-hand if a second member hadn't been following close behind. The pair had easily and quietly restrained the girl and brought her to Tennyson, knowing his fondness for such bold oddities. Their efforts had been appreciated and rewarded, and Tennyson had begun dispatching the girl on small missions. Steal this, discover that. Once she had proven herself to be relatively capable, he'd apprenticed her—in a way—to another young vagrant named Roal. Hafgan didn't envy Morgyn, as Roal had been known to be very harsh. His violence and unpredictability had made him an asset to The House in some situations. However, the traits had also led to his inevitable death in a back alley scuffle.

Since Roal's death, Morgyn had often disappeared for long stretches of time and not been in contact with The House. Associates had been sent to tail her on several occasions, but the girl always managed to elude them—seemingly without even being aware that she was being tailed. Then, Tennyson had asked Hafgan to follow the girl, and he'd shadowed her to the ruins beneath the Plateau. She had found an entrance that someone else had created but apparently abandoned. Hafgan had confronted the girl on her way out, easily restraining her when she'd tried to bolt, and brought her to Tennyson.

Morgyn had been contrite. She had said that she just had a passion for exploring, learning about the old times and the old ways. Tennyson, seeing advantage in having an associate who knew ruins, had given the girl free reign to explore as long as she shared her findings periodically with The House, as well as any trinkets she might find. So, she would leave for long periods of time, exploring and reporting back, occasionally doing small tasks for her superiors, gathering information, pick pocketing, or breaking and entering.

It had only been when the Bull had reported to Tennyson about his assault in Vagabond Way that they'd begun to suspect Morgyn's intentions in disappearing, and that she might be playing a relatively complicated game for one so young. There were some missing links, but with the recent, aggressive rise of *Recherche Oletta*, Tennyson was more than concerned about the possibility of Morgyn's involvement in that organization. There was no one else who was bold—or dumb—enough to blatantly assault a member of The House in Rostane. But, rather than confront Morgyn and remove her from the roster for assaulting a full member of The House, Tennyson had decided to continue using her.

Even at that time, Tennyson had been planning an infiltration of the Plateau through the ruins, though events in Ardia and Escamilla's entreaty had forced his hand. With other plans in the

232

works, Tennyson had sent Morgyn on several tedious reconnaissance tasks in the company of other full members of The House, just to keep an eye on the girl while he dealt with the rise of *Recherche Oletta*, among other things. The girl had been in Algania for almost a month, being babysat by a protector and an enforcer, both of whom had been receiving punishment via the assignment.

By the time Morgyn had returned, things had gotten out of hand for Tennyson. *Recherche Oletta* must have found some powerful allies before making themselves know to The House. They seemed to have unlimited resources for bribes and threats. Their manpower seemed to be greater than that of The House, even. Hafgan did not know how many members there were within his own organization, but there were certainly fewer now. Many had gone missing, starting with some associates and moving on to protectors, enforcers, and even an eliminator. Nobles and landowners, who'd once employed The House for protection and for social mobility through damaging the reputation or physical well-being of others, had instead suddenly broken their ties. Others, who The House kept in line with threats and fear of dismemberment, were suddenly well-protected, agents of The House unable to find entry to enforce their will.

In Hafgan's perspective, Tennyson had mismanaged too many of these relationships and had accumulated too few true and mutually-beneficial relationships with powerful people in Rostane. The House helped maintain a balance among the nobles and wealthy classes, certainly, but it just wasn't an effective organization on its own.

Regardless, here he was, trailing a girl through the gritty, stinking streets of Rostane, getting hungry looks from some of the less fortunate residents of the city. His size, and his spear, kept the rabble at bay for now, but for how long? The girl seemed to be immune to the threats lurking in these streets, trotting forward at a decent pace, not giving any of the roughs or desolates a glance.

Eventually, the pair—one up ahead and oblivious, the other dogging her from a hundred feet away—came to a more populous area. More populous, but certainly not much safer. Hafgan had heard that a pair of bodies had been found in the trash around here just in the past week, jammed behind the Oaken Barrel. Which happened to be the girl's destination.

The Oaken Barrel was one of the least creatively-named taverns in Rostane, which belied the usually raucous crowd that frequented the establishment. The brick-faced building was lit by gas lamps, these now illuminating several disheveled men lounging on the large outdoor barrel tables for which the tavern had been named. The ground nearby was mucky and damp, what one would expect in the back of a stable. Likely enough that the owners had doused a good deal of vomit with sawdust, and then someone had either spilled beer or water atop it to create a muddy mess. Morgyn avoided a messy pile, leaping easily to the dry stone steps leading into the place.

Hafgan sighed, not really feeling like dealing with a crowd but relieved that he'd earlier made the preparations necessary to blend in. He donned a black skullcap, the last portion of his disguise, waited two minutes, and headed toward the tavern.

Luckily, the men up front were so lost in drink that they paid him no mind. This was the time of night, a couple hours preceding sunrise, when most of the violent sorts had already had it out and the dreary, depressed drunks briefly ruled their domain. Some of these men would soon leave the tavern and go to work. In this part of town, many of the men were porters and dockworkers; for them, partaking of drink during work hours was completely acceptable. To everyone but the Yetranians, of course, but even the guiding religion of the country would find it easier to knock down the Tulanques than pull drink from the hands of dockworkers. Other of these men would drink until they passed out and would either be dragged to their boarding houses or charged for sleeping on the floor of the tavern.

234

Hafgan could never understand how men could lose themselves in drink. It was a distinctly human habit.

He entered the Oaken Barrel keeping his face down, looking for the girl from beneath lowered eyelids. He quickly identified her sitting in a corner booth, chatting with a heavyset woman dressed in skimpy clothes. A prostitute, if Hafgan were to guess. Glancing around, he saw another empty booth where he could monitor Morgyn easily without appearing suspicious. He slid into his chosen seat, appreciating the dim light in the room which seemed to be the maximum brightness preferred by taverns at this time of night. It was as if a brighter room would burn the eyes of the severely inebriated patrons, or at least illuminate how filthy the common room had become over the course of the evening.

A short, wrinkled serving woman approached his table, giving him a dark look from under her bushy brows. Not unusual, if she'd recognized him as a Wasmer. Despite the shaving, skullcap, and his other efforts, Wasmer also had longer fingers than humans, and these were very difficult to hide. He ordered some stew—which was likely whatever was left over from dinner, mashed up and cooked in some broth—and an ale. Sipping on an ale helped him blend in, though Hafgan still hadn't developed a taste for it. It tasted bitter, no matter how light of a brew he ordered. He'd mastered concealing his disgust, though.

Morgyn continued to chat with the prostitute for a few minutes until she was brought a bowl of stew and a chunk of bread. The heavyset woman left then, heading for a staircase in the corner while the girl attacked her food with relish. Shortly afterward, Hafgan's own meal arrived, it being a brownish mass of goo with a couple of chunks—presumably meat—floating about. At least it didn't appear that anyone had spit in it this time. Still, despite his famishment after standing in the bushes by the river all night, the consistency of this vaguely-defined stew was such that he could only choke down a couple of bites. The ale was actually a relief, as it masked the greasy taste.

After three quarters of an hour had passed, the prostitute waddled back down the stairs and whispered something to Morgyn. Morgyn paled, hastily scraped her bowl clean, and headed upstairs, leaving the heavy woman to peddle her wares to a nearby bald man who'd been holding his head in his hands.

The change in situation posed a problem. The upper levels of this building were apartments and residences, and Hafgan could not safely follow Morgyn upstairs without suspicion. And, knowing Tennyson, he wouldn't be satisfied with "Morgyn went upstairs above a tavern" as an explanation. Hafgan was not afraid of the man, but he'd rather avoid a tongue-lashing. It was always unnerving from behind that Ultner mask, though Wasmer generally did not worship Ultner as a god. Aversions to silver-faced demons seemed to span race, culture, and religion.

Hafgan slapped down a few small yets, rubbing his face as he left the tavern. Already, he was feeling a fine stubble growing on his cheeks. He let out a sigh.

He stepped back from the Oaken Barrel and surveyed the building. There were three stories above the tavern, each with several darkened windows. He supposed it was possible that Morgyn had, with her coin earned from The House, taken up residence here. She could likely afford it. But the informants had seen her emerging frequently from a low-income boarding house on the northeastern side of Rostane; that was her most likely home.

Hafgan began to circle the building, striding toward a narrow alley separating the Oaken Barrel from a single-story apothecary or herbalist. He examined the upper levels, watching as one of the unlit windows burst forth with orange illumination on the second story, and he could see shapes moving about, silhouetted against the light through some thin curtains.

While it was entirely possible that someone here was an exceptionally early riser, Hafgan had to hope that the light

236

represented a possibility of him gathering some additional intelligence. These windows, in this neighborhood, did not have expensive glass. Rather, most of them were barred, with thin curtains or screens keeping out the reek of the city and the intrusion of nature. Meaning that, if Hafgan could get close enough, he would be able to overhear any conversations going on in that room. The only issue was about fifteen vertical feet.

He glanced around hurriedly. It seemed like the roof of the apothecary was attainable if he could rearrange and stack some old crates. He did so, setting aside his spear, stacking the boxes about six feet high, and then jumping, grasping the edge of the roof and easily pulling himself up without toppling the crates and making a racket. The next part was more difficult. There was the telltale sound of voices from behind the lit curtain, but Hafgan couldn't make out the words. He'd need to get closer, but there was only one way to do that.

Wasmer were generally known as, and expected to be, excellent jumpers, able to leap across crags and canyons in the mountains, and even propel themselves across rivers if need be. Hafgan was no exception to this rule, but it was not something that he enjoyed. Heights always made him uncomfortable. Leaping ten feet through open air to a one-foot-wide window ledge—and silently, no less—gave him some real trepidation. Wasmer were not meant for flight.

But, the *Dyn Doethas* taught that hesitation was defeat. Hafgan chose a dark window immediately alongside the lit one, backed up several feet to give himself at least a small running start, and launched himself into the air. For a brief moment, he was certain he was plummeting to the trash-ridden ground below, and envisioned himself shattering his ankles, breaking his cover, and ruining his career as hired muscle. Instead, the ball of his foot hit the ledge and he nearly tumbled backwards before grasping the window bars and steadying himself.

Feeling relieved and firmly clamping down on the bars, Hafgan crouched in the slowly brightening morning light. The sun would likely be cresting the horizon in less than an hour. With luck, he'd hear a thing or two first.

"…unable to report?" From a somewhat nasally male voice. Hafgan didn't recognize it.

"Errands. I've been on endless errands, to and from Algania. I had little choice." It was Morgyn. Hafgan tried to restrain a burst of excitement. He was exactly where he needed to be, and Tennyson would be thrilled. Or, at least he wouldn't be mad.

"But, now you come to me." Hafgan heard some irritation in the voice, though not anger. "I'm assuming it is worthwhile?"

"Yes, sir. The ruins. They had me sneak into the Plateau through the servants' lift, which was no problem. Then, I helped them smuggle out an important person."

"Them? An important person?"

A moment passed. Hafgan wasn't sure whether it was tension, but after a moment, he heard a jingle, metal on metal.

"They called him Fenrir Coldbreaker. I've seen the man before, but he was changed. In a guard uniform, bearded, bald. He was helping Lady Escamilla and her servant escape. I was to guide them through the ruins," Morgyn said, sounding smug.

"Lady Escamilla? By Oletta, girl!" The man sounded more irritated.

"As if I had a choice."

"Did anyone else see you?"

"They didn't *see* us."

"Speak clearly, girl. You are really starting to try my patience again." That sounded to be the truth, from Hafgan's vantage. The nasally voice was increasingly sharp.

"The guards. They heard us on the way out. We entered the ruins through the western armory. The Coldbreaker man, he made too much noise and brought down the guards. We managed our way through, but the guards were in the ruins, as well. Among other things."

Silence for a moment. The sound of a chair scraping the wood, and then the sharp slap of skin smacking skin. He heard Morgyn cry out sharply.

"Do you know what you've done? Those ruins were to be a secret. A fucking secret." The sound of another blow. "And Lady Escamilla! Cover or not, Lady Escamilla is a lynchpin to The House! You may have undone months of work because of your stupidity, you little..." *Slap.* "fucking..." *Slap.* "Cunt!" Hafgan could hear the girl sobbing.

"I'm sorry. I'm so sorry! I thought my cover..."

"You need to leave the thinking to those with brains. Not stupid little street cunts." Another strike.

"Please..." Hafgan felt, for a moment, pity for this girl. But, with confirmation of her treachery, he managed to shove the feelings down without much of an issue.

Her sobbing, and the beating, were suddenly interrupted by a firm pounding sound, a strong fist knocking on wood.

"Shit!" exclaimed the man. "Okay, you little cunt. If you value your life, and the lives of *others*, you need to make this right. You are to kill Lady Escamilla."

"Yes! I will kill her, Patriarch. She trusts me, and I know where she is going. I won't let you down. I—"

"Enough. Debrief with Ana and head out immediately. Now, get the fuck out of my sight." The man sounded frustrated and tired, if anything. So, things weren't as perfect as they seemed for *Recherche Oletta*. Tennyson would be interested in that.

Another pound from within the apartment. Hafgan heard a door open and close, some quiet speaking, and then some shuffling. Daybreak was really starting to take hold, and Hafgan knew he wouldn't be able to stay here much longer. Hopefully, he would eavesdrop something vital in the time he had left. What he had overheard already had been beyond his wildest expectations. He could retire on this information, assuming he had any interest in doing so.

"Your grace. My lady." This from the nasally man, the one who'd abused Morgyn. It had taken Hafgan some time to understand the complex structure of nobility within Rostane, but "your grace" was an honorific only used for one particular position. For a duke, essentially the ruling class of this country. With one dead as of a few hours ago, one being a duchess, and the third having no reason to be in Rostane, the identity of this addressee was obvious. Duke Samuel Penton III, the Little Duke of Rostane, was colluding with *Recherche Oletta*.

"You continue to find the most disreputable of locations for these meetings. If I wanted to walk through this much filth, I would have just descended to the sewers," the man, presumably Duke Samuel III, said with obvious contempt.

"I find that it has a certain quaint charm." This from the woman. The aforementioned "madam." She had a slight accent. Perhaps not from Rostane, but he couldn't place it. Very slight, indeed. But, her voice was like a harp. Beautiful and subtle.

"Apologies, your grace. My lady." The nasally man, again. He didn't sound particularly apologetic, but then, Hafgan did still struggle with human intonation.

"Now just why—"

"Patriarch. You requested our presence, and we are here." The woman had interrupted the duke! His temper was legendary.

Hafgan braced himself for an outburst. A moment of silence came, with an almost palpable tension. But then... nothing.

"Yes, and far quicker than I anticipated," said the Patriarch.

"Is that a problem?" Now the Duke's anger did come through.

"Absolutely not. I only wish I could offer you refreshments." Again, was that sarcasm?

"The hour grows late, great Patriarch. Or early, as the case may be. Why do you not tell us what you have?" queried the woman. It seemed as if a battle of subtlety was being waged here. Unfortunately, the undertones were far too refined for Hafgan to catch on entirely. He would need to limit his reports to just the facts, rather than surmising the possible underlying meanings.

"*What I had* was contingent on happenings at the fortress. And yet, in the course of an evening, I hear that Malless is dead," said the nasally man.

"Surely an unfortunate accident." Again, the melodic, slightly-accented voice of the woman.

"And, even more recently, I hear that Lady Escamilla has left the visitor's suite and is currently on a stroll through the countryside," said the Patriarch.

"What?" exclaimed the woman, obviously surprised by the latest news. "Penton, how could you let this happen? Are you truly that incompetent?" Hafgan had to choke back a gasp at the last part.

"You had best watch yourself, woman. I am beginning to strongly doubt this partnership all around."

A sick moment of silence. And then, a force, a power that Hafgan could sense even outside of the building. The dawning light seemed to dwindle, and the air thickened to the point that

Hafgan felt a sudden panic as his heart raced. He closed his eyes and sought his center, sought the *hedwicchen*.

"I... I mean..." Hafgan could hear the duke stammer as he gasped for air.

"Without this partnership, little man, you would still be living in the physical shadow of your father instead of just the shadow of his memory." The nasally-voiced man had shed his surface-level deference, and even Hafgan could hear the contempt. The force seemed to lift then, and the world righted itself.

"You... you overreach yourself," the duke warned, quickly regaining his arrogant core.

"I know my reach exactly. And you are well within it."

Hafgan wished he could see through walls, piercing the veil of quiet tension. There was little time left. He was undoubtedly visible from the street, should someone happen to walk by and look up. He straightened a bit to relieve the pressure on his feet.

"Gentlemen, we are all emotional and reactive. I apologize, your grace, if I reacted poorly to this news." She did sound contrite, and her voice was so musical that one could almost believe it. "Let us agree to be civil."

"Agreed. Civility is what sets those with noble blood apart from commoners," said Penton. A pause. "It is true that Escamilla escaped. Evidently, she had some inside help. Several of my men were found dead, not a mark on them. Someone led her through the ruins beneath the Plateau. My guards are currently cordoning them off and changing the locks. How did you hear of this, Patriarch?"

"Though we are partners, I cannot reveal my sources. You understand, of course." There was a smile in the Patriarch's voice.

Another long pause.

The woman intervened. "These problems are not insurmountable. It simply means that we must advance our plans. Do you know what that means, gentlemen?"

A deep sigh. "It shall be war. A much bloodier and more expensive war than we had planned." The nasally-voiced man did not sound pleased.

"Indeed. We already have forces marshalled near the border of Florens. And we still have collateral over Hunesa and Draston—at least enough to delay their involvement until our military superiority becomes obvious," said the duke with some authority.

"But how shall we justify this war without making more enemies within Rostane, itself?" asked the nasally-voiced man. "Our current plans did not account for us being the aggressors."

The woman answered, calmly. "That is simplicity itself. I have just an excellent feeling, a brilliant feeling, that a small village bordering Florens will go up in flames. I also believe that a letter will arrive from Eric Malless, the same day, declaring war upon us. I believe that both of these things will happen by, say, noon today. You will have these documents in hand, and can easily gather the support needed to marshal the forces provided by the nobility to supplement your standing force." She laughed. It sounded like music.

"I suppose that my people will be ready to move," said the nasally-voiced man with some reluctance. "We've enough fighting men to do some damage, assuming an opportunity presents itself."

"And, as always, I shall have a trick or two that will make this campaign a quick success." Another melodious laugh. "However, I want us to move quickly. Events have forced our hand, but it is perhaps a good thing. It is important to unify Ardia as soon as possible against other potential threats."

"I will begin—"

243

"What th' fuck?" shouted a woman, the surprise nearly launching Hafgan—face-first—into the alley below. A woman, a shriveled, gray-haired hag, had bumped Hafgan's leg while emptying her chamber pot out the window. She swung the pot at him through the bars, catching his knee with a surprising amount of force that he just managed to absorb, though his leg buckled.

"You fucking pervert! Get away from 'ere!" She hit him again as he lowered his body until he was hanging from the window and then dropped to the alley below, landing with a splash in the old woman's slop.

Having retrieved his spear, Hafgan darted away toward the headquarters of The House, his head reeling from what he'd learned.

Chapter 17

Approaching Dunmore's chapel, the largest structure in the small
town, Meri's eyes were drawn upward to see that the great bell
had not yet fully settled, though the deep, metallic ringing had
ceased a few minutes before. Illuminated by the white and blue
moons, amidst a strange fog that seemed to have arisen in the
aftermath of the decimation, the windowless white building
seemed almost to glow.

Dear Yetra, who would she find in there? The whole situation
seemed entirely unreal. Impossible. Unfair. She had finally
escaped, finally had hope that her life might someday approach
some level of normalcy. And then this.

Dunmore, destroyed. No more laughter as the Perrigen kids ran
around, fighting off imaginary monsters with sticks. No more
smells of the delectable apple pies that Angie Arlins would make
and set on her windowsill, knowing full well that at least one
would turn up missing, pilfered by those very same stick-wielding
children. No more friendly greetings from Mayor Marsh, and
certainly no more weekly Yetranian ceremonies in this very
chapel. Facing the chapel, Meri was surprised to find that, even
though she wouldn't have attended such services after her ordeal,
the idea that they were gone forever brought tears to her eyes.
But, she could deal with those feeling later, once she found out
who had survived. And once she figured out what had destroyed
most everything that she knew.

Standing on the threshold of the chapel, Meri felt a sudden
reluctance to go any further. Her hand was on the handle of the
door and her heart was fluttering, her head pounding, when she
felt around in the pockets of Sandra's light blue dress—finding
the reassuring touch of her knife. She took a deep breath, grasped
the simple, iron handle, and pulled open the door.

Light flowed from the service room, and Merigold couldn't see for a moment. One arm flung up in front of her face, she walked in. She had entered this chapel so many times before, and she automatically stepped over the large crack that stretched across the entryway stones. Ragen had always wanted to get it fixed…

"That can't be… Merigold Hinter?"

Hearing a familiar, friendly voice for the first time in recent memory, Merigold felt her legs go weak. Tears leaked, unbidden, from her eyes, and her lower lip began quivering. Just before she fell, she was enveloped in strong, soft arms.

"So, we'd been gone for about two weeks. My pa took us with him to sell some eggs, and my ma had built up quite a collection of pottery over the winter," Marissa Punter said, her chubby face illuminated by the flickering flames from the stove.

"Yeah, and my mom had woven some beautiful carpets. You should have seen them, Meri! They looked like they must be from Sestra," said Ola Fial, her rich brown eyes shining with a damp excitement.

The two girls were younger than Meri by several years; Marissa—a chubby blonde girl with a womanly figure—was about seventeen, and Ola—tall and thin as a reed, with stringy chestnut brown hair—was about eleven. Both girls had lived in Dunmore their entire lives, though Merigold knew Marissa much better than Ola. She remembered teaching Marissa, one hot day, how to chop wood correctly. *You don't hit it straight on. You aim for the edge, cutting right along a seam.* But they wouldn't be cutting wood together in the town square anymore.

246

"So we went to town, Ola and her family and me and my family, along with the Hagathorns, over to Ingers and Astin. We made sales, spent some time with relatives and family friends. Everything seemed normal—"

"And then we came back to this!" interrupted Ola, sounding both upset and excited. Meri guessed that, being so young, Ola didn't quite understand the import of what had happened here. She didn't entirely understand *death*. Marissa, on the other hand, seemed to be just barely holding it together, obviously trying to be strong for both Meri and the younger girl.

"Yes, we came back into town via the western road, just after sunset. Things seemed almost normal from a distance—"

"But everyone was dead."

"Ola, please! Yes, everyone was dead. Some were… torn to pieces. Others… just lay there." Meri could see a mirror of her own reaction in the girl's eyes. Stunned. Disbelieving. Horrified. Uncertain.

"You probably noticed the wagons out front." Merigold hadn't. "We went here, to the chapel, hoping that any survivors would come—"

"But no one was here, so my parents and Marissa's paren—"

"Ola! Sit still and tend to the tea!"

"I can't do both!" Ola spread her hands wide.

"Well, then sit still! I'm sorry, Meri. Everyone else went to search for survivors and left us here to—"

"Even our moms! And everyone had weapons from the basement!"

"For the love of Yetra, Ola! Yes, they left us here, and we had locked and barred the doors. My parents headed toward the western outskirts, the farms over there, and Ola's ma and the

247

Hagathorns went to the eastern outskirts. To find anyone still around, and bring them here. To bury… everyone, and figure out what to do next." Marissa's features were tight, as if she were just able to hold back tears. Dear Yetra, the only concerns that Marissa should have right now were wondering who to dance with at the Summer Zenith festival. "We'd both fallen asleep, and the next thing I knew, the bell was ringing!"

For once, Ola didn't interrupt. Meri examined the younger girl, who was now hunched forward, thin hair covering her face and her eyes. She had the posture and appearance of guilt.

"I'm sorry, Marissa. I thought that the bell might guide my ma home through the night, and I unbarred the doors so she could get in if we were sleeping."

"Ola, you need to think! If the people who'd done… this… were still nearby, they'd have heard the bell and come get us!"

"I know, Marissa. I just got scared, and I miss my ma," said the little girl, tears glistening in her eyes. Marissa sighed and pulled the girl close. "It's okay, Ola. If you hadn't rung the bell, Merigold wouldn't have come here. And we are so happy she is here." She gave Meri a wan smile, clearly spent.

"But, Meri. We've been doing all the talking. Where have you been? It's been over two months since we saw you last!"

"Oh, I've been… um…" Meri didn't know what to say. Obviously, she couldn't tell these girls what had happened. Ola was too young, and Marissa was looking more and more overwhelmed. She couldn't heap any additional burdens on them.

"Senida said that you ran off with some man—"

"Ola!"

"It's okay," Meri said grimly. "That's exactly what happened."

"I knew it!"

248

"Ola! Go sit on the bench," pleaded Marissa, gesturing to some seating in the corner of the taneory, where the girls were currently hidden away. The taneory fireplace provided light, and some unwelcome additional warmth, in the summer heat. Meri could see Taneo Marsh's things lying about: his wide-brimmed hat that hid his shiny, bald head. His flexible wooden cane, which Meri was convinced he didn't actually need. Even his silver Ascension necklace, with Yetra portrayed standing over a gray background, arms raised in a "v."

Now, Taneo Marsh was probably lying dead somewhere beyond the chapel.

Marissa leaned forward, a hint of a smile on her face. "Sorry about Ola. But really, you ran off with a man? Was he handsome?" Meri thought about Saren, as she'd used to see him. And, as she saw him now.

"Yes, he *was* handsome," she said.

"Really? I can't wait to find a handsome man. All the boys in this town…" Marissa trailed off, averting her head and scrubbing at her eyes. "But, no one could believe it. Your pa was furious, stomping around town, asking questions. Sandra told him and a bunch of other people in town that you'd been with Saren, and I thought for sure your pa was going to wring his neck. They got in a big argument right in the middle of town! But then Saren said you'd stood him up for someone else, and Paul said he saw you running off late at night with a tall Sestrian."

Merigold shuddered at the sound of both Saren's name and Paul's, but Marissa continued without even taking notice. "We didn't know what to believe! But your pa wasn't having any of it and just kept shouting at folks—especially folks who made implications about you running off, or… darker things."

There it was. The darker things. The witchery. The bullshit that Saren had made up. Granted, Merigold had—in what felt like a lifetime ago—had an unusual ability. To draw energy from others, to help her keep on her feet during the long shifts. But, this had practically been an instinct, like scratching an itch or stretching a stiff limb. She'd never abused it, never drawn too much from anyone, or too much in a given day. And she certainly never had talked about it, so there was almost no chance that anyone knew of it.

But witchcraft! That was nothing like her ability. Witchcraft was something that the Taneos railed against, where witches would imprison children and steal their souls, eat animals alive, and put curses on towns and villages. Babies would be born dead, crops would wither and die, and even stones would turn to dust. These stories had made Meri shiver when she'd been younger.

And none of it mattered, anyway. Merigold hadn't been able to draw since that first night with Saren. She couldn't even feel her own vessel, as she pictured it, or the vessels of others.

"Yes, I wish my father had known what happened to me," said Merigold now, thinking of what Ragen would have done to Saren.

"What happened to your eye? And what's with the bruises?" Ola had been sneaking closer while the older girls chatted.

"Ola! We don't ask questions like that!" Marissa appeared simultaneously appalled and curious herself. She kept her eyes on Meri, head tilted.

Meri brought her hand to her eye. Her socket felt puffy and painfully sensitive, and she imagined it looked hideous to the girls who had been either too tired, too distracted, or too tactful to bring it up earlier.

"I… I had a tumble from a farmer's wagon on the way back here. My eye must have hit a rock." It was a weak story, but the best that Meri could come up with. Marissa considered her face, her own expression thoughtful and maybe a bit suspicious, but she didn't press the matter.

"A wagon? Where did the wagon drop you off? Did you see anyone else? Was anyone hurt? Did—" Marissa cut off Ola yet again. She looked Merigold right in the eyes, her own face grim. It was almost as if the younger girl could briefly see past her own grief to understand Meri's own.

"I'm sure that Meri needs some rest, as do we all, Ola. Let's not pester her with questions. We should all get some sleep. Meri, we have plenty of blankets."

Meri smiled her thanks. "Yes, we should all rest." It might help avoid more questions. "But at first light, I am heading to the Duckling. I need to know if everything is okay."

Marissa briefly frowned. "Please, give some time for our parents to come back. They can help keep you safe."

Merigold gripped her knife in her pocket. "I can keep myself safe."

It was nearly full daylight outside. Meri could see early rays of light filtering down through the bell tower, giving life to the new day. She had not slept at all, but rather kept a vigil over the girls who'd both faded shortly after their conversation, Ola's head on Marissa's lap. Oh, how the two of them reminded Meri of herself and Sandra, falling asleep after a long night of talking and gossiping. She hoped fervently that Sandra was safe.

Ragen, too, had better be safe. Meri touched Marissa on the shoulder, aware that she could feel nothing more than the girl's skin. No vessel, no energy. Marissa flinched at her touch, though, exhaling heavily and waking Ola.

"Sorry to wake you," Meri said gently.

Marissa blinked against the new day's light. "It's okay. I was having bad... dreams. You just startled me."

Dreams. The poor girl was now destined to a lifetime of bad dreams. Meri squeezed her shoulder reassuringly. "I know. But it seems safe here, now. Even so, I am going to head to the Duckling and want you to bar the door after I leave. Don't open it up for anyone you don't know, and *don't ring the bell*." Meri gave Ola a stern look, who at least had the wherewithal to look sheepish.

"Yes, Meri. But you should wait here! My ma should be back very soon, and the Hagathorns too! It will be much safer if you wait," Ola pleaded, grasping Meri's hand. Meri smiled at the skinny girl.

"I will be just fine, Ola. If anyone bad were still around, they would have come back at the toll of the bell. I will be safe, but your parents expect you here. I need to go. But I will be back. I promise."

Merigold gave both girls long hugs, and it seemed as if Marissa would never let go. She did, though, and Meri left the taneory, Ola and Marissa at her heels. The morning sun pouring through the glass-covered ceiling openings illuminated the service room, and the rows of oaken-brown benches faced the simple alter covered in a beautiful lace cloth. Of course, there was the customary statue of Yetra, standing atop her stone, arms raised, that angelic look on her face as her silvery-white hair cascaded across her body. Merigold now had trouble looking at the statue, though she had spent so many days gazing at the goddess, listening to Taneo Marsh's passionate, hypnotic sermons.

A loud pounding at the doors to the chapel made Merigold jump, even as they'd been moving forward. Ola ran straight to the other side of the room with a yip while Marissa knelt behind a bench. Merigold found her hand on her knife, examining the

252

barred wooden doors warily. There was another pound, followed shortly by a deep, masculine voice.

"Marissa! Open up! We're back!"

Marissa, almost disbelievingly, leapt up and bounded toward the doors, looking much like a squirrel as she hopped over and around the benches. She struggled to lift the heavy bar, and although Meri realized that she should help, she found she was somehow paralyzed, unwilling or unable to face more people.

Finally, the bar was removed, the doors heaved open. Marissa threw herself at her father, Leman Punter, a burly forester in his late thirties. Her mother, Jayna, joined the embrace, and Ola wasn't far behind. Merigold felt a pang of jealousy as she stood alone in the service room, seeing the palpable love spread among the family. She tugged at her hair awkwardly, thinking what she must look like.

After a moment, Marissa pulled away. "Ma, Pa. We found a survivor last night. Merigold came back!" Marissa excitedly gestured into the church, and Jayna scowled at her, while Leman gave her a brief, tired smile.

"Aye, Merigold Hinter. Well met," said Leman, either not noticing or ignoring his wife's reaction. "We've found some folks, as well," he said, stepping aside and gesturing with his meaty arm.

Two men strode forward, each having a dazed look about them, looking rather like'd they'd been run down by a horse. The taller man stood with a slight hunch and wore a pair of spectacles—a rare luxury, but a necessity for his profession. Terrin Umber was a scribe, spending his days reproducing copies of *The Book of Amorum* for the Central Yetranian Church out of Hunesa, and he spent his nights reading whatever books he could find in the humble village. The shorter man—boy, really—had wild, brown hair covering his face. Merigold wouldn't have been able to see his face anyway, as he'd immediately hung his head low. Chad Umber didn't want to meet Merigold's eyes.

Rather than feel fear or shame at seeing one of her tormentors in person, Merigold hardened. She felt in control. She was no longer locked in the dark, alone and forgotten. No, Meri was free, and she was strong.

"The Hagathorns back yet?" asked Leman, looking askance at Ola, who was intently examining her sleeve. The Umbers strode into the chapel behind the Punters.

"No, not yet. I'm certain that they'll be back soon," said Marissa, obviously exaggerating her optimism for the sake of the younger girl.

"I cannot believe this," murmured Terrin to his son. "It's unimaginable. Unnatural." Meri still could not see Chad's expression. He was completely focused on his father, keeping his gaze locked anywhere but in Merigold's direction.

"Aye, it is unnatural. Witchery, I'd say. And, isn't it perfect that our resident witch has returned home," spat Jayna Punter, watching Meri from slitted eyes. She was older than her husband by a few years, and had probably never had a haircut in her life. Her mousy braid hung nearly to the ground. "And I hear she is a whore, too. Just look at her—probably beaten by some man unwilling to pay."

Meri flinched at the words as if they were physical blows, feeling tears spring to her eyes. She could see Saren all over again, spitting on her and calling her a witch, a whore. As she had feared, it hadn't taken long for the accusations to begin. After her warm greeting from Marissa and Ola, Meri had almost felt like she was at home, assuming she could forget about whatever had happened in Dunmore, itself. But already, Marissa's mother had denounced her. She gripped her knife in her pocket and took a step back, fighting down her shame and anger.

254

"Merigold Hinter is not a whore! Nor is she a witch!" Help from the most unexpected place—Chad Umber stood in front of her now, almost protectively.

"What do you know, boy? My sister and niece are dead in the square! Did you see Evie out there? No? That's because she was torn to bits!" The woman's voice was raised, discordant. "And now this witch is here, with my daughter! Just like her father—a black soul!" cried Jayna, her voice escalating until she was nearly shrieking.

"Jayna, please," interrupted Lamen. "We know nothing of what happened here."

"Clear as day, it was dark magic!" Jayna said with conviction, her red-rimmed, swollen eyes firmly locked on Merigold, over Chad's shoulder.

Chad's father stepped tentatively forward, but was studying the floor as if it were a tome. "Aye, it was magic. But, there's no dark magic. Magic is only dark if the wielder decides to use it in such a fashion."

Jayna sputtered. "What do you know of magic? Do we have another witch on our hands?" She approached him aggressively, looking like a puffed-up owl trying to intimidate another.

"Stay back from my pa!" said Chad, shifting to cover his father. Meri felt her lip curl at the boy's sudden protective nature. Where was this nobility back in the cabin?

"Jayna! We know the Umbers. They are good people. By Yetra, Terrin spends his days copying *The Book of Amorum*!" said Lamen, attempting to calm his wife with a restraining arm.

"'Evil often wears the guise of good.' Ain't those the words from that very book? 'Trust not what you can see, for surely the truth lies deeper.'" Jayna tried to push aside Lamen's arm, but his muscles were hardened from felling trees. Even a furious woman could not move him.

"We all know the great book, and none better than me," said Terrin, still inspecting that spot on the floor. "There are references to power and magic in *The Book of Amorum*. By cross-referencing these allusions with other accounts of magical power, I can derive at least some informed conclusions."

Merigold stepped around Chad, ignoring his pleading eyes, moving closer to Terrin. She had always wanted to learn more about magic. Perhaps what she did—drawing energy—was magic. Meri suspected so, but had never talked about it or heard it mentioned.

"Though magic has been illegal in Rostane for years, since the reign and unfortunate assassination of King Thontos, some writings still exist that can educate us on these matters." Terrin sounded as if he were in a classroom, giving a lecture to unruly children. "One thing is clear: there is always a cost associated with the use of power. Power does not just appear—" he held out his hands, "—out of nowhere. Rather, those who are able to draw and control power do so essentially by stealing it."

"Sounds dark to me!" snarled Jayna. Terrin drew back, obviously concerned by the feral turn in Jayna's behavior. Lamen began stroking Jayna's back, but she pulled away from him.

"Perhaps stealing is the wrong word. Reallocating? Now, I was saying … I do not know a lot about magic, but it appears that *pasnes alna*, or whatever magic users called themselves at a given point in history, have affinities to draw power from certain reservoirs of life, drawn from different aspects of our world. The ones I know of are plants and the earth, though there are some references to maguses being able to pull power from animals and other living things. A skilled magus might be able to pull some level of power from, say, a bush, without permanently damaging the bush. They could then make use of that power for whatever purposes they required. I'm a little fuzzier about what can actually be done with magic once the power is collected."

"The plants in the green… The dead willow tree on the path…" murmured Merigold.

"Indeed. I've never seen magic before or its aftermath before, but there is one account in *The Book of Amorum* that sounded like magic stolen… reallocated from plants. 'And as they touched the trees, they withered and died, leaves turning to ash, life dissipating in an instant.' This was in regard to the army of Ultner, birthed of Pandemonium to unleash a terrible power upon the world."

"Aye, though the forces led by Yetra fought back," supplied Lamen.

"Correct. There is another reference. 'Theron, a general of Yetra's forces, drew life from the earth itself to halt the onslaught of demons, stones quivering and breaking with his power.' Based on my other readings, Theron may have had an affinity for earth."

"But stones are not living! How can you get power from stones?" asked Chad, seemingly calmed by his father's voice.

"I've exhausted my knowledge of magic at this point, son. I only know enough to say magic was, indeed, used in Dunmore recently. There is no other logical explanation."

There was a silence at this point. An oppressive silence, like a great hand pressing down upon everyone in the chapel as each person thought about what awaited them outside. About their losses, and about how to move on.

Jayna gave a great, sobbing shudder and slumped on one of the benches. Merigold almost wanted to comfort her. Meri understood loss as much as anyone and could relate to Jayna's strong, negative reaction, her desire to blame someone for this travesty.

But, the woman had already condemned her as a witch, and would unlikely want any consolation from such a creature.

Lamen finally broke the silence, his hands on his wife's shoulders, Ola clinging to his waist. "I'd best get to work. There is a lot to be done."

"I'll help the best I can," Terrin said, stepping forward. "I'm not the strongest or fittest, but the people of this town deserve a proper burial." He had the body of a scholar, and hands stained with ink, but he seemed to be the most collected of the group.

"Pa, I will help, as well," said Chad, glancing at Meri and biting his lip. "I can dig."

"Aye, you can, indeed."

"I need to go to the Ducking, to check on my uncle and father. Then, I can come back here to help," said Meri.

"Where have you been, Merigold? Why *are* you coming back just now?" asked Lamen.

"I made a mistake; ran off with a man. A traveler." Merigold had choked on the words a bit. Part of her wanted to scream out what had happened, to bring to light the horrors she had faced. But she had little choice but to embrace the whore story. She was not yet ready to speak of what she had endured, and she knew that these people would not believe her anyway. "I... I regained my senses and came back via the west road, same as you." She had enough of an actor in her to show some shame, averting her eyes. Little of the shame was feigned, though the source of that shame was quite different than what the others would have believed.

Chad's eyes darted between Meri and the adults, his face appearing stricken with emotion. Shame? Guilt? Simple self-preservation, hoping to not be implicated?

"I knew she was a whore," muttered Jayna, just barely audibly. Merigold's anger flared up. She fought the urge to reach out and smack the woman, but settled for a fierce look. She couldn't be around these people right now; it was too much. She needed to get away, to focus on her search for Ragen and Sandra, to use it to block out the fear and the shame that were threatening to overwhelm her.

"I will be back later," she said abruptly, moving quietly toward the door

Just as her hand touched the door handles, a deep voice said her name in a quiet voice.

"Merigold?"

Lamen had come after her as the rest of the survivors huddled together, locked in conversation.

"Yes?" Her fingers locked on the handle, grip white.

"Merigold, you are lying. The story of running of with a man... that didn't seem true. I've known you since you were a girl; that doesn't sound like you. And, those bruises, your eye... Are you in some sort of trouble?" She felt blood rush to her face, the breath catch in her throat.

Part of her desperately wanted to tell the big forester about her trials in the cabin. Tell him about Saren and Paul and Chad, about what they did to her. About how Saren had lied about Ragen and her, about them being witches and so on. It would be a furious relief to unload her troubles on Lamen.

But something held her back. Was it the shame of how she had been violated? Was it the fear that he wouldn't truly believe her? Though Paul might be known as uncouth and surly, people in Dunmore were trusting, and he was one of the village folks. Saren was well-loved among the men in the village, a quick-witted charmer, and Chad was hardly more than a boy, the son of a scholar.

Or, was it because she knew that, if Lamen believed her story, he would find the cabin and find Saren before he succumbed to a lonely death in the dark?

"I told the girls. I'd fallen from a wagon on the way here, bumped my eye and bruised my arms and legs." She didn't meet his eyes.

"Merigold…" Lamen said her name again, almost pleading.

"Lamen! What are you doing talking to that witch whore?" Jayna broke away from the group and gestured violently at her husband.

Lamen's shoulders slumped. "Aye, Jayna. I'll be right there." To Merigold, he spoke more quietly. "When you return, we should speak more. I'll talk to Jayna, too. She's just scared. We all are."

Merigold bowed her head gratefully.

"Thank you, Lamen. I'll be back as soon as I can."

"Please be careful. I would go with you, but the people here need me, and Yetra will damn me if I leave our loved ones, out there, to the vultures."

Merigold left the safety of the chapel and stepped out into the day. In the light of the early sun, the scene before her seemed even more twisted than it had the night before. Such devastation belonged to the dusk, to the darkness of night. Now, the withered, grayed plants, the ash floating in the air, and the bodies lying curled up, either bloodied or untouched, filled her with more terror than they had the night before. She hastened to the northern path leaving town, trying to suppress her emotions while simultaneously offering up an empty plea to a goddess she no longer trusted, in hopes that the divine had protected her family.

Chapter 18

Three miles. Just three miles. An hour of walking at a decent pace. Half an hour at a run. Twenty-five minutes via horse and cart.

These would be the three longest miles of Merigold's life.

She was a witch and a whore now, so far as Dunmore was concerned. Or, what remained of Dunmore. Sandra, her surrogate sister, was missing. She didn't know if her father and her uncle were dead or alive. The village itself—the beautiful, little village, filled with hardworking if superstitious people—was now a dead settlement, unlikely to be rebuilt and reinhabited. Merigold had moved straight from one terror to another.

And what or who was responsible? Magic, some poorly-understood power, had taken everything she had ever known away. Had turned the village square to dust, turned the thoughts and dreams of everyone in the village into nothing. Had turned the sounds of children at play into a heavy silence.

Maybe there was something to *The Book of Amorum*, after all. Any power that could cause this type of destruction *must* be evil, no matter what Terrin said. Merigold was almost glad that she no longer had access to her own power. Almost glad, considering the life-shattering treatment that had seemingly ripped that power away from her.

Halfway to the inn, Merigold's pace slackened. She could see the empty farmlands, bereft of the usual small army of farmers, to her left. Here and there, she could see some cattle and sheep, standing about untended. Spots of blackened grass, though, hinted that the tall corn crops may have hid the remains of those farmers. What would she find at the inn? Would Ragen and her uncle Emmet be…

"Merigold, wait up!" called a voice from behind her. She gripped her dagger and turned, seeing Chad Umber jogging up to her. Her stomach was a nest of writhing snakes at the sight of him.

"Stay back! Stay away from me!" she growled with her jaw tight, not sure whether to stab at him or run away.

"Please, Meri," he stuttered, skidding to a stop a few paces from her, winded from his run. "Lamen sent me to protect—"

"Why would you think, for a moment, that I would ever want to see your *fucking* face again? Why would you think that I would accept protection from such disgusting, vile, subhuman scum like you?" she spat. She had never felt rage like this before, her near instantaneous anger so great that she could feel it in every fiber of her being, and it frightened her.

Chad held his hands out in front of him, hair flapping in his face from the warm, gusting breeze. "Meri, please. I didn't know what to do. Saren, he told us about you, how he had you... well, he wanted us to come with him, to do what... He said if I told anyone, he'd kill me! And he had a knife!"

"What about after? It must have been weeks, after you raped me with Saren and Paul!" she shouted through clenched teeth, seeing him flinch again at the word 'rape.'

"It was twenty days, Merigold. I felt every one of them—each one lasted longer than the last—"

"The days were longer for me, Chad, locked below that cursed cabin. You can't imagine. There. Is. No. Excuse. You sick, perverted..." She felt a sudden urge to cry. But she would not, could not, do that in front of Chad.

"I know, Merigold! I can never understand what it was like for you! But, Saren, and then Paul, said that they would kill me, and kill my *father*, if I said anything. That they would come to our house, over on the outskirts, and butcher him in front of me! They

262

said you were a witch, that you were the reason the Michelson's farm burned down, with the kids trapped inside. That, if I said something, that would make me a witch, too. I thought to tell someone about the cabin, to just direct some random person out that way so that so nobody would know it had been me, but Saren... he *knew* what I was thinking. He said that if anyone came for you, he would assume it was me who told, and he would destroy everyone I loved. I avoided them and never came back, Merigold. But I couldn't say anything—I was scared for my father, and for myself! Gods, I'm sorry, Meri. I'm so sorry." Chad's eyes were glistening with tears, his features twisted with guilt and penitence.

As much as she hated it, Merigold could understand Chad's reasoning for not telling anyone. She would do whatever she had to in order to protect Ragen, even if it meant letting someone else suffer. But she could never forgive what Chad had done to her. Never.

She clenched and unclenched her fists, gazing into Chad's wet eyes. How many times had she thought about visiting vengeance on each of her torturers, using her knife—even her fingers—to tear them to pieces? And yet, here was one of them standing before her, penitent and vulnerable, obviously suffering, and she felt no joy at the sight.

Merigold's anger dissipated like fog in the sunlight. With a great effort, she attempted to let go of the flaming hatred that she had been holding onto for... twenty days. She felt a palpable, physical relief as she did so, also, as if she had set down a tray full of brimming beer crocks.

She took a deep breath and exhaled slowly. "Chad... What you did was unforgivable. It was a crime, not only against me, but against everything that you were raised to value. Against Yetra..." It felt odd to invoke the goddess' name, but Chad winced. "You should have done everything to find a way to help me, to bring justice to the others."

"Meri, I'm so…" Chad began, biting his lip.

Meri held up a hand. "I don't forgive you. But… I know you wanted to protect Terrin. And… family is important. Family is the most important thing in the world," she whispered the last part, thinking about what she might find at the Duckling. "Maybe one day, I can learn to forgive again."

Chad tentatively moved forward, a shy, grateful smile tugging at the corner of his mouth. He reached out and gently touched her arm.

Merigold was back in the cabin then, lying on her back and looking at Chad's closed eyelids. She could hear him grunting softly as he thrust into her, barely feeling any friction since Saren and Paul had already spent themselves inside of her. His hand was gripping her shoulder, boney fingers digging into her collarbone, fingernails cutting into her skin. His hair was slapping her in the face with each thrust, even brushing her empty, unblinking eyes. *Slap. Slap. Slap.*

"Don't you dare touch me!" she shrieked, batting his arm away. Merigold reached into her pocket and gripped her knife, pulling it out and jamming it into Chad's neck in one graceful motion, just as she had practiced with Saren in mind. The boy stumbled back, his body pulling the knife from Meri's hand, and he was there standing for a moment and staring at her with wide eyes before he was falling to his knees, hands pawing at his neck. He tried to say something, but only blood and a small gasp came out of his mouth.

Meri stood watching, horrified, as Chad choked on his own blood. She darted forward and pulled the knife from his neck, blood oozing thickly between her fingers as she clasped the fabric-wrapped handle. Chad fell backwards onto the rocky, dirt road, writhing and contorting as Meri tried to apply pressure to the wound. His open mouth worked silently and his eyes bulged from his head, his unfocused stare fixed on Meri.

What had come over her? How could she have done this?

"No, gods, no, Chad! Chad, I'm sorry, I'm so sorry! Please, Chad! Please…"

Chad slowed his struggles as blood pulsed from his neck, covering Meri's hands and wrists. So much blood. His eyes locked with hers, pleading for help. He gave a great heave finally, his torso lifting off the ground, and coughed blood into her face. Gargling and sputtering, his arms and legs went limp as he faded.

Merigold knelt over his body, whimpering, not even noticing the blood that was soaking into Sandra's dress. Now, seeing Chad lying in a slowly-spreading puddle of lifeblood, she could not imagine him hurting her as he had, perpetrating such a terrible crime. No, this was a child—she had just killed a child!

And now, with the remaining residents of Dunmore already suspecting her of being a witch, could she ever go back? Would anyone believe the "witch" wasn't responsible for his death? Could she even hide it, or lie about it? She was a murderer, now.

Covered in blood and sobbing, Meri wrestled mightily against her emotions, finally snapping into her empty, unfeeling place. Her safe place. Her escape. Then, Merigold strained and struggled to pull Chad into the tall grass. His corpse, rather. She scattered dirt over the blood staining the path, kicking and scraping at it, trying and failing to eliminate the evidence of a struggle.

Leaving Chad's body behind, she stashed her knife in her pocket and continued her journey to the Duckling.

Two of the longest three miles were behind her.

Chapter 19

The inn stood abandoned. The sprawling three-story building, lovingly painted with a fresh coat of burgundy paint every year by her Uncle Emmet, had an empty feeling—a hive without any bees.

It wasn't just the visible lack of people that struck her. There was a heavy, eerie silence hanging about the place. The inn would usually have been bubbling with noise at almost any hour. There was always the telltale sound of chatter among locals: stories being exchanged, deals being made, jokes being told. Travelers would be asking for directions, stabling their horses. Wood getting chopped throughout the day generally made for a consistent 'thud' in the yard, with pots and pans clanging from the kitchen, and Ragen would be shouting to be heard over the cacophony. The sounds of home. Of familiarity.

Now they were gone.

The scene was much the same as it had been in Dunmore. There were circles of shriveled, gray grass, and at least two trees that Merigold could see were completely gray, lifeless leaves beginning to pile around their bases. An ashy mist had formed around the Duckling, leaving Merigold to feel as if she were seeing the world through dirty spectacles. The only thing missing here was the wanton destruction of human life she had witnessed in Dunmore. There was not a body to be seen.

She approached the inn's doors cautiously, one hand clutching her knife that was now stained with the blood of a child. Still, no noise. Merigold was almost surprised to notice that she didn't truly feel fear or sadness. She felt disconnected, empty, acting only for self-preservation. With her free hand, she clasped the door handle and pulled. The door swung open then, and she found the missing corpses.

Bodies were stacked in the common room, over by the white table near the fireplace. They weren't stacked haphazardly, either. They were placed purposefully in an organized pattern. Three at the bottom, head to foot to head, the next layer alternating so that the head of one was at the foot of another. None of these bodies had the shredded, bloodied flesh that Meri had seen in Dunmore. No, they were whole, intact. Almost alive.

Merigold crossed the common room, as she had so many times before, typically while swaying around a milling, carousing mass of customers and friends, balancing trays of food and beer as she danced from end to end. Occasionally touching the people and drawing from them. Just to help her get through the evening.

Now, crossing the room was easier. Meri righted some upended chairs and stools as she passed, and she pushed aside a broken mug with her foot. Dispassionately, she examined the bodies for some sign of her father or uncle. There must have been thirty corpses, many of whom she recognized. Farmer Tinny, a bent, old man with a liver-spotted, hairless head. Linds Emal, an annoying woman who was always coughing and clearing her throat. Both of the Pinkerton children capped the human tower, too small to otherwise fit the ghoulish latticework of the tower.

But no Emmet. And no Ragen. She didn't see his graying hair topping his muscular build. In fact, Merigold, in a detached fashion, noted that none of these corpses were strong and robust folks. There were children, the elderly, and several stringy, thin adults. The strong—like her father and uncle Emmet—seemed to be missing from this grisly display.

Merigold left the bodies untouched and wandered into the kitchen, looking around mutely at the familiar surroundings. Atop the charred metal stove sat a vat of congealed cinnamon porridge, its surface covered in flies that somewhat scattered as she approached. Nearby, she saw some partially-cut apples, bared white flesh turned brown.

267

The sharp cutting knife was missing from the cutting board. Ragen tended to his knives much like he'd tended to Merigold: overprotectively. He sharpened them weekly and generally kept them under lock and key in the big, oaken cupboard on the far end of the kitchen. The cabinet stood open, and she could see a blank spot where the fruit knife should have hung. But, it was gone. Not in the kitchen, not in the cupboard.

Somehow, the missing knife cut through Meri's stupor in a way that the stack of bodies in the common room had not. She began to shake, gripping the edge of the smooth countertop in order to remain standing. With several deep breaths, she just managed to will her feelings away again.

She wandered the length and breadth of the first floor, checking each and every room, including Ragen's. There was no one around, nothing else out of the ordinary. Most of the rooms were untouched, doors unlocked, as if the patrons had simply all met in the common room to die. Ragen's room, too, was flawlessly clean. The normality of it all was a striking contrast to how shattered Meri's world had become.

Meri returned to the kitchen, the heart of the inn. Almost automatically, she began cleaning up the kitchen, clinging to the familiar motions as if they were a chunk of debris and she were stranded in the ocean. She closed Ragen's cabinet, locking it with the key he kept secreted under the washing sink. She set the heavy pot of porridge just outdoors and gathered the leftover fruits in a bag to be tossed into the refuse pile. She washed her hands thoroughly to remove any remaining blood and then fixed herself a salad out of the pantry. The kale was still fresh, as were the carrots and radishes. Vegetables. For the first time in forever. She topped the meal with some oil, and went upstairs to her room.

It was exactly as she'd left it. Her bed was made, an abundance of plush pillows arranged pleasingly, the green-and-gold bedspread untouched. Not a spot of dust on her desk or dresser, and her mirror still stood in the corner. Another gift from Ragen. Once he'd noticed how much she loved the mirror in their village house, he'd had this one imported for her from Hunesa.

Merigold hesitated for a moment, then stepped toward the mirror, seeing her reflection for the first time since... that night. There was a different woman looking back at her, a tired woman. Her hair, usually a near silvery-blonde that regularly shimmered, was matted in places and seemed dull, dry. It was longer than it had ever been and hung limply down instead of falling in its usual waves. Her blue eyes were gray and haunted, hollow circles in her even paler-than-normal skin, her right socket rimmed by a purplish bruise. Even her lips seemed to be lacking color. Sandra's dress, which she had thought fit well the night before, practically hung off of her.

Removing the blood-splattered thing, Merigold continued to examine herself, noticing that each of her ribs stood out like rough bark on a tree, her hipbones protruding sharply below her sunken waist. Her arms and legs were covered in healing bruises, and there was even a fading, brownish-yellow ring around her neck. Her breasts were spotted all over with small round bruises, caused by grasping, prodding fingers...

This was the body of a victim. And also... This was the body of a killer.

Salad forgotten, Merigold laid down on the bed, its soft mattress so unfamiliar to her sharp, bruised body. She found herself on her left side, staring at the wall. Not sleeping. Just existing.

Several hours later found Merigold in much the same position, with her eyes staring blankly, floating in the in-between of sleeping and waking. She sat up suddenly then, heart fluttering, blinking moisture into her dry eyes. Was that a noise from below? A shattering sound, maybe?

Meri pushed herself to her feet, feeling lightheaded. Dear Yetra, she'd last eaten, what... two days ago? There was an untouched, soggy salad nearby. Wait, she was in her room at the Duckling? Whatever had startled her from her almost-slumber must just have been Ragen, preparing breakfast. It was already light outside. What a dream! What a terrible...

She saw herself in the mirror then, still naked, still bruised. Still pale, still sunken, still broken. Still a killer. Yet again, Merigold found herself drawn back to her despairing reality.

Another sound from below. Somebody was here! Somebody was in the common room. Was it Ragen, returned? Or was it whomever had caused this disaster, some sort of magus, come to wreak more havoc upon any hapless individuals who remained?

Merigold hurriedly moved to her closet, carefully avoiding a few floorboards that she knew would squeak as she threw on an emerald skirt and white blouse—her most standard garb for serving. She dropped silently to the floor, flailing around in the pockets of Sandra's bloodied dress until she found her little knife. Scant protection, but at least it had proven to be effective.

Merigold slowly opened her door and, back pressed against the wall, feet working sideways, went down the stairs, treading as lightly as possible. She entered the kitchen and crouched behind the counter. She wondered if she could safely grab one of Ragen's sharper knives from the cabinet quietly enough, but she quickly dismissed that idea. Instead, she crept toward the serving window, little nail-knife in hand, her rough, bare feet making slight scraping noises on the well-worn wooden floors.

Slowly, a fraction of an inch at a time, she raised her head to sneak a glance into the common room. From the window, Merigold could see the common room clearly in the afternoon light that was filling the space. The bodies were no longer visible. They had been covered with burlap tarps, bedding, and towels. Despite the summer heat, a fire had been lit in the fireplace, the familiar sound of crackling, popping wood now bringing some sense of normalcy to the room. Merigold saw something that made her catch her breath then: sitting on chair at the end of the white table was a person, leaning toward the fire, back facing her.

From the short, brown hair and build, Merigold thought it was a man. He (if it was a he) was wearing a simple but well-made carmine shirt with short sleeves, and a brown vest covered his back. His boots, worn and dirty, were placed neatly by the fire, likely with the intention of their drying, although Meri was not aware of any rain that had passed recently. Now that she was focusing on the man, she could smell the distinct odor of cooking meat, and was disgusted with herself that it made her mouth water. He must be preparing a meal over the fire.

Merigold ducked back down behind the window, slumping against the wall while she considered what to do. What was this man doing here? Did he mean harm, or was he waiting for someone? Was it he who had covered the bodies of her neighbors and acquaintances and friends, perhaps in a gesture of respect? Or was he here for more nefarious reasons, to add any travelers to the tower of bodies while stopping for a light meal?

Her dagger was in her hand. A normal person wouldn't dine in front of a pile of the dead. He must mean her harm. He must...

"Merigold Hinter, you are welcome to join me," called a man's voice from the common room. She stiffened, debating whether to bolt, or to charge and attack. This man knew her! His voice wasn't familiar, though, and just why was he here? And how did he know *she* was here? Meri stayed crouching, uncertain what to do.

"My dear lady, if I were out to harm you, I certainly would have done so while you napped, above. But, I could sense that you needed the rest. Please, come join me."

Merigold's mouth was dry as she rose. She cautiously entered the common room, her gaze fixed upon the man in front of her as she slowly moved forward. He turned and stood, a smile on his face, slightly revealing the white teeth of a well-to-do man. He was really a typical looking person, someone whom she wouldn't have given a second glance to on a busy night at the Duckling. Not tall, not handsome, no real defining features. Well, there was a small scar above his left eye, just barely noticeable by the way it indented his eyebrow.

He gave her a small bow and offered his hand. Merigold eyed it, suspiciously, one hand gripping her dagger behind her back and her other held out in front of her, not reaching out to his. The man gave a brief shrug.

"Cryden Rensaw, at your service. Would you like to have a seat?" he asked, courteously pulling out a chair.

"I'll stand," she said, briefly.

"Suit yourself." A small crack in his knightly manner. "You need not be afraid, Merigold. Like I said, I have no desire to harm you. In fact, I am here to help you."

"Convenient."

Cryden sighed and resumed his seat near the fire, flipping some meat in the pan. "I understand your suspicion. Look at what happened here," he said, gesturing toward the bodies. "And I know that something similar happened in the village south of here, though the perpetrators were here first." There was some

272

question in his voice, as if he was somewhat uncertain and desiring of Merigold to fill in the details. She offered nothing.

His fixed smile seemed strained. "My dear lady, we are going to be spending some time together in the near future. It would be best if you were to offer a word or two."

"I don't plan on spending any time with you," Meri said firmly.

"I'm afraid there is little choice. Events are moving around us and there is obviously nothing left for you here."

That was true, painfully true. Merigold decided to try a different approach. This Cryden was right: he could have easily harmed her many times over by now. She went forward and took a seat across from him.

"What exactly happened here?" she asked, warily. "Where are my father and uncle?"

Cryden leaned back over the fire and extracted his pan, dumping the meat onto one of the inn's platters. He brandished a steak knife and began cutting. Meri noticed that the table was already set for two. Again, she salivated. And again, she felt contempt for herself, knowing that the dead were piled up scant feet from her table.

"Of your father and uncle, I know nothing. I'm sorry, Merigold." Meri sighed, shoulders slumping, feeling deflated. "As to what happened here… there were powers at work yesterday. Deadly and dangerous powers."

"That much I gathered," she said, acutely aware of the pile of bodies behind her.

"To those who are unfamiliar," he glanced up at her sharply while trimming off some fat, though his smile lingered, "it is called magic. Magic, my dear lady, is a tool of great use, but also a catalyst for great destruction."

273

"Again, I gathered that," said Meri, growing irritated at his condescending tone.

His smile broke, and Meri felt real apprehension as he stopped cutting and gave her a level glare. It was as if the light had been pulled right out of the room, as if the breath had been pulled from her lungs. The feeling lasted just a moment, but it was enough to fill her with trepidation. She needed to stop baiting this Cryden. It was so unlike her! Although, that girl that she'd used to be was dead. Either lying in a dark cellar or abandoned in the tall grass, just off the Dunmore path.

"Now, if you would please just listen as I answer *your question*... The magic used here was of a prohibited nature," Cryden said.

"I thought all magic was illegal."

"Oh, that? Yes, yes, by the laws of dukes and earls and such, magic is not allowed in Ardia. One will find that those laws are less binding than one would believe, however. No, this is magic that is restricted by the laws of those who actually practice magic. The ruling bodies, so to speak, of the *pasnes alna*."

"*Pasnes alna*?" Merigold asked.

"Apologies." Cryden's good humor and polite manner, feigned or real, seemed to have regenerated. "*Pasnes alna* is an ancient term. It roughly means, "those in touch with life," though an exact translation is beyond our language. It is what magic users call themselves."

Cryden dumped some meat onto the plate in front of Merigold and procured a bottle from a pack under the table, next pouring each of them some deep red wine. Merigold was unable to contain herself, and she dug into the food with relish. The man grinned at her eagerness.

"Now, what was I saying? Oh yes. Prohibited magic. I would imagine you know little of magic, and now is not the time for details. Suffice it to say that, with magic, there is always a cost. Some *pasnes alna* derive their power from plant life, from the green vitality that surrounds our world. Some people derive it from the earth—the minute, but pulsing life beneath our feet. Others still can pull this power from within themselves, sapping their own energy to impact their environment. A dangerous, but not forbidden, practice. Still others draw power from the life of animals and, sometimes, from humans."

Merigold recalled the dead, desiccated rat that she'd avoided while running through Dunmore to Sandra's house. Strange that the vermin stood out in her memory now.

"It is disallowed, by the ancient dictates of the *pasnes alna*, to draw extreme amounts of power from other humans, to utilize the life of others for your own gain. There have been… terrible consequences, in the past, from this. Of course, taking a nip of power, from time to time, might be frowned upon, but is not restricted," Cryden murmured, giving her a meaningful look. She swallowed.

"So, someone… stole… the lives of the people here?" Merigold was horrified.

"That appears to be the case," said Cryden, between bites of steak. "Not their lives, but their power, their energy, their *maenen*. The deaths were a side effect."

"Everyone I know is dead because someone wanted power?" Her voice was high in pitch, anger evident in her tone.

"Not everyone. You examined the dead, no?" Cryden wiped his mouth.

"Yes, and… I…"

"There were undoubtedly people missing. The young, the healthy, the strong. People who can continue to provide power over time. They were taken, to be used..." Cryden trailed off, his eyes clouded.

"Wait! So, people might still be alive? My... my father might... might be?" Merigold pushed away her plate and stood up, already rushing toward the kitchen.

"Merigold!" Cryden shouted after her. Meri didn't heed him. She dashed through the kitchen and up the stairs, and began shoving clothing in a pack. She switched her skirt for durable pants, ones she wore when working in the yard, and pulled on a good pair of walking boots. Her father and uncle might still be alive! Maybe she had not lost everything, not yet. She needed to go after him...

"Merigold, get ahold of yourself." Cryden was leaning in her doorway, one leg crossed in front of another, a frown on his face. "You want to go after those who were taken. You want to rescue them. But there is nothing that you can do. These people have powers that you cannot believe. Look at the devastation here! South, in Dunmore! Merigold, you can do nothing!"

Meri was not about to let this stranger snatch away the first glimpse of hope she had seen since her escape. "You do not know what I can do."

"I have some idea." Cryden's voice was flat.

"How do you know anything about me, Cryden Rensaw, if that is your real name? And how did you end up here, right when all of *this* happened?" These should have been her first questions. Apparently, hope also gave her courage.

"I suppose I will humor you, my dear lady. Like I said, we will be spending some time together, so we might as well build on a foundation of trust and understanding." Cryden gave Meri a small smile. She was unmoved, folding her arms.

"I am a what is called a *cautaton*. A finder. A recruiter. I have the ability to detect those who use magic. I identify individuals who have powers, and I... investigate. This is a relatively rare ability," Cryden added, with some pride. "Some individuals have powers that manifest weakly and have little potential. I do not pursue them, though I do mark their locations. Others are of the sort that we would not welcome into my order. We track them, as well. When I find an individual with potential and character, I recruit them."

"Kidnap, it sounds like." Merigold had no intention of going with this man. Her father needed her help. She didn't know how to find him or how she could help him, but she needed to do *something.*

"Merigold, yours is a unique case. I've been here before, several times, and noted your talent. However, you had already been... marked."

"Marked?"

"I cannot explain this right now, but there are different orders of the *pasnes alna.* At times, in specific circumstances, an order can lay claim to an individual. This is something that is respected across the orders, though we might disagree on many fundamental issues."

"No one can lay claim to me!" Merigold stepped forward. "Not ever again."

"Apologies, Merigold. I had nothing to do with how you were marked," Cryden said, his hands raised. "I felt the power used here from Rostane. Far outside of my usual range, meaning the power unleashed was expansive. I came here, and found... all this. I could sense you resting in your room, and I decided to wait. An event like this... long-standing treaties have been broken. The rules no longer apply. You have a talent, Merigold, and there is nothing for you, here. Come with me and learn how to control your powers."

"I have no powers," she said, averting her eyes.

"I am certain that you do. I am never wrong." A bit of conceit, there, she thought. "I've seen you, weaving in and out of the crowd. A touch here, a brush there. Very subtle. Commendable."

"That was then. I no longer have any powers."

"My dear lady, being able to utilize magic, having a talent, isn't something that goes away simply because it you will it to be so. It is innate. I can sense it within you, right now, swirling about, quite brightly," Cryden said, bright eyes fixed on Meri as if he truly did see some power within her.

"You are wrong. I… used to be able to… borrow energy from others, just a tad, to keep me on my feet during busy days. I used to be able to sense energy within others, even within myself. But now… Now, I cannot see anything. I cannot *feel* anything." Meri licked her dry lips. She'd never admitted to having this ability before. Giving voice to it seemed wrong, but this Cryden obviously knew the truth of it. And, what was the point of hiding it, now?

"Hmmmmm…" Cryden rubbed his smooth jaw. "You can no longer sense *maenen*. This is unusual, but not unheard of. Tell me, my dear lady," he added more delicately, softly, "have you, perhaps, experienced a recent trauma?" He seemed to look at her, *Merigold*, for the first time, eyes flickering to the bruises that riddled her arms and legs.

Merigold hurriedly averted her eyes. She wondered if Cryden could sense her blood-covered clothes, bunched up in the closet. Or the brown and crimson-dyed dagger, its metal surprisingly warm in her pocket. Or even Saren, miles away, injured and frightened, trapped beneath the floorboards of an unassuming, nearly hidden, cabin.

278

"Perhaps…" Still, she was not meeting his eye.

"Like I said, not unheard of. I am certainly no expert on this topic, but at times of great trauma, the *maenen* can become obscured, particularly to the untrained. It is not insurmountable, however. Once we reach Rafón, I'm certain that we will find you help."

"What makes you think I want help?" Maybe she was better off being unable to access this destructive power. Merigold was very acutely aware of the shells of humanity stacked like so much wood in the inn, lives stripped away with the use of magic or *maenen* or whatever this Cryden called it.

"Because you have no way to find those who are lost. Because if you don't learn to control your power, you might do the same, one day, by accident," Cryden said, gesturing in the direction of the dead. "Because there is war in the air and you cannot protect yourself as you are. Because maybe, just maybe, you will have a chance one day… for vengeance."

Vengeance. To do unto others as they had done to her family and friends. To make them suffer, to make them pay. Certainly, the Yetranians would preach against such a practice, but given that Yetra had protected neither her nor the people of Dunmore, not her father or uncle, she gave such teachings very little credence at this point. Perhaps one could not wait for divine intervention to balance the scales. Indeed, lightning rarely seemed to strike at evil. Rather, the *people* needed to be the instruments to help the world find Harmony.

Merigold could not wait for balance to be returned to her own life. She was too far gone, everything she knew lost or taken. But, she had brought justice to Saren. And Chad… Amidst her swirling emotions, a plan began to form in her mind. A desperate plan, but at least it was some direction in her life.

"You are right, Cryden. There is nothing for me here. Nothing. I will come with you, but I make no guarantees that I will stay at this… where exactly do you intend to lead me?"

"We can call it a school, though it is much more than that. Where you will learn to again feel your *maenen,* to control it. We will travel to Rafón by a ship out of Enowl, and then over land to the Agricorinor, the seat of my order."

"Agricorinor… I will come with you, at least as far as Enowl. I expect to learn more of this school by then," said Merigold firmly, having no real intention of boarding a ship. "Now that we are agreed, though, will you please let me pack in peace?"

"Of course, my dear lady. Pack practically. We have many hundreds of miles by land and sea." With a bow, he left the room.

Merigold stuffed some more clothing in her bag, as well as an additional pair of sturdy boots. Travelers coming through the inn always talked about the importance of good footwear. She left her room, glancing back to make sure that Cryden was not watching, and she strode quickly to the smaller linen closet. As quickly as she could, she pulled out her knife and pried up a loose floorboard there, extracting an iron box. Inside the box, stacked in neat piles, were a wealth of yets. Ragen's fortune. Enough coin to buy another, much larger, inn, and with plenty to spare. Enough money to buy a small castle, if one were so inclined.

The path to Enowl would take them through Hunesa. It should be an easy thing, then, to slip away from Cryden and use this coin to hire a group of mercenaries and trackers. With some help, Merigold could pursue the people who took her father and her uncle, magic or no. And then she would have her revenge. No need to wait until she learned to control her power.

"My dear lady, you certainly took your time," said Cryden, standing outside of the inn and saddling his horse.

"You know how women are," Merigold replied dryly. "Where's my horse?"

"Given that I did not know I would be sharing your so-far sterling company when I left, I only thought to bring the one. Silly me," Crydon said, sardonically. "We will have to ride double to Enowl, and plan on doing a good deal of walking. Sargon will need a break. You first."

Merigold tied her pack to the saddle and pulled herself onto the beast, feeling uncomfortable. She had only ridden a horse a handful of times, and they always made her feel uneasy. They had those sad eyes that seemed to say, "Don't sit on my back." And they had those teeth that seemed to say, "*If* you ride on my back, you will lose a finger."

"Just a moment, my dear lady. I seem to have forgotten something." Cryden walked back into the Duckling and was gone for a long moment. Meri smelled something odd during this time. Was it… liquor? Had Cryden stopped in for one last shot of distilled rum, and instead spilled the bottle? The odor was so strong…

Cryden emerged minutes later, a pipe to his mouth, hands cupped around the instrument while he attempted to light it in the increasingly windy afternoon. He shook the match out and took a couple of puffs at the pipe then, closing his eyes and leaning against the building. The smell of kerena wafted over to Meri, stinging her nose. She had already begun to become impatient when Cryden tossed his lit pipe into the Duckling.

There was a near instant inferno as the spilled casks of rum ignited, flames engulfing the floors in the common room and the kitchen. Merigold dismounted in a single move, running toward the Duckling and The Boat as Cryden strode toward her.

"What did you do? What is wrong with you? This is my home!" she shouted at Cryden as she tried to run past, heading toward the well. He intercepted her.

"Don't touch me! Don't ever touch me!" she shouted, swinging hard at his face. With relative ease, he knocked her fist aside and grabbed her shoulders with much more strength than she would have expected from his frame, dragging her away from the burning building.

"Listen to me! Do you want these bodies, the people you care about, to be defiled by animals? Do you want your home to be claimed by squatters, assuming that it isn't claimed by the duchy? No, this is the only way. Let this pyre give some dignity to the deaths of these simple people, to the death of your home."

Merigold pulled away from Cryden angrily, straightening her blouse. She watched the fire rage throughout the Duckling for several minutes, the flames reflecting in her damp eyes. She could feel the heat on her face, especially as the fire took hold on the second floor, roaring yellow and orange with the glow visible in each window, black-as-night smoke billowing thickly from the roof.

When she could stand it no more, Merigold turned her back on the Duckling and again mounted the horse, waiting to leave her home and life behind.

Chapter 20

If she opened her mouth one more time, Fenrir would toss her from the wagon, to land in front of the horses. Or beat her over the head with a stick. Or do anything that would shut her up. That godsdamned Emma was insufferable. Perhaps she did deserve her claw of a hand!

Ever since they'd left those forsaken ruins and met up with Lady Escamilla's men, Emma had been taunting and baiting and generally insulting him. Comments about his beard and his bald head, he would have expected. He didn't much care for his altered appearance (which he did not even need; he'd seen not a single guardsman he recognized at the Plateau, and no one had yet given him a second glance), but the constant remarks about his intelligence and the not-so-subtle jabs about the size of his manhood had really started to grate at his nerves over the last few days. He was confident that neither were undersized, but still...

By Yetra's sagging tits, he was spiraling from one literally painful mistake to the next. First, the blunder with Frommis in Umberton and his subsequent beating by that innkeeper. Then the stabbing, then the follow-up stabbing by the boney, powerful fingers of no-longer-his-father. And that had been nothing compared to the mess at the Plateau. Emma trying to crack him with a vase. That little chit, Morgyn, clonking him in the head and alerting the guards. Their escape through the ruins and the fucking insane fight at the end.

That was another place where he and Emma disagreed. He remembered the conversation they'd had that night on the boat leaving Rostane.

Tilner Pick, Escamilla's man, had been changing the bandage on Escamilla's arm. The bite wound. He had rubbed some herb on it as she winced.

"What exactly happened, my lady?" he had asked, concern evident in his voice.

"Our escape did not go as planned," responded Escamilla, fatigue showing despite her efforts to maintain her regal calm.

"That's an understatement," grunted Fenrir, sprawling exhausted against a crate. Every muscle ached. He had never fought like that before. Sure, there'd been plenty of sparring back when he'd trained, and annual tournament matches with blunted swords. But he had never had to fight such freakish foes, and certainly not with the intention to kill.

It was the first time he had ever killed in combat, too, and he would have expected to feel intense guilt or regret. Maybe both. He had heard from veterans, like Silas, that it was not all glory and slaps on the back, as stories and songs would lead one to believe. No, battle was a chaotic press, men desperately hacking at one another, doing whatever was necessary to stay alive. Silas, at least, had fought against Wasmer, and could tell himself that they were different, wrong, somehow alien. Fenrir wanted to believe that he had also fought against outlandish monsters. But he knew they'd been human, just like him.

A bit more insane, maybe.

The first one, who'd rushed at him out of the blackness, howling as it impaled himself on his sword... it had continued fighting with him, despite two feet of steel protruding from its back. Fenrir had held its thrashing face away from his with a gloved hand, watching the life leave its wild but still all too human eyes. Every feature of the thing had been human. In the light of the lantern, the thing had seemed unusually pale and very unkempt, but that had been the only distinctly odd thing about the man who'd attacked him.

Fenrir estimated that he had killed half a dozen of the things and maybe injured three or four more. But despite the realization that these creatures had, in fact, been human, he felt no guilt. No, he instead felt a rush, knowing that it had been his life or their lives. The blood spilling from their wounds, the knowledge that his strength and agility had been greater, actually gave Fenrir a touch of pride. After years and years of carrying a sword and never using it, he had proven that he knew how to wield his weapon, and it was gratifying. Anyhow, even if his inclination was correct, that they'd been human, they'd been so far gone that it had felt more like putting down animals. He had been practically benevolent.

"I never saw anything like it, Tilner," said Emma. She was familiar with the man. "We were in the ruins and attacked by monsters! I think they were troglodytes. I've heard of those before."

Fenrir hadn't wanted to argue. The adrenaline of the evening had worn off and the exhaustion that mixed with the lingering pain in his shoulder and constant ache in his knee had brought him to the brink of unconsciousness.

"Perhaps," said Lady Escamilla. "But I believe Fenrir thinks differently." *Damn.*

"Yes. They were humans. Far gone, nearly insane, but they were humans," he had said.

"There's no way! They threw themselves at your weapon! After Erlins cut one open, it continued coming at him even with its guts spilling out. They must have been monsters! They were…" Emma had shouted back at him, hushing herself only mid-rant at a burning look from Escamilla.

"Troglodytes are three feet tall, blind, and nonviolent. I've seen them. These were a little taller," said Fenrir, having no real idea what troglodytes were or if they existed, but wanting to be right. Emma glared at him.

285

"You've always had some perception issues, Coldbreaker. I remember you told me that this…" She had held her fingers a couple of inches apart, "was eight inches" Emma finished, smirking. Havert, Escamilla's other man, had chuckled at this as he'd worked the oars, struggling mightily to move upriver while Tilner tended to their mistress.

By mid-morning, they had landed near Hunesa Road and camped for the day. Escamilla's men had arranged for two additional soldiers to meet them off the path with a covered wagon. The wagon had been filled with cages, each one containing a cooing, shitting, twitching carrier pigeon. While they'd rested, Escamilla had written a dozen or more notes, sending pigeons in every direction. Fenrir had not bothered to learn more about these messages. He would know soon enough, or not. Either way, he didn't care.

He wanted to be as far from Rostane as possible, but they'd continued camping a few hundred yards from Hunesa Road while Escamilla had worked. She'd finally fallen asleep by late afternoon and Fenrir had urged the group to load her into the wagon and get moving. They were to head to Brockmore, one of Escamilla's largest holdings, southeast of Hunesa and a couple hundred miles away. However, her men would not budge without her command. Tilner had even partially drawn his sword in an attempt at intimidation. Fenrir hadn't bothered responding in kind. Instead, he'd shrugged and slept fitfully until dawn the next day.

They'd begun traveling incognito, with Escamilla again dressed as a serving woman and secreted in the bed of the wagon. They wanted to keep her out of sight and Tilner had insisted that she rest. Fenrir was the wagon driver, seated next to Emma, playing the role of a moderately successful merchant, silk clothes and all. Tilner and Havert acted as guards (well, they were guards), flanking the wagon, each mounted on chestnut horses while Escamilla's other two men disappeared on errands for their lady. They presented a sight as common and unremarkable as a column of dirty peasants on the long, hundred or so mile stretch between Rostane and Hunesa.

So, Emma had been in close proximity to Fenrir for near a full day at this point, belittling him and mocking him with remarkable regularity. With Escamilla in the back, in the wagon bed, there was nobody to intervene, and Fenrir's efforts to ignore Emma were wearing thin.

"…and you know how we serving girls talk. The term 'limp noodle' came up more than once. And, I heard your nickname was 'the inch worm.' Given that I'm an unclever whore, not worthy of rescue, I can only guess what inch that worm was referring to. I can only imagine that it was your penis," chattered Emma, as if she was having a perfectly normal conversation.

"And, I wonder if that inch is even visible. If I recall, there was quite a bit of fuzz. Actually, it was the consistency of your beard! So, that inch is likely lost in a sea of gray by now!"

Fenrir gripped the reins, his palms turning white. He had thought he was in love with this little ginger-haired bitch, back when he'd been in his loveless arranged marriage with his now ex-wife. Thinking about it, he saw that she'd always been quite acerbic, but he had never been the target before. He'd used to like her biting wit, finding it refreshing after he'd spent his day absently listening to the feigned friendliness of the nobles or the tedious lectures and mutterings of the Scholars at the Enlightenment. Emma had a way with words. She rarely outright insulted her betters, even in the privacy of their chambers. Rather, she could weave a story that, with a simple and subtle use of words, told factual stories in which the real-life characters seemed ridiculous. It had been quite amusing to Fenrir, back when they'd been together.

Now, he'd very much love to feed her to some wandering wolves.

"I've heard that, when the hair starts to gray, the mind starts to go. Indeed, I once knew a man—a decent man—who used to be able to make me laugh with a clever joke, or make me swoon in wonderment with a clever story. But now, only a few years later, the man is essentially a mental invalid, sitting all day, looking straight ahead and drooling, nearly incapable of speech. Aye, the gray has seeped into his brain. It's a real shame," Emma said with sorrow, shaking her head.

"Enough of this, you little cu—"

Havert, a dark eyed and heavy-set Sestrian, rode up next to Fenrir, interrupting his likely angry and witless rejoinder.

"Havert, how goes it?" queried Fenrir with a pleasant tone, thankful for the brief respite from the acid-spitting troglodyte sitting next him.

"Hail, Coldbreaker. We are to take the southern road to Hunesa, so bear right ahead. Sir Pick wishes for the lady to have a warm repast and warm bed this evening, and there is an inn not far along the road. The Duckling, it is called."

"You're fucking kidding me," muttered Fenrir, and Havert raised an eyebrow. "Ah, by Ultner's burning balls, never mind." The guard rolled his eyes and resumed his trot.

At the very least, his disguise might now come in handy. He doubted the innkeeper would recognize him.

Indeed, the innkeeper would not recognize him, as the inn was little more than a charred husk, a blackened skeleton of wood. Supports still stood, as did portions of some of the walls, but that was about all. The common room and kitchen were visible from the path, or what was left of them were, the stovepipes laid bare to the world. Fenrir pulled the wagon to the side.

"What happened, here?" asked Lady Escamilla, stepping out of the wagon, not a single hair out of place. Servants' clothing or not, there was no hiding her regal posture.

"There must have been a flood," drawled Fenrir. Tilner Pick gave him a sharp look.

"You are to show the Lady Escamilla respect."

"I think I will show the Lady Escamilla a way out of the Plateau, through guards and mobs of the insane, and then I will do as I wish," Fenrir returned, getting pretty damn sick of this vainglorious, puffed-up popinjay of a man. Between Emma and this Tilner, Fenrir was about ready to borrow one of these horses in the night and ride off. If it hadn't been for his fear of repercussions from Tennyson, he would have been gone by now.

"You'd best show me respect, as well, you criminal shit," Tilner spat, literally. There were flecks of saliva on his long mustaches. His hand was again on his sword. Quick to anger, it seemed, when Escamilla was in the mix.

"Gentleman, I would beg for respect from all parties. Tilner, this man means no harm. Sir Coldbreaker, if you would please avoid confrontation until after we determine the cause of this fire, I would be more in your debt." Fenrir grunted in acquiescence. Tilner shot him another dark glare and pointedly turned his back.

"My lady, it appears there was a fire. Smoke still rises, so I would counsel caution. The embers are likely still burning beneath the ash." Fenrir managed to restrain himself from making a sarcastic comment, but just barely. Emma must have been rubbing off on him, he thought.

"Investigate," said Escamilla.

While Tilner and Havert approached the burnt-out shell of the Duckling, Fenrir started to rub down the horses. He had no desire to wade in the steaming ashes of a ruined building, so he stuck to a tenet that served him well at the Plateau: those who take initiative to do a slightly unsavory task but look busy doing it are less likely to be assigned even more distasteful work. Though he didn't care for horse maintenance, he would rather not singe his leg hairs.

His work made him think briefly of the horse that he'd abandoned in Umberton. His father's horse, more specifically, that he had borrowed for the outing. Perhaps someone would eventually return the branded beast to his father, which might cause a certain line of questioning, such as how Darian was related to The House. The man had the resources to avoid any real inquisitions into Frommis' hand mutilation, but it would certainly be a thorn in Darians's side. The thought made Fenrir smile.

"What's so amusing, Sir Coldbreaker?" Escamilla had crept up beside him. "Does the thought of burning buildings bring you pleasure?"

"Nothing. Just thinking of family," he muttered.

"Ah, the de Trenton mercantile empire. I have butted heads with your father a time or two while dabbling in the trading arts. I understand you had a falling out?" Escamilla folded her boney arms.

"You could say that." A topic he'd rather not discuss.

"Which is why you took that dramatic name?"

"Yes." He thought it was a bit dramatic, too, but Martis had pushed for Coldbreaker.

"Where does the name originate?"

"My mother." *Quite a few questions.*

"Despite my knowledge of all things related to trade in this county, I know little about your mother. Usually these are arranged things, reducing merchant rivalries or forging bonds to strengthen the business. Correct?" Escamilla raised a single white eyebrow, accentuating the creases on her forehead.

"Why all of the questions?" Fenrir had no desire to speak of his mother. "With all due respect, my lady, I have little desire to make friends. My cup already overfloweth in that area." Truthfully, he had dozens of acquaintances—men with whom he could share a beer or a story. Men who would probably just shrug if they realized that Fenrir was found ripped to bits beneath the ruins of the Plateau, also. How many would show up to his funeral, when it came? Martis, absolutely. Probably Silas. Maybe his ex-wife, primarily to spit on his remains. Certainly not Darian de Trenton. Or Astora. His daughter, named for his mother...

"Well, Coldbreaker. For the time being, we are going to be traveling companions. If you are tasked to keep me safe, I have the right to know a bit about you, don't you think?"

It was probably true. He was a big man and a capable killer, at least recently, and working for a powerful, underground organization that largely ruled by fear. And yet...

"My lady, my past is irrelevant. The fact of the matter is that I am being paid excellently to smuggle you out of the Plateau and to keep you safe in the interim. My background and past mean nothing. I am your man as long as my superiors say that I am." He'd kept his tone respectful, but not so much as he once had, back at the Plateau.

"That is certainly reassuring," Escamilla said with a wry smile.

He gave a sigh. This Escamilla seemed like a decent sort, better than most of the wretched, self-involved, humorless nobles shambling around the Plateau. And, she was right enough: she was stuck with him until a time when he heard otherwise. Perhaps

291

he would be in exile and never hear from Tennyson again. With his father having disowned him, Fenrir wouldn't even have minded that so much.

Except that he wouldn't get paid.

"Coldbreaker comes from the *Srota,* my mother's people, from the far south, from the Domain. Her surname was *Kalabrot,* which translates to 'he who breaks the cold.' My friend recommended 'Coldbreaker,' and given that my former surname was no longer an option, I went with that."

There, that should satisfy her, and maybe she would start to trust him a bit.

Escamilla nodded thoughtfully. "Why did your father disown you?"

Wow, she went right for the throat.

"I don't believe that we are good enough friends to discuss that yet," he said, focusing on rubbing down one of the horses.

"Let's work on our friendship, then. Ask me a question," said Escamilla, leaning against the wagon and scratching at her bandage. Fenrir recalled from Martis that bite wounds tended to linger, the filth in the mouth burying itself into the body. Although, he'd been talking about animal bites. Not fucking-insane-people-living-below-the-Plateau bites.

"Why The House?" he asked now. "Why did you reach out to Tennyson? Obviously, you had been targeted by The House before." The question had been weighing on him.

"Yes, *I* had been the target of The House in the past," said Escamilla, looking askance at Emma. The girl was sitting on a bench near the untouched inn stables, combing her fingers through her mess of red curls. The setting sun shone amber in the sky, reflecting off of Emma's hair, almost as if the heavens were highlighting her beauty. Fenrir found himself staring for a moment, and then he scoffed, remembering his day full of jibes.

"Two years ago, one of my competitors contracted with The House to teach me not to meddle in the affairs of men. I eventually found out that it was a merchant, Yulio de Farns, but that is of no concern." Fenrir knew that name, and remembered rumors that the man was found dead, his eyes burned out and replaced with hot coals. He made a mental note not to cross Escamilla.

"At that time, I learned the value of having such an ally, one who is powerful, but can be controlled through the correct dispensation of money. I began to forge relations with the one you call Tennyson, working through intermediaries and agents. I supplied funding for some of your organization's operations, and they, in turn, protected some of my interests." Perhaps by providing the coals? "We had been in communication for months, particularly as the little duke continued to scheme and maneuver for power."

"You were aware that Penton was planning a takeover of the country?" When Tennyson's agent had given him the details, that he was tasked to retrieve an imprisoned Escamilla, he himself had been astonished. First, that he was going to be involved in another covert type of mission. Second, that the ruler of his home duchy was apparently planning a hostile takeover of the country.

He wondered what signs he had missed over the past few years. He certainly didn't recall any talk of war during his tenure as a guardsman, no special trainings on deploying for battle and so on. But, that had been three years ago, so things may have changed. He had heard a little bit about various Rostanian noble houses standing against Penton from time to time. Not in true rebellion, of course, but rather for tax relief or trading rights or some other political maneuvering that Fenrir didn't understand. But mostly, it had seemed like it was business as usual.

"Indeed. The little duke had begun showing signs of aggression, but on a scale likely not noticeable to the average Rostanian." Maybe Fenrir wasn't completely oblivious. "He was pushing for more support from the larger houses and doing it in unsavory ways. He was demanding higher taxes from those who did not pledge military and economic support to the duchy, and threatening to pull others from power by various means. It was all done very sensitively, through agents, using implications rather than demands. However, for those of us who understand politicking, it was very clear what was happening."

"And yet, you put yourself into his power?" asked Fenrir, finishing his rubdown of the horses, then grabbing oats from the wagon bed. Escamilla followed him, carrying the feedbags.

"Ah, my great mistake. While we knew that the little duke was hungry for power, there were no indications that he would resort to outright abduction. Bribes and threats, I can handle. There is little that the duke can do to me. However, when several ironclad guards escorted me and Emma to an interior room of the Plateau, I had little recourse. I was able to reach Tennyson through covert channels, and he sent me my hero."

"Why do you care whether the duke takes over Ardia? Why wouldn't you just work with him?" Fenrir dumped the oats into the feedbags and strapped the things to the elongated faces of the horses. Years of military training taught a man to take care of his horses. Though he rarely rode, he was not unfamiliar with these duties.

"The economy! War certainly stimulates certain portions of the economy. Metalworking, butchery, food production, prostitution, they would all boom. But, what do you think would happen to sales of my silk clothing in Draston? Or my oysters out of Enowl? Granted, armies do drink a great deal of ale and cider, so my apple orchards might remain productive. Assuming that they were not stripped by a foraging army. And, if I bowed to the little duke, I

294

would be little more than a puppet. A united Ardia, under Penton, would come at too great a cost."

"The economy, eh? So it comes down to money. Interesting how the Lady Escamilla seems to value money just as much as certain elicit criminal organizations, and—"

"My Lady Escamilla," shouted Tilner, rushing toward them, his sword slapping noisily against his leg. "There is an issue. It appears that this was not just a kitchen fire—there is a pile of... human remains... in what was once the common room."

"How many?" asked Escamilla, showing little emotion.

"It is difficult to say. My apologies. It looks like the bodies were drenched in some sort of fuel, rendered nearly unrecognizable. Flesh was... melded... with clothing and bone. And, the ceiling partially collapsed atop them. Maybe twenty? Thirty?" His voice was shaking. The gruesome sight had apparently taken its toll.

Escamilla, however, was all business. "Was there sign of violent death?"

"Too hard to say. The only other noteworthy detail is that we were not the first people to investigate the inn. There were other footprints in the ash."

"We will need to divest ourselves of this location immediately. It is possible that others have reported this incident to the duchy. I need not remind you all that we are not precisely in the clear."

"Yes, my lady. Havert! Saddle up! Let's cover some more ground this evening. Brockmore is a long way away, yet."

Chapter 21

The scene was one of pure and utter chaos.

The crowds were overwhelming, with most men milling about with no obvious direction in mind. Groups clung together smack in the middle of the thruway, speaking in loud, excited voices, and the crowd was forced to part around them, much like a stream running over and around rocks. Unlike with many a stream, however, this flow of people was going nowhere fast. And yesterday's torrential rain didn't help. The usually hard-packed ground was little more than muck, sticking to shoes and boots and coating people, from the waist down, in brown goo. A rickshaw, appearing to be full of provisions, was stuck in the mud, causing further confusion as no one stopped to help. Here and there, commanding voices rang out for order, but these were largely ignored.

Such was the state of the staging grounds wedged behind the Plateau in Little Town. Hafgan found that he didn't need to exert as much effort as others to pick his way through the mess, at least. His stature, hairy face, and slightly elongated fingers were signal enough for the multitudes to give him room. Some manifested their biases against Wasmer by simply stepping back. Others took a more active approach.

"Look, a fucking fuzz-face!"

"Go back under the mountains with the rest of the ugly goats!" Another insult he'd heard, but one that Hafgan had never quite understood. Wasmer did not, in the slightest, resemble goats. And goats lived *on* mountains, but not *in* mountains. Probably just some weak human logic.

"What's slime like dat doin' 'ere? We don't want none o' dem in da army." This from a toothless old farmer, far past his prime.

Hafgan was used to these insults. He'd heard them often enough that it was just the normal way of things. He simply pulled down his broad-brimmed hat to both shield his face from the light and shield the crowd from his face. Again, he should have shaved, but what was the point?

Just two days ago, Duke Penton had issued a decree. All registered citizens, men of fighting age, must report to the staging grounds over a period of six days. Men not of fighting age, but who had the experience or desire to engage in the glory of war, were also encouraged to attend. Based on occupation, physical fitness, and—most obviously—wealth, the citizens would be assigned to a military squad, pressed into service supporting the military, or simply allowed to buy their way out. The wealthy could also buy a commission as an officer, to lead men into glorious battle from the safety of the various command tents. This was simply for the sake of vanity. Hafgan had learned that these golden officers, as they were called, had little real say in the military tactics of the Rostanian military force; at least, this had been the case during the border skirmishes with the Wasmer.

In the meantime, though the purposes of the large-scale conscription was generally unknown, the city was cordoned off. There was no unauthorized entry or exit. Some traders were allowed in, but not out. This was to be a temporary measure until muster was completed, according to the criers. The military likely hoped to outrun the news of the inevitable aggression against Florens.

Hafgan had reported this news to Tennyson days ago, along with the rest of his reconnaissance, immediately after overhearing the duke. Regarding Morgyn working with *Recherche Oletta*, Tennyson had simply replied that they must trust the Bull, Fenrir de Trenton, to protect Escamilla. What man wouldn't be able to repel an assault by a girl who couldn't be more than fourteen years of age? Besides, The House had no manpower to spare in sending a warning. They were all committed elsewhere. Thanks to their recent efforts, several of the smaller noble houses were back in the fold, again paying for protection, and several agents of *Recherche Oletta* had been eliminated in a rather brutal fashion. Their… colorful… remains had been left in very public places.

Tennyson was much more concerned about the conspicuous relationship between *Recherche Oletta* and the little duke. It was obvious, now, where the funding for this group had come from, as well as how they'd had the resources to shield themselves from The House for so long. They must have been working a long-term operation, planning to make themselves known all at once, when the little duke had been ready to move. There was still much that was obscured about the partnership between the duke and *Recherche Oletta*, and the motivations behind this group. Not to mention that woman who had been involved in the meeting with Penton and this Patriarch. But other members of The House were focused on reconnaissance. Hafgan had his own task.

Finally now, he had pushed to the front of the crowd, reaching one of several tables set up in the far square. Despite the crowds, and though these desks were the ultimate goal, lines were short or nonexistent. Perhaps the excitement of being part of the crowd was overcome by the actual fear of enlisting. Regardless, Hafgan approached a balding, piggy-eyed man who was sitting behind one desk and mopping his brow. The sun had baked his scalp a nice, bright red, and the man was none too happy as a result. Or maybe it was just his wretched personality.

"We's got ourselves another goddamned fuzz-face," he muttered, barely glancing at Hafgan. Hafgan stood for a long minute, attempting a respectful politeness. Those in the human military did so enjoy abject respect, particularly from civilians.

"Sir," Hafgan said, growing irritated at being ignored.

"Oh, it kin fucking talk, kin it?" His piggy eyes squinted at Hafgan, showing obvious disdain.

"*It* can indeed talk," said Hafgan, focusing on each word to ensure proper construction. At least one of them would speak the Ardian correctly.

"You're one of dem wit' shaved teeth, eh? Can't stand bein' a goat, eh? Well, you ain't a human, that's clear as good liquor. Godsdamned wannabe."

Hafgan ground his filed teeth together. It wasn't that he was unused to this kind of blatant racial attack. It happened most days that he left his boarding house. It was more that this man was one of those sub-classes of humans, of the type that couldn't even speak the language correctly or treat others with common courtesy. Hafgan had little respect for humans like this. However, he followed cultural protocol and didn't respond to the man's obvious baiting. He had an assignment, after all. And, it was finally an assignment that would utilize his particular set of skills.

He ignored the man's insulting question, and instead retaliated with grammar. "Sir, I am here to enlist in the military." Diction was probably too subtle a jab for the sub-human to comprehend, but no matter.

The man turned his head, sucked snot into his mouth, and spat loudly onto the ground. This was an insult in any culture, and Hafgan had to actively work to restrain himself, his hands longing to grasp the spear strapped to his back and introduce this man to the sharp end.

"I ain't allowed to turn you away, Duke's orders. Kin you write?" asked the man with disdain, sliding a paper forward. Hafgan glanced at it—a standard enlistment agreement. Enlist for one year, payment chits supplied once every two months, desertion punishable by death. The typical military rhetoric. Hafgan signed the document with a false name; it wasn't as if anyone would check.

The man fumbled around with some files, apparently able to read and write. Surprising. With a smirk, he handed Hafgan a square ticket that was covered with a series of numbers.

"We'd got a special unit just for you goats, even you wannabes. Report immediately to camp outside of the west gate." The man stood, and Hafgan noticed that his leg was missing from the knee down, replaced with a hollow iron peg. Again, he gathered snot and spat at Hafgan's feet. Hafgan clenched his fists and bared his fangless-teeth at the man, who stumbled backwards at the sight. Without another glance, Hafgan turned and stalked toward the west gate.

Since leaving the mountains, Hafgan had never seen so many Wasmer gathered in the same place. A makeshift military camp had sprung up outside of the west gate, complete with lean-tos, cookfires, an improvised blacksmith, and an awful smell that was either the cooking or the latrines. There were few humans amidst the dozens, if not hundreds, of Wasmer, and those who were present were shouting out orders, or reluctantly going about their tasks with their heads bowed. Hafgan imagined that working with Wasmer was a duty used to punish soldiers or to haze new recruits. Such did the Rostanians see his race.

Based on how the Rostanian military had historically been run, Hafgan known that the Wasmer would be built into a separate unit from the rest of the military, a unit that operated largely independently, following Wasmer rules and traditions. The separation ultimately made his job easier.

The Wasmer milling about were just as disparate as the humans in Rostane, although most of these humans would never take the time to notice the differences in terms of appearance, interests, talents, and intellectance. Humans had this tendency to see anything different from themselves as a uniform stereotypes with little variation. Hafgan wondered if he'd himself suffered from this shortcoming back before he began living in Rostane. Almost certainly, though, he had since learned his lesson. The Wasmer who he saw in the camp seemed to represent a wide range of trades and skill sets. He saw one, a hulking, hairy brute, working the bellows at the blacksmith, while another short and slender Wasmer poured iron into arrowhead molds. Two Wasmer were arguing in their native, sing-song tongue about Ardian politics. And, nearby, a large ring had formed and two Wasmer were wrestling.

One wrestler was older—the long, braided hair on both his head and his face was mostly gray, although he'd likely been fair-haired to begin with. He was tall and sinewy, moving like a man much younger. And indeed, across from him *was* a man who was much younger. A pup, really. But, a really large pup, rippling with heavy musculature, a blistering scar across his bare, hairless chest. Unlike what most humans believed, Wasmer were just as likely to have, or not have, body hair as the standard Rostanian male. Just another assumption.

The pair circled each other, arms raised defensively, careful not to cross their feet and risk losing their balance. Each fighter made the occasional feint, but the slow circling continued for quite some time, creating a build-up of excitement within the crowd. Just as the crowd began to grumble, the young one lunged, his arms reaching for the gray-haired's leg and simultaneously trying to hook the other leg. A standard wrestling move, and one that the gray-haired one was prepared for. He gave a quick side-step, slapping aside the young one's extended arms and forcing him to stand upright by locking his own arms against the young one's chest. The pup wrapped his much bulkier arms over his opponent's shoulders and the two stood straining against each other. At a casual glance, it was an odd embrace, perhaps a son ecstatic to see his father. But, a trained eye could see the minute changes in stance and pressure; one would push hard to the left, and the other would respond by slightly lowering the hip and pulling on the right side. This stalemate lasted for a time, but the smaller, more experienced man had both inside control as well as leverage. He suddenly dropped his hips, and pulled on one side with all of his strength, flinging the off-balance pup to the ground and landing on him, the gray-haired one's hands forced against his opponent's neck. The young one went limp in submission and the crowd cheered as he stood, offering a hand to the fallen fighter. The pup took the hand, grinning as he stood. There was little shame in losing to a master.

This would be as good a place as any to start. It might even be *the* place to start, judging from the look of things.

After the crowd cleared some, Hafgan approached the elder warrior with a half smile, hands spread in the traditional greeting of the Wasmer. The man began to return the greeting, smile creasing his braided face, but then abruptly stopped. He folded his arms, veins visible across his wiry muscles.

He spat at the ground in front of Hafgan's feet, and his smile altered into a dual-fanged scowl. A lot of spitting, today.

"I do not need a *budredda* in my presence," he snarled, the musical language of the Wasmer flowing from between his clenched teeth. The phrase "budredda" was a new word added to the language—a crippling insult derived from the word "scum" or "filth," but specifically referencing human pretenders. As Hafgan was, made evident by his filed down fangs, and the fact that he responded in Ardian.

No need to be polite anymore, then.

"I imagine it be embarrassing to be in the presence of a better." Not ideal, but clear enough that this Wasmer would understand the insult. Noticing the man's clenched fists, Hafgan knew he had hit the mark. It didn't take much, with fighting caste Wasmer, to get a rise.

"You little shit, daring to insult me. Why are you here? Don't you have enough humans to fuck you in the ass?" he said in Wasmer, stepping forward. The crowd began to re-form around the two of them, other Wasmer stopping their work upon hearing the insult.

"It be me who does the fucking, and I be here to do the same with you…" he reached back and patted his spear, "…with this."

The bravado and insults were relatively standard among Wasmer warriors, but this gray-hair had some real venom in his look and manner. The military culture among his birth people was one of the reasons that Hafgan had left, truth be told. The constant challenges, maneuvering for rank, and infighting. Not that he'd had much of a choice about leaving.

"Weapons it is," called the gray, lithe warrior, pandering to the crowd, who let out a ragged cheer. "I will not be chastised for murder, however, by those we fight with. They shall be blunt."

At a glance, a youth from the crowd rushed over to the blacksmith, procuring two spears without the iron heads— essentially quarterstaves. He gave one to each warrior, first to the gray-hair with deference, then tossing the second at Hafgan's feet with some contempt. To the youth's chagrin, Hafgan caught it perfectly balanced on his boot, flipping it into the air and catching it with little effort.

"I am Siarl Llywelyn, warleader of Wasmer at this camp."

Perfect. Hafgan couldn't have been luckier, stumbling into this wrestling match.

"I like to know the name of the men I defeat, even if they are half-men. *Budredda.*" Siarl hefted the wood over his shoulder, not bothering to check for weight and balance. Such confidence.

"I be... am Hafgan Iwan. You want rest before we are beginning? I not want you to use fatigue as excuse for losing," Hafgan continued, somewhat poorly, in Ardian. He wanted no question about the outcome of this contest, and he wanted to appear unshakable, though internally his guts were roiling. It had been some time since his last challenge, and he loathed these contests.

"I need no rest to set another budredda aside. Easier than cleaning the latrine." Siarl gave a smug laugh at his own joke. "Give us some room."

A great number of Wasmer had gathered by now, perhaps hearing that their warleader was set to fight a budredda with weapons—always a sight. By definition, the warleader was expected to be the most skilled warrior, and rarely did such a challenge arise. The massing crowd was good, though; Hafgan needed as many as possible to see this.

Without any fanfare, the battle began. Siarl took up a fighting stance and began to move to the side while Hafgan just stood still, holding his stave in two hands out in front. Siarl did not wait for Hafgan to prepare as was proper, but instead launched an attack, darting forward with a great sideswipe of the stave, giving him an incredible range and a great deal of leverage. There was a great "crack!" and the crowd visibly flinched at the impact.

Hafgan had shifted, driving his own stave into the ground, solidly catching the blow. Siarl recoiled from the unexpected resistance, but rallied quickly. He used the momentum from the recoil to spin around, facial braids streaking behind him, this time striking low. Hafgan had little difficulty leaping over this predictable attack and then ducking under the follow-up. Siarl stepped back, leveling Hafgan an appraising look, perhaps with some grudging respect in his eyes. Hafgan spat on the ground—it was his turn for a show of contempt—and Siarl leapt forward with a fierce series of attacks.

Had any one of the blows landed, Hafgan would at least have had a broken bone or shattered skull. This was nearly as dangerous as fighting with sharpened weapons. But he found his center, attaining *heddwichen*, the meditative emptiness learned in his *Dyn Doethas* apprenticeship, and pushed down the uncomfortable feeling in his stomach. Though leading in the military might be based on skill with weapons, some—like himself—were given advantages early in life. Siarl, despite his general prowess, had not been trained by the *Dyn Doethas* and was outmatched by Hafgan, though not by as much as Hafgan had expected. Siarl was no mean fighter, his attacks showing adaptation and creativity. And he had not given himself completely over to the rage that Hafgan had tried to ignite.

Hafgan continued to block and dodge, dancing around the circle, occasionally digging his stave into the ground to propel himself forward or upward. Siarl had not slowed, however, and was coming closer to landing a powerful blow that could quickly end the fight. No mean fighter, indeed. Hafgan needed to end this in a hurry, though the feeling of desperation barely breached his *heddwichen*. It was more of a gentle decision, flowing into his mind like a cool, shifting breeze.

He shifted from his defensive stance to one of offense. He began striking back with an apparent fury, his stave moving in a blur as it cracked again and again against Siarl's own weapon. The two continued to exchange blows amidst a circle of onlookers, with Siarl fighting defensively now, having fewer opportunities to riposte. In the back of Hafgan's subconscious, he was aware that there was now a hush over the previously-rowdy audience. The sound of staves slapping together, coupled with heavy breathing and grunts of exertion, was all that could be heard. Hafgan pressed his brief advantage with everything he had, sacrificing protection for a more furious attack.

The fighters flung themselves together, each swinging with force. There was an audible snapping as both fighters simultaneously landed a blow. Hafgan felt his opponent's stave smash into his ribs, bruising or breaking at least one bone, but needing to have made such a sacrifice in order to strike Siarl with the force necessary to disarm him. His own stave broke Siarl's wrist, the man's stave flying into the crowd, end over end. With a grunt, Siarl fell to one knee, grasping his injury. Hafgan stepped forward, teeth clenched in pain, and rested the end of his stave lightly against his opponent's neck.

What most fighters didn't understand was that it was easier to kill than disarm.

Siarl met his eyes, his own gaze filled with anger, pain, and contempt. Hafgan thought, for a moment, that the man would refuse to yield, and he braced himself to fend off another attack. But, the man ultimately lowered his eyes, giving a slight bow of his head in acquiescence.

Hafgan had made a bitter enemy. Truth be told, he had likely made an enemy of many Wasmer in the audience—Siarl was obviously well-respected, and the shock in the faces of the crowd was rapidly being replaced with anger, silence replaced with bitter murmurs. However, he had accomplished his goal, albeit with one additional broken bone than intended. He surveyed the people massed around him.

"What is all this? What's going on?" demanded a loud voice. A *human* voice.

An unarmored man forced his way into the circle, flanked by four armored Wolf Knights who glared at the Wasmer as he passed. He was wearing a wolf emblem above his heart—this indicating a captain's rank in the military—and his clothes were very fine. And he was incredibly thin, but not in the manner of a lithe warrior; rather, he seemed bereft of useful muscle. He barely filled out his clothing; in fact, the scabbarded sword at his side looking almost ludicrously large. Likely a golden officer, if anything. The only other defining feature of the man was his slightly crooked nose, indicating that he had actually been in a fight at some point.

"Why are none of you working? Do you not know that we are preparing for war?" The man gestured angrily, seemingly amazed that few Wasmer gave him much heed. He looked around and finally noticed Siarl kneeling in front of Hafgan.

"In-fighting among soldiers is *not* allowed in the Rostanian military. *We*, at least, are better than animals." A very brave, or very stupid, man, to less-than-subtly insult a race when completely surrounded. Granted, many of the surrounding Wasmer likely didn't speak Adrian well enough to understand the affront, but the man's imperious tone was clear. "If we had the time, I would have you both lashed. There is to be no more of this. Do you hear me?" He turned in a slow circle, surveying the Wasmer. "Who is in charge of this rabble?"

There was a long tense silence, and Siarl let out a growl mixed with a moan as he regained his feet. He twitched his neck toward Hafgan then and stalked off past the crowd, men shrinking from his anger. Hafgan should have felt some pride at defeating the tested warrior, but instead felt only guilt and regret. That was always the way of it. Even when it wasn't a farce, like his involvement in this army. Regardless, he stepped forward, nodding to the crooked-nosed man.

"I be… am warleader here. These men answer to me." His meditative state had faded and his damaged rib felt like a dagger in his side, digging deeper with each breath. But he was unwilling to reveal the pain, even if he did want to curl up on the ground.

The man gave Hafgan, who was at least a head taller than himself, an appraising glance, sniffing loudly from his crooked nose.

"I have the misfortune of being your commanding officer. Captain Sigmund Fitra. Given your rank as… *warleader*… you

307

are awarded the loose equivalent of lieutenant. Congratulations," he said. Even with his limited understanding of the intricacies of the language, Hafgan could hear the sarcasm. Nonetheless, Rostanian military personnel had to be managed with respect if this gambit was to succeed.

"Yes, Captain. Thank you, sir," he said. Elevated from civilian to military lieutenant in just a day. Quite the accomplishment. It was amazing that a second desperate plan by The House was actually coming to fruition.

"What was your name, Wasmer?"

"Hafgan Arkon, sir." Was that the pseudonym he'd used when enlisting? It really didn't matter.

"Well, Arkon... you are to attend me at a staff meeting tomorrow at sundown in the main camp. You'll be..." he regarded the dispersing crowd with some disgust, "...my mouthpiece to this rabble. I trust you can handle this?" He pointed at Hafgan's chest with a gloved hand, revealing a surprising characteristic— the man was four-fingered, a victim of The House. Hafgan wondered briefly how that had come about.

"Yes, sir. I am having military training. That is, I have military training."

"Uh huh." Sigmund was already turning, having no interest in Hafgan's credentials. "Sundown, Arkon."

Chapter 22

Brockmore. A sprawling estate with gently rolling hills that bloomed with pink, white, and red roses. Partially a productive winery, its grape vines produced some of the sweetest fruit in three countries, which was sold at a premium to a relatively limited few who could afford it. It was a great manor house—an architectural marvel—rivaling that of many noble lords and ladies, though this land had originally been developed by merchants. Altogether, one of the loveliest places in Ardia.

Now, it was an armed camp.

As Emma and her traveling companions arrived at the outskirts of Brockmore, she was amazed at the transformation of the estate. Or, the decimation was more like it. The rolling hills were now covered in canvas tents arranged in some relative order, but the order itself had come at the cost of uprooting many of the gorgeous rosebushes, and the emerald, grassy hills had been transformed into beaten-down and browning wisps of turf interlaced with paths trod bare by heavy feet. A perimeter, miles long, was being dug, men swearing and shouting as their blistered hands shoveled the earth aside, this immediately being formed into a barrier just beyond the obstacle. The road, usually made of hard-packed clay, was now a sticky muck sucking at the wheels of their cart. And, everywhere, armed men were roaming about, doing whatever it was that soldiers did. Shouting orders, rattling swords at one another, boasting, and so on.

"What is happening here, Emma?" Lady Escamilla asked, her eyes straight ahead. Given that the road was choked with wagons and soldiers, the two were strolling next to the wagon in the grass, where it was slightly less muddy.

"You are worried about retaliation from Penton, so you have mobilized your forces, stripping your other holdings of soldiers," answered Emma, guessing this was the purpose behind all of the pigeons. "You plan to dig in here while you wait to see whether his army comes after us." The plan seemed reasonable to Emma. The ditch looked to indicate that Escamilla's forces were preparing for invasion, and they had passed a heavily manned wooden barricade on the road a half mile back.

"How many soldiers do I have here and how did I gather them?"

Emma had nary an idea of how to count this many men. She took in the tents, stretching in neat rows beyond her immediate field of vision. She examined the massed groups of soldiers who were cramped in the lanes, as well as the formations maneuvering in the distance. It was overwhelming, and she had no idea.

"Perhaps five thousand?"

"Very good!" Escamilla sounded surprised.

Lucky guess!

"Now, how did I gather five thousand men?"

Easy. "You sent pigeons out immediately after we escaped from Rostane."

"My holdings, estates, and interests are spread all across the four duchies. Issuing orders, moving and arming men, preparing this land for their arrival... This takes more than the couple of weeks that we have been traveling from Rostane." Now, Escamilla eyed Emma, the older woman's mouth twisted in disappointment.

"You knew that it might come to arms some time ago." Emma had attempted to sound decisive, but her comment had sounded more like a question.

"Indeed. I increased my standing defensive staff at Brockmore months ago, when the little duke began acting with more aggression. The first message you sent out, when we became imprisoned weeks ago, was to mobilize my other forces. Many of my holdings are now operating with a skeleton crew, with those men ordered to flee in the event of any sort of encroachment and to alert me here at Brockmore."

Emma was impressed, as always, by Escamilla's foresight. The woman seemed to be prescient. "I would imagine that you invested heavily in military rations of late, Camilla." Emma flashed a quick smile.

"Now you are starting to think like me." Escamilla's own mouth twitched slightly upward, an increasingly rare sight these days. Emma felt a brief surge of joy at the sight.

The small retinue—Emma, Escamilla, Fenrir, Havert, and Tilner Pick—were finally approaching the great manor house. Surrounded by a squat wall, covered in deep-green ivy, the three-story structure rose before them. At each corner stood a graceful tower containing a decorative brass bell. Emma recalled from her visit here, years before, that the four bells chimed with different tones and that, after quite a bit of practice, the servants could play surprisingly melodious songs. The second-story windows were stained glass, and told the story of Yetra. A person could circle the building and see the entire saga, from Yetra's conception by her mercantile parents and the destruction of her city to her defeat of Ultner and his consignment to Pandemonium. All while the pagan gods stood by without interfering.

It was a foolish, magic-ridden story. Essentially a fairy tale that had somehow launched the largest religion in the continent. A religion wrought with political gambits, scheming, and bigotry.

Though she loved the (formerly) beautiful grounds of the estate, the heavily religious theme of Brockmore Manor certainly didn't suit Emma, and didn't seem to be consistent with Escamilla's own religion of choice: the almighty power of Escamilla. Nonetheless, for some reason, she'd done little to renovate or strip the manor of its religious overtones.

Emma sighed. *And, she keeps Ignatius Pender around.*

"Greetings, my dearest Lady Escamilla Breen—home at long last after your great trials and tribulations, rivaling those of the Yetra, herself!" The chaplain had limped out of the great double doors, carefully descending the handful of stairs. His orange robes, overlaid with a green stole that was topped by his balding, grayish-brown pate made him look like an overgrown pumpkin. Emma worked to not curl her lip at the sight of him. The man *never* stopped preaching, and was the very embodiment of hypocrisy.

"Greetings, Ignatius. It has, indeed, been a trying time," offered Escamilla with a brief nod, ever courteous.

"*The Book of Amorum* states, 'When fog surrounds you, and all is obscured in darkness, faith shall sustain you.' Faith, Lady Escamilla, is the cornerstone of all our lives. Without faith, what is life but a series of meaningless gestures?"

"What is life, indeed?" muttered Fenrir, failing to meet the chaplain's eyes. Another glare from Tilner. When Emma wasn't making Fenrir's life as difficult as possible, Tilner was acting in that capacity. Emma appreciated the reinforcement.

"Chaplain." Tilner bowed respectfully, as deeply as if the man had at least been a duke, if not a king. "If you would excuse us, our lady has traveled a long way and is in need of comfort."

"Not to mention a bath," jested Escamilla without any real mirth. Emma agreed on that count. Though she had cleansed herself of blood and ancient dust, she was used to cleaning herself daily with a bucket and sponge, with the occasional luxury of a bath with Escamilla's blessing. By this point in their journey, she was feeling more than a little... ripe.

"Of course, my dearest lady. I would never stand between you and succor after your ordeals. However, if I might, I would speak

with you about the massing of these mighty forces set before us."
He gestured, grandly, to the busy, despoiled lands in front of him.

"Later, Ignatius. I promise. There is too much to discuss."
Escamilla had put him off with grace, though Emma was certain
that the old windbag simply wanted to proselytize about love and
Harmony, without fully understanding the plight that Escamilla—
and Ardia—was in. The man had no concept of "aggressor." If
he'd had his way, all these men would have lain down their arms
and been slaughtered already.

Emma never understood why Escamilla allowed Ignatius to
retain his place in Brockmore at all, even allowing him to join her
retinue to The Plateau on occasion. It had been years ago when
Escamilla had acquired Brockmore. It had been the titular Armus
Brockmore—an aging merchant king—who'd sought to sell his
lands instead of allowing his atheistic and amoral son, Peyton
Brockmore, to inherit them upon his death. Escamilla had showed
immediate interest, purchasing the land even though she'd had to
sell off some of her own assets to afford it. Armus was allowed to
stay in the manor until his death, and the deal had been that
Ignatius would retain his own post throughout that time. Given the
choice, Emma would have sent the man packing the day that
Armus' heart had stopped. Ignatius was ever questioning and
meddling in Escamilla's affairs, not to mention constantly quoting
that damned *Book*. And yet, here he remained.

Just as the group moved toward the door, there was a clatter of
hooves behind them, a man shouting at his horse. An exhausted
messenger—wearing the gold livery of Florens, resplendent with
a river otter under a layer of dust and muck—dismounted and
stumbled toward them.

"I need to see Lady Escamilla. Is the lady present?" His eyes
were drawn to Emma, perhaps expecting her to be the lady. It was
almost flattering, except that she would never have wanted that
kind of burden. She valued her red curls too much to see them go

gray before their time. Anyhow, being a serving girl with a dead mother and an unknown rapist for a father, she lacked the pedigree.

With a tired sigh, Escamilla stepped forward. Her age clung to her more than ever, covered as she was in the dust of the road and still wearing a simple shift, a bandage wrapped around her arm. The bite wounds, though it had been a couple of weeks, were slow in healing. Fenrir had said something about the filth that lived in each of their mouths. Emma bet Fenrir's own oral cavity was dirtier than average.

"I am Lady Escamilla. Word from his grace, Eric Malless, I take it?"

"Yes, my lady."

"Tilner, summon my war council." She said, steely-eyed.

"But, my lady, you should rest—"

"I don't recall asking your opinion," she cut him off.

"Yes, my lady."

'War council' may have been a bit too grand a term for the disparate group arrayed before Lady Escamilla, at least by Emma's estimation. There was, of course, Tilner Pick, his mustaches freshly waxed, staring darkly at any man whose eyes lingered on Escamilla for too long. Guy Empton, the de facto general of the gathered forces, towered over all in the room, his height masking the fact that there was a growing bald spot right on the top of his relatively young head. The five captains—Ezram, Braston, Quentin, Perod, and Garen—Emma could not tell apart. Each was a grizzled, middle-aged, long-haired, slightly-greasy military sort. And, all five had beards.

The sixth captain was more distinct, as she had strikingly brilliant silver hair tied into two complex braids. And also in that she was a *she*. Trina Almark, known as the Silver Lady, was the captain of Ultner's Fist, a mercenary detachment of a few hundred fighting women. The group was infamous across Ardia and beyond, partially because of its success and partially because of the novelty of seeing women who'd been trained to fight. Many men had scoffed at Ultner's Fist only to be handily spanked, or the very bloody equivalent.

Also in the room was the chaplain, Ignatius Pender, reclining in the corner and somehow managing to look both supremely pious and supremely smug. Fenrir stood against the wall nearby, muscular arms folded, stubble on his pale scalp beginning to show, sipping heavily from a flask he'd found somewhere. There were several others Emma didn't recognize, including a young, heavyset man who was maybe twenty years of age and sporting a recently broken nose. Finally, there was the messenger from Florens, still wearing the dust of the road, though he had washed his face and hands. Underneath the dirt, he was a boy, only fifteen or sixteen, and much too young to be trusted with such an important task. And, perhaps, he hadn't been trusted with it at all.

"...and they overtook the six of us in the evening after a long chase. Our leader, Sir Evan Reband, was separated from us, being knocked from his horse early on, his fate unknown. The rest of us scattered... Has anyone else arrived yet? Sir Lewis, or my fath... Sir Reband?" The boy had a hopeful, moist look in his eye—a puppy hoping to avoid a beating.

"Not as of this evening... What's your name, soldier?" asked General Empton.

"Jeffers Reband. I'm not yet a soldier." A heavy silence followed, somehow seeming at odds with the cheerfully colorful

315

light that bathed the great meeting chamber, filtered as it was through the stained glass. After years of peace in Ardia, it seemed there was to be civil war among the duchies. And perhaps the first casualty was this poor boy's own father, this Sir Evan Reband. Emma felt a dampness building in her own eyes, and felt glad that she was obscured, standing behind Escamilla.

It was the chaplain who broke the silence. "My son, 'strife befalls us all. A weak man lets it define him, while a strong man lets it expand him.' In the coming days…" Ignatius, turned, taking in each of them, "…young Jeffers' story will become all too familiar. Children, separated from their fathers. Children, sent to war. Life must be preserved at all costs, no matter what must be sacrificed. Our pride is nothing compared to the value of life, the value of our children's futures."

"And what would you have us give up aside from pride, chaplain?" This from one of the captains, who had a slightly bushier beard than the others. "Should we give up our very freedom so that the powerful can grow even more powerful?" There were grunts of assent from the council, as well as several dark looks from those who likely held the chaplain—and Yetra— in high regard. Tilner was one of those casting such looks, as was one of the captains. Perod, maybe?

"Peace, Braston," said Ignatius. So, Braston had the bushier beard. That should help Emma identify him. "War need not always be the answer. We have not yet bandied words with Duke Penton. For it is said that 'the most noble of wars shed not a drop of blood, and—'"

"You think *words* will make a difference? Penton tortured, cutting and burning, a brave man. Baron Erlins. Penton forced Lord Malless to suicide after beheading his cousin. And Penton thought to kill Lady Escamilla! There shall be no peace!" Emma was surprised to find that hers was the angry voice filling the echoic chamber, echoing discordantly off the cold stones. Even

316

more astonishing was that she had stalked toward Ignatius, and that he had shrunk back from her fury.

"This is not the place for four-fingered *servants* to have a voice. Get the fuck out of here and mind your betters!" Before anyone else could react, Captain Perod—if that was his name— had strode the few steps to Emma and roughly grabbed her arm, his gloved fingers digging into the meat of her forearm. Gods, he was strong!

"Stop this!" shouted Escamilla, stomping her foot, her expensive, amarillo silk dress stirring around her. The man didn't listen, and continued to drag a struggling Emma toward the decorative iron doors.

Suddenly, she found herself freed, so abruptly that she nearly tumbled backwards. Regaining her balance, she saw the most unusual sight, as Fenrir stood over the toppled Perod, the latter of whom was struggling to his feet while holding a hand to his face.

"Stop this immediately!" demanded Escamilla in her most imperious tone. Perod reached his feet, breathing heavily for a moment before lunging at Fenrir, fists swinging.

The man was a fighter, Emma could see immediately. He connected two solid punches to Fenrir's gut, and one partially-deflected punch to the cheek. Fenrir, however, was a big man, and did not go down. Rather, he absorbed another punch to the head in order to grab the man's face and drive it into his upward-propelled knee, crushing the man's nose. In a smooth motion, Fenrir lowered his leg then and swung it directly between Perod's legs, quickly ending the fight as the man again collapsed to the carpet-covered stone, dripping blood onto the expensive, decorative rug.

Those gathered in the colorful chamber were stunned, perhaps unable to believe that such violence had been committed within the presence of the war council. Ignatius' jaw was hanging open while Tilner's fists were clenched in rage. Emma, herself, was rubbing her arm where Perod's fingers had dug into her flesh. She met Fenrir's eyes—glossy and detached though they were—and, for a second, it was five years ago. It was just a second, though, before Emma came back to the present, suddenly becoming acutely aware of her mangled appendage. Shaking her head furiously, she stalked back to her place beside a livid Escamilla.

"This is completely unacceptable! Perod, you are stripped of your commission." The man rolled to his side, continuing to groan, one hand on his face and the other between his legs. "It is I who shall dictate who is, and is not, to be present in this council. It is I who shall make the decisions here. It is I who shall provide the yets to help protect our nation. Do not forget who has been providing you and your families with a comfortable living and safety all these years. Now, you are all called to return the favor. Not for me, but for Ardia." Her eyes were gleaming fiercely, teeth bared and shining with saliva. Her short speech was greeted with an embarrassed stillness, though Fenrir seemed unaffected, disconnected from the rest.

Tilner was also unmoved by the lady's speech. "What about this man?" Tilner gestured hotly at Fenrir. "You dismiss Perod, your loyal captain, a man you have known and trusted for ten years. Meanwhile, this… degenerate… stands among us, close to your person. He should be removed immediately!"

"Care to try your luck?" growled Fenrir, a fierce, detached look still about him. He took a step forward and Emma heart pounded, feeling real fear for Tilner. In that moment, Fenrir looked like a true killer.

"Enough!" Escamilla's voice fell like an avalanche. This time, even Fenrir seemed to take note, his eyes coming more focused and looking somewhat abashed. Tilner certainly appeared chastened. "Tilner Pick, you have no more right to dictate who is in this room than Perod, and you are not immune to being dismissed."

Tilner glared at Fenrir, askance, but returned to his seat. "Apologies, my lady. I would never think to question your decisions." Though his thoughts were clear to everyone in this room.

"Now, if we are done preaching..." She began, meeting Ignatius' eyes, who did not look away, "...or fighting like animals, I would like to hear the news that brought this young man before us."

"Thank you, my lady," said Jeffers uncomfortably. His eyes darted from Fenrir to Tilner to Perod, who was pulling himself to a chair, still in obvious pain and with his bloodied face dripping onto his shirt. One of the other captains was tending to him, wiping his face and whispering something. The two left the room, Perod supported by his former peer.

"My fath... Sir Evan Reband was tasked with delivering this message from Lord Erik Malless, Duke of Florens. We were made to memorize the message, lest we be captured and a letter be stolen." He cleared his throat and began reciting a message in a well-rehearsed tone. "Lady Escamilla, I am pleased that you have returned safely." Malless must have sent these messengers within a couple of days of receiving Escamilla's pigeon-borne note, and Jeffers, at least, must have ridden hard. "As we had expected, Penton has crossed the border into Florens with his advance forces, and several large towns, including Ferne, have already been sacked. Our military forces are scattered around the duchy, currently regrouping in Florens. I have word from our mutual friends in Rostane that a large scale conscription is underway, and thousands have been conscripted or volunteered. We will need reinforcement immediately, as the full force of the Rostanian military will be at our bridges in scant weeks, while the forward forces work to cut Florens off from the outside. Of course, we shall continue to meet their forces in battle wherever possible, but cannot match them. We have reached out to allies in Jecusta, and hope for assistance from there, as well. For now, send your forces as we agreed. We will continue to be in communication to develop strategy. We shall avenge my father and protect Ardia together. Yours, Lord Duke Erik Malless."

Jeffers deflated after his speech, nodding to Escamilla before collapsing into a hard wooden chair, putting his head in his hands. Emma felt an unusual need to comfort the boy, but her feet stayed planted. This wasn't the time or place for comfort. She glanced back at Fenrir, who had resumed his easy lean against the wall, arms folded, his eyes focused on the stones in front of him. Taking another pull from that damnable silver flask.

"This is consistent with our own intelligence," offered Guy Empton. "We were aware that the advance forces had moved across the border." Nice contribution from the general. Emma resisted rolling her eyes.

"Indeed, General," the younger man with the broken nose wheezed. "Our intelligence also shows that the conscriptions have yielded nearly twenty thousand, in addition to the fourteen thousand military regulars. If they mobilize this full force, they would number thirty-four thousand and still have approximately six thousand troops, as well as citizen reserves, in Rostane."

The number of troops was a physical pressure in the room. Rostane was the military power in Ardia. There had never been any doubt of that. However, thirty-four thousand soldiers, marching on Florens... After seeing the five or six thousand troops amassed in Brockmore, Emma could not even imagine the sight of that number. Escamilla's forces had seemed strong at first sight, had brought her hope, but now her stomach was a sour pit.

"We cannot march yet," said one of the captains. "Many of our forces have not yet arrived. By our estimates, we are still waiting on approximately two thousand, two hundred soldiers."

"Agreed. There is little that we can do against such numbers, even with our full forces." Another one of the captains—the bushy-bearded Braston.

After a moment, while the gathered officers continued to digest the unwelcome news, Trina Almark, the Silver Lady, spoke for the first time, her voice much hoarser than Emma would have expected based on her delicate, feminine features. A goddess of war with the voice of a man.

"I do not know your experience with war and battle…" she said with a sneer, her full lips curled upwards, "…but towns have been *sacked*. Penton did not stroll into these villages, politely requesting that any defenders lay down their arms and that civilians relinquish their possessions. No, men were slaughtered in a one-sided battle. Tortured, disemboweled, dismembered, and so on. Women and even children were raped and killed and discarded like trash. I have seen many towns sacked by armies anxious to fight, worked into a frenzy. Delaying our involvement, like cowards, will accomplish nothing other than allowing the bodies to pile up."

"What would you have us do? Add to the pile of the dead by throwing a much smaller force against such numbers?" demanded Tilner, his voice still carrying some of the heat from earlier.

"I would expect you to act like *men* and protect your country, " she spat, literally. Several of the officers, including Tilner, took clear offense and surged to their feet, shouting at the brash female mercenary.

"Enough of this! Do I need an entire new command staff?" Escamilla was nearly shaking with rage. "All of you will sit down. Now! Or you *will* be removed from this council!"

Everyone complied, save for Fenrir, who kept his place by the wall. He hadn't moved in response to the Silver Lady's taunts, and Escamilla didn't point him out. Emma would have enjoyed seeing him tossed from the room, but it was not to be.

"Now, if we can have a civil discussion… Danby, what of Fraunt and Proan?"

The young man with the broken nose must have been Danby. "When we received word of your imprisonment, I sent pigeons and runners in your name to Fraunt and Proan, as well as to many of the lesser nobles across the duchies. Fraunt outright refused to speak with us."

"Not surprising, as Penton has her son," said Escamilla, rubbing her eyes. Her anger appeared to have spent her dwindling supply of energy.

"Indeed. We were able to make contact with Proan, who offered funds but no men. Several of the lesser nobles offered conscripts once there is evidence of aggression. We sent more runners out yesterday. I expect we can raise another fifteen hundred men in the next week. With our estimates of Florens' own strength, we would still be outmanned by approximately two-and-a-half to one."

"What of the armies of Florens?" asked Escamilla.

"They have approximately eight thousand soldiers, though a third of that would be conscripts. More would likely rise to defend the city. Combining our forces with theirs would yield close to two to one odds."

"Bah. Most of the enemy is just untrained rabble," scoffed Trina, tossing her silver braids.

"We aren't exactly well-trained ourselves," mumbled one of the captains. Quentin, unless Emma missed her guess.

"Big talk gets us nothing," said Braston, leaning forward, eyes on the Silver Lady. "This isn't a tavern story, here. Historically, the bigger force tends to win the day. Peasants and farmers can be taught to drive spears and lances into the ground, enough to stop a cavalry charge. Even if they break, which is likely, the charge will be halted. Peasants and farmers often have some skill with a bow, too, and anyone can aim a bow forty-five degrees into the air and release. Supported by professionally trained soldiers, a smaller force would be consumed."

"There have been many cases where that was not true." Surprisingly, Ignatius filled the silence left by Braston's hopeless words. "There are cases in *The Book* where men, armed with their faith, prevailed against more powerful forces."

"Aye, we are aware of those stories. But, Yetranian though *most* of us are, we all recognize that *The Book* occasionally embellishes to teach important lessons. I apologize, Chaplain," Braston added, with a measure of respect.

"No need to apologize, my brother. I have studied the great *Book* all of my life, and I know, probably more than anyone, that embellishments are present. But also that many of the stories are based in historical fact, and several of those are well-documented facts corroborated with other sources. The Battle of Tiernum, for instance, where Amorum the Martyr led the forces of good himself. Several historical writings have shown that they were outnumbered by thousands. Tens of thousands. And yet they prevailed." Ignatius spread his arms.

"Even so, they were defending Tiernum, supposedly a great, walled city, fortified against all manners of assault. Our forces... we've no choice but to go on the offensive. And when, Ignatius, did you start supporting the thought of war?" General Empton brows furrowed, perhaps not trusting this sudden change of heart within the chaplain. Emma certainly didn't.

"I will never support war, or the loss of hundreds and thousands of lives. But, if we must fight, which it sounds like we must..." Ignatius glanced at Escamilla, who nodded. "...then I would prefer that we win." He'd finished with a grin. Emma

323

noticed that her mouth was hanging open at his words. She shook her head; the world seemed upside down.

"What would you recommend, Ignatius?" asked Escamilla, gesturing absently for Emma to fill her wine glass. Emma complied, falling right back into the role of handmaiden.

"The key factor in these battles was faith. Men of faith fight harder, even against difficult odds. Especially against difficult odds." His eyes were shining, but his voice remained calm.

"Ignatius, most of our men are Yetranian, but so are the men of the Rostanian army." Escamilla sipped at her wine.

"Aye, but we must instill within our men a great faith and passion. I ask for your permission to begin teaching the men what they truly fight for, that we are Yetra's chosen. That Penton has broken the sacred laws spoken by Yetra, documented in *The Book of Amorum*. I have several Taneos who would be excellent for this task. Men of passion, themselves."

To Emma, this sounded like the start of a holy war. Religious zealots leading men into battle. And in the histories, that never worked out particularly well.

"Ignatius, this is a dangerous path. As you know, men with too much *passion* can become as dangerous to those who lead them as to those who oppose them," said Escamilla, echoing Emma's thoughts as she leaned backward and placed her fingers in a steeple. "I would not mind some proselytizing, but do not overdo things. I will not have my men become fanatics."

"One can never believe too much. But, I shall practice moderation, my lady." Ignatius inclined his head. General Empton cleared his throat.

"With respect, even with such… faith… our forces are still outmatched by a significant number, and these soldiers are not used to fighting in formations."

"Yes, we need additional forces in order to have any chance," said one of captains in a subservient tone. Ezram, maybe.

Escamilla glanced at Danby, who was staring at his stomach and rubbing it gently. Apparently paying no attention to the proceedings. Indigestion?

"Danby!" she said, sharply.

He startled, but kept one hand on his generous gut. "Yes, my lady?"

"You mentioned earlier to me, some options for more soldiers?"

"Well, yes. There is really only one option, to be true." He attempted to hold back a small, wet belch. "In Hunesa. A large mercenary company called Ferl's Company, newly returned from campaign season in Sestra. They fluctuate, but may number approximately two thousand and–"

"Those fuckers are not fit to lick our assholes. Ferl is untrustworthy scum!" spat the Silver Lady, sloshing her own wine as she slammed down her mug.

"Perhaps the same could be said of all mercenaries. Trust can never truly be purchased, as one never knows when a bigger purse might come along." Tilner obviously had little rapport with the beautiful, hoarse-voiced mercenary captain, his mustaches quivering as he glowered at her.

"Tilner. I have an assignment for you." Escamilla stood, her tone imperious. "You are to ride to Hunesa at first light, tomorrow, and secure funds from Proan to hire this Ferl's Company for the coming engagement."

"My lady…" he stammered, rising to his feet as well, but with his mouth gaping like a fish.

"And, given that you do not trust soldiers of fortune, you will be accompanied by one yourself. Fenrir, you will be leading negotiations with this Ferl."

Fenrir's drooping eyelids suddenly flickered open, the big man as astonished as Tilner. Tilner, meanwhile, was somewhere between broken and furious.

"Lady Escamilla, my orders were to stay close to you and protect you. Though the company would be pleasing..." He nodded to Tilner with a twisted smirk. "...I believe it is in your best interests to keep me nearby."

"Do you believe that you can protect me better than the thousands of armed men camped outside? With your dented sword and your limp? Besides, my agreement with our... mutual acquaintance... was that you will be following my orders. And, this *I order*. Besides, would I not be even safer with two thousand more soldiers?"

Fenrir smirked, but instead of insolent, it came across as charming.

"I suppose I cannot argue with your impeccable logic, my lady. At first light."

Chapter 23

"...and fucking bread! Why can't we get enough fucking bread?" demanded General Lucius, his doughy walrus cheeks jiggling as he bristled with anger.

"It takes weeks, months, to plan for and supply a campaign, my lord! You have given me two weeks! Two weeks to find food and provisions for thousands of men, not to mention transportation for such provisions. And, arming these men, as well? This is an impossible task," argued Quartermaster Polk, his voice very nearly reaching a state of outright pleading.

It was not the first discussion of bread since Hafgan had begun attending these meetings a couple of days ago. Upon his arrival at that first meeting at sundown, Captain Fitra had relegated Hafgan to a corner, which perfectly suited his purposes. To become a common sight, an ornament in a room where people forgot that you were even present: that was the goal of anyone seeking to gather information, and usually a challenge for a six and a half foot tall, hairy-faced Wasmer. But, thanks to his unexpectedly successful and rapid rise through the ranks, that was exactly what had happened.

The Wasmer were an advanced race in so many ways. They studied astrology, and understood the tides and fluctuations in weather. All castes were taught to read and write from a young age, as well as how to both listen and orate. They had even discovered ways to utilize mountain icecaps to proxy the running water systems seen in advanced human cities. At least the mountain-dwelling Wasmer in the Tulanques had done so. However, in all things related to war, they were still so very primitive.

Leadership was for the powerful. The fastest, the most skilled, and the strongest Wasmer became warleaders, with leadership changing on a frequent basis depending on the outcomes of challenges. Challengers were allowed to vie for power at any time, although the warleader could also refuse any challenge. Refuse too many, however, and one might be seen as weak and risk getting deposed anyhow—usually in a less savory way. These contests were only allowed during times of peace, so many warleaders, and particularly those who got lucky in battle, forced battles among other Wasmer clans, or even the humans. Over the past thirty years, there had been a number of border incursions into Ardia, with Wasmer raiding mountain towns and villages in the Rostanian duchy, as well as some of the vassal counties and baronies, under the guise of a border dispute. The loss of life in an already sparsely-populated race had caused many of the Wasmer clans to rethink this ancient tradition, but in a roundabout way.

Most clans were ostensibly guided (and actually ruled) by the *Dyn Doethas,* groups of so-called wise men and women who were most typically priests and leaders of faith. Before Hafgan had been born, just after the border battles with Rostane had started, Taern Llegyn, a wise man of his own clan—*Carreg Da,* Black Stones—had concocted a rather ingenious plan.

Just like humans, the Wasmer were resistant to change. The warlike members of the tribe, generally the lower castes, would never abide by following a lesser warrior into battle, no matter how strategic and intelligent that leader could be. Intellect was not a prerequisite of the job, but strength and individual battle acumen were. Taern posited that such warriors could be created, trained by the *Dyn Doethas* to be both ideal warriors and excellent scholars. They would be trained in all styles of battle and the practice of numberless weapons. They would be trained in war and strategy, studying historical works related to these topics, both written by human and Wasmer. They would learn of faith, of the many gods of the Wasmer people, of the parables and the stories that formed the framework for their society.

With this training, the *Haearn Doethas*, as they were to be called, would guide the people's proverbial hearts, heads, *and* hammers. That was after they challenged and handily defeated the current warleaders, taking their place as the visible leaders of the clan.

All of this with oversight from the *Dyn Doethas,* of course, who would continue pull the strings.

Hafgan had been among the first drafted into this experimental program within the *Carreg Da,* along with several other boys of his age. Each boy had been offered by their parents in return for wealth—the shiny gems used as money among the Wasmer. Under the harsh tutelage of the *Dyn Doethas* and Taern, Hafgan had learned all manner of things, including how to fight the standard Wasmer warleader, who tended to be fast, strong, and predictable. It had been Hafgan's plan, not Tennyson's, for the Hafgan to infiltrate the Rostanian army by rising in the ranks of the Wasmer unit through challenging their warleader. Although, Hafgan had to admit that Siarl was more skilled than he'd expected. Or perhaps Hafgan's four years in Rostane had made him soft.

Hafgan was brought back into the present by the shouting officers, still arguing about bread. As a *Haearn Doethas,* Hafgan also learned the intricacies of provisioning an army, and he agreed with Quartermaster Polk: the situation was nearly impossible.

"You dare raise you voice to me, Polk?" General Amos Lucius sputtered, obviously unused to such treatment. "I could have you lashed!"

There came a universal sigh in the room. Lucius had threated to lash nearly every one of the twenty or so officers in the huge command pavilion, but his well-known fury was only matched by his well-known lack of action. Only during peacetime could a man like this rise to the rank of general in a military.

"Sir, Polk has a point." Captain Ressig stepped forward, his eyepatch setting him apart from all other members of the group,

329

as he had fought, hand-to-hand, in an actual engagement. Word was that he'd lost his eye to a Wasmer spear during a border incursion. Nonetheless, he was one of the few who bothered acknowledging Hafgan, with his manner even bordering on polite. Odd.

"We still know very little about the war we are about to fight. Where is the battle to be fought? Who is our opponent? Who are our allies? Speculation is everywhere and morale is dropping. We cannot train our men appropriately, or lead them adequately, with no information." A competent man. Which was why several of the other officers, golden officers who'd bought their positions, were giving Ressig familiar, contemptuous looks.

"Ressig, with all due respect..." There was no respect in Captain Jeret's tone. "...our men are trained for any eventuality. Rostane is *the* major military power in Ardia. Morale will not be a concern once we point our men in the direction of the enemy. They are just anxious for the fighting to begin."

"Jeret, I don't think—" Ressig began.

"Enough of this bickering!" shouted Lucius, pounding his fists on the table. "As I have said, the direction of this possible engagement is yet a highly-guarded secret, relegated to only the highest circles of the military."

"Sir, we are officers, and need—" Ressig was again cut off.

"Sounds like a spirited, constructive discussion, my lords." Two Knights of the Wolf, the personal guard of Duke Penton, had pushed open the flaps to the spacious command tent and entered, followed by three figures.

The speaker was Savant Iolen. Hafgan had never met the Scholar before, having been invited to the Plateau none too frequently. But, he had heard of the man and his tendency to earn the ire of the nobles. His cynical, mocking tone and his simple clothing matched the description, not to mention his deep, arresting eyes. Accompanying Iolen was Lord Evron Faris, advisor to Duke Penton, his long, silvery black hair flapping in his face as he pushed his way out of the wind and into the shelter of the tent.

The third figure was unknown to Hafgan. A woman, and a beautiful woman at that, with lovely, pale features and raven-black hair tied in a tight bun. She was clothed in all black, with a dark veil pulled back to reveal her reddened, puffy eyes. She was apparently in mourning.

"Lord Faris," said Lucius, standing and giving a quick bow to his superior. The hierarchy of Rostane nobility and military was confusing, with power changing hands as often as a letter being sent to Jecusta. However, Hafgan understood that Faris, given his success in strategizing during the border incursions with the Wasmer, had been made field marshal for this particular engagement.

Faris nodded respectfully to the general, taking a moment to straighten his hair and clothing. Iolen, on the other hand, strode forward and rested his hands on the general's desk, leaning over him like a bird of prey.

"How go preparations, my dear General Lucius?" he asked, hinting heavily that he knew exactly how preparations were going.

"I need not answer to you, Iolen, regarding anything. In fact, remove this man from my tent!" the general snapped with venom. He rose to his feet rather ponderously, his paunchy belly pushing his desk forward so that his chair fell backward. Two golden officers gladly sprung forward, no doubt having been insulted by Iolen in the past.

"Oh, I wouldn't be so quick to make such commands, General Lucius," said Iolen, stepping back with no apparent fear.

331

"Indeed, Lucius," Faris interjected. "The duke has promoted Savant Iolen to a military position as High Strategist. His knowledge of all things military is immense, and strategy will be the key to triumphing in the coming battles."

"This… this…pissant…" the general launched visible flecks of spittle, "…is to be part of my retinue? Absolutely not!"

"No, my dear general. I shall not be part of your retinue. I shall be your superior in all things military." The Savant had turned his back to the general, spreading his arms as if to encompass the entire tent into his embrace.

"What? Absolutely not! I will resign my commission, I will—"

"General, our grace, Duke Penton, was prepared for this response. He has instructed that your contract does not allow for your resignation without imprisonment. You must work with High Strategist Iolen, lest you be punished." Lord Faris was deferential in his tone, but was nonetheless as hard as steel. "Any attempt to countermand his orders will be met with the same chastisement."

The general, cheeks red and shaking with rage, clenched his fists and glared at Iolen's back. And he did not live up to his reputation—great anger and no action. He flung the table over, causing Iolen to stumble forward. He moved around the toppled table then, exhaling like an over-exerted plow horse. Hafgan tensed, ready for Lucius to lunge at Iolen, who had stepped back behind Faris. Faris, however, stood firm, crossing his arms—almost as if he was daring Lucius to try something. But, that was the end of the action.

"I would rather be confined than take orders from this… this… insolent little… fuck!" he puffed. Hafgan imagined that there must be bad blood between the two, but supposed he would never find out. Iolen sat poorly with many of those in authority, but he possessed the favor of the duke.

"Indeed. Well, then, let it be so. Please escort General Lucius to the holding cell," said Faris, gesturing to one of the Knights of the Wolf.

A stunned silence persisted while the general was removed, with the officers, particularly the golden officers, appearing amazed that one of their own could fall so far so quickly, and right in front of their eyes at that. The resulting fear was visible to Hafgan from his corner, though he was no more than mildly anxious. Quartermaster Polk was wiping his damp, balding brow. Captain Fitra was fidgeting with the stump of his finger, hidden beneath an obviously-custom glove. Captain Jeret's eyes were darting back and forth, as if he were looking for the most likely route for escape. But, no one moved until Iolen broke the tension.

"So! What do I have here? The brave warriors of Rostane. The men who have risen to the top through only persistence and true ability." The golden officers especially shifted at this comment. "The backbone of our great duchy, the reason that our enemies will quake before us. And... what's this? Which one doesn't belong? There is a Wasmer among us!" The Savant approached Hafgan, who stood to attention. "Mighty Wasmer, how do you find yourself among your former foes?"

"My lord, I never was fighting the humans," offered Hafgan. "Too young."

"Oh, and a rather excellent speaker! This one may give us the edge we need in the coming trials." Was that sarcasm or sincerity? This man was too subtle for Hafgan to tell. He would need to be vigilant around him, though. He'd been noticed.

"Enough, Iolen," said Lord Faris in his calm, commanding tone. "We now have an army without a general, and we will have to assess our options. But, the purpose of our visit was to inform you of our purpose and destination. I value your patience while making these preparations. And I know you appreciate the reasons for such secrecy." The officers nodded, their number including

Polk and Ressig, who had just been complaining about this very topic. Jaret's little mouth was pursed, a smug smile threatening to escape.

"Our destination is Florens." A small gasp spread through the room, the sound like water being spilled on hot coals. Faris waited a moment, letting the import of his words sink in.

"They are the aggressors in this case. We learned, recently, that men garbed in the livery of Florens sacked and burned Pafferton on the southern border. Since then, Duke Erik Malless has declared war upon our duchy, apparently over the suicide of his father. We have little choice but to bring the battle to Florens before they are able to bring their full military might to bear, as well as that of their allies." Hafgan knew, firsthand, that these were all lies. He wondered whether Iolen or Faris were also privy to the treachery, or if it was localized to Penton and his conspirators.

"Thank you, Lord Faris. Now, please, my noble officers. Listen to the words of this lady to give face to the enemy," said Iolen with a small, mocking bow.

The lady, until now all but forgotten in the midst of the startling news, moved to Iolen's side. Whereas he was all insult and sarcasm, this lady was all somber and shattered innocence.

"Gentlemen, my name is Baroness Farah Erlins, wife to Baron Theran Erlins. For those of you who are unaware, Pafferton falls within our barony, along the border with Florens. My husband…" Her voice broke. It was a heart-wrenching sound, like the last plaintive call of a dove. She seemed to visibly steel herself, though, and moved on. "My husband was taken by the Florensians. They sent a note to our estate, but not for ransom. Rather, they sent a note declaring war, along with…" she shuddered. "…his fingers. I have to presume that he is gone, lost to those bastards in Florens." The officers in the spacious command seemed to be enthralled by the baroness—certainly

334

moved by her beauty, if not her story. Even Hafgan, who had only occasionally found human women appealing, was watching her almost raptly.

Lady Erlins' demeanor changed. Her back went straight and her fine jaw set firmly, her eyes going cold as the frosty caps on the Tulanques. "Gentlemen, I beseech you. Bring the fight to these torturers and murderers. Raze their homes, and kill their wives and children, as they did ours. Make examples of their men with torture, as they did my husband. Rip their hearts out, as mine has been ripped out. Make them pay, if not for the citizens of Pafferton or my husband, then for me. If we do not respond in kind, all of Rostane is open to these unspeakable atrocities."

Hard words from a woman who had likely lived in luxury her entire life, making few decisions aside from which dress to wear. Stirring words, though. Looking around the command tent during her brief speech, Hafgan could see men's faces hardening, resolve burning in their eyes. One man, Captain Jeret, let out a tentative cheer, and several other voices joined the ragged, uncertain din. Hafgan found that he was, in fact, one of those raising their voices.

He was surprisingly engaged in this woman's plight, despite knowing that Pafferton had been burned by Rostanians, by whomever that beautiful-voiced woman was. And that Theran Erlins had been tortured by Duke Penton, apparently lost in the ruins beneath the Plateau—at least according to a brief pigeon-borne note from Lady Escamilla.

"Gentlemen, please take this lady's words to heart. Do not think of these men as fellow Ardians, as neighbors. They are murderers and rapists and would gladly do the same to your families. The only path to protecting our country is to destroy those who would see us destroyed," said Iolen in a uncharacteristically serious tone, meeting the eyes of each officer briefly, including Hafgan.

"Now, gentlemen, spread word among your men of our purpose, our destination. We march in three days." Lord Faris, with a final look, pushed back the tent flaps and left, with the Wolf Knight, Iolen, and Lady Erlins sweeping away behind him.

When he returned to his own camp, Hafgan gathered his small army of about four hundred Wasmer—a relatively ragtag bunch. While perhaps a hundred or so were from the warrior caste, like Siarl, the remainder were porters and laborers, skilled traders and merchants, pressed into service by the draft. He managed to line them into some semblance of even ranks and shared Lady Erlins' message of murder and battle, doing so in Ardian. He had practiced this speech during the hour or so's stroll back to camp, and he thought that he carried off the final version rather well, though he was unable to communicate the emotion of the grieving woman. Not that the Wasmer much cared about the plight of the country. The Wasmer warriors were simply anxious to fight, while the civilians would rather not have been there, regardless. A tale of tears did little to move the men of his small army.

Later, Hafgan found himself in his own small canvas command tent, attempting to wrap his head around balancing his roles as an informant for The House and also a lieutenant of this army. Now that he was in a position to learn intimate details about the movement of the army, he would likely experience a conflict of interest before long. Ultimately, Tennyson desired that the little duke was to be toppled from power. Would that involve orders for Hafgan to lead his army against the Rostanian army? It was unlikely that they would follow. Would he have to provide misinformation to his military superiors? They likely wouldn't listen to him anyhow. Or, was he to simply sacrifice himself in an assassination attempt? He likely wouldn't obey *that* order. His loyalty didn't run that deep.

There was a scratch at his tent flap, followed by a throat clearing. Hafgan hadn't expected any visitors, though had anyone meant him harm, they would have been unlikely enough to announce themselves.

"Enter," he said gruffly.

Two men pushed their way through the tent flaps, both of them Wasmer, instantly making the structure feel cramped. Both had their hair cut short, and one had recently shaved his face, appearing almost human. The men held their arms out, greeting Hafgan with single-fanged smiles. Like him, these men were budredda.

"Warleader." They both nodded respectfully, speaking Ardian.

"We are in the Rostanian army. Call me 'Lieutenant.'" The men grinned, likely appreciating the reference to human culture. Hafgan gave a smile, as well; it was rare that he could interact with those like him. Those who sought to blend in better with the humans. "What do you call yourselves?"

"I be called Paston, and he be called Derek," said the shaved-faced Wasmer. Very Ardian names. Something Hafgan had never been able to adopt—his name was too much of his identity.

"Welcome, Paston. Derek. What do you need from me?"

The two exchanged glances, with Paston looking somewhat abashed. "Honest, we wanted to speak with you. You be like us, and there be so few of us around."

"Yes, there are so few of us. I am glad to see friendly faces in the military." Hafgan was proud of himself for making it through multiple verb conjugations so smoothly. It wasn't a competition, but he was focused very closely, and was far superior in speaking

Ardian. It helped that he was relaxed. His speech was always much better when he wasn't under pressure.

"Indeed, Lieutenant. I need ask—where do you learn to fight like that?" This from Derek, who had a slight lisp as he spoke, sounding like his mouth was full of rice. "I never heard of someone defeating Siarl before. I thought it be impossible, but I be happy to see it." He had a hard look in his eyes, reflecting perhaps the abuse that he had experienced at the hands of the powerful, traditionalist Wasmer. Hafgan hadn't been aware of Siarl's reputation before their battle, but he had generally avoided his kind in Rostane. Warrior-caste Wasmer in human cities tended to lead to trouble.

"I learned to fight from the Wasmer, from the *Dyn Doethas*." Hafgan was brief on purpose. He had no desire to discuss his time with the Wasmer wise men, particularly not with these folk he knew nothing about.

Derek and Paston looked at each other askance, Paston scraping one foot against the opposite calf. The pair obviously wanted to know more or say more. Hafgan sighed. The men were likely timid after seeing his skill with the spear. It was a familiar occurrence, particularly among the Wasmer, where skill with weapons often equated to social status in the lower castes. Most often, weapons masters were surrounded by sycophants and cronies. It made for a lonely existence, lacking true friends or confidants and never knowing if those who attempted to learn from you would later challenge you.

Finally, Derek spoke. "Lieutenant, we wish to learn how to fight. Not those drills that the humans be running us through. The step, thrust, repeat. Step, thrust, repeat. We be wanting to learn to fight like you. Maybe not become masters, but be able to protect ourselves. From all enemies."

Hafgan raised his eyebrows. Now, this was a surprise. The only results of his skill with weapons had been the broken bones, inevitable ire, and occasional deaths of people for whom he bore no ill way. Among the Wasmer, there was never this earnest respect that he saw in the eyes of these two men. Paston and Derek must have felt a kinship with him, for no reason aside from the fact that they all had shaved-down fangs and tried to assimilate with human culture. People, regardless of race, always sought to fit in it seemed.

Hafgan idly wondered if insects or animals had such struggles. He supposed that they did. Rarely did the goat mingle with the bear.

"How many be…" Damn! A slip-up. He couldn't get too comfortable. "…are like us in the military—assimilated?" Hafgan asked.

"Maybe a couple of dozen? I be familiar with at least a few," offered Paston, glancing at Derek.

"I shall train all of you, all assimilated Wasmer. Gather them for special assignment, and be ready a half hour before sun-up, the field to the north, by the solitary oak. I shall teach you to fight." Hafgan was astonished at his own offer. It was unlike him to make a spur of the moment decision like this. Usually, his choices were based on information and knowledge, benefits carefully considered against the costs. Since he no longer had a people, he typically focused on how his decisions could help Hafgan Iwan, perhaps giving him some influence in the world, like he would have been destined to have among the Wasmer if his life had gone differently.

Helping these men was out of character for him.

But maybe his decision wasn't so altruistic. He reasoned that, based on the look Siarl had given him, and the reluctance with which his army followed his orders, it might be beneficial to surround himself with a trained fighting force loyal first to him. Yes, these Wasmer could be his personal bodyguard, devoted to him and trustworthy—perhaps even following him in the event that his orders from The House would put his life in true peril.

"Yes, Lieutenant!" The men were both beaming, excited children who'd gotten exactly the toy they wanted. Hafgan gave a grim smile in return. If he were to teach these men to fight in a short period of time, those mouths would soon be formed into grimaces of pain. Derek and Paston saluted smartly, in perfect Rostanian military form, and rushed out of the tent. Hafgan shook his head, both at himself and the two Wasmer, and then resumed his seat.

Almost immediately, another figure drifted into his tent like a fog, nearly silent and just as obfuscate. Tennyson entered, heavily cloaked despite the summer heat, lantern light glinting off his silver mask. Ultner's face seemed to leer at Hafgan.

"It appears you are making friends," said Tennyson, slumping easily into a seat. Hafgan didn't bother rising, himself, and didn't bother responding. He was not intimidated by Tennyson like so many others, and he took liberties that most of his associates would not dare. The two had a mutual respect, not unlike that between two lions, whereas most people held fear for Tennyson and contempt for Hafgan.

"Quiet, this evening, my Wasmer friend." Still nothing from Hafgan. Very few people, indeed, would be bold enough to refuse a response to this man. However, instead of becoming enraged, he snorted. "You are in a stubborn mood. Shake it off—I do not have much time here, and we've matters of import to discuss."

"It has been some difficult days," offered Hafgan. Exhausting days, first by earning his spot, and then by maintaining his deception amidst hostile Wasmer stares, and disregard, condescension, or outright hostility from the human soldiers. His position was precarious at best, and he was more than aware of the dangers.

340

"Indeed. I heard you fought quite the battle, toying with the Wasmer warleader and then dispatching him with hardly a facial hair askew. Impressive, as always."

It didn't feel impressive. He felt malicious, villainous. Siarl had been doing what he'd been raised—and encouraged and rewarded—to do. Be the fastest, the strongest, and fight better than everyone else, becoming the leader. Hafgan had defeated and humiliated him simply for the sake of a complex ruse. Little wonder that Siarl had been giving him spiteful, venomous glares while he cradled his broken wrist in a sling.

"I be doing what was necessary for this plan of yours, Tennyson."

"Plan of *yours,* my Wasmer friend. I wanted eyes and ears in the military, and you illuminated me on the intricacies of Wasmer military culture." It was true. "Now, what have you learned?"

"General Lucius be… imprisoned when he be… when he learned that Savant Iolen was to be the new High Strategist, his superior. No general at the moment. Baron Erlins' wife, Farah Erlins… Stirred the officers with an untrue tale of rape and murder by the Florens' military. It be seeming that she was duped, but I be… was uncertain if Savant Iolen and Lord Faris were aware of the little duke's deception." Hafgan was barely even trying to catch his mistakes. Too much pressure.

"Any indication of who the new general will be?" Tennyson leaned forward, elbows on his knees.

"No, Tennyson. General Krast be massed with the regulars at the Florens borders. He may be given control of the whole army, but I be hearing it be… is unlikely. Too many men. I am expecting that there will be a promotion from the ranks."

"Right. How many troops are being deployed?"

341

"The regulars at the border number around eight thousand." That had been a tricky bit of information to acquire. "The conscripts from the noble houses, the enlisters, and the local regulars be near twenty-six thousand, at my best guess. Many of these not be fit to fight, though they be training now."

"Fodder," mumbled the silver-masked leader of The House. "Keep your eyes and ears open. Troop movements, unit strengths, disposition of the officers. Anything that might be of use."

"What will you doing with this information?" asked Hafgan, expecting answer Tennyson offered.

"You cannot know, in case you are found out." An unlikely scenario. More likely, Hafgan would be pushed out of strategic meetings or deposed by his own command of Wasmer. "But know that we have allies. Though I would rather not see the destruction of the Rostanian military, a change in leadership is desired. We have some in mind who would be more sympathetic to our cause, and less so to *Recherche Oletta*."

"How be things in the city?" The camp seemed a world away instead of mere yards from the western gate.

"Unrest. The people are nervous, of course. War has that effect, particularly when so many are being conscripted. Rumors are tearing through the city about the war, the people fearing attack from Hunesa and Florens. There are darker rumors, too. A small town not more than thirty or forty miles east and south was destroyed under mysterious circumstances. I am certain that the little duke with blame Florens, though I expect that is quite false. Dunmore, it was called."

Dunmore. Hafgan had never heard of it. "What of The House?"

"We continue to meet strong resistance. Three more of our agents found dead, and one enforcer found fingerless. We have eliminated one agent of *Recherche Oletta* who attempted infiltration. It was… messy." Hafgan would rather not think about that. He did not approve of torture or the grisly, public displays put on by The House in this recent turf war. "We have not been able to locate this… Patriach… that you identified."

Tennyson twisted to his feet, displaying sudden, smooth movements similar to those of a serpent. "Enough for now. I must be going, but first: I need you to do some recruiting."

"Recruiting?" asked Hafgan, rising to his own feet with some grace.

"Indeed. We need more informants among the military. You need not tell them that you work for me. In fact, do not tell them under any circumstances. I'm certain you can be circumspect. They will report to you, and you will report to one of my agents, who will report to me. I, of course, will not be leaving the city again."

"Obviously. And how do I recruit?" Hafgan growled. How much dung did Tennyson plan on heaping upon him?

"Be imaginative. I don't have time to instruct you, but I need more information than you can provide. This should help." A heavy cloth bag dropped to the table with a metallic clink, followed by a second, smaller bag. Hafgan deftly unwound the drawstring of the latter to reveal a modest fortune of yets. Certainly more money that he had ever had held before.

"This is—"

"Plenty to get you started. Money is knowledge. Money is power. Money is loyalty. Of course, that is for you, Hafgan, and the larger bag is for incentivizing your agents. Don't get too excited—these are mostly smaller denominations."

So, Hafgan was now the holder of enough money to, say, purchase a butcher's shop. Or invest in a well-stocked trader's wagon. Or, perhaps simply purchase a big house in a decent part of Rostane, although he would be hard-pressed to find someone to sell a home to a Wasmer in those neighborhoods. His money was worth less than the money of the meanest subhuman. He had rarely considered his larger ambitions or goals here, in human society. Certainly, blending into the human society had been his primary goal. To be able to walk the lanes of Rostane, frequent the nicer establishments and try delicacies, and hold intelligent, rhythmic conversations with individuals who drove the fate of the nation. Without the venomous glares, half-baked insults, angry expulsions of saliva, and occasional threats. But, despite his herculean efforts to both alter his body and his language, fitting in with these humans seemed as likely as the Tulanques crumbling to dust.

What, then, was his goal? Was it to accumulate wealth, and if so, to what purpose? The richest Wasmer in Rostane was still a Wasmer, even if he was a fangless, smooth-faced, well-spoken Wasmer. And, he was budredda, so there was no place among his people—not that he could return to the *Carreg Da*.

"Tennyson, please hold on to this gold for now. Perhaps I will live to retrieve it from you, after all this be said and done."

The mask of Ultner gave him a long, unnerving stare, attempting to pierce the veil that was his mind. And Tennyson gave a shrug, the smaller bag disappearing under his cloak. Without a farewell, Tennyson flowed out of the tent as smoothly as he'd entered, pulling off his mask as he ducked out of the flaps. Hafgan darted around the table and glanced after the enigmatic man, curious to catch a glimpse of his face, but he was already lost in the darkness.

Chapter 24

First light was approaching, though the humid night felt heavy and untouched by time.

It seemed an eternity since Fenrir had last slept on a plush, down-stuffed mattress. At least, it felt that way, though it had really been little more than two weeks. Two weeks of dangerous exploits and, even worse, spending time with Emma, who ate away at his patience like a termite. And now, he could look forward to spending more time with a man who loathed him. Fenrir smiled at that one twist—at least he could displace his frustration with Emma onto Tilner, who was just so easy to bait. Escamilla's trusted retainer especially smarted at the fact that Fenrir and Escamilla had clearly been building some sort of rapport, which was maybe even bordering on a comradeship.

She wasn't a bad sort, for a noble. Perhaps because she hadn't been born into that caste. She'd pitched in with work on the road, helping with the horses (though clumsily), attempting to cook food (though tasteless), and even gathering firewood. Escamilla was willing to get her manicured hands dirty. She did have the tendency to try and delve into his past, but Fenrir had so far managed to neatly sidestep most of these questions. When push came to shove, he'd just bluntly refused to answer many of them.

Fenrir rolled about the lavish bed he enjoyed now, realizing that despite its initial comfort, it was becoming stifling. He kept sinking in too much, and his knee and shoulder were aching. His body was drenched in sweat.

This gods-cursed bed... could one drown in a cloud?

He rolled awkwardly to his feet, briefly stretching out his soreness. Or attempting to, anyway. He remembered the days of springing from a bed, feeling like a stack of shiny new yets. Granted, there'd often been a beautiful woman in such a bed and he'd been springing out to avoid an angry husband or lover. But the point was that he'd been able to spring nimbly, back in the day. Now… Well, there was significantly more creaking and flailing involved.

He limped to the door of his comfortable little room. A walk might calm him a bit and loosen his rusty joints, and then maybe he could hope for a crumb of sleep before jumping onto a horse in the morning. He'd have to be refreshed in order to bandy words with Tilner.

Brockmore Manor was an impressive building. Compared to the Plateau, which was obviously built for functional defense, the architects of this place had had beauty in mind. Even in the empty hallways, where he now found himself wandering, graceful arches rose from floor to ceiling, each displaying unique carvings of knights and warriors, Taneos, and heathens vying for power, or simply standing tall, noble and proud. Great heroes and dastardly villains. The walls were decorated with the odd banner or tapestry and the occasional ornate sword, axe, or lance. The weapons had no scratches or scuffs, appearing never to have been used. A collector, not a warrior, must have amassed these. Probably in an attempt to impress his neighbors or to look like a war hero.

Fenrir, himself, had expected to be given a hero's welcome at Brockmore, having defended its lady from a variety of dangers, risking his own life in doing so (even if the risk had been motivated by coin rather than chivalry). But instead, he'd been met with mistrust, disdain, and outright hostility. Tilner was insufferable, of course, and the other captains shot him sharp looks, with the one even having threatened him before the war council. On the positive side, he had gotten some revenge by braining that jackass, Perod. On the negative side, he had been in one of his weird, disconnected phantom states when it had happened, watching himself engage in the aforementioned braining without really getting to experience it. However, even disconnected, he had noticed that Emma gazed at him with unconcealed lust for a moment, lest he were mistaken. So, that was something.

The moons were high outside, visible from the third-story windows, pale light illuminating a still active, if ghostly, military camp. The tips of the tents appeared as teeth, ready to swallow up the hapless soldiers.

Strolling slowly, lost in thoughts of neglected heroism and weapons and women and teeth, Fenrir nearly jumped when a door opened just in front of him. Out walked—stumbled, really—the messenger boy from earlier, the one with the dead father. His hair was disheveled, and he was buttoning his shirt. At seeing Fenrir, he turned tomato red, color spreading to his chest and evident in the lamp light of the hallway.

"Er… um… Yes, sir," he mumbled, pushing past. Fenrir watched him go, perplexed, amused, and, if he'd admit it to himself, a little jealous of the boy's apparent activity. It had been a long time for Fenrir. Had it been that barmaid from Yetra's Embrace? If so, he barely remembered it, between the awful pain in his shoulder and his alcoholic coping mechanism.

"Ah, Sir Coldbreaker. Enjoying an evening walk?"

Fenrir pivoted upon hearing Escamilla's voice. She was standing in the still open doorway, wearing a shimmering white silk robe, her hands gently straightening and smoothing the fabric over her hips. Unlike her much (much!) younger partner, her hair was exactly in place, and she had no aura of embarrassment. In the lamplight, Escamilla appeared vibrantly youthful. He would never have guessed, at this moment, that she was in her sixties.

"Indeed. My room was stifling. Enjoying some evening fun yourself, my lady?" She merely smiled. "What is that boy— seventeen years old?"

"Fifteen, actually. You know, he is not even a soldier. He was just accompanying his father on his mission, playacting at a

347

military life. His father, a hero to the boy, now mostly likely dead to a Rostanian spear."

"His father was probably in his thirties." He did not know why he was suddenly a guardsman of morality. It seemed somehow… wrong… for Escamilla to have been using the boy, like this.

"Do I sense a tone of judgment? Are you saying that you have never lusted after a much younger woman? A teenager? Why, then, is it wrong for me to do the same? To help assuage the boy's grief with a small gift? Believe me, he will appreciate it this morning, when he might actually find a moment of sleep before the reality of his life crushes him once again," Escamilla said a little sadly.

Fenrir saw nothing sexual about Escamilla. He imagined that it would be like bedding a rock. A cold, competent rock. But, he could not argue with her logic.

It did seem a little pathetic, in some way, for such a woman to be lusting after a much younger man. But, what had he been doing for years? He wasn't exactly a spry youth anymore. Every joint in his body ached, especially his knee and his shoulder, and his beard was increasingly streaked with gray. Gods, from the perspective of others, he probably looked like a slightly younger version of Escamilla with her little soldier boy.

"You have the better of me. Please, continue with your carnal pursuits with my blessing."

"That means everything to me," she said, sardonically, crossing her arms. The pair stood for a couple of moments in a somewhat uncomfortable silence, the sounds of the camp echoing through the open windows.

"So… it is to be war," Fenrir commented, needing to break the silence.

"Yes, there is little choice. Florens will be lost if we do nothing." She frowned out into the night. Perhaps she saw the tent-teeth, as well. And, it wasn't too far of a stretch to say it was her gaping maw about to consume all of these soldiers.

"Chances are, Florens will be lost even if we do something, in addition to thousands more deaths," said Fenrir.

"Believe it or not, I have little desire to go to war. The impact of hiring all of these soldiers and mercenaries, in addition to reducing production in my various holdings, is taking quite a toll on my purse."

"Then why are you going to war?" Fenrir fell in beside Escamilla as she strolled down the decorative hallway. "You told me it was the ecomony, earlier, that you were worried about how war would affect your coffers. That was before I knew you were raising your own army. All this?" Fenrir gestured out the window. "This is inestimable more expensive than letting the little Duke fight his way through the four duchies. There is more to this story, my lady. Tell me, why do you fight?"

"You know the drill, Sir Coldbreaker. You think I haven't noticed that you are about thirty answers short of asking another question?" Escamilla looked at him askance.

Fenrir gave a sigh. He might have to offer something, after all, if he wanted more information.

"What do you want to know?" he asked, reluctantly.

"Why did you join The House?" A loaded question.

"After leaving the guard at the Plateau…" he began, but Escamilla give him a pointed look. He sighed again. "After losing my job at the Plateau, I had few prospects. I drank before, of course, back when I could afford it. Afterward, I burned through my savings on liquor and women, and couldn't hold a job." It was mostly the liquor that had cost him the work, though he'd never

349

likely admit it. "I was never good at much. I had no mind for my father's business and no desire for it, anyhow. Tennyson, he noticed me after a barroom brawl. I don't perfectly remember it, but I was told I threw a rich man through a window and broke the arm of a second."

"That was *how* you joined The House. But *why* did you join it?" Escamilla asked. A tough question.

"You know, I spent nearly twenty years guarding the Plateau, and I was content. I liked my life. I had good friends and good women and I was able to keep my father off my back. There was a solace in that life, the predictability and simplicity," Fenrir said contemplatively, almost forgetting that he was talking with Escamilla." When I lost all of that… It was hard. I suppose that I was looking for somewhere to belong, somewhere I could at least attempt to use the skills I'd gained from years and years of military training. And make some money for good drink."

"So, at least indirectly, I have bought you a drink," she said wryly.

"My lady, you have bought me several kegs worth of drink. I'm certain that my stomach will appreciate it."

Escamilla smiled weakly before pausing at a window, looking out at the rows of tents and the few men still moving about. The forges were still lit, and there was the telltale sound of hammers pounding metal. There was never rest for blacksmiths during wartime.

"My turn," said Fenrir, trying to take the focus away from his life and his mistakes. "*Why do you go to war?* Why do you hide the reasons for raising an army? A woman of your power and wealth could easily leave the country, seek asylum, live off of your amassed earnings in immense comfort. What motivation is there to risk losing everything?"

A pause. Escamilla turned to Fenrir.

"There is more to it than preserving my own wealth. Even more than preserving the country as it is." Her face was dark in the waning moonlight.

"There is some evidence that the Little Duke Penton has some assistance from a covert organization called *Recherche Oletta*. Seeking wisdom, in ancient Auqinen," said Escamilla.

"Not news to me."

"Of course not. You are a vault of information, a walking, talking Englightenment. But let's pretend like you know nothing for a moment. Can you manage that?" Fenrir could, indeed, manage ignorance. "*Recherche Oletta* appeared almost all at once in Rostane. They really became a spear in the side of our mutual friend, *as you know*. But, they also approached many nobles, me included." It might have been Fenrir's imagination, but it seemed that Escamilla shivered despite the thick heat of the evening.

"A man came to me when I was in Draston, tending to some business. He was… persistent. My guards, posted at every entrance to the small estate, saw no sign of him, but he was in my bedchamber one night. He made… threats."

"What did he say?" asked Fenrir, brows furrowed.

"The specifics are not important. But, I know that I cannot run. There was evidence that he had some sort of powers. Magic." Fenrir had never seen Escamilla appear so uncertain. He was shocked. Perhaps there was a breach in the walls of the great lady after all. Nonetheless…

"Superstitious nonsense. There is no magic." Fenrir thought, briefly, of that little Merigold chit from the burned down inn. The one who had touched him.

"My bedchamber, in my Draston estate, is resplendent with foliage. The ceiling is glass and the light shines down to support flowers, vines, and small trees. It *was* my favorite escape; you felt

351

like you were sleeping in a beautiful forest." Her eyes were far away. "As he spoke, the plants began to wither. 'Wither' isn't the right word, however. Some began to turn to ash before my eyes. The man appeared to… I guess *resonate* is the right word… he resonated with a restrained power. Like a bell humming with energy after it has been struck. And then he grabbed my arm, and I felt myself being pulled away. Emptying. And… pain. I can still feel it, inside of me, next to my heart. Always, as if I were somehow marked." This time, she definitely trembled, and Fenrir had the odd inclination to hold her. Perhaps this was why she filled her evenings with young boys—to scare away whatever might be stalking her in the night.

Her story reminded him, once more, of the girl from the burned down inn. Getting slammed in the skull and dumped in a ditch really overshadowed that entire evening, but he remembered her touching him, her blue eyes almost gleaming as she gazed past him, through him. And then, the same feeling Escamilla was describing. A feeling of hollowness, wrongness. He didn't recall feeling any accompanying pain or warmth, but Fenrir had been absolutely certain, in that moment, that the girl was stealing something from him. Had that been magic?

"So, you are fighting this war to..?" Her experience was plainly distressing, but it did not explain her motivation.

"I am fighting this war to protect myself. I am fighting because he gave me an ultimatum, and I do not take well to such choices, whatever the risk. I am fighting because I can still feel his magic, his wrongness, burning on my heart. I am fighting because men like that should not be guiding a nation. And, even if I could run, how long would it be before such a man desired more power? And at that point, with all of Ardia subjugated by him and his ilk, what's to say he wouldn't strike at Jecusta or Algania?" Her fists were clenched, and her weakness seemed to have disappeared. This was a hard woman.

"I see." Fenrir was uncertain how to respond. He had little desire to fight in a war, although it had admittedly been a rush battling in the ruins. That wasn't to say he would go searching for more folks to cross swords with, and particularly not if he were one of thousands, where his chances of survival depended more on luck than skill. Where he could be killed by a stray arrow, shoved forward onto the weapon of an enemy, or even accidentally skewered by the spear of an ally. Tavern stories always portrayed great battles as if they broke down, cleanly, into hundreds, or thousands, of individual duels—tiny islands of combat. However, his time listening to knowing lectures about the horrors of war while on guard duty told him otherwise. He had no desire to be stabbed, pierced, shot, trampled, burnt, crushed, or otherwise killed.

Escamilla resumed her measured stroll down the hall. "Now, Sir Coldbreaker. I have divulged a great deal to you this evening. I've one more question for you, and then we will be even. How… what's this?" She paused, and then approached a window. Squinting in the dim light, Fenrir thought he could make out a rope and grapple on the ledge…

"Camilla, get back!" he shouted as a shadowy figure peeled smoothly off from the larger shadows behind a beautifully-carved archway. Fenrir didn't hesitate for even a moment, launching himself forward toward the short figure while flinging Escamilla back with one arm. The figure stepped backward, shouting "no!" just as Fenrir crashed into him. Fenrir tumbled forward, somersaulting over his assailant, hitting far less resistance than he had expected. He landed on his back as something hit the side of his head. Groggy, he got to his feet just as a second blow connected with his shin. He grunted, unable to get a read on his attacker, a small man circling him, a sort of baton in his hand. With little recourse, being unarmed, Fenrir darted in close, his fist swinging. The attacker dodged Fenrir's first punch but caught his knee in the stomach. Using his far superior weight, Fenrir pulled the man to the ground, punching him in the face once. Twice.

"Stop!" He could dimly hear Escamilla's commanding voice. Three times.

"Stop now!"

Fenrir's arm was restrained as he drew back for another punch. He shook her from his grip but, as he moved back, he saw that the light illuminated Morgyn's bloodied face.

Chapter 25

"Tennyson sent me," wheezed Morgyn, her voice high and nasally as the air was forced through her damaged nose. One of her eyes was bloodshot and squinty, surrounding flesh already turning a sickening yellow that was emphasized by the candlelight in the room. Her lip was split, and the wound had a wet look to it. She lay in a bed—the same bed Fenrir had failed to sleep in—propped up with pillows as Escamilla dabbed at her wounds. Fenrir felt the dried blood on his own shin. No one was fussing over his injury, though he wasn't the one who'd been breaking and entering.

Morgyn's face and arms also had telltale signs of fading bruises. Funny, Fenrir hadn't remembered her getting hurt in those ruins.

"Why in the fuck would you come in through a window?" he asked, voicing his thoughts, which earned him a sharp look from Escamilla. He tried questioning the beaten girl in the hallway, but the commotion of their brief fight had drawn attention. Escamilla had waved other residents of Brockmore back to sleep, sent her reluctant guards back to their posts on the first floor, and spirited the girl back to Fenrir's room.

"They wouldn't let me past the barricade. Said I was a shifty-eyed urchin and that I had no reason to be near Brockmore." She coughed a couple of times.

"Can't say I blame them," Fenrir commented. She glared at him from beneath swollen eyelids.

"Young one…" Escamilla ignored Fenrir, "why did you come all this way? You must have left nearly immediately after us to have arrived so soon." The girl struggled to sit up, but Escamilla pushed her back, easing her to the mattress. "Rest, young one. Give me your message and then you can rest. We can talk more in the morning."

Morgyn paused, rubbing her face tenderly and then withdrawing her hands and examining them. She didn't look up. "Tennyson wanted me to tell you that Duke Penton is working with *Recherche Oletta*."

"We know. He sent agents to meet us just after we left Rostane."

"Yes, and..." Morgyn broke into another coughing fit, covering her mouth and bringing her knees to her chest. She was just a child, Fenrir recalled, a young teenager. How had he mistaken her for an assassin?

"Take your time." Escamilla was stroking Morgyn's hair.

"Yes, and... I... I also worked for *Recherche Oletta*." So, this scheming little chit *was* actually working for the two organizations. Not that it was a surprise to Fenrir; she had attempted to rob him in that filthy alley, all those months ago, even knowing his affiliation with The House. Tennyson had seemed to suspect her, as well, though he'd *still* put Fenrir's life in her hands.

"A dangerous game for one so young." Escamilla did not withdraw her hands, but Fenrir could see a twitch on her face as she clenched her teeth. She asked the only question worth asking. "Why?"

Morgyn's damaged face grew hard. "Do you know what it's like, living in poverty? Rashes from cast-off clothes that never seem to dry. Blisters in shoes that never fit, assuming you can even find a pair. Eating soggy scraps of food from the trash, hoping that it isn't covered in piss from vindictive tavern owners, who try to keep the untouchables from congregating. Drives away the business." Her face was flushed with anger around the bruises. "You wouldn't know, either of you. Both born lucky. Me? I was born to a whore who abandoned me as a cost of doing business." She wiped her now-bleeding lip on the clean, opalescent sheet.

356

"A hard life, young one." Escamilla's face was stone. Immovable. "But do not make assumptions of our backgrounds." Seemed like Morgyn had found an open wound.

"Huh," Morgyn grunted noncommittally. "Well, I wanted more than rags and shit. I started exploring the city, stealing whatever I could. I started leaving the city, exploring the ruins, finding and selling whatever I could find of value. A copper chip here, a silver shaving there, but nothing that improved my life or the life of... others with me. You find yourself in a great deal of debt, buying a crust of bread or a roof for the night. Or paying for *protection*." She coughed again. This was a very different Morgyn than Escamilla and Fenrir had met in the ruins. Gone was the talkative, eager girl. The enthusiasm and guilelessness must have been an act. Fenrir's throbbing shin could vouch for the girl's dearth of innocence.

"And, The House? *Recherche Oletta*?" Escamilla's arms were now crossed, her lips pulled into a tight, colorless line.

"Both found me. First, The House started 'training' me. They helped pay down my debts. *Recherche* contacted me some time later. Wasn't *Recherche* back then; I thought I was just making a bit of extra money, working for a few folks trying to make their mark on the city. And then, recently, a man took charge of the group, called himself the Patriarch. We started targeting The House. That's how I met my friend, there." She raised a tired hand toward Fenrir who glowered in response.

"That's all well and good, but why are you here now, girl?" growled Fenrir. Her story was getting a bit long-winded, and he still thought to catch a couple hours of sleep before leaving. Maybe there was a bench, somewhere, that would be more palatable than his now-occupied bed.

She cleared her throat, eyes shifting from Fenrir to Escamilla, again transforming into a little girl. "I... Do you see these bruises? The old ones? These were from the Patriach, for helping you escape." Her eyes were wet, reflecting the orange candlelight. "I am trapped, being crushed between two powers, Tennyson and the Patriarch. I can't deal with it." Openly weeping now. "I'm scared. I thought you might help me, Lady Escamilla. You seemed so kind. It's been… so long since someone was kind to me."

For a moment, Fenrir felt a twinge for this girl. She was a scared kid, over her head, much like Fenrir at that age. She had people who wanted to hurt her. Who had hurt her. Again, like a younger Fenrir (not to mention an older Fenrir). And, she was around the age his daughter would be, today.

Her wet, choking sobs filled the lavish guest room for several moments, and for the second time that evening, Fenrir was urged to comfort someone. He even took a reflexive step forward before catching himself with a small shake of his head. He glanced at Escamilla; she hadn't noticed his movement.

It was unclear if the older woman was moved by the girl's story, by her tears. The lady's face was impassive, her eyes clouded, her mind obviously somewhere else. Her arms were still crossed, and she almost appeared to be hugging herself. She shook her own head to clear away whatever was tearing at her, and gave Morgan's hand a quick squeeze before rising slowly to her feet.

"Young one." Escamilla moved toward the door, waving for Fenrir to follow. "Rest. We will talk about this tomorrow."

"Evidently, first light has arrived," sighed a drained Fenrir, standing outside the bedchamber of Lady Escamilla. Beyond the windows, the blue of the sky was becoming visible, cloudy

358

streaks slicing gray and orange across the heavens. Ornery sergeants were kicking reluctant soldiers out of their bedrolls, mobilizing them for the morning drills that Fenrir had so loathed in his youth. And a new group of fighters trudged down the muddy road toward the camp, dragging their feet as they marched out of formation. Obviously, they'd gotten as much sleep as Fenrir.

"Yes, you had best be off to Hunesa. Me, I plan on catching up on rest. It has been a trying few nights." Escamilla flashed a smile, though the black bags under her eyes, as well as the fact that the wall on which she was leaning was bearing nearly all of her weight, betrayed her true exhaustion. At least twenty years Fenrir's senior, still recovering from serious bite wounds, and coming off nearly two weeks of travel, he couldn't blame her.

"Yes, you had best rest," he said, sincerely.

"Sir Coldbreaker, please give Tilner a chance. He is simply protective of me and sees you as a threat. He is a good, honest, honorable man." Traits that tended to get men killed.

"Erm," Fenrir grunted, noncommittally. "While I am gone, take care around that Morgyn. She seems authentic, but I've learned not to trust so easily. There's more to her than "

Escamilla gestured to the windows, at the expansive land currently being trampled by an army. "We are currently standing in one of several of my manors, located all over the country, just a piece of all that I own. Tens of thousands draw pay from my coffers, and there are few within Ardia who do not know my name. Believe me, Coldbreaker. My assets and reputation were not built on trusting my competitors."

"Fair enough. Nonetheless, I am charged with your protection, and I'm certain Tennyson would not be forgiving—were you to end up batonned to death by a child."

"I will take care; perhaps even make a true ally out of the girl. I suppose I will have to start stationing guards outside of my chambers, though they might not like what they hear. Well… Put it out of your mind." She exhaled heavily. "Sir Coldbreaker, I want to thank you for all that you have done for me over the past weeks. I understand that you are being paid for this, but know that if you stay in my service, you will want for nothing. I can even grant you a command, if that would suit you."

Fenrir Coldbreaker, Captain of the Guard for Lady Escamilla Breen. One thousand fiercely loyal men, well-trained and well-mannered, aside from some occasional dicing and drinking—which Fenrir would overlook, particularly when he was involved. He had to admit, it was an interesting notion. But even as he considered Escamilla's generous offer, he knew he wouldn't be accepting it.

"I'm yours, for now, my lady. But only as long as Tennyson deems it so." In reality, Fenrir had been wondering how he could escape this situation entirely. Surely, Tennyson was distracted enough by the war that he'd not miss a recently-demoted enforcer who happened to get lucky in a rescue mission. Fenrir had already pilfered a bag of expensive ornaments from his guest room, as well as an obsidian dagger with a bejeweled handle to fence in Hunesa as some insurance. Tennyson hadn't paid him for the rescue job yet, and all of his coin was otherwise hidden. He had little trust for banks. His father—the man who provided the seed for his birth, rather—had lost a great deal of money when a reputable bank had turned out to have less repute than anyone had thought, and Fenrir had heard him rail against banks more times than he could count.

"If you change your mind…" She left the offer open. "In the meantime, is there anything I can offer to you in thanks? Anything within my power."

If not Captain Coldbreaker, maybe he could solve a problem that had been nagging his thoughts for weeks, and particularly now that things had slowed down.

"It seems that you have an extensive network of spies..."

"I wouldn't call them 'spies.' Information gatherers, let's say." The corner of Escamilla's life twitched.

"Whatever you like, my lady. But, something recently happened to me. An attempt on my life." He tugged at the collar of his shirt, revealing the ropy, pink band of raised flesh that ran across his shoulders. Even with the excellent suturing of Martis and his subsequent medical care, it was a scar that would never fade in any sense of the word.

"Ah, a papercut. I did not realize you were a scribe." Escamilla chuckled at her own joke. She certainly needed a nap.

"A large, pointy piece of paper, driven into my shoulder by a man wearing black. I want to know who. Not who tried to kill me, but who arranged it."

"Not much to work with, Sir Coldbreaker. But, I will have my *information gatherers* listen for your name. Danby will interview you about the details before you embark for Hunesa. Of course, it may take some time."

"Well, luckily, I am with you for the foreseeable future." Assuming a better option didn't come along. "I wish you a pleasant rest, my lady. I had best join the proud Tilner Pick on our noble journey to enlist a band of utterly trustworthy mercenaries to bolster our already-powerful forces."

"May Yetra guide you."

Fenrir raised an eyebrow at the blessing, but Escamilla had already turned around and shut her door. Fenrir shrugged, sighed, and trudged wearily off toward the stables.

361

Chapter 26

The room was swirling—wood paneling, cheap furniture, and even cheaper artwork coalescing into a sickening, multi-colored blur. It was so hot, so very hot, and yet Merigold lay under the covers in a cold, beading sweat. All at once, though, the spinning became too much for her, and she lunged to the side of the bed, grabbing a chamber pot just as thick, acidic vomit forced itself out of her mouth. It was like pushing a burning candle through her throbbing throat and out of her blistered mouth.

Merigold's hair hung limply, liberally spotted with flecks of regurgitated bread, while she waited for the spinning and the waves of nausea to die down. It had been a week since the constant nausea had kicked in, and she knew by this point that the only option was to wait it out. Unfortunately, she also knew it wouldn't entirely go away. This seemed to be her new normal.

The first bout of nausea had hit her when they'd been on Hunesa Road, after they had broken their fast with some bread and oatmeal that Cryden had prepared. The pair had barely talked since the Duckling at that point, and Cryden had done little to comfort her as she knelt against a tree, palms rubbing raw against the bark as her modest breakfast reappeared in a wet puddle. She walked most of the day, which apparently irked Cryden, as it meant that they spent another night on the road. The next morning was the same, as was the following, although the setting changed from a populous roadside campsite to a cheap Hunesian inn.

As the sick feeling finally faded somewhat, Merigold slumped back to the bed, closing her eyes in relief and letting out a heavy sigh. She fully intended to wash up in a moment, after just a short rest, and start her day, but she felt her eyelids growing heavy despite her efforts. A moment later, she was jolted awake as the door thudded open, Cryden Renshaw strolling in with his customary smile. Groggy and panicky, Merigold rolled away from the door, landing roughly on her knees as she groped under the mattress for her little knife, knocking the chamber pot aside and spilling the acidic contents of her stomach across the floor as she did so. Just as her fingers clutched the handle, Cryden spread his arms wide.

"My dear lady, my most sincere apologies for alarming you." His smile grew wider, not exactly oozing sincerity.

"I told you to never, *ever,* come into my room unannounced!" Meri spat viciously, her breathing heavy. She slowly stood then, straightening her rumpled night dress and running a hand through her sodden, disheveled hair. She could almost laugh as she thought about how she'd used to care, so much, about her appearance. Worrying about her eyes being too far apart. Always carefully styling her shining blond hair, even while working. Tinging her lips and eyes with berry dyes to give her some color. Begging her father to buy her the gaudy, silk clothing of a noble lady.

Now, she stood in front of a man she barely knew in her night dress, her hair filthy and her breath rivaling the stench of the midden heap behind the Duckling. Oh, how her life had changed.

"I tried knocking and you did not answer. I became worried, but I see I have nothing to worry about. You, my dear lady, are as safe as a cantankerous little scorpion in the desert."

Merigold didn't understand his reference, but decided to take it as an insult. "What do you want, Cryden?" she asked, venom still apparent in her voice. As had happened at the Duckling, Cryden's smile faded and his eyes darkened, and the air was seemingly forced from the tightening room. Her outrage leaked right out, leaving her feeling hollow and spent.

"Now that you are awake…" And, like that, his smile was back. "…I wanted to give you an update. It will be another six days until we can depart from Enowl. My acquaintance needs to wait on his cargo and I'm not spending the coin to convince him otherwise." Meri had learned little about Cryden in their short time together, but she did know a few things with certainty. First, he had an apparent temper that rose to the surface at the slightest hint of disrespect. Second, he was well-learned, and enjoyed the sound of his own voice. Third, he was cheap.

Nonetheless, his desire to save a few yets worked to Meri's advantage. She still planned to slip away and find some fighters for hire, including a tracker or two, and to hunt down the people who had taken her father. The people who'd murdered near everyone in Dunmore, leaving corpses—whole and shredded— discarded carelessly across the town.

Hunt them down, rescue Ragen and the others, and then slaughter their captors.

"Surely, you understand that I am in no rush. I'm still recovering from my stomach illness, and I'd rather be fully recovered before boarding a boat," said Meri, hands on her stomach and a small embarrassed smile on her face.

"A ship, my dear lady. Not a boat. A ship will be much larger, have a crew of five or more skilled sailors, and will even be carrying boats of its own," said Cryden, hands measuring out the size of boats versus ships.

"Yes, of course. A *ship*." As much as Meri had always enjoyed listening to the stories of others, learning of Ardia and beyond, Cryden's pompousness and self-importance was really beginning to fray her already razor-thin nerves. The fact that her stomach was beginning to roil again did not help matters.

"Now, I would hate to leave you alone, here, in an unfamiliar place. But, I felt the echoes of heavy *meinen*… magic… radiating in the city, and I must investigate. Sworn duty and all that," he said with a wink. Cryden also rarely ceased to discuss his ability as a *cautaton*. He provided few actual details, but certainly lauded his own talent and threw around technical magic terms with relish.

"I'll be fine, Cryden. I simply wish to rest today and continue recovering," said Meri.

"I trust you are feeling better?" Cryden didn't seem particularly interested, as if her health was an afterthought.

"Practically like new." It took a teeth-clenching effort to push back her most recent, and hopefully last, surge of nausea.

"That is excellent to hear." Smiling, his white teeth gleaming, as always. "Can I get you anything before I leave?" He was already half turning toward the door.

Merigold wanted Cryden gone from her room, but she did need something from him, particularly this might be her last opportunity. Information.

"I don't need anything, but... Cryden, what is it like, to sense magic? What does it feel like?" She hated offering him a reason to lecture, but if she was to be combating magic users, and maybe, someday, using this strange power herself, she might as well learn.

"Finally, a bit of curiosity." It was true that Meri hadn't spoken to Cryden much or asked many questions. It may have had something to do with the overwhelming events of the past weeks. She woke at least once every night, shaking and terrified, in a sheer panic that she was still locked in the cellar. Realizing that this was not the case had brought less joy than she would have hoped. The reality of her life now was little better.

"We prefer our students to be curious," he said, leaning easily against a flimsy chair.

"I do want to learn." Merigold felt resolve building within her even as the nausea faded. She would learn as much about magic as possible, whether from Cryden or elsewhere. It was a tool that she could use in getting back her family. In getting back her life.

"I am not regarded as an *aerus,* a teacher, but I can spare a few minutes to speak of being a *cautaton.* What you and others ignorant to the intricacies of the world label 'magic' suffuses the world. Anything that contains life in even its barest form has a hint or more of magic. Animals, people... Of course, you know this. You have felt it and used it yourself." Merigold shifted, recalling how she'd before been able to see a person's vessel, as she'd perceived it. And how she would skim just a bit of the energy or power or life force for herself.

"Hmmm," she murmured, noncommittally. She slowly crossed the room to a wash basin and sat down next to it, never taking her eyes off of Cryden.

"Trees, vines, grass, weeds... plant life radiates its own form of power. More minute than that of animals, but significantly more plentiful. The earth, itself, contains traces of life that a *pasnes alna* can utilize, depending on his or her *pasen.* Passageway, I suppose, you might call it. There are other, much rarer—and even forgotten—forms of *miernes,* the broad term for what you might call magic, that people have been known to utilize."

"And what kind of... *miernes* can you use?" Merigold began brushing out her hair as he spoke, brush becoming caught on the countless knots in her once silken hair.

Cryden laughed with perhaps just a hint of mockery. Merigold couldn't be sure.

"That is something that *pasnes alna* do not share with outsiders. And you, my dear lady, are an outsider. For now. Suffice it to say, when a person has a particular *pasen,* they can sense *miernes* related to that *pasen.* Although this takes both training and concentration to do consistently."

Sometimes, back when she'd still had the power, Meri *had* been able to see others' vessels when she touched them, gleaming buckets of power, different colors. Other times, she'd been blind to this.

"And you can sense all types of *miernes* in others?" Her stomach was settling as she went through the routine of brushing her hair, and she was starting to feel an edge of hunger. Her last meal had been a weak stew and some hard bread the night before, and whatever her body hadn't absorbed was now on the floor and in her hair.

"Ah, that is not how being a *cautaton* works. I can sense when people are accessing *miernes*. If I am close enough, I can even sense magic that someone has never consciously used. It is difficult to explain. Particularly to... someone like you." Another subtle, condescending insult, but Meri would be gone soon enough, so she let it slide.

Cryden straightened from the chair, gesturing as he spoke. "It's a sense on its own, like sight, smell, or sound. The perceptions are unlike anything you would have experienced, but have an emotional aspect. Let's say that someone is actively drawing *maenen*, the type of *miernes* associated with animal and human life. The *miernes* that you can access, my dear lady. I get a sense of warmth and fear and aggression, though it cannot be precisely described. The stronger the draw, the stronger these feelings. These feelings are constant—many more people are accessing *miernes* than you would imagine. Most *cautatons* are driven mad before they are found and properly trained. Those who are surrounded by active draws of *maenen*, particularly, tend to go on bloody sprees of violence." Cryden mimic a knife stabbing downward.

Merigold shivered, thinking of such poor men and women, constantly bombarded by emotions unrelated to their own lives, emotions they didn't understand. She could understand how they might go mad, and be driven to lash out at others, to hurt them, to even kill them. Most people, however, had no excuse for such behavior. Briefly, she thought of Saren and wondered whether he had starved to death in the past weeks. And then about Chad, his lanky body rotting in the tall grass just off the path where she'd left him.

Now that her sky was no longer a patchwork of wooden planks, such thoughts filled her with a sickening, aching guilt.

"What do the other types of *miernes* feel like?" Meri set down her hair brush and began gently washing her face. Cryden did not seem irritated by her multitasking. Uncharacteristic for the conceited man.

"You are asking the right questions. Impressive. The *maen*..." He drifted off, eyes vague and glassy, focusing on something that Merigold could not perceive. He stared at nothing for maybe thirty seconds. Merigold cleared her throat, which was still vaguely burning from her earlier sickness. Dear Yetra, she needed to drink some water!

Cryden blinked rapidly, as if clearing spiderwebs from his eyes. "Apologies, my dear lady. We will have to continue this lesson later. I really must be going." With a polite nod and a distracted smile, Cryden left as abruptly as he had entered.

Oh, but he was a strange, pompous man that she would not be missing.

Merigold finished washing as best she could, tying her hair into a tight braid. Digging through her pack, she found a serviceable pair of breeches (too loose, but tied with a bright scarf) and an unassuming, dull-white shirt. She also pulled out a smaller pack which contained Ragen's fortune, and spent a moment running her fingers over the careful stacks of large-denomination octagonal yets—everything that Ragen had worked so hard for in his life. Perhaps it had been meant for his retirement or even her dowry. Her eyes grew misty at the thought, and her lower lip quivered.

She shook her head and clenched her fists. The only way that she would see her papa again was if she helped him. If Marissa was accurate, Ragen had never given up on her when she'd been trapped, despite the rumors of her whoring. She would never rest until he was safe again. Until they were reunited.

First things first, she needed to get a quick meal and calm her stomach. Then, she could find some mercenaries willing to work for Ragen's money. In a city of this size, there was bound to be any number of warriors willing to do anything for a yet or two.

Then, once she recruited a small army, she would find a herbalist or wise woman or fringe physician.

Somebody who could help her smother the life growing inside her. The bastard spawn of Saren, Paul, or Chad.

Hunesa was unlike anywhere Merigold had ever been. Of course, that list was relatively small—Dunmore, the Duckling, and three or four of the nearby villages that were similar to Dunmore in nearly every respect. She had always dreamt of visiting one of Ardia's four great cities. Rostane, Hunesa, Draston, and Florens, each with its own wonders—at least, according to the ever-flowing hoard of travelers through the Duckling.

The City of Wayfarers, as Hunesa was known. The Crossroads of Nations, as Duke Proan attempted to market it to travelers, though the name had never stuck. The city was the closest to a major border of any of the great Ardian cities, just scant miles from the thick forests denoting the somewhat transient boundaries of Algania. With the port town of Enowl within its jurisdiction, and with trade goods streaming from both land and sea, the city was a true blend of peoples, cultures, and styles. It was certainly a lot to take in for a village girl like Merigold, who had never seen more than one or two hundred people in the same place at any given time, and even that only during celebrations like Ascension Day or the Bright Harvest Festival.

She'd expected it to be cleaner.

In Dunmore, the houses were sturdy, well-built, and relatively uniform, lining the village square as well as several small lanes. In Hunesa, it seemed that the city planner had been as mad as a horse covered in big, black flies. There was no main roadway, but rather dozens upon dozens, if not hundreds, of smaller streets that converged and diverged, almost randomly, as she strolled. If a city map existed, it would have shown a spiderweb, but one spun by a spider who was quite drunk and none to bright to begin with. The buildings themselves seemed to follow no one style. Cultures clashed, with a noble, white stone-domed Sestrian building looming precariously close to a garishly-colored, wooden… something. And between such buildings huddled masses of unhappy, dirty people, shielding themselves from the light rain with lean-tos and makeshift tents that didn't seem to be terribly effective.

The major wonder of this city, the thing that brought visitors from all over the country and beyond, was the Hundred Markets. But what defined one market from another was as ephemeral as the shoreline of Dunmore Lake during the wet season. As Meri strolled through the city, feeling exposed and insignificant, she encountered her first market, if it could be called such a thing. She turned onto a crooked street, and three vendors, in worn clothing and with equally worn faces, started shouting after her. The three shared a single, long stall, but did not seem to care much for each other. And all sold some sort of food.

"Crayfish stew—the best in the world! You must try! You must!" The balding vendor was shoved back by a meaty woman with ponderous jowls that flapped wildly as she shouted.

"His is swill—those are not crayfish. Just water-bound dung beetles! This, you must try! Delicious, delectable—"

"Horsemeat! The crone sells horsemeat from the oldest and stinkiest horses! Now, if you want real food..."

Merigold covered her face with one hand, embarrassed by the attention and made nervous by their aggressive tactics. She hurried past.

Mere minutes later, she stumbled into the second market. And was stunned by the sight.

She'd been in the general store in Dunmore, of course. And she had shopped many, many times from traders' wagons and even from some small caravans that they'd had at the Duckling. Meri had thought that she had quite an eclectic understanding of what one could purchase and own. With the way that Ragen had doted on her, she'd had many nice things that her neighbors did not.

But this market made her gasp, stopping and gaping like the village yokel she actually was. Among the many, many stalls and storefronts, she saw both marvels and horrors. In one heavily guarded stall, diamonds and rubies and sapphires glittered on necklaces, bracelets, and arm pieces. She self-consciously touched her hand to one of her far less significant sapphire studs—so glorious in Dunmore, but clearly next to nothing in Hunesa. Another stall seemed to be selling animal parts. Not the parts that one would typically eat, but rather the garbage bits. And patrons were lined up, pushing and shoving to get the attention of the butcher, if that was who this man was. A third stall simply sold sweet-smelling perfumes, while the smell of decay radiated from a fourth stall, the vendor loudly claiming to sell a potion that would eliminate wrinkles. Old and young women crowded around. Every one of her senses was overwhelmed, though Meri seemed to be the only one of hundreds affected. She was shoved, jostled, and knocked about among the purposeful and frantic mob of shoppers.

The city was big. Much bigger than Merigold had anticipated, so that she was uncertain where to start on her seemingly overwhelming mission.

This was Meri's first time out and about since arriving in the city. Mostly, she had been feeling ill and wallowing in her room, trying to fight the emptiness that was attempting to consume her. Thinking about Saren and Chad and Ragen. Thinking about being alone in the damp darkness. Thinking of bloody remains. Thinking of the untouched bodies, seemingly sleeping. Thinking about the demon child growing within her, the product of a man who'd raped and imprisoned her. Maybe a man that she'd killed— one left to starve, the other stabbed in the neck. Maybe a man who'd been killed by the magical attack in Dunmore, or who was still alive, somewhere, out there. It was easier to escape into herself and just be a shell, the same way she'd coped in the cellar.

Cryden had mostly left her alone those first few days, going about his business, booking passage on the ship and whatever other enterprises concerned the arrogant *cautaton*. Almost unerringly, however, he'd checked in on Meri with regularity, typically dropping in around mealtimes. And she knew that he could sense her, just like he'd managed at the Duckling. She'd gone down to the common room one evening, drawn to the familiar sounds of imprecise voices, laughter, and the kitchen. Almost catatonic from the memories, she had sat in a chair and just stared at nothing. Remembering, maybe, her old life, when she had been untouched by any true grief aside from the loss of a mother who she could not remember.

A greasy, skinny man had approached her, pulling a chair up to her table and sitting backwards.

"Hi, sweetheart. I'm thinking you're going to need some company tonight. No one with you?" Meri had barely glanced in his direction, not responding.

"Hey, bitch! I'm talking you to!" He had grabbed her wrist then, his hand unknowingly encircling the exact spot where Fenrir had left a bruise so long ago. She had lost control.

A few moments later, Cryden had pulled her off the man, blood under her fingernails, her hand reaching back for her knife. The man had staggered backward, clutching his bloodied face.

"You psychotic cunt! I'm getting the guard!" the man venomously spat.

"No, you aren't." Cryden's tone had been ice. Merigold hadn't been able to see his face clearly, but the man had blanched, mumbled something, and left. Cryden had turned to her, stern and commanding.

"You are not to leave your room without me. Hunesa is a much different place than Dunmore and your little inn. People mean each other harm here. Especially upon women."

"Cryden, you cannot control me," Meri had said fiercely, blood still aflame from her assault on the greasy man.

"My dear lady, I *can* control you, but I choose not to do so. I was hoping that we could be amicable about this situation. I simply do not want anything… untoward… to happen to you while we are here. Please, it will be much safer in your room. You don't want me to find you fighting again."

Another man trying to lock her away from the world, ostensibly for her own good. Merigold had supposed that apparent compliance would allow him to relax his guard, give her an opportunity to escape.

It had worked, too, and now Merigold was moving about freely, overwhelmed by the sights, smells, and sounds of this

373

massive city. People here didn't seem to mean her harm. Rather, they seemed oblivious to her. Oblivious to everyone except for themselves. Locked in their tiny lives, lost in a massive place, having little or no impact on the world around them. At least in Dunmore, even a smile would travel a long way. Here, a smile would be stamped on, spit on, or, more likely, just completely ignored.

"Excuse me. Pardon me." Merigold couldn't get anyone to stop and listen to her. She decided to try a different tack. She approached a small metalworking stall where the vendor—a lovely girl about her age, though appearing quite damp and irate in the misting rain—was threading tiny beads onto a twist of wire. Seeing Merigold approaching, she set her work aside amidst cheap jewelry and an array of small knives and daggers. Merigold had learned, upon entering the city days ago, that only guards were allowed to bear swords or spears. All weapons with a blade longer than their hilt qualified as a sword, and all weapons longer than five feet qualified as a spear, according to the law. As a result, the devious had devised a weapon called a hapler, a weapon with a two-foot hilt and a two-foot blade. Many people wore these openly, and evidently the lawmakers in the city were in a gridlock and had not yet passed a law to forbid the weapons. This girl had mostly knives, though one wicked-looking hapler was leaning in the corner of a stall.

"Whaddya need?" The girl's gruff, irritable voice belied her pleasant looks. Maybe she would not be easier to approach and work with than a male vendor. But, she was lovely…

"Some information, if you don't mind." Merigold put on her sweetest face, the one she would have worn if she'd wanted a large tip. The girl sucked snot into her throat and spat behind her.

"Information don't pay my rent. You gonna buy? Or you gonna leave." The last was a statement of fact.

"Um... well, I could use a small boot... knife? I can pay..." The girl's demeanor changed immediately as Merigold pulled out a small, jingling purse (separate from Ragen's money—she wasn't *that* ignorant of a peasant).

"Yes, miss! We've several of those! Which you wanna see?" The suddenly enthusiastic woman pulled out several, each appearing identical under Meri's inexpert analysis. She brushed her fingers against them, cold metal so unlike her rusted, slightly-bent little knife, secreted on a leather thong around her neck and occasionally scratching raw the area between her breasts. "We've sheathes, too, that clip right into your boot. No one'll know you've a little more protection hidden down there."

"Um, let me see that one." Merigold pointed, and the girl handed her a small knife. Meri made as if to admire it, testing the grip and balance, though she knew nothing of weapons.

"This one should do... By the way, do you know where I can find some men for hire?"

"A girl like you don't need to hire men! Men must swarm you!" The woman winked bawdily.

It took a minute for that to sink in.

"Dear Yetra, no, not like that! I need *soldiers* for hire. I figured that, you selling weapons, you might have an idea." Color was in her cheeks, and the girl had a wide grin.

"Ah, mercenaries. There's always mercenaries in Hunesa. Why do a girl like you need fighting men?" the girl asked while searching for the appropriate sheath.

Meri's face darkened. "That is my concern."

"Tight lips. Well, fine. Probably your best bet would be to check the Cleanly Hog. A big inn and boarding house, by the northern gate to Enowl. But, you mightn't want to go alone. The

375

men're rough, down there, and the guardsmen don't care much to contain 'em."

"Well then, maybe I'll need a second boot knife."

Chapter 27

The name "Cleanly Hog" was obviously a pun. The place felt…
sticky. As Meri pushed open the heavy, wooden door, in the
process passing several rough-looking, leering men who were
loitering outside of the building, she felt dirtied simply by
crossing the threshold. The air was stale, and it reeked of beer,
vomit, and what smelled like eggs. And not fresh eggs. The
wooden floor was warped from spills and her boots stuck to the
panels—a disgusting squishing noise working its way out with
each of her steps.

At the Duckling, Meri had seen many a road-weary traveler,
covered in the dust, muck, and dirt commonly acquired when
trekking from one place to another. She had seen mercenaries and
other fighting men before—honor guards, traveling soldiers, and
the like. Ragen had even, at times, opened up rooms to the
destitute, men and women who had fallen on hard times from
Dunmore and beyond. The men (and few women) in the Cleanly
Hog, however, were unlike any Meri had met. Here, she was filled
with a deep unease.

The common room was spacious, much larger than the
Duckling's. Wooden benches stretched across the room, and all
furniture seemed to be firmly attached to the ground or a wall.
There were none of the decorations—paintings and wall
hangings—that one would expect to see brightening a common
room. Judging from the oft-patched stucco walls, any decor had
already likely been destroyed by the rowdy, raucous groups of
mercenaries. The mercenaries, themselves, could not so easily be
described. Fat, wiry, muscular, gray-haired, brunette, or blonde;
Sestrian, Ardian, or Rafònian; there was no standard look.
However, there was a standard feel. The men radiated a confident
ferocity, having the clear appearance of those who had committed
violent acts in the past and would have little problem doing so in
the future.

Meri had once seen two hawks battle for an injured duckling in the brush outside of her home in Dunmore. The two predators had dived for the duck simultaneously, almost on cue, tearing through the wind at impossible speeds. Instead of going straight for the duckling, one of the hawks had smashed into the other, and both had been knocked from the air by the impact. They'd fought brutally, bloody feathers littering her yard, and the echoes of bestial rage and pain had filled the village. Eventually, the hawk who'd attacked first had stood over the corpse of the other, hiding its own pain under puffed feathers. With a stumbling leap, it had then flown off, wobbling in the air.

The duckling, having instigated the battle with his mere existence, had been left unharmed, and hobbled off no worse for wear.

These mercenaries were hawks. Predators. There was something about how they held their bodies, something about their eyes. It was more than the occasional visible scar or missing appendage (though a man with a shifted bandage, revealing an oozing ear-hole, particularly repulsed her). A feeling of confident brutality filled the room. These beings were men who would rather kill each other over some loot than share. These were men who would visit violence on an enemy without trying to talk out their issues first. These men were killers.

Meri steadied herself, thinking, *This is for Papa. This is for Papa.*

It became a mantra as Merigold stepped fully into the inn, the doors closing heavily behind her like they guarded the entrance to a crypt. It had seemed like such an easy thing, finding some fighting men, paying them some money, and having them lead her to her father and the people who'd destroyed her life. Now, looking around, she was overwhelmed, and scared. Most of these men appeared to be at least as capable of atrocities as Saren, and at least as unrestrained. She wondered if it was too late to turn

378

around, walk back to her cheap inn, and go off to learn about magic with Cryden. She even paused and turned around, but someone stopped her.

"Girl. Whatchaneed?" asked a squinting, bent man who was presumably the owner of the establishment.

This is for Papa.

"Pardon me?" she asked.

"What. You. Need," the man growled through his surprisingly intact, white teeth.

Merigold steeled herself. "I need to talk to whomever is in charge here, of these fighting men."

The man gave a creaking chuckle. "'Whomever.' We got a duchess here." He peered around for an audience and, finding none, he continued. "Girl. A little advice. These'n't men to tangle with. If they didn't bring me so much coin, I'd stay clear, myself."

This is for Papa. She took in a quiet breath, finding just a smidgeon of courage. "I don't need advice, good sir. What I need are fighting men. Direct me to the leader here."

The man grumbled, but waved for her to follow. Merigold exhaled, her feigned confidence having been exactly that—fake.

"Sergeant Paran. A girl," the man said, leaving her at a corner table. He caught her eyes for a moment, almost seeming to plead with her. She met his eyes in return, though, hopefully appearing unafraid. He sighed deeply, and walked back toward the door.

The sergeant didn't look any different from the other mercenaries, except that maybe his clothing was a bit finer, and that the others seemed to give him the slightest touch of deference. He was middle-aged, his face and head completely hairless, a thick scar running just above his right temple. It was as wide and long as a finger, pinkness standing in stark contrast to the pallor of his skull.

"What're you looking at, chit?"

"Um, nothing, sergeant," she stuttered, remembering his title. Apparently, she'd been openly staring.

"That's right. Nothing. Now, what could a little blonde piece like you be doing in a place like this? We usually only get a very… specific type of woman in here." The sergeant, and his two cronies, laughed at that, and one stood up and gestured with his hips at a scantily-dressed, rather voluptuous woman sitting on the lap of a fighter nearby. Merigold gulped, knowing full well what he was talking about.

This is for Papa. "Sergeant, are you the man I speak with to write up a contract for service?"

Paran smirked, which somehow stretched out his head-scar, making it harder for Meri to avoid looking at it. "I'm as close as you're going to get." Meri's mouth was as dry as ash.

"Fine. I have need of experienced fighting men, brave and honorable soldiers like yourselves. Trackers, too, if you have any—people who can follow an old trail."

The three men glanced at each other, and then laughed uproariously, one coughing and sputtering as his ale went down the wrong hole.

"If you are looking for honorable men, you're in the wrong place. Look around." Meri didn't. "If you want scoundrels, thieves, murderers, you're in the right place. If you want men who would stab someone in his sleep, or who would steal a child from his mother, we are what you want."

Merigold shivered. But, this was for her papa.

"In that case, I need scoundrels, thieves, and murderers. I need killers. I need vengeance." The ice in her voice surprised her. Merigold had never before said, out loud, that she was out for revenge. Rather, it was for Papa that she was doing all of this, to save her father and anyone else she could from Dunmore. But it was more than that, she now admitted to herself. It was to bring agony to those who had ruined her life. It was to balance the scales in a way that Yetra had not, could not, or would not. To make those who'd visited suffering upon others experience their own suffering in whatever way that she could.

Wasn't it true that Saren had been punished—by her hand—for his terrible misdeeds against her? As had been Chad, though she tried not to picture his surprised, young eyes, the way they'd looked as his blood had washed over her hand and soaked his clothing. She was willing to balance, create Harmony, where Yetra was not.

After all, one couldn't expect a bolt of lightning to strike someone who'd committed an evil deed.

She felt more certain, more resolved, than she ever had in her short life.

"Strong words from a small girl. Come. We never talk terms in the common room. Musk, outside. Woody, you're with me."

Strange names for strange men. Woody, she saw, had probably gotten his nickname from a poorly-fitting set of wooden teeth. Based on his youth, the man had probably lost his teeth in a battle, and instead wore a constant grimace due to the oversized implant. Musk… Well, she didn't get close, but he *looked* like he had an odor about him. Looking around as they walked to a back room, Merigold imagined that most of these man would carry quite a foul scent. For a man to be nicknamed "Musk," he must be very special indeed.

Down a hallway to a small office with a few chairs and a table. Musk stayed outside, giving Woody a resentful glare. *Must be upset not to be the favorite.*

Merigold sat down opposite Sergeant Paran, with Woody flanking her, folding her hands in her lap to resist the urge to tug on her sapphire studs or her braid. Though she'd been feeling slightly more courageous, today's ordeal was far from over.

"So, girl. You have my interest, something that doesn't come for free. Nothing is free, in this line of work. Let's see the color of your money, or we'll go no further." Paran leaned forward.

This is for Papa.

Merigold pulled out her larger coin pack, slowly opening it to reveal the majority of Ragen's fortune. Paran grinned, and she could hear Woody sucking loudly on his teeth.

"This will do. Woody."

Woody reached down and grabbed her arm, not gently, as Paran snatched the pack from her grip. A few coins slipped loose and tumbled to the rug-covered floor with no sound.

"What? Stop this!" Merigold shouted, jerking to the side as she stood, just managing to escape Woody's grasp.

"Didn't I just tell you? We are not honest men. We take what we want, when we want it, and that's that." Paran didn't even glance up at her. He was absorbed in the neat stacks of coin before him.

"Sarg, I'm thinking I want a little bit more from this deal," Woody said, sucking his teeth, a mean look in his wet eyes. Merigold shrank back.

"Don't get greedy. We've enough here, to never have to draw a sword again."

"Ah, Sarg. I think I'd like to draw just one more sword." He gestured meaningfully at his crotch. Woody was between Merigold and the door, her only escape. *Dear Yetra. Dear, dear Yetra.* She would not be hurt like this again.

"Fine, Woody. Just be quick about it. I'm going to do some counting, so try to keep quiet, too." With a mere dismissal, the sergeant gave permission for his man to take Merigold.

The hawks who'd fought, back in Dunmore... The beast that had struck first, unexpectedly and with great commitment, had been the one who'd survived, leaving his opponent bloody and dying in the brush. Though Merigold was more like the duck...

She pushed herself against the wall as Woody approached, working on unlacing his pants, sucking his teeth again in obvious anticipation. Merigold made as if she were terrified (which she was) and crouched down, cowering.

This is for me.

Just as he released his pants, she drew her boot knife and rammed it, to the hilt, into his stomach and left it there.

The man was stunned, transfixed by the knife protruding from his paunch. He grasped it with one hand and fell to his knees with a gurgling scream. Woody spat out his wooden teeth as he hit the ground and they bounced off Merigold's boot. Heavier than she would have expected.

A strange thought to have.

Paran, who hadn't noticed the exchange until the scream, knocked his chair over as he jumped up. The door flew open as Musk entered, also alerted by the scream.

The hawk, back in Dunmore, had only fought one opponent. And he'd still been grievously wounded by the end of it. Merigold had no hope. Her hands began to shake as Paran pulled out a hapler, its wicked, razor edge gleaming in the lantern light of the room. Musk had pulled a curved dagger from his belt.

"What happened?" asked Musk, locking the door and gesturing at Woody. The man was now on the ground in a growing puddle of blood and intestinal filth, curled around Meri's knife like a fetus around its umbilical cord.

"This cunt stabbed him! I told him not to be greedy," said Paran, squinting at her, his scar stretching on his pale dome.

"What do we do?"

Musk seemed uncertain. Could she jump over Woody's form and make it past Musk, through the door? Probably not, unless she wanted that curved dagger to pierce her flesh. The same way that her own knife had torn through Woody.

"Woody drew his own lot, but we need to teach this cunt a lesson," said Paran.

Woody moaned and sobbed. Paran stepped up next to him, not looking down. "Bitch, take off your clothes."

"I have more money," said Merigold, her voice quavering. Maybe greed would save her.

"Pft. What you've given us already is more than enough."

"She gave us money, Sarg?" Musk licked his lips, looking at Paran.

"We took a few coins from her, it's true," lied Paran. Musk's eyes darted to the pack still lying open on the table. He licked his lips again.

"That looks like more than a few. You holding out on me?" he demanded.

Paran darted a glance over his shoulder then. "You'll get your share, Musk," he practically growled.

"But, if Woody weren't lying dead there, I'd be gettin' nothing!" Musk gestured at the man writhing slowly in his own blood.

Woody moaned, not dead, but as good as. Musk again ran his tongue over his lips.

Two hawks, fighting instead of sharing. Please, Yetra, allow for some hope. Let her be the duck.

Paran turned his back on Merigold, perhaps realizing that the bigger threat was behind him. He twirled his hapler skillfully in one hand, the long-hilted blade whirring softly through the air.

"You want to try something, Musk, you shit-sucker? Remember what happened to Three-Fingers?"

Musk stepped back, hands up. "No, Sarg. I was just saying…"

"That's right. And don't forget who's in charge here," spat Paran, turning back toward Meri just as she crouched to reach her other boot knife.

"No, no, no, bitch. You think I can't see you reaching for your boot? Toss the knife aside." He levelled his hapler at her, stretching over the fallen Woody. Woody's growing puddle of vileness and blood was now staining Merigold's boots, and he was barely twitching. Still occasionally coughing and sputtering, but perhaps unconscious.

Dear Yetra! There was no other choice.

"Drop it, cunt!" snarled Paran, waving his weapon at her.

She tossed the knife into the corner.

"Thatta girl. Now, do the same with your clothes."

This was just like the cabin, her prison. Dear Yetra, not again. Only, these men were likely to kill her after.

385

She took a breath and tried to find her empty place, her escape, just as she had with Saren, Chad, and Paul. Tried to send her mind somewhere else, and just leave her body—a shell of meat—here in this office room.

The emptiness eluded her.

She slowly removed her blouse, subtly moving her little nail-knife with it, leaving it covered by folds of fabric. The boots, pants, and underthings came next. She set the clothing down carefully on the table, leaving the weapon covered but easily accessible. As if that would help her against two armed mercenaries. Tears were starting to squeeze from her eyes. Unbidden, like a leaky dike.

"Come around this. I don't want to step in that slime. Good."

She was standing face-to-face with Sergeant Paran now, smelling strong liquor on his moist breath, so close that she could see each of the wrinkles around his cruel little eyes. He stroked her cheek with rough, calloused hands, resting his thumb and pointer on her chin.

"It's a shame, girl. You are such a pretty little thing. All you needed to do was comply with Woody over there, and you'd be out of her safe and sound. Certainly much poorer, but you'd have your life," Paran said, quietly, almost gently. Then, impossibly fast, he drew back his hand and cracked her across the face—knocking her against the wall, but not off her feet.

"But, instead, we're going to hurt you. Pandemonium, when we are done with you, we might pass you around to the men. Haven't they earned it?" Paran addressed Musk.

"Aye, Sarg. That battle in Sestra was quite tough. Quite tough, indeed." Always licking his lips. Merigold wondered idly if they were chapped.

"Perfect. Get over here, cunt." Paran grabbed her arm and jerked her towards him.

Thoughts of rape and darkness flashed through Meri's mind. Cold, damp, alone, nauseous, abused.

No. This would not happen again. She would never again submit to the touch of a man, never again allow someone to use her in that way.

Merigold again delved inward to find her escape. But, this time, she did not seek a protective emptiness. She sought power.

And she found it.

It was as if the lights flared vividly to life in the room. She could see Paran's disused vessel of power, cracked and drained, a dull sludge sunk deep inside of him. Glancing at Musk, she noted that his vessel was not as decayed, but lacked the shine that she had seen so many times in Dunmore and at the Duckling.

For a moment, time paused. If a fly had been in the room, Meri would have seen each individual wing flapping, would have been able isolate every spasmodic leg twitch. Drool was dripping out of Paran's mouth, suspended in the air like an aborted raindrop. She gripped his pale, bare arm with all of her strength, and then she began to draw from him, flinching as his filthy *maenen* coursed into her own vessel, overflowing, sullying her, contaminating her. But she continued to draw, despite the filth.

Paran's pupils dilated and he made as if to strike her. But instead, he fell slowly to his knees.

"What the f–" he wheezed, air escaping from a tea kettle.

He went fully to the ground, Merigold crouching to maintain her grip. He was gasping like a fish stuck in the shallows when the water receded, his eyes bulging in the same way.

"Sarg! What's happening?" cried out Musk, uncertain of whether to help or to flee. A coward. But, a coward with a curved knife.

Merigold tried to turn her attention to him but, all at once, it was too much. The *maenen*, Paran's *maenen*, filled her body with a great, burning pressure. Such a pressure! It was as if the sky had settled directly on her body, crushing her against the earth. But, in a way that was also tearing her apart. The agony was unimaginable, almost unrecognizable as pain. She needed to discharge this pressure... she needed to...

Musk had taken a step toward her, and she glanced up from under her half-closed eyelids, eyes glowing both black and red. She raised her free hand, and with a long, piercing scream, released the putrid power from her palm.

A barely-visible, uneven beam of light streamed forth, tearing free from her hand like a rabid, cornered animal seeking escape. The beam, the dull black and red of Paran's *maenen* mixed with the brighter turquoise of her own, slammed into a stunned Musk's chest.

For a moment, Musk stood still, transfixed, watching with wide eyes the absurd, the impossible, happening just in front of him. He even slapped at the stream of light, trying to knock it away.

Then, Musk exploded.

His body was torn apart from the core, limbs shredded into pieces, torso rupturing, the mess shooting across the room. The fleshy parts of his head combusted as his skull launched through the air, ricocheting heavily off the wall before landing near Merigold's feet. She didn't even notice.

Too much! Just too much! It was a roaring river, caught against a wall with nowhere to go save a single egress. Not a river. A sewage pipe, ending in a mortared-stone barrier, a finger-width

388

hole the only escape. The barrier could not hold against such vile pressure.

Dear Yetra. Dear, fucking Yetra.

Merigold fell to her knees, her nails drawing blood from Paran's arm.

No, she wasn't on her knees. She was standing over a man who resembled Paran, though with short, scraggly gray hair. More wrinkles around his face. And Merigold held the spear that was piercing the man's heart.

It wasn't a spear... It was a crutch that she was leaning on, watching as her brother was brutally lashed by the man she'd seen earlier, skin and flesh torn right off of his back. Her father? Her brother? No, that wasn't right. She reached out...

...And was holding down a crying, bruised woman—a girl, really—as she fucked her virginity away. A spindle of drool hung from her mouth, straddling the area between her chin and the girl's bare breasts...

This was wrong! This was so very, very wrong.

The hands around the girl's neck. Scarred, with hairy knuckles and dirty fingernails. Not her hands.

Merigold tried to hold on to some semblance of self. Ragen, smiling at her from across the common room, his weary face wrinkled, primarily around the upturned corners of his mouth. Meri felt her own reciprocated smile turn into a mockery of a grin as she lunged at him with a sword.

No!

Sandra, brushing Meri's hair as she cried into her hands, upset that no one had invited her to the Harvest Festival. Meri turned back to Sandra, reaching out as if to embrace her. Then she

389

propelled Sandra's head into the wall, the light leaving her eyes as she crumpled to the ground.

Taneo Marsh delivering a moving sermon, transfixed by an arrow released by Merigold's bow. Marissa Punter hugging her in the chapel, stabbed through the throat by Merigold's knife.

There was little of Merigold left. There was violence. There was Paran, and...

Saren. Saren, kissing her outside of the Duckling, a moon's light dancing playfully across the misty evening. Saren forcing her legs apart, mouth opened in a slimy grin as he worked to penetrate her. Saren watching impassively as she washed over the bucket. Saren, hurling curses up at her as she closed the cellar door on him.

Merigold released her death grip on Paran's wrist, power dribbling out of her other hand like a spent well pump—blue, red, and black dissipating on contact with the wooden-planked floor. She fell forward onto her hands, her disheveled braid resting on the bloody floor, soaking up crimson like the brush of a demented painter. She was gasping for breath, sobbing without tears as she fought to retain what remained of herself.

Just as Meri began to fade into unconsciousness, she had some vague awareness of the door slamming open, the sharp report of the lock snapping from the wall. She stared up then, without really seeing.

"What in the fuck–"

"–by Yetra and Ultner!"

"So much blood."

"What is she..?"

"Who is she?"

Merigold Hinter.

Serving girl.

Quiet. Liked to listen..

Ragen. Papa. Taken.

Saren. Kidnapper. Rapist.

Merigold Hinter.

Killer.

Amidst confused and outraged voices, Merigold slumped to the wooden floor, her naked body warmed by the slowly congealing blood.

Chapter 28

"What in the fuck?" exclaimed Fenrir. He was kneeling in blood, having slipped after ramming his shoulder through the locked door and into the office.

"...By Yetra and Ultner fucking twisted genitals," whispered Ferl, standing just behind Fenrir.

Fenrir's stomach was a sour knot. He'd never seen anything like this. He imagined very few people had ever witnessed a such a sight.

It was a small room, identical to so many other cramped meeting rooms in random public buildings around Ardia. But this room was unique in that the walls were splattered in blood and gore. There were bits of humanity covering the room, some of them recognizable and others grotesquely ambiguous. Near Fenrir was what looked like a knee, and on the other side of the desk was, based on Martis' description, a chunk of human intestines, somehow affixed to the wall like some gory, demented piece of art.

Off to the side lay a man, probably a mercenary, in a separate, more concentrated, pool of blood mixed with vileness. The stench of the whole ordeal made Fenrir want to vomit, his stomach being clenched by a great, imaginary fist. The merc must have been stabbed in the stomach or intestines. Martis had taught Fenrir about common battlefield wounds during their long talks together, and he didn't need to see the source of the vileness on the floor to know where the wound likely sat—not based on the blood and the smell. It was possible that the injured man was still alive, but for his sake, death would be better. Fatal infection was practically unavoidable with gut wounds, and the pain would be immense— all for an inevitable passing in a day or two.

In the opposite corner was another absurd sight. A girl, completely naked, had just flopped forward as he'd broken in the

392

door, and she lay face-down in the gore. She must have been the source of that piercing, pain-laced scream that he and Ferl had heard while walking back to negotiate the hiring of Ferl's Company for Escamilla's purposes. A man leaned on the wall near her, his glassy eyes fixed in a thousand-mile stare. Fenrir could see his stomach moving with his breathing. Alive, then, his wilted cock hanging from his unlaced breeches. So, his intent was clear enough.

Ferl, and one of his lieutenants, still stood behind Fenrir. The lieutenant had just finished vomiting loudly in the hallway. Fenrir was glad he hadn't shown that weakness himself, though his body was tempted to betray him. Luckily, he had somewhat fortified himself with rum beforehand. But there wasn't enough rum in the world to make this scene bearable.

"Sir, what do we do?" asked Lieutenant Christoph with an acidic cough. The scarred, graying mercenary squinted into the room. "I think that's Sergeant Paran, there!"

"Fucking Paran," mumbled Ferl. He was a wiry, athletic man, both shorter and younger than Fenrir would have expected of the leader of a rather infamous mercenary company. Even Fenrir had to admit that Ferl was a handsome man, too—his strong jaw, cleft chin, and ocean-blue eyes probably made him popular with both the ladies and clients alike. Right now, his face was twisted up with disgust and anger.

"Coldbreaker, Christoph, go in there and look around. Check on the bodies," said Ferl. Ah, leading from behind. A true leader.

Of course, Fenrir was so accustomed to taking orders, he'd barely batted an eye when Ferl told him to break down the door. An idiot move, both because now Ferl would assume he had authority over Fenrir, and because who the fuck knew what could have been going on in this room?

393

But, considering that his breeches were already soaked in blood and viscera, Fenrir followed the order. Christoph stepped into the room, as well, but turned around immediately to dry-heave when his boot slipped on some unnamed internal organ. Some professional soldier. Though, granted, this was far from a normal battlefield sight.

Fenrir first checked on the man curled on the ground. He'd been stabbed in the gut, as Fenrir had suspected, and must have pulled the cheap boot knife free, curling around the wound. Then, he'd bled out and died.

Stepping around him, Fenrir's foot knocked a couple of loose coins off of a rug. He crouched (with a groan as his knee clicked) and saw a small pack that must have been knocked to the floor by a chunk of human remains. In the bag was a wealth of coin.

Shit. Fenrir had already pawned the stuff he'd stolen from Brockmore, but this gold could make a flight much easier and more comfortable. If only he could smuggle it out of this room. If he had an opportunity. But, that was impossible. He instead grabbed a stack of yets and shoved it into his sock as he stood with the pack.

"Looks like we've got some money, here. A good deal of it," he called to Ferl.

"Fucking Paran," Ferl said, more loudly this time as he sullied his own boots by stepping into the room, motivated by the gold. He took the pack.

"Godsdamn. He was going rogue. Not unexpected. Check the bodies."

Considering Christoph had never reentered the room, apparently the order was meant for Fenrir. He shrugged and checked on Paran first. As he'd thought, the sergeant was still breathing, though he was unresponsive.

"He's alive."

Ferl drew a dagger and casually, slowly, plunged it into Paran's neck, the sergeant unresponsive as the dark red lifeblood flowed from his severed jugular.

"Must have been killed before we got here." Ferl gave Fenrir a flat glare to accentuate the pronouncement. A dangerous look.

"That's what I saw." There was something of Tennsyon about this young mercenary captain. A willingness to do whatever needed to be done. The ability to consign a person to death with a word or a thought. And, a lack of remorse for doing so.

Fenrir wasn't strictly scared of the captain, but he certainly would rather avoid crossing him.

"The girl?"

Crouching somewhat painfully again, Fenrir shifted the girl's face out of the crimson liquid. She sputtered, coughing up some blood on reflex, but remaining unconscious. There was something familiar about her. When he'd walked in, she'd been on her hands and knees, looking up at him. Her eyes… she'd seemed to be in such pain, both physical and emotional. She'd appeared terrified.

"She's alive."

"The dead don't usually cough. Thanks, though," Ferl said drily.

Fenrir was briefly irked, but let it go. Always the better option. Besides, he was not the sole proprietor of sarcasm. He lifted the girl up—she was surprisingly light—and set her on the chair. Usually, he'd have appreciated an opportunity to survey a young, naked blond girl in her twenties. But even Fenrir, a well-known debaucher, couldn't see the girl as more than a victim, or near victim, of rape. He'd never resorted to such a vile crime, though he'd sometimes paid for his pleasure. Half the fun was with the chase, but not in a literal sense.

And still, he couldn't shake the feeling that he'd met this girl before.

"*Pasnes alna*. Only explanation," said Ferl.

"*Pasnes alna?* A magician?" Fenrir had some passing knowledge of the order of magicians, those who called themselves *pasnes alna*. His father… Darian de Trenton, rather… had had some dealings with these world-bending weirdos, despite strict laws forbidding the use of magic, or the presence of magic users, in Ardia. Fenrir had overheard many a tedious lecture and passionate debate regarding the morality of magic while standing guard in the Enlightenment, keeping visiting Scholars safe from imaginary foes.

"Yes. I've seen similar sights before, though not quite so… colorful? This girl must be a *pasnes alna*." A witch, then. Someone who could manipulate the world through the use of powers that Fenrir could barely understand.

Wait. This girl, a witch. Something about an inn. Getting clunked in the head…

Fenrir burst out laughing at the absurdity of it, the pure low probability and scant likelihood that he'd have run into this girl again. He drew Ferl's dead-man's glare, the captain fingering the hapler at his side. Fenrir shook his head.

"This girl isn't a *pasnes alna*. She's a fucking barmaiden."

The girl, Merigold, was lying on a cot in the corner dressed in her old clothes, which had amazingly escaped the worst of the human explosion. Fenrir had dressed her himself, noting the fresh bruise on her face as well as a crisscross of partially healed bruises all over her body. She'd been poorly treated, and recently, too.

When he'd grabbed her clothes, Fenrir had also found a sort of make-shift weapon, a long, rusty nail, wrapped in a copper-stained bit of cloth. Merigold had been poorly treated, but she wasn't quite helpless. Together with the weapon, the dead men in the Cleanly Hog's office attested to that.

Fenrir wasn't squeamish. He'd cut off at least enough fingers to make a new pair of hands. But, looking at this bruised and beaten girl, remembering the utter fear and pain in her eyes before she'd lost consciousness, Fenrir had felt his age very acutely for a moment.

And for a second moment, he had thought of Emma. She'd been mistreated, too. Maimed in a very painful and very obvious way. Being four-fingered (or worse, in Emma's case) was typically a death sentence for a servant-class woman. Sometimes, people would simply murder a four-fingered. But, more often, being branded by The House consigned such victims to a life of ostracization, derision, and unemployment, until they slowly wasted away from hunger or disease. Emma had been lucky that Escamilla had kept her on. Her life would be very different right now otherwise.

Her life would also be different if Fenrir hadn't entered her room that night, if he hadn't held down her hand and swung his knife. If he had disobeyed his superiors, forfeiting his chance to work with The House and perhaps even his life. Then, maybe not, Fenrir corrected himself. If he hadn't performed the deed, then some other enforcer would have played the role, and probably done a more accurate job. At least with Fenrir's mistake, Emma wouldn't be automatically flagged as four-fingered. It could have been a kitchen accident or some birth defect that had maimed her. In fact, Fenrir may have done Emma a favor by botching the job.

And, of course, he had made a stack of yets.

"We'll have to report the victims to the guard. The *two* victims," Ferl was saying to Fenrir. Hunesa, despite appearances on this side of town, was a city of strict law and order. Ferl, himself, could be prosecuted if his men were implicated in these murders, as he was technically their commanding officer even between engagements. Ultimately, it was easier for Ferl to simplify things in this situation—two men fought over a woman and some money, with one killing the other, and then the woman killed the second in self-defense. No need to mention that a third man had been blasted across the walls.

Ferl had left Christoph to guard the site of the macabre massacre, and he'd pulled several of his men to clean up the mess as much as was possible. Fenrir didn't envy their task: mopping up as much blood as they could, collecting the quivering globs of humanity spread across the room, and disposing of all of it at random places around the city. Ferl seemed to know exactly how to hide the fact that a supposed magician had exploded a merc.

"No one is going to miss Musk, anyhow. I don't know where he's from, and it's likely nobody else does, either. It's typically a safe bet that no one in my company will be missed in the unfortunate case of an early demise," said Ferl with a wry grin. He was reclining in his chair, seemingly recovered from any anxiety over the brutal death of his men.

"What about the other two?" This business of casual murder intrigued Fenrir. The House was very covert in its pursuits of human termination, whereas Ferl's Company seemed quite practiced at getting away with murder in the open.

"Sergeant Paran was a liar and a thief. Not necessarily a disqualifying factor in our line of business, except that he lied and stole from *me*. He wasn't authorized to negotiate deals with the kind of money we found in that room." Fenrir suddenly noticed the feel of the cold coins against his sweaty ankles. "Clearly, he

398

planned to take that money and run. And obviously, the three of them planned to rape that girl."

"Wrong decision, evidently," observed Fenrir.

"Indeed. There's a time and place for that sort of behavior. My men know that. They also know that to rape between engagements is a hangable offense—at least, it is in most cities. If local authorities didn't take action, it would have been handled internally. Paran and Woody consigned themselves to death, regardless of that girl's actions. I just hastened Paren's demise while simultaneously allowing us to protect this girl."

Ferl didn't seem like the sort who was big on sheltering the innocent, and Fenrir's skepticism must have shown through on his face.

"Ah, yes. I'd generally care little about keeping some city bitch safe. The rules are in place for the reputation of my company. You think that city leaders would want to hire, or house, or allow to visit, a group of rapists and murderers? This girl, however, is a special case. Killing a *pasnes alna* can bring the wrath of their kin. And, as you can see, they certainly have the power to dissuade persecution of their kind."

"A few months ago, this girl served me eggs in some backwater inn. I'm telling you, this is no career magician." Even as he spoke, though, Fenrir recalled her strange touch. How she'd seemed to steal something vital from him. But, it just seemed so unlikely.

"While I've no doubt that you saw this girl…"—but despite his words to the contrary, Ferl appeared quite doubtful—"…it isn't impossible that she is also a *pasnes alna*, a *metsika*, or at least has some magical potential."

"Magic, and its use, are illegal in Ardia." Fenrir answered, realizing that he sounded much like those peasants and bumpkins who he'd often entertained with war stories.

"And to think, I took you for a shrewd and intelligent man, despite your appearance," Ferl said with a small smile.

Jackass, Fenrir thought idly.

"Stealing is illegal. Do people steal? Do people lie and cheat and avoid paying taxes? People have far less control over the manifestation of magic abilities than they do over their own behaviors. I've heard that one in a hundred people are born with some magic ability. Think what that means. In Hunesa, a city of maybe one hundred and twenty thousand souls, twelve hundred of these people can use some form of magic. In such a cosmopolitan area, with travelers and wayfarers streaming in and out of the city, there might be two thousand people within thirty miles of us who could replicate the scene in that office! *Pasnes alna*—schooled magic users. *Metsikas*—untrained, but potentially powerful magicians. Wild ones, as they're called. Or those who have weak abilities and have not been detected. All flitting about, mucking up the world."

Chances are, then, that Fenrir knew somebody who could use magic. Thinking of the mess in the other room, he shivered.

"How do you know so much about magic? In Ardia, books on the topic have been taken off the shelves, far as I know. Burned, if the stories are true." Fenrir was still playing the ignorant peasant, but would have hated to admit that it was not entirely on purpose.

"I've traveled the world, and many places are more open-minded than Ardia. In fact, *most places* are more open-minded than this backwards country." Fenrir felt a sting at the jibe. It was a weird feeling. He hadn't realized that he had nationalist tendencies, particularly after being ejected from the Rostanian guard. "I've also got six soldiers, regulars, who have some ability. Five are minor *metsikas*, all of them, too weak to merit interest in any of the *pasnes alna* schools or organizations. The sixth is… well, Ashland is a special case. All six are greenies, and even the *metsikas* know enough to be more than useful."

400

Metsikas. Pasnes alna. Greenies? This conversation—this day—had taken quite a turn. A simple negotiation turned into dissecting the disgusting aftermath of a magical battle, followed by a lesson about magic. Time to get back to business.

"Speaking of useful, we should talk business," Fenrir responded with all the subtlety of a cavalry charge.

"Excellent transition." Ferl was sharp. Tilner was going to hate this man. This thought, at least, brought Fenrir some pleasure after the stressful day.

"Now, tell me, what can Ferl's Company do for you?"

Chapter 29

Crack!

Hafgan blocked a clumsy overhead attack, nimbly disabling his opponent with a quick jab to the stomach. From within his *heddwichen,* he then heard heavy footsteps in the grass behind him. Hafgan dove off to one side, feeling the breeze and hearing a *woosh* as a weapon just missed his arm. He swung his spear blindly behind him at gut level, flicking his wrist for some extra force. A grunt told him that he'd struck true, though he was already spinning his spear up front to face his next two assailants.

Most men, when outnumbered, would assume a defensive stance, sitting back and waiting for an opening or a riposte. The *Dyn Doethas*, however, taught that hesitation could be fatal. Indecision only gave your opponents more time to communicate and coordinate their efforts while you would become less certain, more anxious.

Hafgan danced to the left, swinging his spear low until it was partially deflected by his reactive opponent's own spear. He continued to flank the men so as to effectively face only one at a time. With two hands, he next flung his spear, lengthwise, into his adversary's face. The surprised man raised his sword to protect himself just as Hafgan's heavy boot connected with his stomach. Hafgan scooped up the previous opponent's dropped sword as he leapt over the man, deflecting a wild, astonished swing as he landed. His final opponent was so off-balance after Hafgan's riposte that he stumbled and fell to his back. Hafgan was on him in an instant, digging a knee into the fleshy area below his sternum as he raised the sword.

Finally, he touched the blunted sword, gently, to the man's neck. Then, pulling himself out of his *heddwichen,* Hafgan helped the dazed man to his feet.

Eight Wasmer were in various states of injury around the training ring. One was on his hands and knees, gasping for breath. The others were rubbing bruised limbs or egos as they formed up, standing at rough attention after their handy beating by the weapons master.

Hafgan had gone completely untouched during the training battle, though he'd used all of his skill—and a bit of luck—to do so. Nonetheless, he could see the growing awe in the eyes of his men, this group of twenty-seven misfits who he'd been training for two weeks now, even after the march had begun.

But there was no pride to be found in defeating eight men who had never touched a weapon before a couple of weeks ago.

Each morning, before the sun came up, he led these men in intense calisthenics—jumping, diving, changing direction quickly—so hard that at least one person vomited up the last night's supper during each session. Afterward, he would teach them of the spear, going through proper handling and the multiple uses of the weapon. A spear was not just used for jabbing from behind a shield. A spear could be used to swipe and butt and trip, to block and dodge, to confuse and misdirect. Of course, it took time to master, but competence could be achieved much more quickly than proper handling of a sword or axe, and it could ultimately be more dangerous in the hands of an amateur than most any other weapon.

"Men, what did you see?" Hafgan asked of his gathered misfits.

Silence for a second.

"A fucking beating," muttered Derek then, rubbing his arm. There was scattered laughter, and Hafgan tried to hide a smile.

"A fucking beating, *Lieutenant*," corrected Hafgan.

403

"Yes, sir!" Derek saluted smartly, the 'sir' exaggerated with his chronic lisp.

"Aside from a fucking beating, what did you see?" He was growing comfortable speaking in front of these men, and it was easier to find the correct wording.

"Lieutenant, you fought with more than just your spear." This from Elan, a well-spoken, wild-haired, over-enthusiastic youngling. He hadn't fought in this training battle for that very reason. He needed to learn to cool down and fight with his head, and so he needed to learn through observation. And, as it turned out, he was surprisingly astute.

"Correct. How many of you be injured by my spear?" Half raised their hands. "The rest of you were harmed by fists, shoulders, and your own weapons. The lesson?" For Hafgan, speaking in front of Elan was the hardest, as the boy had been born and raised by Wasmer in Rostane, meaning that he'd learned the Ardian from birth. It was unnerving, knowing this and trying to find the right phrasing, though the boy seemed not to judge him. In fact, the boy was in utter awe of Hafgan and followed him around in a quite irritating fashion, a puppy begging for scraps.

"Surprise," said two of the men in unison. Hafgan had been preaching this message since the start. The best way to achieve victory, both in individual battles and with armies, was to do something unexpected. A skilled boxer might take down every opponent in an organized tourney, but faced with an inebriated opponent in a tavern, he could be overwhelmed simply due to the unpredictability of his adversary.

"Correct. Always change the rules. Fighting toe-to-toe with a skilled warrior, you will be losing... you will lose. But, surprise that warrior, and you may yet live."

"Lieutenant, why–" began one of his soldiers, but was cut off by another.

"Lieutenant, we won't be fighting like you ever. Why bother watching you beat on us? For that matter, why bother training like this? There is nothing to be gained." Enric was older than Hafgan by maybe ten years, and kept his face and head completely shorn of hair. It took a great deal of time and maintenance for a Wasmer. He was also the most reluctant of Hafgan's little crew—muttering complaints during the training and questioning his advice, shirking duty whenever possible. He was the rotten piece of fruit that could corrupt the entire bucket, but Hafgan was reluctant to toss him aside completely. Likely, as with most others in this group, he'd probably been abused and mistreated by humans and Wasmer alike, and was simply used to rejection—it was why he claimed to have joined. Hafgan needed a way to strengthen this man instead of reject him.

Hafgan strode toward Enric, standing scant inches from him, locking his gaze. Enric, surprisingly, didn't back down. He had courage, if not confidence.

"*You*," he began scathingly, concentrating on speaking carefully, "…will never attain my level of skill. Perhaps you should leave this group, and train with the regular army. With the fodder. As it is, you are the least of those assembled. Even…" he scanned the crowd, "…Paston could best you."

Paston stepped forward, if uncertainly. He had become Hafgan's right-hand man, a sergeant in duty if not name. He had promise of being an adequate fighter, but his true value lay in his organizational abilities. Before being drafted, he'd worked for a small, overseas trading company, keeping their books. He had a head for numbers and paperwork—something that was so incredibly valuable in a disorganized army on the move. He'd managed to get their unit needed supplies and weapons through bureaucratic obscuration, something that Hafgan only half understood. Considering his dual role here and in The House, it shouldn't have mattered to Hafgan whether his Wasmer unit was well-supplied, but it somehow did.

"Bah! I be having nothing to prove and no quarrel with Paston," said Enric, hairless face uncertain now.

"Truly, the words of a budredda coward." There was an audible gasp as Hafgan uttered the most insulting term that could have been used for these misfit Wasmer. Filth. Trash. Midden.

Less than Wasmer. Less than human.

Without reacting to the crowd, Hafgan tossed his own spear at Enric, who was bristling at the disregard and insult. Hafgan turned his back to the man then, showing further disdain for his abilities. He grabbed another practice spear from a stack and handed one to Paston, giving him a level stare. Hopefully, the intelligent man understood what Hafgan was doing.

The two faced off within the loose ring of would-be fighters who silently awaited the outcome. This was the first time that Hafgan had allowed a battle between his men, and the practice was strictly forbidden by the human generals. Since Hafgan had taken Siarl's place as warleader, several others had been lashed for this organized infighting. His own eight-against-one battle just now would probably also be condemned, were anyone else to hear about it. Nonetheless, Hafgan knew this had to be done.

Paston, shorter and wider than Enric, with a small, protruding gut around his middle (despite two weeks of hard training and a forced march), began to circle the other man calmly, holding his spear with two hands in front of him in a defensive stance. Enric, on the other hand, was obviously angered, baring his filed-down teeth as he brandished his own weapon. In the first tentative pass, Hafgan, his arms folded—overseeing the fight like Traisen, the god of war—noted at least six mistakes. Footwork, grip, weapon-handling. To him, this was two children play-fighting in slow-motion, wielding fake weapons. But he remained silent as the two made another awkward pass. And then a third.

Paston, despite his paunch, was the faster of the two, sidestepping and even rolling, once, to dodge an attack. But Enric was superior when it came to handling his spear, and much stronger. He wore away at Paston's stamina with quick, jabbing attacks, forcing him to clumsily dance around the ring. Paston, to his credit, managed several controlled ripostes, one of which narrowly missed Enric's skull. Ultimately, though, the outcome was made apparent as the fighters became more engaged.

Enric pressed his attack, sensing Paston's faltering energy. Paston blocked the wide swipe, holding his spear with both hands, and the two were locked together, padded wood against padded wood, newly-formed sore muscles straining to their peaks. Suddenly, Enric fell back and inexpertly kicked, nearly losing his balance as his foot collided with the stomach of the off-balance Paston. The kick lacked force, but was enough to stun the smaller man. Enric cocked back his spear to finish the fight, aiming squarely for Paston's exposed head, and swung.

His spear was sent spinning through the air, end over end.

Hafgan lowered the wooden sword that he had picked up in a hurry upon seeing that Enric was lost in battle madness. He easily could have killed or brain-crippled Paston, and Hafgan had had little choice but to intervene. Enric turned to face him, body heaving with his fierce breathing. For a tense moment, it seemed that he would attack. Hafgan crossed his arms nonchalantly, waiting for the man to calm. After a minute, Enric straightened himself and unclenched his fists.

"Perhaps there is the makings of a man within you yet. Well-fought, soldier," said Hafgan with sincerity in his face, looking Enric directly in his eyes.

The next morning, when the men went through their usual exercises, Enric sweated as much as anybody, and didn't utter a word of complaint during the spear drills.

407

"–still lagging behind General Krast's forces by several days," said Captain Ressig, scratching at his eyepatch.

"That impetuous fool was to wait for us at the border!" snapped Captain Jeret, his pompous voice filling the commandeered farmhouse like the crowing of a self-important cockerel calling for a mate when none were interested.

"Hold your tongue, Jeret! *General* Krast outranks you, if you haven't forgotten." General Sigmund Fitra was resting his head in one hand, tired and overwrought. Perhaps because he had no business being a general or leading men, in Hafgan's learned opinion.

But, as it turned out, when an army had no way to provision itself on short notice, and one of the most powerful merchant lords in the city offered to sponsor the campaign, that man ended up having an inordinate say in the appointments of said army. And when that merchant lord was Principal Darius de Trenton, he assigned someone who was wholly his creature. Hence, Sigmund Fitra had become a general of the armies of Rostane.

It was not going well.

"My apologies, *Lord General*," said Captain Jeret, rancor barely masked behind a chipped and rapidly peeling facade of respect. Apparently, this golden officer either had a personal grudge against General Fitra or was upset because he'd himself been passed over for promotion. Regardless, tensions were high when the two of them were in a room together. Which was daily.

Luckily, the quartermaster intervened before this situation could escalate, though his choice of topic was less than tactful.

"Sir, the reported desertion count for today is fifty-four, with forty-nine of those being conscripts and the remainder being career soldiers," interjected Quartermaster Polk.

"Fucking deserters! Why would career soldiers possibly wish to desert? This... this is their fucking job!" The general slammed his four-fingered fist into the hard oaken table and then immediately grasped it in pain, which seemed to only make him angrier.

"Lord General, most of these men signed up for the military during peacetime. They never planned or expected to fight. Some others have family and friends in Florens," offered Ressig. One of Hafgan's new informants had reported that Ressig was from a small town near Florens' capital. A town that was likely already sacked by the advance forces.

"We need to stop this. The army is leaking men like a barrel of water full of holes," said Lieutenant Itham. A portly, red-faced, pock-nosed blacksmith-turned-soldier, Itham enjoyed stating the obvious whenever he could get a word in. Itham was one of only three lieutenants in the room, including Hafgan. Apparently, each was in charge of a 'special' force, and somehow merited presence in these meetings. Itham led a group of sappers. Terence was a lieutenant of an engineer corps, specializing in siege equipment. And Hafgan was in charge of the Wasmer, though he was not certain how they merited being called a special force. Probably because nobody else wanted to speak to the fuzz-faced goats.

"Once retrieved by our outriders, I might suggest lashing the career soldier deserters and garnishing the wages of the conscripts," said Ressig, massaging his temples.

"No. Once we retrieve them, the career soldiers will be stripped, dragged, and beheaded, if they're still breathing. The conscripts will be lashed, stripped, and forced to march barefoot in units across the army. The men shall see the price of desertion," said Fitra as he leaned forward, lips pressed to his steepled fingers. Being dragged was an old method of punishment in the Ardian military. Unfortunate victims were stripped and tied to horses near the front of the army, usually by their feet, with their free limbs being bound tightly. Such men were then dragged over the rough roads and terrain, unable to protect their bodies from the ravages of the journey. Even on a hard-packed road, like the one between Rostane and Florens, the dirt and gravel were enough to shred a man's skin and flesh to nothing. A stray, jagged rock could disembowel a man. There were few survivors of this practice, and those few were mercifully beheaded—the next morning.

By design, the rest of the army had to both listen to the sounds of the dying men for hours and march through the gore—at least, through whatever wasn't covered in dust—as a rather heavy-handed reminder of the price of desertion. This practice had not been used in over a hundred years, and was considered to be inhumane and brutal by modern standards.

"Lord General, isn't that a bit... harsh?" asked Captain Yanso, rubbing his veiny forearm with an oversized hand. Yanso was ostensibly Hafgan's superior officer since Fitra's promotion had come, though the career militant had only spoken three words to him in the last weeks. The 'Fuck you goat', in that case, had been punctuated with a fake lunge designed to make Hafgan flinch. It hadn't been successful.

"I've got a war to win. And I'm not going to win it by hemorrhaging spoiled soldiers between here and Florens. And beyond, as is likely the case. No, His Grace Duke Penton authorized me to use whatever means necessary to make this march a success, and I intend to do so," said General Fitra, speaking slowly and meeting each captain's eyes in turn.

General Fitra's proclamation was greeted with silence, the twenty or so staff officers who were present either being stunned by his brutality or unwilling to voice their approval. Considering

410

most of these men knew only peace-time, Hafgan suspected the latter. The fact of the matter was, the dragging would be effective. In the military accounts that Hafgan had read and memorized during his training as a *Haearn Doethas*, death by dragging had had a near-perfect success rate in deterring desertion just so long as the morale problem was not extreme (which could lead to a revolt). More merciful leaders had also tied the rope around the neck of the victim, allowing them to die of either a broken neck or strangulation. Not exactly painless, but a far stretch better than being slowly torn and flayed open by the ground.

"Gentlemen, no need to stop speaking on my behalf," said Savant Iolen, pushing into the farmhouse. Escorted, as always, by a pair of Wolf Knights. Lord Faris was not far behind with his own retinue.

"You are late, High Strategist," said General Fitra, eying the learned man and the duke's advisor with irritation. Iolen looked anything but repentant.

"Certainly, you qualified men of war need not wait upon our presence to discuss the trivialities of a march. With your expertise, we have been able to travel fully five miles per day!"

"Shall we neglect training the conscripts and simply send them into battle to be slaughtered? Or, should we instead ensure we are *prepared* to fight a battle?" retorted Fitra.

"Of course. Speed is not a factor here, though we have an enemy army marching with great haste to Florens at this moment," said Iolen, slumping easily into a vacant chair.

"An outnumbered, ill-prepared army! Lead by a trumped-up old woman. High Strategist, perhaps if you were to share an alternate *strategy* instead of showing up at random and simply insulting—"

"Apologies, General." Lord Faris, ever the peacekeeper, had cut off Fitra before he said anything he might regret. "We were tending to separate matters of national security. If you wouldn't mind calling this meeting to an early close, there are urgent matters that we must address."

"Fine. Officers, off to your units. We've not much longer to get this rabble into some semblance of a fighting force, so continue with the same training every morning," sighed Fitra, glaring askance at Iolen.

"Captain Yanso, please stay for a moment. We may have a special assignment for you and your men," said Faris, taking up a comfortable chair as one of the captains moved.

The officers filed out, still apparently stunned by Fitra's pronouncement. Hafgan lingered as long as possible in hopes of overhearing Yanso's assignment, but was eventually forced to leave his corner with the rest of the staff. Outside, the officers huddled together in small clusters, discussing the pressing matters of the day—none so important as the dragging. He inched toward the group with Ressig, the only officer who afforded him even a hint of respect. Hafgan stood just outside the circle of officers.

"–must we follow the orders? These are people, Ressig. Like you and me. They're just scared."

"Is there a way to fake it? Or to save these men? Can we instruct the outriders to ignore any deserters that they find?"

"No, that would be treason, disobeying a direct command and countermanding our general." This from Ressig, to whom the other captains clearly deferred.

"There must be a way—"

"Eight of those are my men—"

"I can't do it!"

"We must follow orders, gentlemen. I don't like it any more than you do, but this is war. Blood will be spilled. Any of us here may be wounded or killed in the coming battles. At least this bloodshed might serve some purpose, keeping this army together and perhaps reducing our casualties overall." Ressig was firm, though his eyes were clouded. A man of reluctant duty.

Hafgan tried to push into the circle, and when two of the captains realized it was the Wasmer, they hastily parted. Suddenly, he was in the group with plenty of room to spare. None of the captains made eye contact with him, save Ressig.

"Sir, I have a suggestion." *Enunciation.* He needed to focus in order to be treated seriously, particularly by the golden officers.

"I've a suggestion for *you*, goat. Why don't you go fuck…"

Ressig cut off Captain Roneth—the cavalry commander—with an abrupt wave of his hand. Roneth stunk of horse, as always. "Wasmer, let's hear it." It wasn't necessarily deference that Ressig gave him, but it was far better than Hafgan was used to getting.

"Spare the dragging men the pain. Tie them by the neck. A broken neck or strangulation be… is much quicker a way to go. Give them three mouthfuls of devil's claw root to numb the pain, as well. Or, slit their wrists while binding them—up-and-down the arm, not across. The effect will be the same for preventing deserters, and it will be a mercy compared to death by dragging."

The group of men eyed Hafgan, not sure what to make of his advice. Ressig, however, gave him a wan, tired smile.

"Excellent idea, Wasmer. It shall be done as you suggest. Ithum, procure the devil's claw root from the quartermaster. We will cut the wrists. Less painful and far quicker than strangulation." Ressig nodded in respect and Hafgan returned the gesture.

413

He headed back to the Wasmer camp then, his only consolation being that he'd managed to spare some condemned men a day or more of agony.

To cap off Hafgan's day, there was more trouble.

As Hafgan neared the Wasmer camp, set purposefully a mile or so east of the main army in an effort to reduce racial tensions, he saw that a crowd had formed, jostling each other and raising their voices in both the Wasmer and traders' tongues. In Hafgan's experience, crowds rarely gathered for something positive, and the tone of this one was certainly aggressive. Getting closer, he heard a great shout—a war cry, really—and sprinted the last hundred yards through the bushy grasslands.

In a brief gap through the bodies, he could see a melee.

Shouting ignored orders as he shoved through the crowd, Hafgan managed to reach the front just as a body was hurtled at him, tumbling hard into his shins. He crouched down.

"Paston?"

The Wasmer's mostly-shaved face was matted with the blood pouring out of his nose, and one eye was already swelling shut. He seemed confused, and his eyes widened with the recognition of his commanding officer.

"S-sir," he slurred through cracked lips.

"What be happening here?" Hafgan demanded, surveying the scene before him. At least eight Wasmer were fighting. Brawling, was more like it. One of his soldiers knelt on the chest of a downed man, pummeling the fallen man in the face. Another was ramming his shoulder into the stomach of a tall Wasmer. The taller soldier wrapped one arm around his attacker's midsection and punched him repeatedly in the ribs. Two more were engaged in a cautious fistfight, maneuvering around the body of a fallen man as a barrier. A couple of tents had toppled and a brazier was on its side, its smoldering contents spread across the makeshift field of battle.

"Well, there be a disagreement." Paston coughed, splattering some blood on Hafgan's formerly pristine Rostanian uniform. Hafgan frowned, both at the words and the blood. He took an inexplicable pride in the condition of his military garb.

"What disagreement?" Hafgan growled, watching the fight. At least no one had resorted to using weapons.

"Um… One of Siarl's traditionalists be goading one of our men. Called him budredda. Started fight," mumbled Paston, rolling painfully to his knees and wiping his face on his sleeve. The inevitable break between the traditionalists and his misfits. Hafgan was just surprised it hadn't started sooner.

"Who struck first?"

"I… can't say, Lieutenant." So, one of his men, then.

Hafgan took a deep breath, prepared to shout more orders when one red-headed Wasmer yanked a spear from an onlooker and plunged it into the back of a fallen man.

The crowd immediately hushed, and the fighters who were close enough to see what had happened also froze. Hafgan, however, did not hesitate. He launched himself forward, covering the space in an instant and knocking the brawlers aside. His fist slammed into the side of the killer's head, intercepting his spear as he fell, its tip dripping with the blood of the fallen. He immediately reversed the tip so that it was brushing the killer's neck.

"Stop this at once!" he roared, his voice carrying through to the remaining men who were fighting. They slowly came to a stop, and the gathered mass of Wasmer was near silent. The sudden silence was tangible—a taut line just waiting to break.

"Check on him," Hafgan said to one of his misfits. The soldier jumped to action, rolling over the fallen man. The body belonged to Elan, the hot-headed, well-spoken youngling who followed Hafgan around and idolized him as if he were Traisen reborn.

"Dead, sir," said the soldier quietly. The words were absorbed by the gathered men like a plague.

Most soldiers refused to meet Hafgan's gaze as he looked around, glancing away like children who'd been caught stealing sweetmeats from the kitchen. One young soldier—a traditionalist messenger boy from Rostane named Elgin, if Hafgan recalled correctly—was openly weeping at this point. Another one, one of his misfits, was vomiting quietly behind a short shrub. Siarl, however, stood tall with his arms crossed, staring squarely at Hafgan who stolidly returned the gaze. Neither of them broke eye contact until the man on the ground squirmed, pressing against the tip of Hafgan's spear.

"What be your name, soldier?" Hafgan demanded of the killer. The red-haired man twisted slightly, looking to Siarl. Siarl didn't respond, continuing to watch Hafgan, surrounded as he was by his traditionalist followers. The man on the ground turned his head back to Hafgan, glaring at him up the shaft of the spear.

"Why did you kill this man?" Hafgan spoke slowly and with as much conviction as he could manage. The man spat a reddish blob to one side. He must have bitten his tongue when Hagan had hit him. Hafgan applied a slight pressure, the tip of the spear digging into the man's neck, sounding out a slight pop as the tip just punctured the man's skin. Blood of the victim mixed with the blood of the killer. "Speak."

416

"You are fucking budredda scum! You spurn our traditions, our lifestyle, our very race! To do what... dally with humans? You are no longer Wasmer, and you will never even be human. You are a boil to be lanced from the body of the Wasmer!" The red-haired man's voice, speaking his native tongue, carried in the dying light, and the hate was as contagious as a plague. The gathered Wasmer began muttering their angry assent, particularly those near Siarl. The traditionalists. Meanwhile, the assimilators were clumped together, eying the crowd with a wary fear and expecting to be attacked, run out of camp, or killed like poor Elan.

These men, these misfits, lived their lives in fear. Always searching for belonging, but instead finding little more than suspicion and hate. Each one, Hafgan knew, had a story. Perhaps he didn't fit in, or wouldn't accept, his place in the strict Wasmer caste system. Born into the warrior caste and wanting to be a baker? Madness. Or, perhaps he'd been born among humans and learned early of humanity's derision for the Wasmer people. So, these men all found themselves pushed away from Wasmer culture and drawn to that of the humans. The Wasmer were not sorry to see them go.

However, such Wasmer rarely found welcome from the humans. No matter their efforts to assimilate, they were, at the least, ignored and ostracized. At the worst, they were incessantly insulted and abused for their hairy faces, their height and long fingers, their difficulty in mastering the traders' tongue. For being different, alien. So they made changes. Most would file down their second set of dogteeth, changing the shape of their faces and allowing themselves to more easily form the syllables of the traders' tongue. Some shaved their faces in a truly endless battle to camouflage their heritage, at least at first glance. Others, taller Wasmer, would wear long cloaks and hats, and develop a hunch, to mask their height.

And yet, even Wasmer who made every effort to integrate into human society were treated poorly, far worse than the servants' caste. Called "wannabes" and "pretenders," or, probably more commonly, "scum." Few humans would employ such people, and usually only at severely cut wages. Human men assumed that the misfits were little more than animals who wanted to fuck their women, so many fights broke out. The women would simply scorn them. Parents gave them dirty looks, afraid that the Wasmer would mate with their children. And the children were afraid that the Wasmer would kidnap and eat them, tearing into their flesh with double-fanged monster mouths. Or so the stories went.

These wannabees, these scum, these budredda. Each searching for some sense of belonging or community, but instead only greeted with contempt, abuse, and derision from both Wasmer and humans. Now, marching to a war where, no matter the outcome, they would only see loss.

These men *deserved* a place in the world. Whatever the purpose for which Hafgan joined the army, he was now here for these men.

"Soldier, you have murdered a member of the Rostanian Army. The penalty for murder is death. As the officer of this division, I am exercising my right to carry out the sentence immediately. Do you have any last words?" He'd spoken in the traders' tongue, focusing on each word.

The crowd was as silent as a catacomb. The fallen killer, his red hair burning in the waning sun, twisted with desperation, looking to Siarl. However, the gray and grizzled warrior did nothing to intervene, merely meeting the soldier's eyes with a gaze that betrayed no emotion. Perhaps the killer gained some strength from his brief glance at his leader, though. He turned back to Hafgan, little fear in his eyes, pushing himself into a seated position despite the spear at his neck.

"Fuck you, budredda!" he shouted, the curse ending with a gasp as Hafgan pushed the tip of his spear directly into the killer's heart, easily avoiding the ribs. A study of human and Wasmer anatomy had been a core part of his *Haearn Doethas* training.

Hafgan ripped the spear from the man's chest in a smooth, easy motion. With an equally easy motion, he pushed the killer's body backwards, the man falling to the ground with a hollow *thud*. Hafgan held up the spear and slowly surveyed the crowd, lifeblood dripping onto the grass and the man's body. He turned in a full circle, meeting the eyes of many of the men, starting and ending with Siarl. The traditionalists could have taken this opportunity to overwhelm him, but nobody moved.

"This is the price of murder." Hafgan sank the spear into the ground, next to the unnamed man who had already gargled his last, bloody breath. "There will be no treason in the Rostanian Army. Any hint of treachery, and any move against your fellow soldier, will be punished without mercy. And furthermore—" Hafgan gestured to the huddled group of misfits, "—these men are *my personal guard.* Any insult to them is an affront to me. And I will not allow any insult to me or my honor."

The men—*his men*—flanked him, hands on weapons where they were available. He noticed that they seemed to stand a bit taller, that some of the fear seemed to have dissipated. Again, the crowd murmured, and Hafgan heard the term "budredda" repeated several times.

"I hear you, men of the Rostanian Army, calling us names. Budredda. You say it as an insult. It is not. We are fighters and soldiers. We are the best. We are brothers. We are budredda!"

Paston, worse for wear, took up the cheer. "We are budredda!" Hafgan's other men followed, first tentatively and then with growing fervor. He saw the men's jaws set with determination and purpose, eyes glistening with tears. Perhaps for the first time in their lives.

Despite the two dead men at his feet, despite the cheering voices of men with newly-found hope… Despite the fierce, killing glare from Siarl as he and his traditionalists stormed off, Hafgan could only focus on one thing.

An entire speech, under pressure, and he hadn't made a single grammatical error.

Chapter 30

By Ultner, these mercenaries could drink!

A few days out of Hunesa, Ferl's Company, at nearly two thousand strong, had arrived in a disorderly mass at Overton, a moderately sized market town of a few thousand, on route to Brockmore. Needless to say, they'd swarmed the taverns like beer-guzzling locusts, scaring locals into their homes and mobilizing the outnumbered and outmanned town militia. Apparently, the mercenaries hadn't had the time to spend their most recent earnings before leaving Hunesa, following the incident with that girl, Merigold.

She was still sleeping, Merigold was. The girl didn't appear to be in any pain, nor did she appear to be dreaming. She simply slumbered peacefully on a cot in a covered wagon, not unlike a young girl who looked to be taking a nap. Fenrir was drawn to her, spending most of his days in the wagon at her side. He would put her into a sitting position and force water down her throat, as well as the flavorless oatmeal that the mercenaries passed off as food. Fenrir tried to convince himself that he sat in the wagon for the sake of comfort, so he wouldn't have to be jolted about on a horse and be exposed to the rain. But, there was more to it. The helpless girl, not much more than a teenager, ignited memories that Fenrir had worked hard to quash. Mistakes of his youth, and mistakes that had continued through his adulthood.

So, tonight, he drank to suppress those memories.

"Slow down, Coldbreaker. This is not a race," said Ferl, his deep blue eyes shining with repressed mirth. If Fenrir hadn't known any better, he would not have believed that this handsome, charming man could kill in cold blood. If he hadn't seen the dagger plunge into Sergeant Paran's throat, of course.

"If it was a race, he'd be losing," joked Christoph, the older lieutenant who was quaffing his own ale to prove his point.

"Certainly, but at least I'm doing better than Mustaches, here." Fenrir gestured at Tilner Pick, who'd insisted on coming along but refused to take a drink. He rolled his eyes at the 'mustaches' comment, refusing to be baited.

The four sat in the corner of Overton's largest tavern, watching the raucous mercenaries carouse and drink—a couple of angry, sober sergeants keeping them from growing too rowdy. Even as Fenrir watched, though, a fist fight broke out between two small men, one bashing the other's face with a pewter mug before a sergeant could intervene. Nearby, other soldiers laughed uproariously.

"Sir Ferl, we really should finalize the terms before the evening grows any later," insisted Pick. He had been after Ferl to finalize the contract for days now, and Ferl had continued to put him off. Fenrir suspected it was a negotiating technique. It wasn't like Escamilla's army could send the mercenaries away after they'd marched a couple of hundred miles; not when the bolstering forces were desperately needed.

"Just 'Ferl' will do, Tilner. Mercenaries typically forgo formal titles. Mostly because we don't earn them," said Ferl, meeting Pick's eyes over his glass as he sipped his Sestrian red wine.

"Regardless, the price you continue to propose is too high. Though your men have experience in battle and…" Pick trailed off, watching the ruckus unfolding nearby; the unconscious body of the man who'd been smacked by the pewter mug was being dragged toward the door. "…an obvious lust for combat," he finally continued "the typical rate for a force your size would be roughly half the amount."

"There is no force like mine." Ferl gestured grandly to the various cutthroats and roughs filling the tavern. The smell of the road seemed to permeate the building, smothering any delightful smells that might have originated in the kitchen.

"Sir Fe…" Pick cleared his throat. "Ferl, in my experience, there may truly be no force like yours by design. These men of yours are undisciplined, and you have conducted no training exercises while on the road. Military protocol dictates the importance of practicing formation and command responsiveness in times of war," said Pick, obviously working to maintain his professionalism. He had managed to obtain funding from Duke Proan for the military force, but confided to Fenrir that it would not cover the mercenaries' exorbitant fee.

"They have talents that you have yet to see." Ferl was pure confidence.

"Fucking scary talents," muttered Christoph, glancing at a cloaked and hooded woman who sat with a couple of well-dressed men. This group was not nearly as boisterous as the other mercenaries, and they seemed to have a protective bubble around them. No one approached, aside from a terrified serving girl who generally seemed set out of sorts by the entire situation. Somehow, Fenrir's eyes were continuously drawn to the hooded woman's feet. They were completely bare, her pale appendages standing out like the moons on a clear night.

Tilner followed Christoph's gaze and took in the strange group at the table. He traced a circle in the air, beseeching divine protection from Yetra. These people had to be the greenies that Ferl was so proud of. *Pasnes alna* that were not *pasnes alna*. People of power.

Tilner tore his eyes from the magicians. The man was a fish out of water, clearly distressed by the ignoble mercenaries and their various dark powers. He took a deep breath and visibly composed himself before resuming his negotiations.

"Regardless, if you are unable to lower your rate, we will have to make a final decision upon arrival. I will make no guarantees as to Lady Escamilla's disposition," said Tilner firmly.

423

Ferl just continued to grin his small, self-assured grin, saying nothing.

"So what's your story?" Fenrir asked of Christoph, attempting to fill the gap in conversation.

"My story, eh?" Christoph scratched at his graying beard, glancing up at the ceiling. He folded his arms, revealing that they were criss-crossed with scars. "I don't suppose it's anything special. I was born in Algania—not particularly far from the border of Ardia, truth be told. My father was a smuggler, and my mother was... well... unhappy that my father was a smuggler. The usual story. She ran. He found her. He killed her. I killed him."

Christoph paused to light a well-polished cherry pipe. The smell of kerena, a herb often used to dull the senses, wafted across the table and tickled at Fenrir's nose.

"The Alganian guard found me, but didn't begrudge me my actions. I worked with them for a while, still young. Turns out they were as corrupt as my father. There was a fight between me and a couple others. I killed them. I ran."

"A lot of killing and running," noted Fenrir.

"Aye, that's been my life. Eventually fell in with Ferl, here. It's been a few years, now. I hope to avoid more running, though killing will probably be necessary," said Christoph with a puff at his pipe.

"A reluctant killer makes an excellent officer," commented Ferl. "The best armies fight the least."

"Reassuring, given that we are paying you to fight. A lot of fucking money," mumbled Tilner, finally pouring himself a glass of wine from the decanter. He gulped it down, and then immediately helped himself to another glass. He glanced darkly at the barefoot women from time to time, betraying his nerves.

"And Ferl, what's your story? How do you find yourself leading an infamous company of mercenaries?" asked Fenrir, waving to a serving girl for another beer; he'd never been much for wine. Ferl raised an eyebrow at his inquiry.

"I was born to it," Ferl said, leaning onto his elbows and resting his chin on his thumbs. He met Fenrir's gaze as if daring him to probe more. Christoph was pointedly watching the beginnings of another brawl while Pick was working on his third glass of wine, seemingly oblivious to the tension. Apparently, the captain of this venture was not prone to speaking of his past.

Fenrir leaned forward himself, mimicking the captain's posture and manner. "We're all born to something. Might as well be something that would pad your purse."

Ferl continued his alpha glare for another moment and then barked a laugh, leaning back in his chair. "I wonder if there's more than bluster in you, Coldbreaker," said Ferl.

"I supposed I could be wondering the same about you." Fenrir had found bravado to be an excellent tool for diffusing taut nerves.

"I think you will find my record quite impressive. I'm certain Sir Pick, here, can corroborate my company's various exploits." Ferl gestured at Tilner, whose well-groomed mustaches were now stained with the Sestrian red.

"Oh, certainly. We have it that Ferl's hired company was victorious over the rebels in Nislea two years ago, crushing the fisherman with the might of arms—to better serve their greedy dictator, Manus Enis. Oh, and they also destroyed the small, independent tribal nation of Oshwon, nestled near Farrow's Hold, capital of Jecusta, at the behest of Lord Unael. Not to mention the Battle of Eneval." The wine was chipping away at Tilner's ability to hide his disgust.

"Battle of Eneval?" asked Fenrir. Eneval was a large city on the oft-disputed border of Algania and Jecusta. The soil was rich there, ideal for high-yield crops like corn and tomatoes. "There was no Battle of Eneval."

"Exactly," said Ferl, smacking his fist on the table. The serving girl who'd been refilling their decanter jumped at the sound. "The best battle is never fought. Lord Unael was intimately aware of our prowess, so when the Alganian Assembly hired us, Unael did not press his claim to that land. Treaties were signed, and blood was not shed."

"And so, we find ourselves hiring men who are unwilling to fight," said Pick, his voice bitter. "Except, of course, fisherman, farmers, and savages."

"Watch yourself, Pick. I don't know you, but I will tell you, we do fight. You think Oshwon was easy?" This from Christoph as he'd surged to his feet, knocking his chair to the ground with a rattle. He stalked around the table, stabbing at Pick with a furious finger.

"They came at us every night as we slept, slitting the throats of our pickets, murdering men in their tents and on their bedroles. These 'savages' knew their valley, every ambush point, killing ten of us for every one we managed to catch and kill. Our soldiers were stolen away, left mutilated along our path. Mutilated but alive. You cannot understand what that was like, seeing men begging for death because the prospect of living without fingers or toes, without eyeballs or cocks, was simply too much. The blood was too much."

Pick didn't rise from his seat, nor did he shrink in the face of Christoph's face-twisting rage. He simply considered the older soldier, pointedly examining the scars that tattooed Christoph's arm. He gave a rueful smile.

426

"I pray to Yetra, then, that your people can bring that same courage with you, Lieutenant. We face insurmountable odds and, though I do not expect much deceptive stratagem, I expect blood. And, it will be the blood of my own countrymen, regardless of who wins."

Tilner drifted off, staring at his wine glass. Somehow, Fenrir liked Pick better for his inebriation.

Christoph's shoulders slumped slightly as the anger leaked from him, and he moved to slump back into his own seat. His brows were furrowed, and his veteran face appeared quite old at the moment. Probably remembering the various macabre sights from his time in Oshwon, or even the recent blood-painted walls back in Hunesa.

Moving on, the group ate their meal of cranberry chicken stew and roasted potatoes in a contemplative silence, conversation being limited to the recent rainstorms and the resulting supply logistics. Topics that Fenrir was rather disinterested in, so that he instead focused on his beer. A bit too yeasty for his taste, but the hops lingered nicely in his mouth.

"So, Coldbreaker, what about you?" asked Christoph, a while and several beers later. The veteran lieutenant was in better spirits, and even Ferl was more talkative. "You're obviously a soldier of some sort. What's your story?"

"Less exciting than yours, Christoph. Not worth going into." He didn't care to talk about his time as a guardsman in any context, let alone with a stranger. And, discussing The House was strictly unnecessary.

"I don't know. I think his background is *faintly* interesting," said Pick, giggling uncharacteristically. He was outright drunk now, and Fenrir no longer found the quality to be endearing. In fact, he wanted to punch the smug mustaches right off of Escamilla's hanger-on.

427

"Come on, Coldbreaker. Tell us your story," encouraged Christoph, face awash with his own drunk smile.

"Yes, Coldbreaker. Enlighten us as to how you find yourself a messenger boy for a rebel army," said Ferl, his expression and mannerisms untouched by the Sestrian red even though he'd consumed at least as much as Tilner.

Fenrir fidgeted, hand in his pocket, accidentally poking himself with Merigold's little makeshift knife. He'd held onto the thing since that night in the Cleanly Hog. He had a sense that it was more than a weapon to the girl. It had the feeling of a talisman, an artifact or a charm of some sort. Fenrir had done a lot he wasn't particularly proud of, but somehow discarding this little weapon seemed like sacrilege.

"I was a guardsman at the Plateau. Now I am in the service of Lady Escamilla. That's it," Fenrir said, somewhat coldly.

"I think there is more to it than that," said Ferl, eyes shining with interest.

"There certainly is. Coldbreaker, how about you share *why* you left the guard," said Pick, high on wine and humor.

The fucker must have known his past, Fenrir realized, either from Escamilla or Emma. It was certainly a well-kept secret otherwise; the nobles were not prone to talking about something that caused as much embarrassment as that night would have. "I would rather not, Pick," Fenrir growled, eyes alight with pointed anger.

Pick, in his cups and apparently in a crisis of both religion and patriotism, ignored the warning. "I'll share, then. Fenrir Coldbreaker, the great warrior you see before you, *fainted* during the Ardian Council. He was the reason why the Council disbanded, in fact. It is said that…"

428

Tilner found himself on the ground, a heavy-breathing Fenrir looming over him, fists clenched. Tilner shrank away, scrambling backwards and attempting to regain his feet. Fenrir took a deep, shuddering breath.

"You need to learn to hold your wine better, Pick. And your tongue."

Fenrir, dizzy from the anger and alcohol, tossed down a handful of yets, stepped over Pick, and staggered out of the tavern. He was unaware of whether Ferl and Christoph were laughing at him, but assumed so. Apparently, there was no escaping that part of his past. New career. New name. Pandemonium, he was even in a new city. His goddamn weakness would always be there—a cancerous mole on his back, an infected blister on his foot.

Pick. That Ultner fucker. That shitting little fucker.

Fenrir managed to make it back to his tent outside of town amidst the carnival-like atmosphere that seemed to have overtaken the mercenaries. This was the last decent-sized settlement they would pass, as they'd next be heading overland to catch up with the Army of Brockmore. The shouting and singing and drinking just pissed Fenrir off more as he vomited up the contents of his stomach scant feet from his tent flap.

He thumped his spinning head down on his bedroll and closed his eyes then, attempting sleep, though he knew that his throbbing temples, anger, and regret were conspiring against him.

Fenrir hit the ground. Hard. The metallic clang of his helmet on the flagstones reverberated dully through his skull as he attempted to recall where he was and what had happened,

429

gasping and bewildered as he was. His tabard had twisted up over his face, obscuring his view, and his scabbard was hopelessly tangled in his legs. Still foggy, Fenrir managed to straighten his garb and struggle to his knees amidst a storm of angry shouts.

"Assassin!" a grainy voice bellowed. "He murdered a guard!"

The situation was rapidly building toward a state of chaos. Nearby voices combined into a cacophony, with several nobles shouting conflicting orders in imperious tones while others simply screamed and wailed in sheer panic. The din grew even louder as guards rushed inward from the perimeter of the room, herding the unarmored occupants together and leveling their shields in a protective maneuver. It sounded for all the world like a stampede of heavily-armored, braying donkeys bearing down upon the hall. Steel raised in anticipation, the formation of guards turned in unison, facing Fenrir, their eyes scanning the surroundings to locate an attacker.

Fenrir, disoriented from his fall and knocked further off-kilter by several rushing guards during the scramble, finally found his feet. At the heart of the great council chamber stood more than forty fully-armored guardsmen, eyes and weapons trained keenly upon Fenrir, and with almost double that number of nobles clustered tightly behind them. Fenrir, head thumping to the rhythm of his racing heartbeat, shifted his feet at the sight in front of him. Solid, practical pillars; rare, colorful tapestries with a Yetranian motif; and bewildered, frightened faces all returned his stare in the brightly-lit council chamber. The thunder of voices and feet had faded to an uneasy, murmuring quiet. Foggy and still trying to work out exactly what had happened, Fenrir stepped forward toward the safety of the guards, his comrades-in-arms. The guards shifted uneasily in response, bracing themselves behind their shields, swords and spears glinting in the lamplight.

A moment later, a commanding voice broke the tense stillness. *"What is happening here?"* demanded Duke Henrik Malless, the ruler of Florens. With Duke Samuel Penton the Second recently taken ill and Samuel the Third at his side, Henrik was the highest-ranking, or at least the most assertive, man in the room. From behind the relative safety of the shield wall, he shouted, *"Where is the assassin?"*

"That guard, there—he was attacked by an assassin!" cried Baron Erlins, gesturing toward Fenrir. The burly, pock-faced baron had his own ornate ceremonial sword drawn in readiness, though the flimsy, curved blade was likely to snap in the unlikely event that it ever saw battle.

The reminder that an assassin might be lurking about caused renewed agitation within the crowd. More of the nobles began to draw swords as they shuffled anxiously behind the guards. Some simply backed up to the tapestry-laden rear wall of the hall, looking uncertain and nervous. Fenrir was more uncertain and nervous than anyone, having not even dared to move from where he'd taken his last step. His chest, face, hands—all felt like they were on fire, though they were slick with sweat.

"Stop! Erlins, you others, stand down. Guardsman, what happened? Where is the man who struck you?" shouted Malless, addressing Fenrir with his questions. His deeply resonant voice, well-honed from years of ordering others about, once again controlled the attention of the crowd and stirred Fenrir toward attention.

"I... your grace... that is, I'm not sure," stammered Fenrir. His head was almost clear, and his body was starting to cool down. In fact, he was feeling a bit too cold. Between his fall and the cumulative stress of having over a hundred people staring at him, Fenrir had begun to shake beneath his gilded breastplate and decorative tabard, emblazoned with the slavering Wolf of

431

Rostane. His underclothes—linen shirt and wool pants—were soaked through with icy sweat.

"Guardsman, are you hurt? Speak up, man!" commanded Malless.

Fenrir took a few steps in place, rolled his shoulders and flexed his arms. Aside from his weak right knee, which had been paining him for nearly twenty years, he couldn't identify any particular injuries. The back of his head hurt, of course, from his fall, but he supposed that the nobility wasn't interested in that small detail.

"Your grace, I do not appear to be injured in any way," replied Fenrir, starting to feel more himself and falling in to the rehearsed formality he'd acquired from decades of working with the nobility.

"Well, then. What happened to you? Was there an attack?" queried Malless, his bushy eyebrows coming together in consternation.

Fenrir tried to recall. The nobles, the most notable people of Ardia and beyond, had been embroiled in a deep, forceful discussion about some treatise. Though the first Ardian Council in thirty years was supposed to be monumental, Fenrir hadn't been paying much attention. Retreating to a state of blissful unawareness was one of the primary skills required for being a successful guard. Or at least being a sane one. Next thing he'd known, he had landed on the ground, head aching and ears filled with the sounds of confusion and panic.

"Your grace, I am uncertain…" Fenrir trailed off, his voice echoing hollowly in the great chamber.

"If I might interject, your grace."

A man of indiscriminate age had stepped forward. He might have been in his mid-thirties like Fenrir, or he might have been a hale fifty. Clad in dull, maroon robes uncharacteristic of the bright, garish colors of the majority, the man had dark—nearly black—engaging eyes that appeared to take in everything around him. Some of the less bold nobles eyed him with uncertainty or maybe even distrust, although Fenrir was hardly in the best position to make that judgement.

"By all means, Savant Iolen. You know that this council respects your opinion. At least, some of us do," added Malless, not exactly under his breath.

"Look at this man." Iolen spread his hands theatrically as he gestured toward Fenrir. "His skin is mottled, pale and splotched with red. He has obviously perspired through his underclothes, and is shaking either from these sweat-soaked clothes or from the unparalleled power of all of your noble glares." He drew out the last part ever so slightly, the words carrying just a hint of irony. A handful of nobles grumbled at his tone, and Baron Erlins even took a step forward, that useless sword gripped in his hand.

"It is obvious that there is no assassin in this room. Assuming an assassin could have gotten into a walled city on high alert due to the presence of this very council, he would have had to approach the Plateau without being spotted. Then, he would have to avoid the fine guardsmen and retainers who are currently overcrowding this fortress, enter this room through its only entrance, and strike just this one single guardsman," said Savant Iolen with a just-so-subtle hint of mockery.

Fenrir nervously shifted his weight from side to side, beginning to understand. He removed his helmet, showing that his short, brown-blond hair was soaking wet, his head showing indents from the tight straps that had held the gear in place. It was a relief to feel the air on his head, cloying though the chamber was. His head clearing, he had reasoned out what had happened, and now he braced himself for the almost inevitable outcome of this international spectacle.

433

"No, this man was not the target of an incredibly skilled, practically-invisible, world-class assassin. There is a much simpler explanation. It is hotter than Pandemonium in this room, and the man is wearing at least sixty pounds of armor." Iolen paused, almost as if to give his audience time to draw their own conclusions. He smiled.

"This man simply fainted."

The sounds of the rising mercenary army—tired soldiers grumbling and weary officers shouting orders, creaking wagons being loaded with supplies, and the clanging of iron pans—woke Fenrir from his uncomfortable slumber. The hangover was a commonplace feeling, though he'd been sober long enough that the experience felt worse than he remembered. His skull was being crushed by rocks, and his mouth was full of fetid cotton.

Much how he'd felt that day during the Ardian Council.

He'd simply fainted. Hence had come the proclamation from that Savant Iolen, and who was Fenrir to dispute the learned man? Not that he'd had much of an opportunity; he had been immediately dismissed by Captain de Hosta, the old officer seemingly reluctant to do so and yet having little choice. Fenrir's sudden unconsciousness, in reality, had made for an intranational incident, the fall heard around the country. The panic and fear raised by his toppling, armored body had caused not only a disruption of the Ardian Council, but also caused one overweight earl to badly sprain his ankle while fleeing, and also brought one of Duke Proan's daughters—the attractive one, at that—to wet herself quite publicly.

Luckily, the embarrassment of nobles had worked in his favor. Instead of admitting to themselves and others that the alarm had been raised entirely over a fainting guardsman, many had maintained, afterward, that there truly *was* an assassin in the room that night. Indeed, many had ignored Savant Iolen's pronouncement and vehemently blamed dark magicks. Even with no evidence, many still maintained that a guardsman had been felled by a *pasnes alna*, one who'd been aiming to kill the gathered nobility of Ardia. It had been helpful, as the contrary mistruths clouded the factuality of that day, and few knew of Fenrir's exact fate.

The only positive outcome of the entire situation had been that it caused his father quite a bit of shame.

Afterward, Martis—as a friend, not a physician—had checked Fenrir over. Again and again, in fact, as the physician was nothing if not thorough. Fenrir's older friend had maintained that he could find no hint of weakness, nothing that would predispose him, a healthy man in his thirties, to suddenly lose consciousness. Fenrir had, after all, spent hundreds, if not thousands, of hours standing guard in full armor, and rarely felt anything near syncopic. And yet, somehow, everything had gone black that day.

Fenrir had thought about it nearly every day since. Rage took him if any of the rare people who knew of the episode—aside from good friends, of course—even hinted at his weakness. It had led to more than a couple of tavern fights following his dismissal, as Fenrir had attempted break the teeth of any guardsmen who'd commented about his secret. Soon, he'd been banned from the typical haunts of the Plateau's house guards and had to drink in less reputable establishments. He was still quick to fight, but the quality was more common—and even desirable—amidst that population. Such fights usually ended with bloodied knuckles, some chipped teeth, and an occasional broken bone. Fenrir had ached to prove himself, to prove he was not weak.

Maybe that was why he'd joined The House… to affirm to the world that he was not fragile or impuissant. That he was not, as a now-broken-faced man had once told him, a cockless, spineless lady of the night.

"Sir? Coldbreaker?" A hesitant voice at the mouth of his flap.

"Yeah. Galen, right?" The disheveled head of a young Rafónese boy had popped into the tent at his response.

"Ajay, sir." The boy's voice was tight.

"That's right. What is it?"

"You asked me to alert you when the wagon train was prepared. We'll be moving soon, if you want to resume your position in the wagon bed. With that girl." He touched three fingers to his cheek—likely a ward against evil.

Fenrir felt for Merigold's own little ward in his pocket, rolling the chill, rusted metal in his fingers. Like Fenrir, this girl was not content to be a victim of circumstance. Fenrir reached into his slept-in boots, pulling out his heptagram. He examined the sharp, multi-pointed star for a long moment, and then removed the symbol from its chain, pocketing the chain with Merigold's knife and sticking the loose heptagram back in his boot.

"Sir?" Ajay was impatient.

"Aye, I'll be there. Break down my tent and have it packed with the wagons. And get me some leather, thread, and a strong needle. The saddlery back in town should have it."

"Sir." A definite rancor there.

Can't make everyone happy.

436

Chapter 31

The Army of Brockmore was on the move.

Six thousand, seven hundred-and-sixty-two men had been pulled from Lady Escamilla's holdings across the whole of Ardia. Fifteen hundred-and-four of those were mounted cavalry, if that term could be used for men mounted on plow and domestic riding horses. Nine hundred-and-eight were longbowmen, equipped with the signature yellow yew bows of Jecusta. Emma wondered what deal Escamilla had made to secure those bows, as they were never seen outside of the Jecustan military, but she'd somehow had them stockpiled at Brockmore prior to the arrival of her forces. The woman was truly a mystery.

The remainder of Escamilla's forces were infantry. Each of these footsoldiers was equipped with a short sword, a halberd, and a small shield. How Escamilla had managed a standard arsenal for each infantryman, Emma had no idea. Sadly, she hadn't been able to work the same magic with their armor. The men were wearing anything from leathers to bronzes and irons. The patchwork nature of the infantry was largely covered by off-white tabards, each emblazoned with the crimson apple that had become Escamilla's standard years ago. Escamilla claimed that she had never authorized a standard, that her men had simply created it out of love for her, trying to capture the fairytale of her beginnings by going back to that bag of fruit which a young Escamilla had sold for a profit. In fact, when the apple standard had begun appearing around her first holdings, Escamilla had had to appease the nobility by 'punishing' the men responsible. Escamilla, of course, was not a noble lady, and would *never* make an effort to create a crest like that—it could be seen as an act of treason. However, she'd been unable to root out this standard and keep it from popping up all around the ranks of her men.

Emma, however, knew Escamilla better than many, and also understood that men's loyalties lay as much, or more, with people as with banners. Escamilla had almost certainly authorized the apple standard and then pantomimed efforts to stomp it out.

And now, a small army of seamstresses were creating apple tabards so that the army could have some unity through their common garb.

Behind Escamilla's forces marched the two mercenary armies. The Silver Lady's Fists of Ultner, women all, marched easily in even ranks, silver fists emblazoned on their matching tabards. Six hundred-and-forty of them. Behind them, in looser ranks, came the least disciplined but probably the most battle-hardened force marching toward Florens. The nineteen hundred-and-twenty-one members of Ferl's Company served as rear-guard, joining the larger army on the road. Fenrir and Tilner had made record time in retrieving this force and, apparently, their task had been made easier by some legal troubles faced by Ferl in Hunesa. Something about some violent murders.

"As of this morning, there are nine thousand, three hundred, and twenty-three soldiers marching to Florens, not including high-ranking officers, the baggage train, or camp followers," recited Emma, responding to Escamilla's inquiry. Emma had taken a varied, undefined role that included running messages and conveying orders, as well as keeping track of numbers, unit dispositions, equipment, and supplies in order to provide Escamilla with quick answers, and she was also managing some of Escamilla's financial affairs, at least as they related to the military. It was almost as if she had been trained for this very role from years of working with the lady, spying and gathering information, and keeping track of a massive amount of material without writing it down.

At the same time, she'd been given a wardrobe to match Escamilla's, a quartet of guards who shadowed her everywhere, and essentially limitless authority as the voice of Escamilla. Men

438

bowed when they saw her coming, and she was afforded only the best treatment.

For so long, Emma had simply been an observer of great people and great events. She had been nothing to these people. Background. Furniture. An oddity, sometimes, given her disabled hand. She had watched quietly as dukes and barons and rich merchants discussed matters of national security or the dispensation of tens of thousands of yets.

She'd had no utility, no influence on such events, and she'd wanted neither. It had been a hard life, but usually a safe life. It had been the life of a servant. And now, she had been thrust into this position of authority, given true power and responsibility.

She felt considerably overwhelmed.

"And have the outrider reports come in yet?" asked Escamilla. The two rode together near the middle of Escamilla's forces, which stretched more than a mile down the road. It was a straight shot from Brockmore to Florens—at least, it was if you didn't mind a little off-roading through grassy fields and farmlands. Given that time was a factor, that was exactly what the army was doing. Farmers watched, stunned, as their livelihood was trampled underneath the boots of men marching to war. These farmers' children might starve this winter, and the army had not yet crossed the borders into the duchy of Florens.

At least Escamilla and her staff had strict rules regarding foraging, looting, and misconduct. Four men had been lashed already for sneaking off to a tavern at a small town, near which the army had camped. They might have gone undetected, too, had one not started a bar fight, causing hundreds of yets worth of damage. Two separate men had been hanged for rape that same night.

Three others had been responsible for beating to death an old man thought, by the locals, to be a heretic, a worshipper of Ultner.

439

The report said that they hung the man by his ankles over a fire, taking turns beating him with burning brands. This had gone unpunished. The Army of Brockmore was marching for Yetra, after all, and such acts were nearly unavoidable.

Emma liked to think that they were fighting on the side of right and justice, but she'd read enough of the disciplinary reports to doubt the justice part. Sometimes, it seemed, bad men were needed to do the right thing. And these reports hadn't even included Ferl's Company.

"The rear outriders from Brockmore have caught up, yes. That's what I came to report. Two hundred-and-twelve more men have been equipped and are marching to catch up as of thirty-six hours ago. At our current pace, it's unlikely that they'll catch up until we meet the enemy." *Meet the enemy.* Emma had said it so casually, though the prospect held nothing but uncertainty and death. As it was, even including the Florens army, they were outmanned and probably out-trained. Though a chunk of Rostane's army was made up of conscripts, many were career military. Escamilla's men, though soldiers in their own right, were primarily guards and peacekeepers, largely untested in battle and certainly not trained in fighting as a cohesive unit (aside from what little training they'd gained over the past few weeks, which wasn't much).

And yet, they were what stood between Duke Penton and Florens. Perhaps all of Ardia.

"What of the forward scouts?"

"Let me think—" said Emma, reluctant to share this part. Escamilla, though unbowed, was wearing the strain of the march on her face.

"Emma. Now," Escamilla said sharply.

"The Rostanian Army has halted its desertion problem. They… dragged… several men to death, and lashed dozens more, to the

440

bone. One of your spies, a camp-follower, saw the bodies. They were, her missive reported, shredded beyond recognition."

"Brutal." Escamilla said, reacting less than Emma had expected. Her mask was firmly fixed, as it was most of the time, these days.

"Yes, quite brutal." Emma shuddered. She couldn't imagine. "The Rostanian Army has finally caught up with their forward forces, and they are scant days from Florens. There is a messenger, newly come, from Malless, who seeks to speak with you. He wouldn't share his message with me."

Escamilla sighed. Another problem needing an answer, no doubt. Malless had been sending out multiple messengers daily, requesting that the Army of Brockmore arrive with all speed. Each messenger would report only to Escamilla. At this point, it was an annoyance.

"Another one. I'll meet with the man when we make camp. It's time we finalized our strategy for the coming battle. No more dawdling and wavering." Escamilla's eyes had a distant look in them, and they rode in silence—or, whatever silence could be found in the midst of a marching, swearing, and shouting army. Several quiet minutes passed.

"Camilla, what's on your mind?" asked Emma, seeking to break the silence.

"What, aside from war, death, destruction, and the rapid depletion of my fortune?" she asked with a weary half-smile.

"Yes, aside from that," Emma returned the smile.

"I'm an old woman, Emma. An old, tired woman who wanted to spend the end of her career quietly relaxing in one of my estates. But, instead, I find myself organizing and leading an army, fighting an unwinnable fight against a much bigger force. I'm not cut out for this, Emma. This is young people's business. I don't have the energy, anymore." Escamilla's eyes were fixed straight ahead, but clearly her mind was elsewhere.

"You're not old—you've many, many years left! You were never going to retire, and you're sprier than someone half your age," said Emma. It was unnerving for her to hear Escamilla speaking like this. She was too strong to talk as if she was already defeated. And, Emma didn't want a reminder of the hopelessness of their situation.

"Spry? My knees ache, my hands are stuck to these reins, and I am dying to relieve myself right now."

"Yes, spry! Do you remember catching that vase that I was going to clobber Fenrir with? Or, remember the way you handled that spear, when those monsters attacked? I, in my youth, was paralyzed in fear, and you struck true. Where did you learn to handle weapons like that, anyhow?" Emma asked the last somewhat offhandedly, hoping to change the subject from whatever was ailing Escamilla.

Escamilla was silent, her face suddenly hard. She didn't say anything in response.

"I'm sorry to offend, my la—"

"No, Emma. No 'my lady' right now. 'Camilla' will do," Escamilla said wearily.

"Of course, Camilla," said Emma, watching Escamilla ride through the corners of her eyes.

"You have never asked how I ended up where I am: a wealthy, powerful old woman."

"Everyone knows that, Camilla. Your father died and you sold his last bag of fruit for far more than what it was worth, giving you more yets to work with. You sold and sold and sold, until you ended up with land, and so on." Emma gestured to the apple

442

standards and tabards. "We are surrounded by reminders of your first sale and first major venture."

"And how did my father die?" Escamilla asked, looking at Emma askance.

Emma didn't know. No one ever mentioned the Garrick Breen part of the story, aside from the fact that he'd been a poor merchant.

"You don't know, Emma. No one does, as the truth is not worth telling. My father was a thief, a drunk, and a liar. No one would deal with him where I grew up, so we took to traveling. Him, my sister, and my mother."

"You have a sister?" Emma was stunned at this. Escamilla had never mentioned family, not a single time in their years together.

"Had a sister. My father sold her to slavers in Rostane when he needed money for liquor." Escamilla said in a monotone.

"There aren't slavers in Rostane!" Emma said, unwilling to believe this story. It was terrible—to sell your child for extra spending money?

"Silly girl," Escamilla said, with some affection. "Anywhere there is water and ships, you will find slavers. Either for galley slaves or domestic household slaves in Sestra or Algania. I don't know where Alesha ended up. I've since spent a good deal of money trying to track her down, but to no avail. You can't track nothing, and slaves are less than nothing."

"I'm so sorry, Cami—" Emma began, but Escamilla cut her off, her voice finding some urgency, some emotion.

"And my mother? She was a wisp of a woman—would never have stood against Garrick's wishes. She knew about his plans for Alesha, and yet she did nothing." Escamilla was growing heated, gesturing as she rode. "She had opportunities, plenty of opportunities, to report him to authorities. He beat her, you know.

The same way he beat me. And she never said a word. Not for herself, not for me."

"Camilla, I—"

"It caught up with her. He knocked her down one night at a campsite, and she hit her head on a rock. Something broke in her brain. After a couple weeks of hauling her around while I cared for her, he left her behind. Or, at least, she wasn't there one morning.

"So, when we traveled with a caravan, I spent time with the guards. Learned how to handle swords and spears, even if I had to pay a price. Of course, I had no money to offer, so I whored myself out for a year. It's alright, though, because Garrick already gave me practice at that."

Emma was horrified, but Emma did not stop. This had been building for years and years, a festering excess of bile and ichor that finally had an escape.

"I could have killed Garrick in his sleep. The man drank himself into a stupor enough nights. But, that would have been too easy. He wouldn't have known why he was being killed, or who was doing the killing. So, one night on the road, just me and him, I confronted him with a spear I'd secreted in our little rickshaw. He *laughed* at me. Laughed, the old bastard. He said he should have sold me, too, but I was a younger and softer version of my mother, so he'd kept me around. He grabbed the old sword that he carried around from when he served, briefly, in the military. I could have stabbed him in the back, but I let him arm himself. He came at me, trying to kill me. I wore him down, bled him with a dozen tiny wounds. When he fell, exhausted, I looked him in the eye as I drove the spear, slowly, into his gut. He swore and ranted and screamed and begged for his life, but I didn't give it to him. I watched him die. It was one of the sweetest sights."

444

Escamilla was openly weeping now, tears streaming down her cheeks as they rode.

"The next day, I waited for a passing caravan, told the story of how a robber had murdered my father while I hid in the woods. Who would think that a petite seventeen-year-old girl would have murdered her father in cold blood? They helped me bury him, that bastard. And I took what remained in his rickshaw—not a single bag of fruit among the goods, mind you—and sold it near Florens."

She finally stopped, quickly and unobtrusively dabbing at her eyes with the white-laced sleeve of her crimson riding habit, designed to match the apple standard in every regard. There were of her guards nearby. Escamilla and Emma rode underneath an ornate tarp suspended by poles that were held aloft by four horses, which were minded by pairs of foot soldiers. It had not yet rained today, but judging from the gray weight of the clouds, it would not likely hold off much longer. Some of the soldiers were glancing over, having heard their liege lady's voice raised with emotion. A couple even had their hands on their hilts.

Escamilla took a deep breath and composed herself.

"Camilla, I don't know what to say. I am so sorry all that happened to you. But, it made you who you are. It made you strong," said Emma in a near whisper, simply shocked at the story. She didn't know what else to say—what could she say?

"You say that as I am wiping snot from my nose and tears from my eyes. My apologies, dear. This is what happens when I'm exhausted and surrounded by weapons of war. I think about the past." Her voice was again calm, though it held a bit of a scratch. "But, think nothing more of it. You, my dear, have faced just as much adversity in your young life."

Yes, she had faced something like that. Never knowing her father, a pretty standard situation for the daughter of a servant.

445

Her mother had been tight-lipped about it, but he'd probably been some guardsman or minor noble. Losing her mother to the stomach flux. Racked with guilt for not being at her side when she died, and for being anxious to get her stinking body into the street for the corpse wagons. And then the ordeal with Fenrir and her hand.

She examined her mangled appendage—her thumb, pointing finger, and little stub of a middle finger attached to what remained of her hand, hidden under her custom-designed black glove. The surgeon, Martis, had saved her hand, though she recalled the pain following the surgeries being worse than the pain when she'd woken the morning after the attack. And now, the man who'd done this to her was scarcely a mile away, marching with the mercenaries. She clenched her little claw for a moment, and then relaxed it with a deep breath. Like Escamilla had told her, time and time again, she needed to push her emotions aside.

"But, maybe it is better to keep the past where it is and focus on the future."

"You are becoming a very smart girl, my dear. Let us both focus on the future today, starting with finalizing our strategy. Let Malless' messenger know that I will meet with him in the command tent when we camp this evening, and make sure he is rested. Until then, we have plenty to do to occupy ourselves."

"Yes, *my lady*," Emma said, tongue-in-cheek.

"Funny, too. I wonder why you are unmarried." Escamilla's voice was flat. "Come to the command tent this evening when you are done with your other duties for the day."

"My other duties?" Emma had thought to ride with Escamilla for the remainder of the day.

"Yes. I'd like for you to check in on the girls."

Chapter 32

Merigold was tired.

It seemed that she was always tired since awaking amidst this army marching to war. Fatigued and achy, her joints felt like rusty hinges that hadn't seen oil in ages. And, every morning, she was still torn with nausea no matter what she ate. Even most afternoons found her stomach in knots.

Unfortunately, the baby had survived Merigold's ordeal.

Much of what had happened in Hunesa was vague in her mind—more of a general impression, a flashing of images. Dear Yetra, but her life had been a blur since her imprisonment. None of it seemed real, but her thin, weakened body and the few artifacts left from Dunmore told her the truth. Everything had changed. Again.

Days ago, she had regained consciousness in a covered wagon, the man Fenrir at her side. She had recognized him instantly, although he had changed since she'd met him at the Duckling— hair trimmed short, beard and temples grayer than she remembered. He'd jumped to his feet when she finally stirred, either in shock or excitement; which was unclear. He had seemed happy, although she'd noted that he didn't smile.

He'd told her that she'd been attacked in Hunesa when trying to hire mercenaries. That *had* been her plan, hiring mercenaries to help her find Ragen. She recalled that idiotic idea. A young girl, heaving around a sack of octagonal, high value yets, walking into a nest of thieves, murderers, and rapists. She'd essentially been asking to be assaulted.

She recalled her head swimming at the vague memory, feeling herself almost shifting to a different consciousness. She'd had a vision of herself, of rough hands holding down an overweight, blond girl… Those thoughts! She'd never touched a woman like that… Those hadn't been her hands!

Fenrir had shaken her out of the brief trance and, at the feeling of his hands on her body, controlling her, Merigold had felt a swift, panicky desire to stab him in the neck. She'd managed to choke down the urge, though, and force her mind and body to relax. She'd only pushed Fenrir's hands away from her shoulders instead, and he'd jerked back as if burned by her touch. Maybe he had remembered what touching her cost him in the Duckling. Or, maybe it was something she'd done back in Hunesa.

Merigold probed him about what had happened in that inn with the mercenaries. He'd been tight-lipped about it, only telling her that she had used her *powers* to escape from the men, but used too much and lost consciousness. She had some remembrance of the feel of the magic, the blackened vessels of the mercenaries, and of tearing out their life force, and using it to… and that was where she couldn't remember anything more. Some fleeting memories of Fenrir and some other men talking, and then nothing, until she'd woken up here.

Throughout the next couple of days, Fenrir had visited her in the wagon while she'd regained her strength. They didn't talk much, but he watched her often. Not in the way that Saren had, or even in the way that Fenrir himself had in the Duckling those months ago, but more in the way that Ragen had. For some reason, she wanted to tell Fenrir what had happened to her, to Dunmore, and to her family. But giving voice to those events would make them too real, creating phantasms that she wasn't ready to face.

One evening, after they had spoken for a few minutes about the disposition of the army, and a little bit about Rostane, he'd left abruptly, leaving behind a small pouch without a word. In the bag had been her dagger, her little nail-and-linen make-shift weapon, attached to a small silver chain, the blade in a folded piece of

448

leather made to be a sort of sheath. She had kept it around her neck since, and it gave her some comfort while she was surrounded by these soldiers. Her little weapon, returned to her. How had Fenrir found it? How had Fenrir known?

A Lady Escamilla had visited her also—a formal older woman who was apparently leading this army. She had asked Merigold a lot of inane questions about her life and had smiled a lot, wrinkles creasing her angular face. Escamilla had said that the army was going to keep Meri safe while she recovered, and would give her shelter and protection. It seemed so altruistic.

Merigold did not trust her, of course. She was essentially a prisoner, once again, though a better fed and cleaner one than before.

The well-dressed noblewoman had inquired about Merigold's powers and abilities also, subtly and not without kindness. Had Merigold not already been suspicious and on-guard, she may not have noticed. But Meri had given nothing away, and managed to learn that she had committed some acts of great violence against the mercenaries. She still didn't have any details, but she'd gleaned enough to know that she was capable. Capable of taking care of herself.

And maybe capable of helping her father after all.

She just needed to figure out how this damn magic worked. It had the power to destroy her home and her family, but clearly, it might also have the power to give her revenge.

Since then, Merigold had begun *trying* to rediscover her powers, to figure out how to manipulate them to some extent. Early in her life, drawing had just been something that she could do, like breathing or laughing. She could focus, almost without thinking, and see the power—the *maenen,* Cryden called it— residing within everyone near her. Meri could then tap into it with a touch and a thought, instinctively knowing that drawing more

449

than a thimble's-worth, so to speak, would attract attention. Of course, she had occasionally drawn a little too much in the past, with her target flinching or looking around, confused. But she had never before drawn so much as she had from Fenrir that night at the Duckling, and her experience with the mercenaries was too hazy for her to remember.

Something that had been so simple and effortless had grown so difficult. What had Cryden said? That her ability to sense *maenen* in others may have been obscured by her trauma? The moment she'd needed the power the most, when Saren had bore down upon her, it had failed her. Since then, she had only accessed her power once—again when she was in great danger. Merigold understood neither how she had tapped into her magic on the latter occasion, nor why she had been entirely unable to access the magic once and then found it so effortless the other time.

So, she worked at it. Merigold would peek out from her covered wagon, seeing the loosely-packed men marching behind her, dust rising to obscure the sweltering summer sun like a hazy fog. The nearest soldiers were maybe ten feet away, their crimson apple tabards showing the dirt of the road more and more, especially since the storms had come. With great concentration and a throbbing focus, Merigold could manage to sense their *maenen* intermittently, flickering like an oil lamp running low on fuel, though the efforts left her with a splitting headache behind her eyes and a feeling of nausea that was unrelated to her blasted pregnancy.

Meri had even managed to draw some *maenen*, just a sliver, from soldiers helping her in and out of the wagon at mealtimes. But, so unlike before, it filled her with a disconcerting feeling of dread, leaving her weak and shivering. It offered an unnerving juxtaposition against the rejuvenating effect the *maenen* had previously had. Every instinct told Meri to stop drawing, but she persisted, continuing to push through these awful feelings, continuing to practice.

She would need to master this talent before she could seek escape, and then vengeance.

"I'm supposed to stay with you for now," said a young, short-haired girl, vaulting into the moving wagon with little ceremony and a great deal of dexterity. Merigold was startled from her seat, hitting her head against one of the bows suspending the tarp as she leapt up. The girl ignored her, immediately hunkering down onto a bench.

"Who in the name of Yetra are you?" asked Merigold.

"Morgyn Coldwater," the girl said abruptly, glancing toward the opening.

"And what are you doing in here?"

Morgyn said nothing, and just continued to watch outside, askance. She was soaking wet, her white maid's dress clinging to her lithe, adolescent form. The summer storms had been raging unabated for days now, turning the fields to muck. The army was marching cross-country at this point, having crossed the border into the duchy of Florens, and making far worse time than expected. Merigold had overheard the soldiers complaining of extreme chafing, and some men were marching much as sailors were rumored to walk, legs bowed to avoid their thighs rubbing together. It seemed altogether unpleasant.

Today had been the first day where the sun had poked through the clouds in a week, giving the soldiers hope that they would dry out. But that hope had been smashed like raindrops upon the rocks as renewed sheets of water had begun falling an hour ago, making up for the few hours of relative dryness.

"Excuse me, Miss Coldwater. I would ask that you—"

"There you are! Gods, Ignatius. You were supposed to be watching her!" Two more people were suddenly pulling themselves into the wagon, the space seeming suddenly cramped. The speaker, a woman of maybe thirty, had trouble navigating the hatch, her crippled hand awkwardly gripping the wooden support. Her gorgeous red hair was flattened to her face, probably blinding her completely. The last person to board Meri's previously-empty wagon was a rather overweight older man, balding, who also struggled to enter the slowly-moving wagon, his left leg moving stiffly. He wore orange robes and a green stole, as well as a great, golden Ascension medallion, which spun wildly as he finally managed to heave himself fully into the wagon.

"Morgyn, this isn't a game! I was just trying to talk to you!" said the red-haired woman. Merigold remembered her; Emma, it was. She had hung in the background when that Lady Escamilla had interrogated her.

"And I told you that I didn't want to talk!" shouted Morgyn, folding her arms and dropping her head into the go-to pose of a teenager. Meri remembered striking that pose quite a few times with Ragen. But Merigold's own long platinum hair had covered her face like a security blanket in those situations, while Morgyn's short hair did little to obscure her features.

Emma sighed with exasperation and gave Merigold a wan smile. "Hi again, Meri. I'm Emma. I was going to come by and see how you're doing, too. I work for Lady Escamilla. I'm her... I'm not even sure right now."

Merigold had immediately felt drawn Emma. The woman seemed to be in over her head, just like Meri. And, she was stunningly beautiful, which always helped. She had a lot of features in common with Sandra. That hair... curly where Sandra's was straight, and Sandra's had been noticeably lighter and blonder, but both had some red. And both had green eyes, another rare feature. Put them together and, well, Emma just made her think of Sandra, of home, and of happier and simpler times.

"Hi Emma—it's nice to see you again. It seems like you're having a pleasant day," said Merigold, her voice hinting at irony.

"Indeed! This little one is a runner," Emma said, gesturing at Morgyn, who was continuing to sulk. "Oh, I am remiss. This is Ignatius Pender, the Chaplain of the Army of Brockmore."

Meri might have imagined it, but there seemed to be some tension between Emma and the religious man. The high-ranking Yetranian official gave a quick nod, though, and flopped down across from Morgyn, rubbing his thigh.

"Apologies, my girl. This weather really wears at my old leg." His voice was hoarse, and he coughed wetly for a few seconds. "And this preaching has my throat as raw as the uncooked meat they feed the soldiers. So many, however, are seeing the light of Yetra and the glory for which we march. The glory of her, and her ideals. 'For it is faith that truly feeds the bellies of the masses, not meat or bread or wine. And the satiation of faith endures, though renewal is required,'" Ignatius quoted.

"Fowles?" Merigold blurted out despite her best efforts to forget *The Book of Amorum*.

"Oh, you are familiar with *The Book*, my girl? You must be very much so, as 'the Filling of Faith' is a relatively obscure reference. Where did you learn of *The Book*?" asked Ignatius, continuing to massage his thigh but now looking at Merigold.

"I am from Dunmore, a small—"

"Dunmore, with the duck eggs! I have visited, though you were probably only an egg at the time, yourself. Does Taneo Marsh still lead the congregation?"

"No. He… passed away recently." Meri looked at her feet, unwilling to meet the eyes of the chaplain lest she lose control of her emotions.

"That old chunk of granite? We overlapped at Rosewan together. Might I ask how he passed?"

Merigold remembered Florence Marsh, Taneo Marsh's wife, leaning over the hedges, wearing the flowered gardening dress that she was so proud of. Dead, seemingly untouched. Not far from her had been a body that had been torn to bloody bits— clothes, skin, flesh, and organs shredded beyond recognition. Taneo Marsh had rarely strayed far from his wife's side.

When she had been picking her way through Dunmore, so soon after her own escape, Merigold had felt numb, stunned at the sight of things. Then, she was bound with depression, a cancerous growth infecting her every move, her every thought. Now, reflecting on it, she was angry. Filled with rage, fingernails digging into her palms, drawing blood. How dare something like that happen to good people? How dare *Yetra* let that happen to good people?

"He is dead. His wife is dead. The entire village of Dunmore is dead, murdered by dark magic," Merigold's voice had become more rapid as she spoke, more strangled as her anger bubbled forth at this simpering, pious man. "Most every man, woman, and child left for the buzzards. Some seemingly untouched, some torn beyond identification. Good men and women, and all children are innocents? Tell me, Chaplain. You are a man of Yetra. Tell me why these people were allowed to be killed. Tell me!" She was breathing heavily, on the precipice of tears, glaring at the chaplain through blurry eyes.

Aside from the omnipresent sounds of a marching army and the clatter of the rain on the cover, the interior of the wagon had gone silent. Painfully silent. Emma fell onto the bench next to Morgyn, while Morgyn stared openly at Merigold. The chaplain

454

ran his hands through his damp, thinning hair and took a deep breath.

"Please, sit, my girl. Meri." Merigold hesitated, but let herself lose her balance when the wagon hit a particularly rough bump, landing heavily on the bench.

"I am truly, truly sorry for your loss, my girl. I will pray for you, every night, and the people of Dunmore, taken according to Yetra's plan. For Yetra does, indeed, have a plan for all of us." Ignatius had spoken in a calming voice, as if he were delivering a sermon. This was obviously not the first time that he had discussed the topic of death.

"And Yetra's plan was to allow everyone to be murdered? Good people? Children, even?" Meri could not fully contain the anger in her voice.

"This is a classic philosophical debate; why do bad things happen to good people? Thinking men, religious men, great men, and small men have spent their lives in pursuit of the answer. I cannot presume to know better than all of those who have come before me. However, I am reminded of Yetra's own story. I imagine that we are all familiar with her origins?"

"Of course," said Meri, half-scoffing. She had most of *The Book of Amorum* memorized at this point. There'd been a copy in every room of the Duckling, including her bedroom.

"You others?" the chaplain asked, raising an eyebrow.

"Well, my duties at the Plateau had typically precluded my attendance to your ceremonies," muttered Emma. It was poor form, in Ardia, to miss services.

Morgyn was now hugging her knees on the bench. "No," she said simply.

"Well, I suppose a quick education is in order so that we can relate to our sister here. As we all know, the world was formed at

455

the crux of Harmony and Pandemonium, two unstoppable forces that ever have, and ever will, wander the Cosmos, drawn to each other like iron and a lodestone. Early images showed Harmony and Pandemonium as having human characteristics, great beings inevitably warring with whatever great powers were at hand. Many now conceptualize Harmony and Pandemonium to be more forces of nature, realities of existence, that seek to impose their aspects upon their surroundings without will. Others still believe that there is a consciousness behind the forces, a powerful desire to shape reality. I suppose that we shall never know the truth. Regardless, I digress."

Merigold was sitting and listening closely, just like she would have during her weekly service. Her anger was fading in the face of this man's soothing and authoritative—though slightly sore— voice. Emma was working at her fingernails with a small file. Morgan, still clinging to her knees, was watching Ignatius from beneath lowered eyelids.

"The world was initially created as a battleground between Harmony and Pandemonium, and life was created to serve as the soldiers in that battle. No creature on earth was beholden to either of the warring forces; rather, these forces influenced innate, subconscious motivations and needs. Each of us have a touch of Harmony and Pandemonium within ourselves, each vying for dominion. These feelings, of course, are not as strong as when the great forces were present, before the battle had been won on this world, before they left for other worlds. During this time, humans evolved from primitives, living in small groups and tribes, into societal people, gathering in greater numbers, building villages and towns and cities. Learning more about how the world works and harnessing powers of magic and science."

Ignatius paused, coughing into his sleeve. He cleared his throat.

"With technology, with the rise of magic, comes violence. Wars were waged on an unimaginable scale; the loss of precious life, extreme. Pandemonium reigned for a time, and the scales tilted toward the destruction of Harmony and peace, at least in this world. Truly, these warring forces could never be destroyed. The—"

"Chaplain, could you please reach the moral of your story? There is a war to be fought, strategies to be determined, and I'm certain that these girls have more important things to do," said Emma. Ignatius frowned, an expression that seemed unusual on his jovial face.

"Girl, perhaps you should focus on this story and care more about your salvation into Yetra's loving embrace. Lest people begin to think you a heathen." The two glared at each other. Emma clutched her disfigured hand with the other, while Ignatius held his medallion, perhaps as a not so gentle reminder of his station.

The tension was too much for Meri.

"Yes, with the world out of balance, a personification of the power of Harmony was born upon the planet. Yetra," said Meri, finishing the story.

Ignatius shot one last withering look at Emma and then smiled at Meri.

"Exactly. Yetra was born human, however, not an all-powerful goddess—the Champion of Harmony, as we know her. She was shaped by her life and experiences, and her childhood was integral in her development to be a proper host. With Pandemonium reigning in the world, danger was omnipresent. Yetra was born in a place called Auqine, a town that had the capability to protect itself from the chaos that raged elsewhere. A stout wall, many skilled soldiers who defended it in the name of peace and

457

concord. Yetra was born to loving parents and average prosperity. That did not last."

Morgyn was no longer feigning indifference. Her head rested in her crossed arms, and her brown-flecked eyes didn't leave the chaplain.

"When Pandemonium holds sway, all are at risk. Even good people could become corrupted. And that is exactly what happened. Auqine rotted from the inside, with several men and women conspiring to open the gates at night to the forces of Pandemonium, warriors who sought to sow chaos and attain equilibrium through subjugation." Ignatius again cleared his throat. Merigold offered him her canteen, from which he gratefully sipped.

"Yetra was outside the town with a small group of soldiers and women, gathering ingredients in the forest for medicine and foodstuffs. When they returned, the village had been destroyed. Her mother had been savaged and her father had been tortured and killed, his body nailed to his home's doorframe like so many others. Many bodies were not found—survivors were made slaves to serve in the armies of Pandemonium.

"Without this terrible event, the goddess that we now revere, Yetra, would have remained living in this peaceful town, likely happy and ignorant to the ways of the world, dying before achieving godhood. However, this event tempered her, forged her into the hardest steel. She learned the difference between fighting for peace and fighting for subjugation, spreading harmony versus dischord. She led a small group of survivors to recover the slaves and soon built up an army, ultimately defeating the fractured forces of Pandemonium. You see, the suffering of many was required in order for Yetra to achieve her potential and to save the world. The suffering allowed her to ascend and become the goddess who now guides us." Ignatius finally took a breath.

"I am not likely to become a goddess, Chaplain. What could the suffering of Dunmore be worth?" asked Meri with sincerity. *Please, let him have an answer.* She needed an answer.

"No, my girl. There is one goddess who directs our lives. But perhaps you are meant for another purpose, and these events were meant to forge you, as well. The goddess has altered our reality so that the lessons learned in her mortal life apply to our world. Suffering does not occur without purpose. For Yetra knows, as do we all, that there is a balance to be maintained. Perhaps you were chosen to fight Pandemonium, and this was an effort to strengthen you. Perhaps you are meant to provide unflinching support to others who wage this same war. It is beyond us to understand."

Merigold Hinter, chosen to fight Pandemonium. It was nearly laughable, viewed from most angles. Even before her trauma, Meri was nothing more than a fixture in the lives of travelers, living a life that had little impact aside from filling the bellies of those moving between big cities. Afterward, having visited such a large city, Meri could see just how miniscule any individual person could be. How could any one person, particularly a serving girl from an out-of-the-way village, be chosen for anything of importance?

Yes, the idea of being "chosen" should be laughable to Meri. But, as Ignatius spoke, she felt something warm building in her stomach, a forgotten feeling. Hope, maybe? She had forced a sort of balance into the world. Meri had killed at least four people, bad people, who had sinned in some way. Saren, Chad, and—if Fenrir had been accurate—two unnamed mercenaries. Perhaps she *had* been chosen to be one of Yetra's hands on earth, destroying those who committed crimes against Harmony (as all four men surely had), restoring balance. Yetra had to work *through* those on earth, as she had ascended beyond the physical plane.

Merigold had been for some meaning for all of the atrocities that she had been through over the past months. She had been faithful, but had turned away, swinging far from Yetra's image. Now, she felt herself being unwillingly pulled slowly back, and she clung to the chaplain's ideals like a drowning woman clinging to a bit of debris.

Even as she realized that the debris might not save her.

"Where do Ultner and the pagan gods fit into this? Riaon? Oletta?" asked Morgyn abruptly, as if she had been holding in the question. Meri was pulled from her hopeful revelry.

"That is a dark topic, young lady. Perhaps beyond what should be discussed here," Ignatius said, his voice holding a warning.

"We've discussed rape, murder, and wholesale slaughter. Little can be darker than that," said Emma with some sarcasm, earning yet another glare. "But, perhaps you could be even briefer than before."

Ignatius' face clearly showed his consternation for a moment before he found his composure. "Ultner is the counterpart to Yetra, the human-born aspect of Pandemonium. As Yetra began to unite the world under her banner, Ultner was born. By the time he grew older, moving into power, Harmony nearly held sway and peace was falling over the land. He again brought war, destroying so much that Yetra and her people had built, again bringing the world to the brink. The Martyrs sacrificed their own lives in order to hold him at bay, and eventually Yetra managed to subdue Ultner, resulting in her ascension. The world was in shambles, the very face of the earth change, but Yetra has since guided our hands in the path to revival and rebirth."

"And the pagan gods... Oletta?" pushed Morgyn, her eyes glittering.

"The church does not acknowledge them," said Ignatius.

"But—"

"The pagan gods are nothing more than imaginary idols, created by people in an effort to subjugate others," Ignatius spat, finality in his voice.

"Hmmfff," grunted Emma, noncommittally. Meri wasn't sure of the implications of her grunt, but Ignatius clenched his fists and his face turned red. If Emma had offered an insult to Yetranians, then Meri should feel angry herself. But, she couldn't muster the energy.

"Okay, I think we have had enough of a history lesson." Emma reached forward and grasped Meri's hands. "Meri, I am so sorry for what you have been through. Please know that you are safe now, and that anything you want will be yours."

"Thank you, Emma." Merigold felt a flush at her touch. Emma's hands, despite her fancy clothes, were just a little rough.

Emma smiled. "I will be back to speak with you one-on-one again soon. Unfortunately, duty calls, as it ever does." Emma did seem reluctant to rise. "Morgyn, come along. We need to let the lady rest after her ordeals. And no running, this time. When you avoid questions like that, it only seems suspisicous. And you don't need to steal! We'll give you whatever you want. And furthermore..." Emma grabbed Morgyn's arm and lead the reluctant, sullen girl out of the wagon and back into the storm.

Ignatius rose to follow, though with more difficulty and a slight grunt.

"Chaplain, please wait. Can I have a private word with you?"

"Of course." Ignatius appraised her for a moment before flopping back to the bench. "I won't mind an extra moment to stay dry."

Merigold had already trusted this man with most of her story, the first time she had given voice to the atrocities of Dunmore. He had given her some small hope, again, that her life might have meaning, that she might have the strength to do what was needed. She might as well seek his advice on one final matter, as difficult as it might be.

"What is on your mind, sister?" he prompted, kindly. All signs of his anger with Emma had disappeared.

Merigold wrung her hands in her lap, nervous to breach the subject. Who, indeed, liked to talk about being abused?

"During... while Dunmore was..." A deep breath. "A man imprisoned and... and raped me for months, and, before I escaped, I became pregnant with his child," Merigold blurted out all at once, lest she not finish at all.

Ignatius, to his credit, only flinched a little at the unexpected statement, squinting his eyes. He shifted in his seat, seeming markedly uncomfortable, but he did not turn away. "Meri, you have been through so much in your young life. My heart bleeds for you," Ignatius said with sincerity. "How can I assist you?"

"Saren. He was a bad man. A monster. He forced me to do... things... that I am so ashamed of. Things that, if I think about them in the daylight... I am appalled with myself. If I think about them at night, I can't stop crying. And, he even brought others to... to violate me while he watched. Paul and Chad. All monsters... all *fucking* demons," Merigold choked out the last part, unable to believe she'd cursed in front of a holy man, but unable to dredge up any guilt. No words felt strong enough to convey what she had experienced.

The chaplain simply watched her, his face as still as a common room after the lunch rush. And, just like in an empty room, Meri felt an urge to fill the silence.

"I don't know who the father is. There is no way to know. Saren, Chad, or Paul. Regardless, the father is a rapist and a liar. A demon. The child growing inside of me... He is the spawn of an evil, sick man. Chaplain, I know that ending life in the womb is a

462

practice frowned upon in the church, if not explicitly forbidden. But… the child will be evil. And, no matter who the child resembles, I could never love it. Never." Tears were streaming down Meri's face now. Though she had thought about ridding herself of the child, this was the first time she had voiced the option. And she felt like a monster, herself. But, she could not go through with this, with having such a baby.

Again, Ignatius considered her for a long moment, searching her face for something. Or perhaps trying to understand her thoughts. Meri, herself, was unsure what she wanted from this conversation. Just someone to talk to, to confess her sins to? Did she want Ignatius' support in ending the baby's life?

Or, did she want Ignatius to instruct her to keep the child?

"The world, Merigold, is filled with more people than can be counted. They outnumber the stars. And, like the stars, each is a little different. Of course, that applies in terms of physical characteristics. You, my dear, are quite slight, whereas I… " Ignatius patted his ample gut "…am of larger proportions. These differences are what makes us special. 'For we should celebrate our differences rather than let them divide us, lest we be split in twain and separated from love.'"

"Eonor," Merigold murmured, recalling the frequent verse intoned during readings, particularly popular during binding ceremonies.

"Yes! Such a well-learned young lady you are. You should have considered the church…" Merigold's face darkened at this. Only virgins could be confirmed as Maids of Yetra. Ignatius realized his mistake immediately and, flushing, cleared his throat.

"These differences, however, are deeper than just our physical appearance. People have unique fears and wants, needs and desires. People are infused with Pandemonium and Harmony at birth. The father, Merigold, whomever it is, let Pandemonium

463

grow and fester within him, controling his life and behaviors. You, my dear, are filled with Harmony, chosen by Yetra for something great. As are all men, here, currently marching for war. Marching for her honor, to combat the Pandemonium that spreads across Ardia."

Merigold recalled hearing, from one of the soldiers immediately behind her wagon, that an old man had been beaten to death by some soldiers for supposedly being a pagan.

"We are all born with the capacity for good and evil, Harmony and Pandemonium. However, the course of a person's life is not set at birth. No one is born a rapist or a murderer. Or a saint, for that matter. The experiences in their lives—their family, their friends, the events experienced as a child—all feed either this internal Harmony or Pandemonium. Children born by good parents awash in Harmony have a propensity for Harmony, of course. An internal drive for peace and love and protection. But, if they spend time with greedy, vicious friends, surrounded by evil, they will, themselves, become tainted and corrupted. However, the reverse is also true. A child, born with the propensity for Pandemonium, if raised by a loving mother and family, shown the correct path to faith and decency, will grow to be a good person." Ignatius voice was passionate, full of conviction. Meri felt herself moved by his words, just as she used to be moved by Taneo Marsh during service. A lifetime ago.

"But, I have no family left. I have no friends. I am sitting amidst an army marching for war. And… I don't know if I could bear to see the reflection of the father in the face of the child." In fact, Merigold was not certain which man's likeness would be most terrible to see. Saren's, the man who'd beaten and violated her, the man who'd brought others to abuse her. Paul's, her father's age, who had always made her uncomfortable and *seemed* to be the most innately evil. Or Chad, a boy who'd tried to apologize to her, but instead been killed by her own hand.

464

"My dear, there is a strength in you. The fact that you are still moving forward after all that you have been through tells me that. Just as Yetra did, despite her losses, you have the infinite capacity to love. You will hold that baby, when he or she arrives, look into its eyes, and see the Harmony within the child and be at peace. Good people will be drawn to you and will support you. *Balance*, my dear. There will be balance in your life. Yetra will let it be so." Ignatius smiled gently as he spoke, reaching out to hold Meri's hand.

Merigold had forgotten the sheer comforting power of a kind ear. It had been months since she had met a soul to confide in, months where her own thoughts, own emotions, had been imprisoned within her mind with no escape. Fenrir was a reassuring presence, but he brought back memories of violence and simply bolstered her resolve to pursue a path of vengeance unburdened by a child. She had been so filled with anger, sorrow, fear, and hate that avoiding the birth of this child seemed like the only option.

But Ignatius Pender continued to dole out hope in generous portions. He spoke with Merigold for hours, through the delivery of the afternoon meal, past even when the army stopped for the evening. He turned away messengers and put off his own work to listen to Meri and to provide his perspective, his wisdom. He told stories and parables from *The Book*, stories that Merigold already knew, but not the way Ignatius told them. He related accounts from his own life, which was surprisingly diverse for a man of faith, spanning two continents and a half dozen countries from his years as a sailor before finding Yetra. And not a single time did he instruct Meri how to live her life, tell her what to choose.

It was with the calming, focused words of the chaplain that Meri decided that she had the strength. Merigold would keep this baby and raise it as her own.

Chapter 33

Emma took a deep breath in a vain attempt to gain some composure. Her two escorts—a hulking, silent brute called Hammer, and his smaller, droll brother who went by Nail—did little to give her courage for her task. Strong arms and shiny armor would do nothing to help her this evening.

Somehow, this tiny undertaking felt insurmountable. But if she could fight monsters and escape through a ruined temple, if she could confront a holy man and his hypocrisy, she must have the strength to deliver a message to Fenrir.

Because of the build-up of muck from the storms, the army had made camp early. Navigating the messy lines of tents and lean-tos, Emma and her escort eventually found Fenrir's tent, pitched within the confines of Ferl's Company's camp. The mercenary camp felt... unsafe. The men seemed unpredictable, like knives thrown by a juggler, just as likely to cut as be controlled. Perhaps this was an appropriate place for Fenrir, at the side of that slimy Ferl.

Emma had little trust for leader of the mercenaries. Ferl was too handsome and well-spoken. Too confident. And there were more murderers in his army than soldiers.

Emma was not the only one who disliked the mercenary captain. The Silver Lady, Trina Almark, constantly insulted him during meetings, tossing out implications about his honor and manhood, and in particularly how both were lacking. Emma had quickly realized that Trina and Ferl's interactions mirrored her own with Fenrir in many ways, and she felt a connectedness with Trina because of it. There was almost certainly a history between those two, but Emma would likely never know the truth. Regardless, Fenrir was currently acting as the mediator between the mercenary company and the Army of Brockmore, and had been given some vague officership where he did not necessarily have a command of his own, but could issue orders to units in both Escamilla's military and the mercenary company. Part of the terms of the contract.

Emma gestured for her guard to stay outside the tent and straightened her wrinkled riding dress. The poor garment had gone through a cycle of being soaked from the rain and dried in the hot, humid air, and as a result, it was now significantly less striking in appearance than it had previously been. The hem, beautifully embroidered with a floral pattern, was stiff and splattered brown with the omnipresent mud. Her mass of hair was in a similar state.

Making herself presentable was a lost cause.

Emma closed her eyes and scratched at the fabric of Fenrir's tent.

"Yeah. Enter!" called a distracted voice. *Cocks*. Emma had fostered some small hope that she could avoid her former lover.

Flanked by a servant, Fenrir was sitting at a thin table, his head resting on his hands while his fingertips worked at his temples and he peered down at a stack of papers. Orders, probably. Or requisitions for the quartermasters on behalf of Ferl's Company. The most decisive battles of any war were fought with paper. And Fenrir appeared to be losing.

His eyes glanced upward slowly from under his lowered brow, but she noted that his head popped up fully when he noticed the identity of his guest. Fatigue dripped from the bulky man just as rain had near ceaselessly dripped from the iron-shaded sky. His eyes were red-rimmed and framed by dark circles, and he rose from his chair slowly, as if exhausted. He wiped his hand across his forehead and one eye.

"Emma... what could I have done to earn such a delight?" he sighed.

"Hello, Fenrir. Or should I say '*Captain* Coldbreaker'?" Emma responded, mirroring his sarcasm.

"I'd prefer Fenrir. By Ultner, I'd prefer to be back in Rostane. Now, will you sit down?" he asked, slumping back into his chair. Emma followed his example. She wasn't exactly brimming with vigor, herself. And, oh, did her legs and back ache from the riding! Horses truly were a terrible way to travel. It took her a few seconds longer than usual, but she managed to work her tender backside into the seat without betraying too much weakness.

"A moment." Fenrir scrawled something onto a scrap of paper and handed it to his servant, who gave a quick bow and left the tent. Fenrir then took a quick swig from a hidden silver flask, grimacing as the liquid evidently burned his throat, and only then did he give Emma an appraising look.

Emma realized that she was alone with Fenrir for the first time since the night that he had mutilated her, all those years ago. They'd certainly spent a lot of time together as they'd traveled from Rostane to Brockmore, but there had always been Escamilla or Tilner Pick within earshot to serve as a buffer. Looking at him now, older and weary, she wasn't sure how to feel. Instead, she decided to let actions drive her feelings.

She quickly stood from her chair and leaned across the small table, putting as much of her body weight as possible behind an open-palmed slap. She'd connected solidly with Fenrir's jaw, catching him completely off-guard as he staggered out of his chair, knocking it to the ground.

"You little…!" he shouted, bringing his hand to his face. Already, she could see a red mark beginning to appear. She met his anger with resolve, her spine stiff in emulation of Lady Escamilla during a negotiation. Inwardly, she was wondering if her escort would reach her in time to stop the muscular man from throttling her.

468

"Damn, that stings!" Fenrir pounded his other palm onto his table, sending papers flying and an inkwell plummeting to the ground. He rubbed his jaw, breath hissing as he sucked in through clenched teeth while he righted his chair and slowly slumped back into his seat. "I suppose I deserved at least that," he mumbled, barely audibly.

Emma had expected anger, but his sullen acceptance? She wasn't sure how to react to it, and crouched halfway between standing and sitting for a moment before re-taking her seat.

"I don't remember you being so strong," Fenrir said in a weak attempt at humor.

"When you're forced to use one arm for everything, you'll find that arm becomes much stronger," she said firmly, and Fenrir flinched at the remark.

The two sat in uncomfortable silence, Emma fidgeting with her hands, Fenrir rubbing his reddening cheek and tapping on the table.

"So…"

"I…"

They both drifted off. What had he been about to say? Emma waited, but Fenrir seemed to be deferring to her. Another quiet moment stretched out in the air, reflecting the gap between the present and the time when they'd been lovers, years ago.

After several painfully long moments, Emma broke the stillness—if not the silence—by reaching into her satchel and pulling out two envelopes, each stamped with Lady Escamilla's apple insignia. She held the first one over the table and Fenrir grabbed it, opening it blindly. She realized that his eyes were now focused intently on her.

"Why did Lady Escamilla send *you*? I gather that you are quite an important lady in this camp, Emma. Far too important to be delivering messages to the hired help," Fenrir said, working the flap free of the seal and pulling out the missive inside.

"Oh, I *am* quite influential in this operation. I speak with the voice of the Lady Escamilla. Officers and soldiers and servants follow my orders, and men *bow* when they see me coming. In fact, I could likely demand that you walk off a cliff and my escort would help me enforce the order," Emma said with a half-smile. Fenrir gave a hint of a smile in return, showing small wrinkles at the corners of his eyes. She'd either never noticed them before or they were new.

"I understand. This pin—" he gestured to the apple insignia affixed to his shirt, "—grants me access to the circles of the powerful. And a shit-pile of paperwork, too. Frankly, I'm exhausted," Fenrir said with yet another sigh.

"You look it," said Emma, pointedly appraising him.

"Thanks for noticing. Now, you didn't answer my question. Why are you delivering notes?" He began reading the missive.

"Because there are certain elements within the army that cannot be trusted with…" Emma stopped suddenly. Fenrir had suddenly gone almost deathly pale. His mouth hung open, his eyes wide as he frantically scanned the contents of the letter. The rest of his body seemed frozen in time, the only motion coming from his chest, which rose and fell in a rapid, shallow rhythm.

"Fenrir? Fenrir, what… Gods, what is the matter?"

Her voice seemed to shatter the paralysis that had gripped Fenrir so abruptly. He hurled the paper away and scrambled backward, looking for all the world as if the letter had turned into a venomous spider about to sink its fangs into his palm. The leg of his chair must have gotten caught during his frenzied motion because Fenrir half tumbled, half leapt out of it. He was now standing next to the chair, one hand on its back while his other

470

hand worked awkwardly across his forehead, down to his mouth and back up again.

"Fenrir!" Emma cried. She was growing genuinely fearful of what the letter portended. Had some unexpected threat arisen? Were they all in danger?

Fenrir gulped a lungful of air and stopped fidgeting. He reached down and grabbed the letter, turned back to Emma, and placed it in her hand. He seemed suddenly cold as stone, but she noticed that his arm shook almost imperceptibly as he held out the paper. Emma read the letter as Fenrir began to pace behind the desk.

"Wait... Someone tried to have you murdered?" she asked. Something about the name of the assassin's employer seemed familiar... Aiden de Trenton. De Trenton?

"Wait, is that *your brother*?" Emma asked. At this, Fenrir ceased his pacing.

It couldn't have been his brother, though! She remembered, long ago, lying intertwined with Fenrir in his bed, talking about their families. Fenrir had always been reluctant to speak on the topic, but he had consumed a good deal more rum than was typical even for him, and he'd been more forthcoming that night as a result. He had two brothers, Aiden and Ethan, both older, both born from a different mother than his own. But when he'd been a teenager, before he'd joined the military, both had passed away. There'd been suspicions that there was foul play involved in their deaths, an attempt to harm Darian de Trenton and his mercantile empire, but they had never been proven. The details of their deaths had been suppressed from public knowledge, and Fenrir had clammed up if she attempted to probe.

Fenrir met Emma's gaze for only a moment. He had seemed so hard, so stoic a moment ago, but the brief gaze betrayed a turmoil

471

beneath the surface. He looked away quickly. Emma touched his arm and felt a tremor before his muscles tightened up. Such pain.

Emma moved around him, her hands resting lightly on his arms, and peered into his face. His eyes were clenched shut, but even though he was facing away from the light, she could see thick tears squeezing from beneath his lids. She was shocked by this more than anything else. Something was terribly, terribly wrong here.

"Fenrir…" she said, gently pulling him into an embrace. He stiffened at first, his whole body taut with restrained emotion. A whisper of a moment later, he broke. Fenrir gripped her tightly, burying his face in her neck, sobs wracking his body.

How could she be holding a man who'd hurt her so? A man who'd been able to look into her eyes while he mutilated her? A man whom she had loved, despite him being married.

A man who'd likely had little choice in the matter of what he'd done to her.

He jerked back suddenly, wiping at his eyes with his sleeve.

"Escamilla's intel must be flawed. My brother… Darian's son, rather, is gone. He is gone," he repeated, as if trying to convince himself. "I need to talk to her. I need more than this." He gestured to the brief, crumpled note.

"Fenrir… What happened with your brothers?" Emma asked quietly.

"I cannot discuss it." His voice had hardened. It had been worth the attempt to try, though. Emma made a mental note to ask if Escamilla knew anything significant about the de Trenton family. No matter how hard the nobles and powerful merchants tried to conceal their lives, there were always spies.

"What are you going to do?" Emma asked.

472

"What can I do? Someone's trying to kill me, and I don't know who." So, he was in denial. "But, here we are marching to a battle that we probably can't win. So, I guess I'll see which kills me first."

"Why do you stay, Fenrir? I get that you helped us out of the Plateau for a stack of yets. But, is it worth it?" Emma truly wanted to understand, but so far hadn't been able to figure out what was driving him.

"Fah. You think I've seen a single yet from that job? In fact, everything that I had hidden at the boarding house is likely gone by now. There's nothing to my name." He laughed, a noise empty of true mirth. "By Ultner, I don't even have my *name* to my name!"

"So you stay because you are poor?"

"I'd leave in a second, even without a yet to my name. However, the people I work for… You do not want to cross them. I haven't heard a word from them, but, if they were to call upon me and find me missing…"

So, Fenrir was actually afraid of these people. Emma looked down at her hand, embittered. He was right to be afraid.

"Regardless, Emma. I need to get to a staff meeting with Ferl and his scounderals. What was that other missive that couldn't be trusted to just any messenger?" He was acting as if the past several minutes had never happened. Emma was both concerned and impressed by the man's ability to ignore reality.

Resigned, Emma handed him the second letter. She already knew the contents, and had explicit instructions to ensure there was no confusion. He began reading as she recited.

"You are to gather seventy-five of the most skilled mercenaries from Ferl's Company and, along with an additional seventy-five soldiers from The Army of Brockmore under the command of

473

Tilner Pick, travel northwest tonight, splitting from this force with utmost secrecy."

He stopped reading and just stared at her, his mouth slightly open.

"You are to lead a covert operation and attack the rear of the enemy camp on the evening of our first engagement. Our spies report that the little duke has joined the rear elements of the Rostanian army, hoping to witness the fall of Florens in person."

Fenrir dropped the missive, which fluttered dejectedly to the ground. He rubbed his tired face.

"Your force is to infiltrate the enemy camp, guided by our spies and scouts." Emma paused, and then added, "You are to kill Duke Samuel Penton."

Chapter 34

Hafgan tried to pretend everything was normal.

As always, he ran the budredda through their morning drills, teaching them balance and stance, lunging and swiping, blocking and dodging. And he began to teach them of the *heddwichen*—the emptiness, the center, the core—that allowed good fighters to achieve greatness. It had taken Hafgan months to learn and years to master, so obviously his men struggled and grew discouraged. Not really a teacher, Hafgan in turn grew frustrated with their lack of progress. So often, doers cannot teach, while teachers cannot do.

The general military training for his Wasmer unit had ceased, though, as they were now on special assignment. The day following the murder of Elan, Captain Yonso had sent the several hundred Wasmer on a forced, double-time march overland for four days, the Wasmer moving much faster than the Rostanian Army. Yonso even accompanied them, though he and his group of thirty human bodyguards were mounted and kept themselves well apart from the Wasmer.

And now they were in a very unusual place. A frightening place, if Hafgan was being honest with himself.

The Wasmer were guarding a wall. An eight-foot tall, tightly-built wooden stockade that was just over a mile in circumference, exactly in the middle of nowhere. Where this wall had come from, well off the path and in the thick forests southeast of Florens, Hafgan did not know. There was no evidence of the myriad laborers who must have spent a great deal of time and sweat in constructing it. Hafgan would have expected a logging camp, lumber mill, or something similar, but there was nothing. However, the wall was relatively new, and the stumps of trees were freshly cut.

The greater mystery was what was beyond the barrier. It very well could have been a logging camp, but Hafgan doubted it.

His unit had met up with a small group of twenty Rostanian soldiers, all appearing exhausted to the point of collapse. They had evidently been guarding this compound and were no longer up to the task. Men had been deserting daily. Hafgan realized why during his first night.

There were noises coming from the walled compound— strange sounds that intermittently punctuated the silence of the night, haunting the mind like a barely-remembered nightmare. They were always just on the edge of hearing, but Hafgan could swear he heard loud pounding sounds and howling, distant screams. Human screams? Of pain? Of fear? Of passion? Even with his training, even by achieving his *heddwichen*, Hafgan was unable to suppress a shiver at the sounds. His men had barely been sleeping and were constantly on edge.

Their main task involved serving as unmounted scouts, traveling in groups of about fifteen to prevent anyone, by any means, from discovering this compound. So far, the Wasmer had killed two messengers from Florens, both of whom had been seeking help from Draston. They had also killed one scout from this so-called Army of Brockmore that was marching to Florens. The army would reportedly arrive at Florens three days after the Rostanian forces had begun their siege, if the city managed to hold out. Both armies were moving slowly due to the storms, though the Rostanian Army—which trained away most of each morning—was as speedy as a mountain goat in winter.

The compound, whatever it was, must be hiding a weapon for use against this marching army. There was no other explanation.

The unease of his soldiers was not Hafgan's only problem. There was also the fact that he had completely lost contact with Tennyson, and that he no longer had access to the majority of his own contacts within the military. He was uncertain of what to do.

Should he maintain the disguise? Try to thwart whatever was hiding within this compound? Or should he simply desert rather than risk his life?

The risk was becoming greater as the battle approached, and not only from external forces. Siarl and the traditionalists continued to rail against his command in less and less subtle ways. Men weren't rising at the designated time, were ignoring scouting group assignments, and even openly disobeying direct orders. Hafgan had had to use force to impose order on more than one occasion, while Captain Yonso did nothing to assist. He'd simply set up camp with his men a half mile away from the barricade, eating the best food and drinking the best ale, and staying dry amidst the rolling storms. He obviously resented this assignment, having sullenly described the mission in as few words as possible to Hafgan before retreating to this camp.

Lastly, four of the Wasmer—traditionalists all—had been reported missing. Likely deserters.

The whole situation was, as the humans would say, a big pile of shit, and he was without a shovel.

"Lieutenant," said Paston, for a second time. Hafgan pulled himself from his brooding state and paid attention to the present. The scouting parties were dispersing in every direction while he, Paston, Enric, and a few other budredda stayed at the base camp, near the sole, gated entrance to the compound. Since their arrival, nobody had entered or exited.

"Yes, Paston?"

"A fifth man could not be accounted for this morning. Bedwyr…"

"You mean…"

"Yes, our Bedwyr." Hafgan was astonished. Bedwyr was one of the budredda, the oldest member of his little bodyguard.

Bedwyr had not been conscripted like the rest of the budredda; he had decided to join the military. He'd before been a water runner foreman, running a crew of orphans and urchins in filling several of Rostane's many great water barrels. A job with little glory and less pay, and he'd even been disrespected by homeless children. He'd enlisted voluntarily, perhaps swayed by the stories of heroic military exploits and the camaraderie associated with soldiery. His pride as a budredda compared to the greatest peaks in the Tulanques.

The fact was, Bedwyr would never have deserted. Not after he'd finally found some measure of belonging.

"That is a problem," said Hafgan slowly.

"Sir, Bedwyr would not be deserting us. He be our brother," said Paston, echoing Hafgan's thoughts.

"Indeed. Paston, something is happening here. It may be this thing we are guarding, or it may be Yonso and his men. But, something is wrong and we are in danger," Hafgan said thoughtfully. Despite his distraction, he still spoke Ardian with little issue. It was becoming less and less effort now that he was becoming accustomed to his leadership role.

"Sir?" Paston prompted him nervously. "What do we do?"

"I have... friends... outside the Rostanian Army, who need to be informed of these happenings, of this location."

"Sir, that is treason!" said Paston, shock evident in his hushed voice. Their entire mission hinged on secrecy.

Hafgan brought his own voice down to a whisper. With most of the men on patrol, they were unlikely to be overheard, but it never hurt to be cautious in these situations.

"Paston, you must know more than anyone. We need not be beholden to Rostane. The duchy has rejected us. The army has rejected us. This assignment be... is... stinking of treachery, as if

478

we Wasmer are expendable. I have learned, in my time with humans, that you cannot trust them to have your interests in mind. They will do whatever they can to hold you down, belittle you, keep you weak. No, Paston, you can rely only on yourself. *We* can rely only on ourselves. And we must do what is necessary to keep ourselves safe." Hafgan found that he believed every word that he'd said. These budredda had grown on him, and he wanted to keep them safe. Even keep them out of the coming battle entirely, if at all possible.

And get them away from this place.

Paston's met Hafgan's eyes for the duration of his little speech, and then tilted his head back as if beseeching the gray early morning sky for answers. The soldier was certainly torn with indecision—he took his oaths seriously, and committing to Hafgan meant betraying military secrets. But, Hafgan knew that Paston's decision was a foregone conclusion.

"Sir, you be right, of course. Please, tell me what we must be doing," said Paston, lowering his head and again looking to his superior. There was only trust in his clean-shaven face.

Hafgan sighed and pursed his lips. These men would follow him anywhere. That was a heavy weight to bear. A mountain, even.

"Find me two men that we can trust above all others. We need to get word to my friends…"

Chapter 35

Florens had been under siege for three days, though there was little evidence of it. From afar, the city was a pearl on the water. White buildings—painted wood—sprawled over the gentle hills that were the foundation of the city. Ships floated lazily along the great Ingwine River, and even fisherman were out with their nets; Florensians had to eat, after all, even during a siege. And, above the city rose the Amphitheater of Spring, a great circular structure carved in the likeness of intertwining trees, branches forming arches to allow entry to those interested in such spectacles. Florens was known for its love of the arts: the epic plays, famous singers, and massive orchestras. It may have been Emma's imagination, but she thought she could hear a few gentle notes carried along the breeze.

Perhaps the reason that Florens was still standing is that the city had a very unique defense compared to Rostane and most other Ardian cities. Originally, Florens had been built on the sharply-curving south bank of the great Ingwine River, which was a half mile wide. As the town had grown into a city, its growth propelled by the constant trade resulting from its proximity to the river, the local government had realized that there was an increasing need for defense. Prosperity drew conflict like meat drew maggots.

However, because the city was so far from the Tulanques or any decent quarry sites, the cost of a hewn stone wall had seemed prohibitive at the time. A ten year public project had begun as a result, whereby a wide, deep ditch was dug, curving around the southern reaches of the city, leaving room for growth. The ditch was eventually flooded with the waters of the Ingwine, essentially creating the island city of Florens, protected on all sides by rushing water. There were docks on the west end of the city, and two wide, floating bridges on the north and south ends. The bridges could be pulled into the city with relative ease for protection, and sections could be removed to allow for the passage of larger watercraft. In retrospect, the city founders had realized that a stone wall would have cost far less, but such is the way with hindsight.

The Rostanian Army was busy preparing to assault Florens from the north—across the Ingwine—while simultaneously repelling Escamilla's forces from the east. Engineers and laborers were constructing siege engines—ballista and onagers—as well as building dozens of flat-bottomed rafts. There was a small, six-foot retaining wall along much of Florens' shoreline, but Malless did not have enough men to defend against a diffused assault, not with the possibility of soldiers swarming over the city from a hundred landing points. Meanwhile, the Rostanians were creating an earthen bulwark to repel Escamilla's forces. Thousands of men with shovels could make a small fortress, though the soaked ground and still-dripping clouds had been hampering these efforts quite significantly.

When Emma had observed the marching forces of the Army of Brockmore, it had been difficult to imagine losing the coming war. Ten thousand men—matching armor or no—made for an imposing site, and the glint of steel weapons could do little else but inspire confidence. The soldiers, too, had the conviction that they were marching to fight for what was right, that they'd been chosen by Yetra to combat Pandemonium given flesh through the corrupting, power-hungry influence of Little Duke Penton. How could such a force, fighting for such a reason, be defeated?

That was until Emma had seen the forces arrayed against them. According to the most recent scouting reports and word from Escamilla's spies, the Rostanian Army now numbered close to forty thousand, not including the many armed members in the baggage train. They must have conscripted soldiers along the way, stripping bare some of the larger towns and cities that they'd passed through in Rostane, and perhaps even forcing conscripts in Florens. The camp was practically a city; it spread from just a hundred years north of the Ingwine to beyond Emma's sight, north and west. Banners were scattered throughout the camp—the four stars of Darinston, the red leaf of Doring, the grinning fish of Serant. Dozens of banners from noble-ruled towns and cities around Rostane were represented, and all the colors and designs looked, for all the world, like a patchwork quilt.

Even growing up in the busy streets of Rostane, Emma had never seen so many people gathered together for a sole purpose. Escamilla's little army would be swallowed by this behemoth; Emma could feel her heart pounding like a drum. Little wonder that the Rostanians turned away Escamilla's emissaries without a word. This conflict would not be solved with diplomacy.

"Is it time? My men, like their horses, are chomping at the bit," said Captain Anew Opine. He had replaced Captain Perod after his attack on Emma and his subsequent beating by Fenrir and demotion by Escamilla. Opine was of noble blood, the Opines ruling their own barony. They'd thrown in with Escamilla after *Recherche Oletta* had assassinated the matriarch of their clan, Baronness Rosalee Opine. It was a small addition to the army—around two hundred inexperienced soldiers—but Opine had proven to be a capable officer, so much so that he now commanded a unit of seventeen hundred cavalry.

Opine did have one very peculiar, and rather annoying, affectation, though. He spoke like a storybook hero, all courage and confidence and bluster. If he hadn't also been competent, Emma would have beaten him senseless by now.

"Soon. We are just waiting on the sun. The morning is on our side," said General Guy Empton, his arms tightly clenched behind his back, betraying his nerves. He was resplendent in full iron plate mail, wearing a crimson cape and looking every inch a commander. His appearance was meant to reassure and strengthen their men, and it seemed to have had its desired effect. All of the officers were wearing specially made armor for this very purpose, aside from Trina Almark, who was adorned in glittering silver mail, and Ferl, who wore clothes that would have befit a merchant of middling success. The two stood as far as possible from one another.

Emma and Escamilla were both ceremonially dressed for war, as well, each sporting ornate and specially-made black-and-crimson leather armor. There was no differentiation between lady and servant.

The highest-ranking officers stood atop a quickly-built raised platform that sat on a small hill, providing an excellent view of the soon-to-be battlefield, the sky above it finally clearing after weeks of storms. Emma had studied the battlefield and their strategy on paper, though it was much more difficult to conceptualize troop disposition and maneuvers even from her vantage. The Army of Brockmore was to attack from the east, the southern flank protected by the Ingwine and thick forests, and the northern reinforced and anchored by their best soldiers. She could see them now—the infantry moving in units of a thousand, ten deep. The cavalry was nowhere to be seen; they were being held in reserve in concordance with their strategy. A strategy that Emma hope desperately would carry the day. She found her legs shaking in anticipation of the battle, and she had to neither fight the enemy nor order others to engage.

General Empton was nodding at the slow formation of infantry, gesturing to one of his runners. There was a horde of runners at the bottom of the command platform, ready to disperse orders that could not be projected by the trumpeters. And then there was a separate ring of steel-clad Apple Knights, Escamilla's personal guard, providing further defense for the leaders. Emma should have felt reassured by the organization and the protection, but it certainly was a beacon to the Rostanians, shouting "command post—attack here."

483

Aside from the officers, also present were the girls that Escamilla seemed to be so fond of. Merigold, the petite blond who'd been through so much and who might, if whispers were true, have some dark magical powers. And Morgyn, the little street-rat turncoat. Both girls had Escamilla's sympathies, though the purpose of their presence in this council of war was unclear. Knowing more about Escamilla's past, Emma suspected that the older woman was simply sympathetic to them, these girls being a reminder of her own beginnings and struggles. Maybe she needed these reminders right now, as men were going to die for her today. Hundreds or thousands.

Ignatius—pompous as always—wore only black. He'd said it was to mourn the great loss of life that would occur on this day, and then quoted some pious dribble from his little book. And of course, most of the men had seemed to buy it.

"We are waiting too long!" said Captain Ezram, fingering his sword's hilt. "The sun will be too high soon, and we'll lose our advantage!"

"Be patient," murmured Escamilla. "Our plans hinge on timing. We must wait until the designated time to strike, even if the sun is a bit higher than we would like."

"How do we know we can trust our allies?" asked Captain Quentin. The bearded captain betrayed his nerves with constant motion, moving from his heels to his toes. Unbecoming of a commander, but no one aside from Emma or her lady were likely to notice. Escamilla had drilled her to always focused on body language, regardless of setting.

"Because, if we cannot trust them, we are doomed regardless," chimed in Emma. It used to be that she would never have dared to speak in front of such men. But, in a scant few weeks, with her new authority, Emma had grown more confident in her dealings with all things military.

"Indeed. We need just be patient," repeated Escamilla. Her back was as straight and strong as the great broadsword Guy Empton wore slung along his back. Straighter than the front ranks of infantry even, who were nervously shifting about. From what Emma could see with the eyeglass that Escamilla had given her, the enemy's line was similarly uneven, soldiers shifting behind their earthen bulwarks, fingering pikes, swords, and bows, anxiously awaiting the coming charge.

This was a battle of amateurs. Even of the career soldiers on both sides, few had had any real combat experience. The Rostanian Army had some veterans of skirmishes with the Wasmer, while Escamilla's own army veterans were nearly all confined to the mercenaries, half of them seeking to avoid the brunt of the battle by taking tenth rank positions (for Ferl's Company), though Ultner's Fist carried the flanks, per their contracts. Otherwise, men unused to wielding weapons in battle and anger were about to collide, and Emma expected it to be disastrous. She fiddled with her hands, not unaware of her own nervous habit.

From the wooded foothills to the west, beyond the massed Rostanians, Emma swore she saw a flash of light. Without further warning, it caught Emma right in the eyes, leaving a flashing afterimage. It disappeared, briefly, and then caught her eyes again.

"The signal! Escamilla, the signal!" Emma shouted. Their allies were in position.

"Sound the horn. Advance and commence bombardment!" ordered General Empton, his voice iron even as Emma's legs turned to water. It was beginning.

The trumpet played several clarion notes, and the call was repeated down the line. The men had drilled for this, back at Brockmore. Would that training hold in the face of an actual enemy?

The infantry began to march, closing the mile-wide distance between the armies. It was a slow march, meant both to intimidate and to conserve energy. The enemy line was swirling with activity as officers shouted orders, and men notched bows and braced their pikes. Their ranks were twice as deep as those of their attackers, and part of the army was still entirely occupied with siege preparation. They obviously didn't see Escamilla's forces as a true threat.

At three hundred-and-fifty-yards out, the first few ranks took a knee, and nine hundred Brockmore longbowmen notched their bows, drew back at a forty-five degree angle, and let loose. The war arrows were lost to the enemy in the sun, and then fell among the Rostanian soldiers. With her eyeglass, Emma could see arrows slinging into their ranks, soldiers clustered so closely together that it was difficult for the archers to miss. Some men sought cover under small shields, but not all had shields, and not all of those who did got them up in time. Soldiers fell across the line. As Emma watched, an arrow took one in the eye, and he grasped at his face awkwardly before falling. Another, several feet behind this one and to his left, took an arrow to his shoulder, the velocity of the falling projectile enough to pierce the leather of his armor and sink in several inches. The soldier started at the sudden growth dully before pitching to the ground in pain.

Another volley fell while the Rostanians recovered from their shock and prepared their own longbowmen. More soldiers fell, killed or wounded, while the longbowmen notched arrows and pointed skyward. Emma cringed as the Rostanians released this concentrated volley directly at the Brockmore infantry, the sky darkening as two thousand arrows rushed toward their victims.

The arrows fell nearly a hundred yards short, though, skewering nothing but the already-trampled farmland.

The yellow yew bows of Jecusta, obtained by Escamilla at some unknown, but probably great, cost, fired with unprecedented range. The Rostanian bows could not match them, and it took two more volleys before the Rostanian soldiers realized that their weapons were having no effect while death continued to rain down upon them.

It took some several long minutes for the officers of the Rostanian Army to coordinate a general advance. A weak, wavering line of Rostanian infantry began a slow advance then, stumbling over their own defensive wall of earth, men with small shields taking the lead. A number of writhing and motionless bodies were left behind.

"How many Rostanians are down?" asked Captain Braston, the only captain without an eyeglass.

"Perhaps a thousand and some hundred—it is hard to estimate in that mess," replied Captain Garen, squinting at the Rostanian forces.

"Not nearly enough," muttered Emma.

"All too many," sighed Ignatius.

Gods, but Emma hated the man. The purpose of this war was to kill, and he worked his men up to a religious froth to massacre their enemies while, at the same time, denouncing the act of killing. *Hypocrisy, thine name is Ignatius Pender.*

Even with their ranks thinned, the shambling mass of men still blanketed too large a swatch of the field of battle. Emma's heart fluttered. Though more than a mile separated her from the Rostanians, the thin ranks of Escamilla's infantry and archers seemed woefully insufficient. She could not begin to imagine how the front rank of inexperienced soldiers felt.

"All conscripts," muttered Empton. "They think to defeat us with conscripts." He gestured to a messenger and scribbled something onto a piece of parchment. The runner sprinted to his horse and took off toward the front lines at a full gallop.

487

At two hundred yards, the Rostanian archers again let loose their own volley, and the Army of Brockmore experienced their first casualties. Men fell, transfixed with arrows, and the battle line wavered. The Rostanian infantry continued to march under this arrow cover, and both sets of archers got off two more volleys before only fifty yards separated the lines. Escamilla's archers began a disorganized retreat then—first in ones and twos, and then by the dozens. None abandoned their bows, but the archers sprinted away from the battle as if terrified.

No one in the command post reacted to this sudden, seemingly undisciplined withdrawal.

But, the withdrawal seemed to have a demoralizing effect on the middle of the Army of Brockmore's line, and it began to bend even before the Rostanians closed the final distance. There was a hush before the lines collided—no roaring of determined men, nor any chanting of warcries. Just the rumble of pounding feet.

Then, the Rostanian conscripts slammed into Escamilla's own green troops.

It was utter chaos. The carefully-practiced, shoulder-to-shoulder collaborative combat was apparently lost in the push. The spear line in the center began to fold even more, simply pushed back by the momentum of the Rostanian behemoth. The soldiers on both sides were crushed together in the churning mud, the battlefield like a fenced pasture cramped with cows who were unable to take a step in any direction. The rear ranks of Rostanians pushed on the backs of the men in front of them, forcing their frontline into the spears of the Brockmore soldiers, and their second line over the bodies of the first. The soldiers in front, on both sides, were pressed against each other, immobilized and ineffective. Soldiers simply struck and bashed in all directions, the need for self-preservation outweighing their scant training. Men were falling to the weapons of their allies as often as not.

The middle of Brockmore's line continued to tremble, though the flanks held strong, anchored by the experienced fighting women of Ultner's Fist who were laying about with their short swords as if this battle were a holiday. The Silver Lady stood, hand on one hip, her body tilted slightly. She was quietly confident. Ferl was similarly casual, nearly the mirror image of Trina Almark. For him, his men dying meant more gold in his own pockets, as his mercenaries were primarily family-less, and few had any provisions in their individual contracts to reallocate their funds in case of their demise.

All at once, the center of the Brockmore line broke, the rear ranks beginning to run. First a trickle, then a rush. Before long, the center of the line had completely collapsed, split through by Rostanian infantry, pushed back far beyond the flanks. The battle line was a log split by an axe.

The command post was a whirlwind of activity as each of the captains and the general were writing down orders and shouting for messengers while Ignatius and a couple of his Taneos shouted prayers for the dead. It wasn't a panic, though; it lacked that underlying sense of fear. It was an ordered sort of chaos.

Emma, for her part, moved off to the side lest she be as annoyingly underfoot as Ignatius. There was nothing that she could contribute to this battle now that it was joined; all she could do was impotently watch and hope that their strategy would win the day.

"Do you think we could have done anything differently today?" asked Escamilla, moving closer to be heard over the din of the command post. Her hands were held folded in front of her, and her voice was as placid as always.

"Yes. We could have moved far, far away. Sestra, maybe. Or Morgos, far across the Vissas. Maybe taken up farming," said Emma. Escamilla's face creased in a smile despite the thousands of hostiles advancing on their position.

"My old back would be poorly suited to such an occupation," Escamilla added. "I suppose this is the best alternative. Girl, why are you crying?" This last was directed at Morgyn, who was at Merigold's side.

"Because I'm scared! Those men are going to break through and kill us!" The little urchin was holding herself tightly, appearing especially vulnerable.

"Hush, little one. That's not going to happen today," said Escamilla in the same soothing tone Emma had seen her use on spooked horses.

"Where is our cavalry?" asked Merigold abruptly. "Surely, we should be bringing all we can to bear upon the enemy."

"Smart girl. You will have to wait and see. Tell me, are you not afraid?" Merigold did not appear to be afraid, but rather seemed distracted.

"I don't know. No, I don't think so. It seems to me that if we were in danger, you and the general there would seem more… urgent. Until you panic, I need to assume we are safe. Besides, Yetra is on our side," Merigold said, glancing at Ignatius, who had his head bowed in apparent prayer. Emma assumed he was just napping and trying to determine where he'd get his next meal. Fat bastard.

"Observant and smart. Tell me, If the Rostanians were to break through, could you use your magic to protect us?" Escamilla asked almost offhandedly.

It suddenly made more sense why Escamilla had invited this girl to the command post.

Merigold went stiff at the question, though, and did not meet Escamilla's searching gaze. Emma thought the girl was going to ignore Escamilla, but she finally responded.

"No." Merigold did not elaborate.

"Do you not know your power? Do you not know what you are capable of?" Escamilla continued to probe. Again, Merigold paused before responding.

"I do not remember," she said quietly.

Escamilla nodded thoughtfully. "Well, you will bear witness to such power in a moment. A fraction of your capability, if my guess is correct."

Meri started at the comment, and her eyes darted back to the battlefield, her face intensely focused on the battle. Emma followed her gaze.

The center of their battle line was simply gone. Rostanians flowed through the gap in the line like a river, mirroring the Ingwine just to the south. Escamilla's center was in a full rout, men sprinting to the back of the flanks. Even Emma, savvy to the strategy, felt the urge to run. But, she attempted to emulate her lady as always, watching over the battlefield with feigned disinterest.

Six small units of Ferl's Company detached from the rear and moved to fill the breach. In the center of each unit was an unarmored man, each adorned in whatever clothing they preferred. One was wearing all black, while another was wearing what looked like a sleeping robe, and was wearing short pants and… barefoot?

"My greenies," offered Ferl, his voice betraying a hint of pride.

The units reached the breach, and the center man in each unit—excluding the barefoot one—took a knee and dug their hands into the ground. Around them, in a growing circle, the grass and trampled wheat began to wither and darken. Some circles were no more than a few feet across, while the barefoot man's— wait, woman's—circle grew to nearly twenty. The kneeling men stood, and the bodyguards parted, creating a clear path to the enemy. This all happened in a matter of seconds.

491

Then, Pandemonium was unleashed.

The leading Rostanians were torn to bloody shreds. Power shot from the hands of the greenies, slightly different for each. Two tossed spinning blades of emerald power, slicing through armor and skin, limbs and decapitated heads falling to the ground. Another seemed to be shooting small green and yellow spikes, which lacked the bloody visual impact of the blades, but were just as effective. The barefoot woman simply launched a sustained, white beam of energy, tearing through flesh and baring wet, dripping internal organs to the open air.

Oh, cocks. Fucking cocks. Emma tossed aside her eyeglass and vomited, as did Captain Braston. Escamilla was white and breathing rapidly, but she did not tear her gaze from the battle. The command post was near silent as the leaders of the army observed the outcome of their decisions.

"This is an abomination!" roared Ignatius, his face messed up with anger. "This must be stopped, at once. It is written that "the powers of the earth shall never be used to shed the blood of man!"

Ferl sneered. "It's our blood or theirs. What do you think we are here for?"

"No wonder you scavenging pieces of human filth manage to win an occasional battle," spat the Silver Lady. "I'd heard rumors, of course, but discounted them. But, now it finally makes sense how such a useless man can—"

"Commence bombardment!" bellowed Guy Empton, his voice cutting through the arguments and the awe and the disgust.

At the sound of the subsequent trumpet, the archers, who had previously appeared routed, darted forward and formed a line two hundred yards back from the magic-ravaged Rostanian forces. With the Army of Brockmore now split cleanly in two, they were easily able to target the massed Rostanian forces without much danger of hitting their own men. The greenies continued to blast the front ranks, moving on to untouched vegetation and spreading their destruction. Three of the them had collapsed in exhaustion, while a fourth had retreated. Two, including the barefoot one, pressed the attack. The greenies had done little real damage, considering the size of the enemy force, but the psychological damage on the Rostanians was immense.

Emma heard a low moan, and glanced at Merigold. The girl was was pale and shaking, silent tears streaming down her face. She was tugging on a sapphire stud in her ear. Emma could only imagine the thoughts running through the girl's head, given that she had recently murdered a couple of mercenaries in the same way.

The Rostanians were breaking. Beset by unknown and devastatingly violent powers, cramped together and unable to defend against the rain of arrows, the conscripts could not take it anymore. But, they had nowhere to go.

"Wait, what's that?" asked Morgyn, gesturing at the Rostanian camp, having grabbed Emma's eyeglass. Emma, steeling her stomach, snatched it back and held it to her eye, examining the enemy fortifications.

The enemy camp was an ants nest. On the north side, the Rostanian calvalry was attempting to mobilize, largely unsuccessfully. Perhaps due to carelessness or conceit, few of the animals were saddled, and soldiers and grooms were struggling to ready the creatures. Emma saw little threat, there. But, on the southwest side of the camp, a pitched battle was being fought. Their allies had finally struck!

The gold coats of Florens were visible, and they were tearing through the engineers and laborers, burning rafts and onagers. So distracted were the Rostanian forces by the battle against Escamilla's army that Malless' forces had managed their surprise attack with only token resistance. However, the career Rostanian military was mobilizing against this threat, with surprising quickness, and beginning to bring the fight to the Florensians.

The signal for retreat sounded over the din, officially recalling the already-routed Rostanian infantry conscripts who'd still been struggling to extricate themselves from the Army of Brockmore.

"Forward, cavalry!" shouted Empton to the bugler. Several clear notes rang out.

From behind the command post, previously hidden by a small crest, over a thousand mounted men began to trot forward on their mismatched horses, heading toward the devastated Rostanian forces.

At a hundred yards, they readied their lances. At fifty yards, the horses were spurred into a thundering canter. A number of the untrained horses balked, and riders were left clinging to the rearing animals or were flung to the ground and crushed beneath the charging hoofs. But the larger portion of horses continued to roar forward, now at a gallop, further mixing up the bloodied sludge of the battle into a reddish-brown slurry.

They slammed into the backs of the fleeing Rostanian soldiers, impaling dozens on the tips of lances, trampling the fallen and the wounded. Few fought back, having already lost their spears and their nerve. The cavalry soldiers, however, were ill-trained for the realities of a concentrated charge, and several fallen horses caused the animals behind them to trip while others were just barely able to stop. The writhing mass of horseflesh and humanity was awful to behold.

Somehow, Emma found the plight of the horses more painful to watch than that of the men on either side of the fight. The horses, it seemed, had had little choice in the matter of this slaughter.

Despite the losses to the Brockmore cavalry, the damage was done. The conscripts fled the field in their remaining thousands, tossing aside weapons and sprinting toward their earthen fortifications under a hail of covering fire.

"Stop march!" growled Empton, his voice having lost some power from shouting commands for the last... had it only been a couple of hours? The sun was not even fully overhead yet, but so many had already died. Emma tried not to look closely at any of the bodies.

Meanwhile, the Florensians continued to fight through the southwestern edge of the Rostanian camp, meeting stiff resistance from the experienced Rostanian military. However, they slowly neared their destination.

"They will have done a great deal of damage to the war preparations. Soldiers can easily be replaced, but engineers are invaluable," said Escamilla, her voice tight. "We have won the day, but the war is far from over. Tomorrow will be far more trying."

Tomorrow would, indeed, be more trying. Emma knew, from the war meetings, that they had little strategy planned beyond the first engagement. But, at least things had gone near perfect, today. The calculated "retreat" was convincing, the greenies were devastating, and, though the cavalry charge suffered from many self-inflicted causalities, it at least further shaved down the number of their enemies. Even the Florensians did their part. Emma continued to watch the gold standards move their way through the Rostanian camp toward their destination. Wait... wasn't the bridge to the city supposed to be extended by now?

"Escamilla, I think there's something wrong!" said Emma, her voice cracking.

Malless and his men—seven thousand strong—had sailed under the cover of darkness to a position well west of the Rostanian camp. They'd managed to conceal themselves until early morning, aided by the distracting Army of Brockmore and a force of a thousand or so that had been left behind in Florens to make loud and visible preparations. The attack had been meant to destroy the siege preparations, targeting the engineers, and then create as much death and havoc as possible, depending on the Rostanian response. Then, they'd intended to cut through the enemy, ending at the floating bridge that connected the mainland to Florens. The bridge, of course, had been partially retracted in advance of the siege, but at the beginning of the surprise attack that morning, the token force in Florens had been meant to extend the bridge, and cover the retreat back into the city from the shore and from several ships.

However, what Emma had seen was that, though Malless's forces had begun to cut through to the bridge, leaving burning siege equipment and bodies behind, the bridge had not been extended! There was fighting at the city end of the bridge, near the great white marble towers that welcomed visitors to the city. And the ships! The ships were firing crank-bows and ballista bolts *at* Malless' forces!

"General! What is happening?" demanded Escamilla, grabbing Empton's plated arm.

"I… I… don't know," said Empton in a hushed voice. His now-colorless face was shiny with perspiration.

"There is fighting at Floren's gates! Someone is preventing the bridge from being extended," said Trina Almark, pointing at the fighting that was raging in the city. "Those poor fucking Florensians are trapped."

"Without the bridge, Malless and the Florensians are doomed." Ferl agreed with the Silver Lady, his regularly-smug expression replaced with one of concern. "The Rostanians must have had sizable forces within the city to pull something like this off. More likely, they had some help, and some insight into our strategy. Someone on the inside, maybe a confidant of Penton."

"They've… we've been betrayed?" Empton was rubbing his eyes, as if unable to comprehend. "What do we do now? What… now?"

"You're the fucking general, Empton!" snapped Emma, risking a glare from Escamilla that never came. "You tell us what to do." Empton didn't respond.

Braston spoke up. "We need to retreat! Our strategies hinged on Malless and the Florensians. If they are gone, then the city is gone. If the city is gone, we've nothing to fight for." He waved messengers to his side, his gestures urgernt.

"It is because we resorted to the use of dark powers!" said Ignatius, his voice oozing with sanctimonious judgment. Two of the captains—Quentin and Ezram—were nodding their agreement, making the sign of Yetra in the air. "As it is written in *The Book*—"

"Ignatius, now is not the time!" Escamilla cut in. The chaplain strode toward her in response, his orange Yetranian stole askew, his face crimson with fury.

"Now is the only time! You have greatly blundered, you ignorant fool. You have angered Yetra—"

Emma slapped him full in the face with her good hand, sending him reeling to the side. "Shut your mouth, old man!" She grabbed at his collar, bringing her face very near to his. "We tolerate you as a military strategy, as a way to boost morale and give the men some faith. But you will not speak to my lady that way! You will *never* speak—"

"Enough, all of you! Enough!" Escamilla's voice broke through the panicked cacophony that was the command center. "You speak as if our defeat is a foregone conclusion. It will be, if we simply languish as the men of Florens are slaughtered. Shall we retreat, leaving these brave warriors to meet their deaths at the shores of the Ingwine, victims of betrayal and our cowardice? Or, shall we act, protect our ally and protect our country?" Escamilla met the gaze of each officer, and some, including Braston, had the decency to look abashed. General Empton was staring dully at the enemy camp, eyeglass shaking. Ignatius, however, met her gaze solidly, and ripped out of Emma's grip. The man had grown obstinate and strong-willed since he had grown in power and spread his faith among the men. His false humility may have fooled others, but not Emma.

"We have a tired, but freshly-victorious army still on the field of battle. An army fortified with faith." Escamilla, ever the politician, nodded to Ignatius in obvious appeasement. "The Rostanians are disorganized and afraid, and our hope lies in creating a united force. We must shield our allies!"

For her part, Emma felt bolstered by Escamilla's speech, and she felt a surge of pride for her lady and friend. Other officers gave a ragged cheer, though Empton was still gazing across the battlefield in glassy astonishment.

"General Empton?" Emma asked, bringing the man back to the moment.

"Yes?" His tone was flat.

"What are your orders to provide relief to the Florensian forces?"

"Um... we must... ahem..." He was holding his left arm, and his face was strained, as if he were holding a great weight above his head.

"Empton? Guy? Are you okay?" Escamilla asked irritably. Empton collapsed with a metallic clatter, his great sword coming loose from the scabbard as he pitched forward. Officers and Apple Knights rushed to his side.

"Oh, cocks," swore Emma before she could stop herself. The other officers, and even Escamilla, were struck with a visible uncertainty laced with a splash of fear. Why now? And what now?

Anew Opine spoke first, the third son of the baroness and most junior member of the command. "Guards, to me! We must form a corridor along the Ingwine before it is cut off by the Rostanians. Cavalry shield to lead the way, reinforced by Ultner's Fist on the southern flank, all with covering fire from the archers. Hopefully, Malless has the sense to cut toward us in response to this betrayal. I will gather the cavalry reserves and deliver the orders myself!" All of this from Captain Anew Opine, third son of the baroness. He didn't wait for permission, but instead dashed to waiting messenger horses, followed by several Apple Knights.

"Ambitious, but rude," murmured Emma to Escamilla as she watched the rest of the officers finally find some semblance of control over the deteriorating situation.

"Smart, though, and manners matter little in moments such as this. Let's hope he is the hero he fancies himself to be. If this works, then I will grant him general's pins myself."

"And, if it doesn't?"

"Then we had best follow Ignatius' example and pray."

Chapter 36

Hafgan and his budredda sat crossed-legged around a great bonfire, Derek turning a make-shift spit to roast a wild pig that one of the men had stumbled across earlier in the day. The thing was old and gamey, but the smell was mouth-watering, and the anticipation of relief from the tasteless dried meat and iron-hard bread to which they were accustomed of late was almost too much. Hafgan had eaten well during his time with The House and had grown used to richer food. His men were similarly anxious, the entire group silently watching the slowly spinning meat like sailors gazing at a harbor after months at sea.

The anxiety, of course, was not solely due to hunger. Word had come, late in the afternoon, that the Rostanian military had engaged with the forces of Lady Escamilla and Florens. Despite the overwhelming numbers of the Rostanians, the Army of Brockmore had managed to secure a notable victory, easily outsmarting the overconfident conscripts. The Florensians, on the other hand, lost a major piece of their army, and that army was now *outside* of the city. Duke Malless had apparently organized—rather successfully—a surprise attack with the goal of destroying the siege equipment and rafts, as well as killing as many engineers as possible. Lieutenant Itham, the officer of the engineers corps, had fallen in this attack.

But, the Rostanians had allies inside of the city who took this opportunity to stage their own attack, preventing Duke Malless and his forces from escaping back into the city across the bridge. If Hafgan were a betting man, he would wager that this was the work of *Recherche Oletta*. The conversation he had overheard between Penton, the Patriarch, and that woman seemed to indicate that *Recherche Oletta* had fighters in Florens. Trapping most of the Florensian army outside of the city, surrounded by Rostanians, was likely too delicious of an opportunity to overlook. As a result, thousands of Florensian soldiers were lost, trapped between the river and their enemies.

Even so, the Florensian army could have been destroyed completely, had not some quick-thinking officer from Escamilla's forces created an effective cavalry screen to allow Malless and his forces an escape route. Half of the Florensian soldiers had been killed or captured, but Malless was not counted among the dead, and the Florensian forces remaining in the city had managed to overcome the presumed *Recherche Oletta* fighters. The result was a larger combined force and a still somewhat-defended city, and the Rostanians had no siege weapons of which to speak.

But, the Rostanian forces still outnumbered their enemies more than two to one, though, and most of their losses had been poorly-trained conscripts. The enemy—the Army of Brockmore and Florens, rather—still had little chance at being ultimately victorious, especially now that they were in the open field.

Hafgan sometimes caught himself actually thinking of Escamilla's forces as the enemy, and he even felt a catch in his throat when he found that the Rostanians had been defeated on the field of battle. It wasn't right, though—he was working to undermine the Rostanian armies. Or at least, he *had been* until he'd lost all contact with The House. Simply put, Hafgan currently had too many masters, and none had his best interests in mind. The officers in the Rostanian military would just as soon see him dead, as the Wasmer were disposable fodder. Tennyson saw him as a useful tool, certainly, but one that could be replaced for a sack of yets. Hafgan wondered, again, why he remained loyal to any of these people.

His immediate superior certain did not instill loyalty. Captain Yanso had summoned him hours ago to reluctantly share news of the battle for Florens and to distribute new orders. The muscular, hateful captain had handed him a missive and given him a few moments to read it, to take in the details of the battle, the

501

disposition of the enemy. Then, the conversation had gone something like, "You and your fucking Wasmer will march tomorrow morning. Hit the flank. Rest up. We're done here."

The big man had then entered the compound near sunset, taking four of his guards with him. All of them, including Yanso himself, had seemed reluctant to enter—particularly as the wooden gates had only eased open a couple of feet, and there'd been no gatekeeper to be seen. It was now an hour after sunset, and none had yet returned.

But, there were more horrible, intermittent noises coming from the compound. Noises that his budredda were trying to ignore.

"That pig be ready yet?" asked Derek, scraping the butt of his spear against the ground. "I be dying here."

"I *am* dying here. You need to conjugate to present tense. Rarely do you actually use 'be' in reference to the self," said Hafgan distractedly. Several of the men had asked him for coaching in the traders' tongue, and he was happy to provide tips. One did learn best by teaching, but as with instructing fighting, Hafgan got irated at times.

"I *be* cutting a slice in a moment here," said Paston, and the men chuckled good naturedly.

"You *be* getting me the first cut, I *be* right?" asked Osian, the smallest member of the budredda, but one who was well-regarded for his appetite. There was another round of chuckles, but it was forced. The howling from the compound again split the air, cutting through their merriment like a bitter mountain wind. Even bereft of the keening howls, true merriment was beyond the grasp of the Wasmer this evening, given that the Wasmer unit was supposed to march to war come morning. Not exactly a thrilling prospect for the men, though Hafgan himself had no plans to allow the march, at least not for his budredda. Sometime after high moons, Hafgan would wake the men and lead them away from this camp, away from the army. He would not allow these men to be killed fighting another's war.

Though, where they would go was certainly a question to ponder.

For a time, the urgent howling ceased. The crackling of the fire and the sizzling of the pig were again the only sounds in the small camp of budredda. Each man seemed lost in their own thoughts. Perhaps they thought of the battle in the morning, or perhaps of the mystery of the compound. Or, maybe they were lost in memories of their own personal ghosts; gazing into a fire in the darkness tended to force a person to reflect on their past. Hafgan had to fight to avoid those thoughts, himself. Memories of his time with the *Dyn Doethas*, of the atrocities that he had committed, tended to infiltrate his mind when surrounded by the dark.

"Lieutenant, you say we be… we are marching to battle tomorrow," said Derek, shattering the thick silence with his lisp. "What… What is battle like?"

Hafgan had no intentions for Derek—for any of them—to see battle come morning, but he might as well be honest. Some would balk at the suggestion of desertion, so filling the men's empty stomachs with a hefty serving of fear might quell such hesitation.

"I have never experienced something on this scale, with thousands fighting thousands. But I have been in battles with dozens, if not hundreds." That was a small lie. *Battle*, not *battles*. "It is a convergence of impossibilities. Men who should live, die, and men who should die, live. Luck and fortune serve as well as skill, though if you have neither, you are a dead man. A stray spear, deflected off a friendly shield, could skewer your organs. A spent arrow could catch you in the eye when you happen to look up. Or, you could stumble backwards and drain your skull on a rock. I could tell you that, by remembering your training, you will

survive. But, I do not want to lie to you. Many of you will die
tomorrow—"

"Many of you will die *tonight*," a voice interrupted Hafgan,
speaking Wasmer. Hafgan twisted to his feet along with the rest
of the budredda, and all reached for their spears. Hafgan had
insisted that they keep their weapons within arm's length at all
times.

Hafgan's eyes adjusted quickly to the darkness ringing the fire,
and the shapes came into focus. Wasmer, armed.

Siarl stepped into the light, his gray hair tied in a topknot,
facial hair in traditional Wasmer warbraids. He held his own spear
loosely in his wrapped hand, the long, twisted cloth the only
provision for his injured wrist. Several men flanked him—two
with swords—and there were other figures coming just-visible in
the immediate darkness. Hafgan heard the crack of a stick behind
him, the rustle of the underbrush to his left. The budredda were
outnumbered and surrounded.

Hafgan had let the traditionalists sneak up on them.

"It has come to this then, Siarl?" Hafgan asked in traders'
tongue. "You dare to commit treason? You risk execution at the
hands of the Rostanians." His men were forming a circle as he
spoke. He needed to buy some time so they could set up some
semblance of a perimeter. They had drilled for this.

"Bah. The Rostanians? We are done with the Rostanians. They
want us out of the way or dead. Tomorrow, attacking the flank
with five hundred? A suicide mission," Siarl said.

"That, at least, we can agree upon. If you are leaving then,
there is no reason for bloodshed here. Let us go our separate
ways." Hafgan had little hope for it, however. These men had
blood on their minds. It was evident in the way they held their
weapons; Siarl had vengeance embedded in the minds of his men.

504

His empty stomach—like his budredda, he'd never even gotten a bite of the pig—was turning in knots. He began taking the deep breaths necessary to attain his *heddwichen.*

"No, budredda. We refuse to follow you, and we refuse to allow you budredda trash to continue besmirching the name of the Wasmer. Rostanian whipping boys is all you are. Human fuckers. We are true Wasmer, and I will not… We will not stand for you budredda play acting as human soldiers. Rather, it is better that you be put down," Siarl snarled maliciously, baring his dual canines.

"You say 'we, but I see only a portion of the traditionalists. It seems that your decisions, your hatred, might not be shared by all. It is a weak Wasmer who would rather attack under the cover of darkness than issue a formal challenge," Hafgan said in a monotone. His own men had formed a circular perimeter and seemed ready for battle. Even so, they were obviously outmanned and probably terrified. Hafgan thought he smelled urine. In his *hedwicchen*, these thoughts and sensations were disconnected from his actions. He was already planning out fifteen possible next steps, depending on Siarl's strategy.

Siarl pointed at Hafgan with his spear. "A bedrudda is not a Wasmer, and therefore cannot be challenged. I should have not allowed that farce back in Rostane."

"You thought to embarrass me, back then. Now that you know that I am your better, you resort to treachery," said Hafgan. Siarl did not react, but Hafgan noticed that a couple of his men flinch at the remark. "Fight me, and leave these men out of this." Little chance of that, but Hafgan had to try.

"No." Siarl shook his head grimly. "You are not Wasmer and neither are your dogs. Enough talk—men, forward!"

The attacking Wasmer rushed at the ring of budredda. Hafgan braced himself for Siarl's rush, but the gray warrior held back while his men surged forward. Two Wasmer came at Hafgan simultaneously, both tall and broad, wielding sword and spear— likely the best traditionalist warriors that Siarl had to offer, given the honor of fighting the best of the bedrudda.

They lasted less than a minute.

When outnumbered and lacking a defensible position, one must attack. Hafgan left the circle of budredda, thrusting at the face of the attacker on this left. Evidently, the men had expected Hafgan to hang back and defend his position; he caught the first attacker directly in the eye. With a gurgle and a spray of blood and brains, the big man was pulled forward as Hafgan retracted his spear, his blade only briefly stuck in the eye socket.

The second Wasmer warrior swung a great bastard sword at Hafgan's gut as Hafgan recoiled from his first attack. He dropped to his stomach, the sword sweeping just over his head. In his *hedwicchen*, he recognized that it had been a close call, but that knowledge did not cause him any hesitation. Instead, Hafgan rolled to one side, ending up behind the soldier as he overswung and stumbled forward. The man had likely expected to cut Hafgan completely in half with the blow. As he propelled himself to his feet, though, Hafgan thrust his spear right through the man's lower back, into the gap between the bottom of his leather cuirass and his belt. The spear tore through the soldier, exiting out of his stomach.

If his *hedwicchen* had allowed him to grieve, Hafgan would have done so. These men were victims of their traditionalist beliefs, beaten into them at birth and further reinforced by Siarl. They didn't deserve an ignoble death at the tip of his spear.

Hafgan took a fraction of a second to survey the battlefield from his *hedwicchen*. Siarl's remaining cronies stared, mouths agape, at Hafgan and the bodies of the soldiers, while Siarl simply watched with folded arms. Hafgan had a moment before they gained the courage to attack him. Behind him, his men were standing firm against the onslaught, thrusting their spears to keep the enemy at bay and working in pairs to wear them down. Though their camp had not been chosen for defensibility—who would have predicted an attack like this?—the positioning of the trees prevented a full-on rush from the Wasmer traitors. So, skill would play more of a role than luck.

Several howls split the air as they fought, overlaying the sounds of battle in an orchestra of rage, pain, and passion.

Hafgan stepped back into the ring of his budredda. Immediately next to him, Derek was fighting a losing battle against a smaller, faster man who spun his spear with great skill. Derek was already bleeding from a severe gash on his forehead, the streaming blood obscuring his vision. Hafgan cracked the attacking soldier in the back of his head, sending the man flying forward into Derek's waiting spear.

"Thanks, Lieutenant. I *be* needing your help on that one," Derek said as he grinned, his teeth white islands in a sea of red as the blood from his head flowed down to his mouth. The smile remained for another second, as an arrow materialized in his neck. He went down without a whimper.

Hafgan began to twirl his spear with ferocious speed while he surveyed the field for the archer. There were only a few in the entire Wasmer unit. If there were more than one engaged in this attack, the budredda would be doomed regardless.

Crack! An arrow was deflected by his spear. Hafgan pinpointed the archer; he was just outside the ring of light, about twenty yards to the left of Siarl.

As the humans would have said, a*ss-fucking Ultner*. He would have to expose himself on all sides to disrupt the archer. But, if he didn't, his men would be dead, brought down one at a time from a distance as easy targets silhouetted against the firelight.

His *hedwicchen,* however, did not permit these fearful thoughts to dictate his actions or control his mind.

He stopped twirling his weapon and dashed forward. There were surprised shouts as he barreled one attacker over with his shoulder and then skidded under a hasty swing thrown by another.

The archer already had an arrow notched. He simply needed to draw back and shoot. If he had any acuity as a marksman, it would be difficult to miss a charging, six-and-a-half-foot tall Wasmer warrior.

But, having seen Hafgan easily dispatch two huge warriors a short time ago, the archer lost his nerve. He threw his bow in Hafgan's path and began to run. It was an easy thing to slice through the man's hamstring and then impale his fallen body.

Then, Hafgan was on the ground, falling to his knees. Blinding pain in his left hip, only partially masked by his *hedwicchen.* He spared a quick look.

No arrow, but one must have been deflected by his hip bone, as a small amount of blood was soaking through his breeches. Perhaps a bone was chipped in there; he couldn't be certain right now. And there was no time for an examination, as he heard footsteps rushing toward his position.

Four Wasmer began to spread out around him as Hafgan twisted to his feet, trying to mask the pain like an injured predator.

Siarl, grim and fierce, buried the point of his spear into the ground.

"Your budredda are dying. I will call off the attack and let them go in peace if you surrender yourself to us," Siarl said, the melodic Wasmer language a stark contrast against the violence in these woods.

The pain was great, and Hafgan was having trouble maintaining his *hedwicchen*. "Last I checked, the bodies of your traitors formed a barrier around my budredda. My brothers—the dogs, as you called them—will never give up the fight. While you be fighting for hate, we be fighting for brotherhood." His monotone was breaking, as was his grammar. This had to be quick.

"Fine, then. No blunted weapons this time, you budredda sc—"

Hafgan jabbed to his right without looking, his spear only stopping when it hit the spine of the soldier trying to sneak up on him. Blood sprayed out of his severed neck like the great fountain in Rostane's Periway Square. Hafgan hurtled over the falling body, grimacing as he landed on his injured leg.

Three left. More howls filled the air from the direction of the compound, louder than before. Perhaps riled up from the sounds of battle?

An arrow hit a tree to his left, nearly ricocheting into Siarl.

"Stop shooting, fool!" roared Siarl, stumbling away from the projectile.

One less problem, at least.

Hafgan tried rushing one of the warriors as they tried to flank him, but the man was ready, deflecting his attack. Siarl thrust at Hafgan then, but he managed to knock the spear aside with his hand, holding the spear with his other. The third man broke through his guard, his spear tip leaving a deep cut in Hafgan's left side, just above the bleeding hip. The separate pains blended together in an agonizing fusion.

In the next pass, Hafgan managed to position a tree between him and the left-most warrior, and this time, he lunged at Siarl. Siarl easily batted his thrust aside, but it had been a feint. Hafgan gripped onto the spear with one hand and jabbed at the warrior's face with his other. He managed to jam two fingers into Siarl's eye, felt a pop, and yanked him forward by his war braids as his arm retracted. Siarl pitched forward with a scream, and Hafgan would have impaled him if the other men hadn't coordinated their attacks. Another deep cut across his shoulder blade.

Siarl pushed himself to his feet, a great grimace on his face, one hand pressed over one of his eye sockets. In the dim light, Hafgan could see liquid running from under his hand. Maybe tears, maybe the humour of his eyeball.

"You three are in my way. Back!" Siarl growled, gripping his spear, his eye clenched shut and pulling his face into a dangerous snarl. His cronies backed off and Siarl rushed forward with a great warcry.

Rage had finally overtaken the lithe, gray warrior. Rather than lose himself, however, he struck with a deadly strength. Hafgan, his own strength flagging from blood loss and his injured leg less and less able to bear his weight, could barely keep the former war leader from landing a blow. He blocked two-handed now, less able to dodge with his wounds. Siarl smashed Hafgan's fingers against his spear, and Hafgan heard a sharp snap as a bone shatterd. He managed to retain his grip through the pain, though just barely.

His *hedwicchen* was failing him. The number of injuries were forcing him from the center.

More shapes became visible nearby, vague even in his Wasmer vision. More enemies? His budredda? Had the Rostanians finally bothered to investigate the sounds of battle? Not much help there, as they'd likely start killing indiscriminately.

He managed another block and a weak riposte. Just as he swung his spear at Siarl's legs, he was jostled from behind and stumbled. He began struggling to his feet, awaiting a blow from Siarl. But, the gray warrior's gaze was fixed at a spot behind

Hafgan, his one remaining eye wide with confusion. Hafgan had started to turn his head when he was driven forward into the dirt again, a heavy weight bearing him to the rough ground and further tearing open his lacerated back.

His spear was lost somewhere in the darkness.

Hedwicchen broken, desperation and training fueled his body to react. Hafgan thrust backward, sharply, with one elbow, allowing the momentum to carry him around. The elbow contacted with something hard, and he spun unevenly to his feet, breathing heavily. His assailant stumbled backward only briefly, though, and then lunged forward with a cry that cut through Hafgan's pain and made him shiver to his core with fear.

The sound was pure malice.

Training alone kept Hafgan fighting. The white-bodied attacker threw himself at Hafgan, but Hafgan managed to grab an arm and twist as the form hurdled by him. The sound of a bone breaking was cut off by another great scream—pain, rage, and hate filling the air like a noxious, sinister fog.

The creature spun around and surveyed Hafgan for a moment, finally giving Hafgan a good look at his assailant.

He—it—was humanoid without a doubt, but pale of skin, and its eyes were nearly completely white. It was thin, thinner than Hafgan would have thought from the force that had slammed him to the ground, but lithe with muscles and sinew. Its mouth was wide open now, and it was baring its teeth like a wolf intent on its prey. Despite the arm that dangled awkwardly at its side, the creature seemed unaffected by the pain. Its bare, hairless chest was smeared with Hafgan's own blood, a grisly warpaint.

A quick glance at Siarl saw him on the ground, struggling mightily against two of these creatures. A third lay bleeding from a ghastly stomach wound nearby, but it was crawling toward the melee.

Hafgan's own opponent suddenly sprinted forward, moving far more quickly than Hafgan would have expected. The thing swung its broken arm like a club, catching Hafgan in the side of the head. It bore him to the ground, smacking his temple against a root. Hafgan strained against it, his wrist across the thing's neck as it gnashed its teeth at him, spittle splattering all over Hafgan's face.

His strength was fading, blood soaking the already damp dirt behind him. And his leg was stiffening; every time his attacker knocked a knee against it, he saw colorful stars burst in his vision.

The thing snapped at his neck, and he could feel its breath on his skin, its teeth brushing the stubble of his facial hair.

And suddenly, abruptly, Hafgan was straining against nothing. Looking up, he could see the stars, and a sliver of the blue Glasas, staring down at him from a gap in the trees. A black shape covered the scant light of the sky, and Hafgan braced himself for another attack as the figure stretched for him.

Paston reached down and took Hafgan's wrist, pulling him to his feet.

"Lieutenant. You look like Pandemonium," Paston said, coughing and wiping blood off of his own face. Next to him was Enric, his hairless head wreathed in drying blood, and Osian, whose small figure appeared surprisingly clean and whole. Several more of his budredda were nearby, and two were still driving their spears into the thing that had attacked Hafgan.

There were a handful of Wasmer standing side-by-side with his budredda. All stood at the ready, gazing into the frightening night that was full of the sounds of fighting, screaming, and dying. They stood in the eye of the storm.

"You do not look so good, yourself, Paston. None of you do. Report."

"The battle against Siarl's traditionalists be raging—"

"*Was* raging," corrected Hafgan, absentmindedly. He was searching the ground for his spear.

"*Was* raging. We budredda held our own, Lieutenant. Several of our brothers be... were down early, but we held and gave it back worse. You stopped the archers for us, charging at the enemy, giving hope." As always, Paston's eyes held only awe. "Without warning, a wave of these creatures swarmed our battlefield. There must have been dozens, if not hundreds, judging how it be soun... how it sounded. Some had weapons, some came at us with only their hands"

"How many budredda are left?" asked Hafgan. He found his spear and leaned against it like it was a crutch. Enric, unbidden, cut through Hafgan's shirt and began wrapping him tightly in long cloth bandages, quenching the flow of blood from the wounds covering his torso.

"The pale ones only stopped to fight us where we be in their path, like we be just an obstacle. Otherwise, we would all be gone. The traditionalists who were fighting us turned to meet the new threat, as well. Otherwise, again, we would all be gone," repeated Paston, looking away.

"How many?"

"We are twelve, at least that we've found. We can thank Enric for our survival—the bastard be... was wild." Enric said nothing, hanging his head. Nearly two-thirds of his brothers were gone.

"Eight of the traditionalists still fight with us. And we have some wounded," Paston continued, gesturing around.

One of the traditionalists knelt over the body of Siarl. The gray warrior lay dead, his throat ripped out by the teeth of one of the

513

creatures. A rough iron dagger also protruded from his side, and there were numerous other wounds. Any could have been the deathblow. Three of the creatures were dead nearby.

One of the budredda—Edwine—spat on the body of Siarl, and the grieving traditionalist jumped to his feet, bristling. Hafgan limped forward and slapped his own man down, though without much force. He gestured hotly to Siarl.

"This man was a true warrior, a great fighter. He is what the Wasmer made him, and cannot be blamed for his prejudice. I understand you are grieving, but he shall be afforded respect."

"Yes, Lieutenant," Edwine said, his back stooped in shame. Hafgan checked a sigh and placed his hand on the man's shoulder.

"We must always afford our enemies respect, though it be… is a hard lesson to learn. I have made the same mistake." Hafgan made a point to meet the man's wet eyes.

The sounds of fighting and howling grew dimmer, the terrifying enemy now a pale, deadly river rushing to the northwest. The Rostanian camp, judging from the direction of the sounds, must have been overrun. More souls claimed by the night. Something about these creatures tickled Hafgan's memory, but his head was too foggy from being knocked around, not to mention all of the blood loss.

There was a grunt of pain nearby then, and the Wasmer turned to the sound in unison, weapons ready. A large shape, limping and holding its arm across its ribs, drew into focus, illuminated enough by the moons to be visible to Hafgan.

"Captain Yanso?" Hafgan asked incredulously.

"Wasmer," Yanso said, speaking the word like a curse, pain evident in his eyes. The captain was bleeding from a dozen minor wounds, some of them obviously bite marks. His steel breastplate—the only piece of armor he wore—was newly embellished with a huge dent. That bit of metal had probably saved his life.

"Enric, tend to the captain. I will be fine." Hafgan didn't feel fine. He kept his feet, but only because his men, and the other Wasmer, were watching. The power of social pressure could not be underestimated. Pandemonium, it could keep the nearly-dead standing.

Yanso was silent, but let the Wasmer tend to him. The captain saw no difference between the budredda and the traditionalists— all were trash to him. He must have been in true pain to allow a member of a race he despised to give him assistance, especially when that assistance required touching his person.

"Captain, what happened tonight?" Hafgan asked, limping over to the captain as he reclined against the tree, being wrapped in bandages.

"Ha. Why should I tell you?" His weak laugh lacked any enthusiasm.

"Because your men are dead. You'd rather we left you in the woods? The smell of blood, and all these bodies, would draw wolves before long. Wolves at the very least," said Hafgan, stiffly crouching next to the man.

"The fucking *pasnes alna* lost control of these things. Fucking Fitra, sending me out here. Goddamn weasel-faced dick sucker. Ultner-fucking shitbag," Yanso growled, hands forming fists.

"*Pasnes alna?*" Hafgan's stomach felt like a stone dropped in a well. The memory that had recently been so foggy was beginning to materialize.

"Yes, fucking *pasnes alnes*. Magic users, you ignorant shit. They kept these things underground and used their powers to compel them forward after I delivered orders, toward the Army of Brockmore. But, they pushed too hard or didn't care that we were

515

in the way. As soon as Alexan, Pinetoe, and me left the compound, *they* came rushing out, flowing over the walls and busting through the gate. That screaming…" The big man was breathing heavily. "Alexan tried to run and was borne down in an instant. There was nothing recognizable about his body afterwards. Pinetoe turned to fight, the fuck-eyed fool. I pressed against the wall and most of the creatures streamed over me. A few, though, noticed me—" he stopped speaking and gestured to his wounds.

Hafgan had stopped listening toward the end. The bigoted captain's words had fully cleared his head.

During his time with the *Dyn Doethas*, he had studied the histories. It had been the part of his training where he'd easily excelled and could avoid beatings more often than not. That was, until he'd delved too deeply, into the forbidden libraries reserved only for the sworn *Dyn Doethas*, never meant for the *Haearn Doethas*. His opinion—that his masters should have been impressed with his initiative and his ability to sneak through guarded, locked doors—had only been greeted by a severe, bloody thrashing, and confinement to the *Pwoll,* a deep hole the size of a closet, with no room to even turn, for a week. Some did not survive their time in the *Pwoll.*

Before being caught amidst the great stone shelves, Hafgan had found a great, hide-bound book sitting on a pedestal, its old, nearly rotten pages crumbling to dust unless he used the lightest of touches. He couldn't resist looking, though. He'd lusted for knowledge like the poor lusted for wealth. How stupid he'd been, back then.

It was a book of deep histories. Forbidden histories that contradicted every Wasmer convention. Arwinyadd Anerin had been killed by the *Dyn Doethas* for his hubris, not by that human expedition. The first war with the Ardians—back when the country had consisted of loosely-banded tribes and groups of settlers who called the region Ardialos—had not been a result of food and resource depletion in the Wasmer towns. No, these resources had instead been hidden to instigate a justified war against the human frontier. And, as he had suspected even back then, most of the holy dictates and divine messages from the pantheon of gods, directing and guiding the Wasmer over the years, had simply been manipulations by the *Dyn Doethas*. That revelation, written in the words of *Carreg Da* founders and those who'd come after them, had crushed his already-wavering faith in the goodness of their gods.

Even deeper histories discussed Wasmer wars with an entirely different group of humans, before the Ardians and the Ardiolos. A much younger Hafgan had only been able to skim the faded, peeling writing, trying to absorb as much as possible before he was caught. But this war, it involved an incalculable number of human *pasnes alna* who devastated the land around the Tulanques, while the *sibrowd gwintan*—Wasmer Wind Whisperers, ancient practitioners of since forgotten magics—sought to protect the mountains.

The purpose of this battle had been obscured, but Hafgan now recalled a reference to endless armies of creatures like these, pale and wild men driven only by the basest of emotions—rage, passion, and hatred—and controlled by *pasnes alna*. Some were said to go into battle unarmed and completely naked, arousal evident on their bodies. Others, those who still had some control, would be equipped with light armor and light weapons. All would fight with a strength, speed, and fury that belied their size and armament. There were references to these creatures tearing out throats, as they had Siarl's, and battling far beyond injuries that would have sent a normal man, howling in pain, to the ground.

The book had called these creatures the *gwagen*.

The empty.

The soulless.

In the margins of the book near this selection, a newer pen had scrawled a note, and Hafgan still remembered every word, it having been burned into his memory like a brand in the flesh of a hog.

When the gwagen come again, the gods shall be reborn, and the world shall be made anew through darkness.

A prophetic message. There'd been something of magic about those words. Though he'd never been superstitious, and had little faith—particularly given his insight into the de facto ruling class of the Wasmer—these words had turned Hafgan's blood to ice, his mind to jelly. Though he'd never quite been able to explain why, he believed, with his whole being, what had been written there in that margin.

And after seeing these *gwagen*—for that is what they must be, he thought—and feeling the crippling terror of their calls even through his *hedwicchen*, witnessing their fury and strength and their unwillingness to bow to pain… this vague prophecy flared to light within his mind once more, filling him with the forgotten fear from his youth.

Hafgan pulled away from a sullen, now silent Yanso, and limped over to the creature that had attacked him, kneeling by it painfully. He rolled the body to its back, examining the face. The broad jaw, the downy hair on its face. He pulled back the creature's lips, revealing the dual dog teeht that he recalled being bared at him during the fight. The dual canines of a Wasmer.

He rose with difficulty, Enrir and Paston rushing over to help him.

"Paston, gather the men. It seems that the danger has passed for us, this night, but others may still be out there. We will gather what survivors we can—budredda, traditionalist, or human. Tomorrow, we bury the bodies and begin our march."

"March, Lieutenant? Surely you don't still be meaning to attack the flank! We are devastated," said Paston, panic rising on his face.

"I suspect there will not be a flank, come morning. No, we march to Hackeneth, the seat of the *Carreg Da*," Hafgan said with a deep sigh, feeling the weight of the mountains settle on his shoulders.

"With respect, sir, why the fuck would we be doing that?" asked Enric, still scratching dried blood from his scalp.

"To warn them."

The *gwagen*, it seemed, had returned. And Hafgan would do whatever he could to prevent an encroaching darkness, even if it meant returning to Hackeneth. Even if it meant returning home.

Chapter 37

"If we're going to die, we might as well be a little drunk. Here, it'll take the edge off."

Tilner Pick slapped the flask away from Fenrir, sending the silver container whirling into the trees, sloshing flecks of liquid onto several men along the way.

"Hey, that was good stuff!" said Fenrir with mock anger. It had been nearly empty, or he might have actually been upset.

"You'd best focus on the task at hand. I do not even know why Escamilla would send you, you goddess bastard," said Tilner through clenched teeth.

Fenrir, Tilner, and their one hundred and forty soldiers—the elite of Ferl's Company and the Army of Brockmore—stood in a dark clearing a mile west of Ingram, a small town north of Florens that was currently occupied by the little duke and his guard, at least according to Tilner's intelligence. Always a questionable thing.

"I do," said Fenrir, pulling another flask from his belt and taking a long pull, savoring the burn of Ultner's Piss, a strong Hunesian whiskey. Always good to carry a back-up, particularly during wartime.

"Why, pray tell? Is it because you are a heroic, noble warrior, a god among men? Coldbreaker, a man who spreads love and wisdom everywhere he goes?" Sarcasm dripped from Pick's mouth.

"No, it's because I'm expendable." Fenrir liked Escamilla. He really did. But, he was also realistic. Everyone in this army was a tool to that woman, from him—a hired hand that she wasn't even paying—on to that adolescent messenger she'd taken to bed. You could trust Escamilla, sure. Could trust her to look out for herself.

By Ultner, she was fighting this war to protect herself from her little shadow assassin.

"You would imply that I am expendable, too? No. I am here to ensure the mission will succeed. You are as likely to desert as anything," said Tilner.

Truth be told, Fenrir had thought about running more than once. He should have lost Tilner in Hunesa, before contracting Ferl's Company. Or feigned receiving a message from Tennyson, saying he'd been recalled. Or just stolen a horse and ridden east as fast as possible. Surely, Escamilla couldn't have spared anyone to find one bastard of a man. And, surely, he could have found *somewhere* that was out of Tennyson's reach.

But, instead, he found himself here, again ready to risk—and probably lose—his life because someone had told him to do it. Was he so accustomed to taking orders that he'd die because someone had pointed him at a cliff and told him to walk? Ultner's shriveled balls, Tennyson was right in calling Fenrir a dog.

"No, you are here because Escamilla doesn't love you," Fenrir answered the other man. And from the corner of his eye, Fenrir could see that the barb had hit home, as Tilner's jaw clenched in the light of the waxing moons. "Can't you see it? It's obvious to the rest of the world. You watch her constantly, seek to touch her whenever possible, to protect her when she doesn't need it. Why do you think she sends you away whenever she can? You are a shadow she doesn't want. Her tastes run much... younger."

With a strangled grunt, Tilner spun and stomped off. Fenrir smiled, grimly self-satisfied. He'd spent little time with Tilner since the drunken fool had proclaimed his weakness in front of Ferl and Christoph in Overton. Tilner, as ever, had been at Escamilla's side while Fenrir had spent most of this time with the mercenaries. Ferl and Christoph never spoke of that night, never discussing Fenrir's alleged fainting spell. But Fenrir could swear laughter played in their eyes when they spoke to him, and that

Ferl, particularly, occasionally smirked when the group would meet.

Now, certainly, he had hurt Tilner right back. The twisting pain in the man's usually stoic face had been evidence enough of it. In fact, was it hatred that had burned in Tilner's eyes?

Fenrir made a note to keep an eye on Tilner in the upcoming battle. Falling on a "friendly" sword was the last thing that he needed.

He could just add Escamilla's retainer to his pile of problems. His aching knee. The fact that his supposedly-dead brother was trying to have him killed. His ex-lover giving him orders, and him still wishing, if he were honest with himself, that he could bed her. Oh, and there was the fact that he'd probably be dead in an hour or two.

From a breathless messenger, they'd learned that the Battle of Florens had been a surprising success, despite a few hiccups. As a result, their mission was even more critical. The last coded missive had been closed with the phrase, "At least, incapacitate as many high-ranking officers as possible." "Before they kill you" had been implied.

"Captain," said a man as he came sprinting out of the night. He must have passed their pickets without notice, Fenrir thought; if they weren't doomed all doomed, he'd recommend the lash for those men.

"Payton. Report."

"It's Denrick, sir." Oops. He'd never been good at names, but commanding officers never were. Perhaps he'd been born to lead, after all.

"Your name doesn't change the order. Report."

"Where is Sir Pick?"

522

"Away. Now, report." Denrick pursed his lips, but proceeded with the report.

"Ingram is relatively quiet, sir. Most of the duke's guard—several hundred men—is camping a half mile outside of the town and not on high alert. They don't appear to expect an attack."

"Penton?" Fenrir asked.

"He is most likely holed up in the inn. The Graceful Arms. It's really the only inn in the town, and it's certainly the nicest and biggest building. The place is ringed in steel, though, front, sides, and back. Wolf Knights have the place surrounded."

"The balls don't stray far from their cock. What?" he asked, seeing that Denrick was giving him a look. "It's an old saying. Now, listen, what else is in the town?"

"Not much, sir. The town mostly caters to travelers heading to Florens who are unwilling to travel the last few miles late in the day. There's a stable, a whiskey distillery, a couple of bakeries, a few dirty boarding houses, a general store, and an herbalist. Maybe I saw a clothing store, too. A bunch of tightly-packed houses, of course."

So, a few hundred men within a ten minute march, and an inn ringed by elite soldiers. Not to mention that Fenrir had to figure out a way to get into that inn to kill the most powerful man in the country—and hopefully find a way to get the Pandemonium back out.

Denrick had a small frown on his face, and he was fingering his sword hilt absentmindedly, as if thinking the same thing as Fenrir. The inevitability of his death in a few hours and all that.

"Denrick, you are from Rostane, no?" asked Fenrir abruptly, noting the man's inflections. Even within Ardia, dialects changed from duchy to duchy.

"The duchy, yes. The city, no." Denrick shifted his weight.

"Why do you fight for Escamilla? Against your countrymen?" he asked next, legitimately curious.

"I… she pays well, and would take care of my family. Five years' wages are promised to my wife, to be paid in the case of my death." Ah, the death contract. His wife would be rich, would have plenty of money to use in seducing other men. Fenrir didn't have the heart to tell the man, or to remind him that, if he died and Escamilla lost the war, his wife wouldn't get shit.

"Very good. Well, go gather the sergeants and find Pick. I have a plan…"

Certainly, setting fire to the distillery had *seemed* like an excellent idea at the time. But, admittedly, Fenrir had been, and still was, relatively drunk. The biggest surprise was that no one had really contradicted his plan. Not even Tilner.

It was far enough from the center of the town that the act would not likely be perceived as an attack. Distillery fires were known to occur with some frequency, which was why distilleries were so often in small towns like this. It would be a nice, bright blaze to draw the eye of any defenders, to distract the townsfolk as his forces attempted to infiltrate the inn, kill the duke, and run back out into the night.

That was, until the first explosion shook the town to its very roots. And then the fire spread to several nearby houses in a heartbeat.

The town was fully illuminated now, glowing as brightly as a vault full of gleaming yets, and there was no hiding in the brightness.

Well, so much for subtlety. Fenrir was as bad at strategizing as he was at stealth.

"Charge! To the inn!" His twenty-five and Tilner's twenty-five rushed the rear of the building, a sprawling and somewhat dingy two-story structure that was guarded by several Knights of the Wolf who were decidedly *not* preoccupied by the fire. Fenrir's remaining hundred men were supposed to stage an attack on the encamped bodyguards as soon as the alarm sounded, as a distraction, and Fenrir hoped they followed that order. They'd be outnumbered at least five to one.

By the time they reached the inn, five of his men had been taken down by crank-bow bolts and a trumpeter had already sounded a shrill "distress" song, recalling the encamped forces into town. And the kitchen door was already barred, the Knights of the Wolf having retreated after expending their shots.

Godsdamned distillery. And still, the fire continued to spread throughout the wooden town like a contagious disease.

"Windows!" Fenrir commanded. "And get that wood and break down this door." Four men grabbed an uncut log from a nearby wood pile, and three returned with it, one caught by a bolt shot from the second level as he moved.

Two of his men broke through the glassed windows, and then one was stabbed while trying to crawl in. He reeled back, vomiting blood before he lay, twitching, on the ground.

Fenrir didn't want to die. The reality of this battle—the barricaded inn, hundreds likely converging on his location—made the outcome seem inevitable. He needed to focus, though; he needed to survive.

In a fizzing wash of color, Fenrir was looking down at himself amidst the chaos, his eyes squinting in the brightness of the fire as it continued to spread throughout the town. Phantom-Fenrir thought his body looked tired, but Body-Fenrir no longer appeared frightened. He shouted out orders, recalling the men from the windows and focusing on the doors. At the very least, Body-Fenrir appeared to be radiating the cool competence of an officer.

The men broke through then, and Phantom-Fenrir was inside the kitchen, watching the battle develop. His men—mercenaries and Escamilla's best troops—stumbled over the discarded log, and Phantom-Fenrir saw the first two being cut down. The next two, however, managed to get a foothold, forcing back the sword-wielding Knights of the Wolf with their spears. The kitchen was no place to swing a sword, though, and soon those knights had fallen. Body-Fenrir and Tilner entered last, Tilner ordering two men to cover the door. Phantom-Fenrir could feel malice when Tilner glared at the back of Body-Fenrir's head, but he made no aggressive move. Phantom-Fenrir knew, dispassionately, that Tilner was too honorable to strike a man from behind, even if that man had treated him poorly. There was no question of that.

Phantom-Fenrir flitted to the common room just in time to witness a massive cluster of shit. His men had a foothold here also, but were fighting off twice as many men. Chairs and benches were on the ground, and roasted garlic pheasant stew was splattered all over the room, mixing with the blood of the fallen. An odd detail to notice, the flavoring of the stew, but Phantom-Fenrir simply knew.

There was also the strong… *feel*… of liquor in the air. The Knights of the Wolf had been imbibing heavily, probably choking down the swill from the very combustible distillery nearby. Bad form, for a bodyguard. Few were armored, but nearly all held weapons. Better equipped knights with crank bows were trying to enter through the front door, but were having trouble joining the melee through the throng.

The little duke was nowhere to be seen, nor were any of the high-ranking officers. Had Fenrir been one of these officers, he would have either fled or barricaded himself upstairs. The path upstairs was open, too, the stairway nestled next to the free-swinging kitchen doors. Body-Fenrir waved forward two soldiers and Tilner Pick, and led the way up himself, leaping over the body of a bleeding, gasping Rostanian soldier as he went.

Only one enemy soldier barred the upper landing, resplendent in his gold and green Knight of the Wolf's garb, short sword raised in front of him defensively.

"Fenrir?" the man asked incredulously, lowering his sword.

Phantom-Fenrir recognized Silas immediately, his stocky build, his wide, jovial features. Last he'd seen the man, Silas had been guarding the southern gate of Rostane, giving Fenrir a friendly warning. A good friend, Silas had always been. Phantom-Fenrir recalled the shorter man pulling military recruits off of a younger Fenrir, saving him a more severe beating.

Last they'd met, Fenrir had promised himself that he'd treat Silas to an ale in the near future.

Instead, Body-Fenrir's sword lashed out, taking Silas in the throat.

His friend's sword dropped as his hands clutched wildly at his neck, trying in vain to contain the blood that spurted forth in a thick sheet. His eyes were surprised as he met Body-Fenrir's dispassionate gaze, sliding against the wall to the ground. Body-Fenrir stepped over him without a second glance.

There were two Knights of the Wolf at the end of the wide hallway, and Body-Fenrir sent his men ahead to take care of them. One of Fenrir's soldiers, an old, one-eyed mercenary from Sestra, fell immediately, but his body pulled the sword from one knight's hand. The disarmed man was quickly slain by Pick's Brockmore solider, and Pick himself skewered the second knight as he tried to escape through the locked door behind him.

527

Phantom-Fenrir found himself on the other side of the door just as his body slammed through the wooden barrier, fragments of the door knocking one guard off of his feet and causing a second to stagger backward. That guard fell to Tilner's spinning sword, his arm mostly severed above the bicep. His men rushed in, finding themselves at the sword points of a semi-circle of eight men.

It was a large conference room, a long, oaken table bolted to the ground on the far side and surrounded by solid, ornate chairs. There were two large emerald green rugs, each with a white chevron pattern along the borders, covering the entirety of the floor.

The still-burning town was visible through a great window that spanned the length of the wall, though the Rostanians, or the remaining villagers, had formed a bucket brigade. Shadows from the great blaze danced around the room in a seeming masquerade ball of chaos.

"Gentleman, please lower your weapons," came a condescending voice from behind the wall of knights. "I would like to meet the conductors of this daring raid. After all, we are in no *true* danger, are we?"

Four of the Wolf Knights moved reluctantly aside, their armor creaking, and Phantom-Fenrir could see five men revealed in the flickering light. Savant Iolen, the High Strategist, was the speaker, wearing his characteristic dull maroon robes, hands concealed in his pockets. Fenrir would recognize that voice—and the sardonic tone—anywhere. Flanking him were Lord Faris, dark and noble, clasping his hands behind his back, and General Melwin Krast, the sixty-plus-year-old general of the Rostanian military regulars. He'd been a captain when Fenrir had been a trainee, and he'd always seemed competent and just, but far too inflexible to be a true leader.

The little duke, Samuel Penton the Third, was just rising from his plush chair. He was not wearing the muscular breastplate or cape that had typified his jaunts around the Plateau even before he'd been made duke. He seemed diminished without them, a shadow of the man he pretended to be. His young face was tired, but his eyes flashed at seeing bare metal pointed in his direction.

The duke's voice boomed across the chamber. "General, why have your men allowed this rabble into my presence?"

The final man, the one being addressed, was one whom Fenrir recognized without any conscious thought. Even Phantom-Fenrir, usually a dispassionate observer of Body-Fenrir's exploits, felt a surge of red anger at the sight of him.

Sigmund Fitra, made a general of the Rostanian forces by the money and false generosity of the man who had once called himself Fenrir's father, stepped forward.

"I apologize, your grace. But the Knights of the Wolf are not under my purview. Captain de Hosta has that honor." *Always a fucking slimy weasel.*

"There is no need to assign blame, your grace," said Lord Faris, his voice calm, as always. "As Iolen said, there is no danger here."

"Indeed, my lord. Indeed! Oh, what do we have here? I feel like I recognize this beast of a man." Body-Fenrir ignored Iolen, holding his sword at the ready. "Please, my friend, lower your weapon."

Body-Fenrir pointed the tip of his sword at Sigmund, grating out one word, his deep monotone filling the room. "Siggy."

Sigmund paled, clenching his fists. One hand was four-fingered. So, Tennyson had actually done him a favor. Phantom-Fenrir vowed to give the man a great hug, Ultner's mask or not. Though Fenrir was unlikely to survive this encounter—nor would he survive such a hug.

"Your grace, I know this man! He is the exiled son of my benefactor, Darian de Trenton! A scum who worked for The House and is now apparently in league with our greatest enemy. Calls himself Fenrir *Coldbreaker* now." Trying to curry favor, as always.

The little duke slowly approached Body-Fenrir, glancing askance at Iolen and Faris. Faris gave a quick nod, and Penton stopped a few feet away.

"I have heard of this man. You worked for my father, no?" Penton raised an eyebrow. "Perhaps, had you been better at your job, my father would still walk among us. You know, they say it was poison, just before the Ardian Council."

"They also say you were the poisoner," spat Tilner Pick, lunging forward with a great, sudden thrust. He was prepared to trade his life for the duke's.

No one moved to intervene, though, not even the duke. Instead of seeing his sword tearing through the duke's chest, Tilner froze mid-step, every one of his muscles appearing to tighten simultaneously, and he toppled to the ground like a statue, its stone base eroded by time.

His sword clattered to the ground, and Sigmund scuttled to the duke's side to retrieve it. Tilner managed a strangled, sobbing grunt.

"Silly, insubstantial man. You think to harm the future king of Ardia?" The duke tittered wanly, the farting sound a noble made when amused. "Who is this man?"

"Your grace, this is Tilner Pick, one of Escamilla's captains and advisors. Perhaps a lover. He's been seen often in her company," offered Krast.

"Oh, perfect. Assuming she survives the night, his head would be an excellent gift for our dear lady. When should we hear of our victory, by the way?" asked the duke.

"Soon, my lord. Our colleagues promise success, and we've little reason to doubt them," said Faris.

"Excellent! Now, let us tend to this lover of Lady Escamilla. Perhaps we shall send his withered jerky as a special treat for her, as well." Penton again laughed, extremely amused with himself.

"It shall be done, your grace. As soon as the fighting dies down below, and we can leave for the safety of the camp. I fear that those flames will continue to spread," said Lord Faris, glancing at the burning town outside.

"No. Do it now," ordered Penton. "We will leave this place immediately after we deal with these fools. The sight and smell of blood does not offend me, and I care little for these garish rugs."

Body-Fenrir braced himself as Sigmund, the stick of a bastard man, stepped to Pick's side and started to raise the man's discarded sword, its blade unreasonably large compared to Sigmund's gaunt frame.

Phantom-Fenrir could perceive the glee in the duke's eyes, mirrored by the obsequious malice in Sigmund's face. The remaining Brockmore soldier darted forward in a vain attempt to save his officer, but this man met the same fate as Tilner, his affected body betraying him as he tumbled to the ground. At a gesture from Faris, one of the Wolf Knights casually thrust a sword into the soldier's back. The man could neither struggle nor scream, an insect left to the mercy of a sadistic child.

Fenrir was a dead man. They all were. At the very least, he would not see a good man killed in front of him, not without putting up some sort of fight. Phantom-Fenrir *willed* his body to act.

531

For the first time, the body listened, its front leg twisting in preparation for a lunge.

Phantom-Fenrir perceived a great pressure, the feeling of a powerful wind crushing him against a wall. Of a mountain collapsing atop him. Being buried alive. His ethereal body was being compressed, and he felt an indescribable pain seeming to tear out his very essence. In the edge of his intangible consciousness, though, he could also see his body continuing its forward momentum, if slowly, as if through a swampy muck.

He had the strength to resist this! His phantom could protect the body, a shield against this strange power, allowing his body to strike.

The duke's arms were folded, a lazy smile on his face as he waited for a head to roll at his feet.

Sigmund raised the sword, again. Ready to strike down Tilner after the brief interruption. The leather-wrapped hilt was visible through the gap where his ring finger used to be, and his crooked nose was twisted in a snarl.

Sigmund, the bastard who had abused him as a kid. The bastard who had, with his brothers, shattered his knee, condemning him to a lifetime of pain. Sigmund, who'd mocked his foreign mother in audible whispers. Sigmund, who'd taken his place as his father's son.

For an idle second, through the inescapable, crushing pain, Phantom-Fenrir's thoughts flickered to that scared girl, Merigold. Blond hair in a braid, tired and alone. And then Emma, bouncing red curls surrounding him as she grinned in pleasure.

Fenrir's body lunged forward, forcing itself through the stillness as his phantom provided shelter from the strange force. His sword was driven straight through the unarmored man, an easy kill, the bar of steel suddenly protruding from his back.

Little Duke Penton fell limply to the ground as Body-Fenrir retracted his sword, and the Wolf Knights surged forward as Sigmund dodged back behind their iron fastness.

Then, in one easy motion, the knights toppled forward in the same way Pick had before them. A graceful, coordinated, metallic avalanche. The sounds of battle had faded below, and an uneasy quiet stretched out as Phantom-Fenrir tried to make sense of what had just happened. Even the fire, outside in the village, had begun to dim as a gentle rain began to fall.

All at once, his phantom was forced back into his body, and Fenrir fell to his knees, the exhaustion and pain and emotions of this battle all striking him at once. He felt heavy, sluggish, his limbs aching as if he had just run from Rostane to Draston and back.

"Very good! Very good!" called Iolen, true amusement in his voice as he stood clapping his hands lightly. "I remember him now, Faris. Where was it?"

"The Ardian Council," said Faris, his hands still clenched behind his back. He was granite, unmoved by the bloody events in this room.

"Ah, yes. The fainting guardsman. Let's hold on to this one. He may yet be of use to us." Fenrir remembered Iolen, the fucking senior Savant at the Enlightenment. His cocky, goading tone echoing through the council chamber as he'd pronounced the death sentence on Fenrir's career, not to mention his comfortable life.

"With respect, High Strategist, Lord Faris. Principal de Trenton may take offense if this murderer is brought into the city," said Sigmund, a hunch to his shoulders as if he realized that Fenrir could have easily run him through instead of the duke. Ultner's pointy cock, Fenrir *should* have targeted him.

"Enough, Fitra. The duke is dead, and certain cautions must be exercised. See to these men; they should be recovering in a few minutes," Iolen replied.

"And this Tilner Pick?" asked Krast from the back of the room.

"There is no need to dirty the carpets. Unlike his grace, I quite enjoy the pattern," said Lord Faris. "Keep him for now."

Iolen walked toward Fenrir, who barely had the energy to look up. Lord Faris joined him, black and silver hair falling over his face while he examined the kneeling man.

"Coldbreaker, was it?" asked Iolen. Fenrir tried to gather the energy to spit in his direction, but his mouth was as dry as those ruins beneath the Plateau. Instead, he merely hissed.

"Feeling faint?"

Fenrir's head began to pound, black spots filling his vision. He was sweating, soaking his cotton shirt in an instant. His legs grew weak and he slumped to the ground.

The last thing he saw was a dead, desiccated rat lying discarded in the space between Lord Faris and Savant Iolen.

Chapter 38

"Our chances particularly increase if Pick and Coldbreaker succeed in their task," said Escamilla, rubbing her face in a fashion that mirrored Emma's own exhaustion. It was well past midnight, and the command staff had not yet agreed on their tactics, on their next steps. Though, there was only one viable option.

"This is not acceptable. We would have sacrificed so much for nothing," said Erik Malless, long, lightly-greased raven hair framing his young, angry features. Like his father, Malless was a large and well-built man. Just barely more than a boy, really, thrust into an impossible position long before he'd been ready.

"Sacrifices must be made in war. I lost one hundred-and-fifty of my soldiers today. A fifth of my force," said the Silver Lady, taking a sip of her wine. She still wore her silver breastplate, though the hour was late. Her eyes were rimmed with red.

"Yes, and I lost thousands, mercenary. But I am not ready to tuck my cock and run!" shouted Malless, perfect white teeth clenched.

"We have won a major victory," repeated Escamilla for the fourth time. "But our tactics relied on being able to split their forces between a well-manned, fortified city and our own camp. They couldn't commit to one without leaving themselves open to another, particularly with the destruction of their siege equipment. We've slaughtered half of their conscripts, but not without losses of our own. Our cavalry is decimated, mostly of its own accord, and the enemy has not yet brought theirs to bear. As you said, your grace, you have lost nearly half of your forces, and there is only a token left in Florens."

"I cannot leave my city to be razed! What about your damned magicians? Can't they even the odds?" asked Malless.

"My greenies are exhausted. They turned the tide of the battle, but need at least a day of rest," said Ferl, who had his feet propped on a second chair.

"With respect, your grace, it is either Florens or Ardia. Despite the bravery of the men today, our strategy has been upended. The Rostanians will not pursue us before taking Florens, and it will take at least a few days for them to rebuild their floating armada. We can use that time to create some distance between us and them, and plan our next move," said General Opine, the hero of the day. Empton was still alive, but he was confined to the medical tents. Half of his face was paralyzed, and his heart was beating weakly. The poor man was not even forty years of age.

Emma would hate to say that Empton's near death had been a good thing, but Opine was clearly more competent, if insufferable.

"What about their cavalry? They'd not need their horse to take Florens, and we'd be cut down on the road," said Captain Braston.

"We can only *hope* they send their cavalry, further dividing their forces. With scouting and outriders, we could surely set up an ambush and massacre them. At Edwin's Gap, for instance, or Atwater. We've myriad options." Opine was confident, his handsome face unflappable.

"So, already you plan your route, boy? We have not yet agreed—" Malless began.

"Your grace, I will not consign these soldiers, and therefore the only hope of Ardia, to defeat. And that is exactly what will happen if we take the field. They are too many, and we are too few." Malless clenched his mug, fingers white and shaking, at Opine's logical words. The duke did not get on well with Opine—who was probably only a couple of years older than him—despite Opine having orchestrated the rescue of the Florensian forces. Or, perhaps *because* he had rescued them. You never knew, with men.

In the corner of the massive command tent, amidst generals and nobles and officers, there was a snorting noise. Morgyn lay in a ball atop a blanket, fast asleep—a cat bored with the affairs of the evening. Escamilla smiled at the sound, and Emma wondered whether her lady planned on adopting the girl.

Malless sighed, his eyes bloodshot and his hand still shaking as he took a sip of Sestrian red. He'd likely not slept for days and, though he'd managed to escape injury in the melee, the deaths of his men had clearly affected him deeply.

"I know, in my head, that retreat is the only option. But, my heart bleeds for my people. I have failed in my duty to protect them. My father—" he choked. The death of his father, though weeks ago, was still an open wound. He hunched over his stone cup, hanging his head as if defeated. He appeared extremely young in the lamplight, and Emma thought she saw a solitary tear fall into his drink. The other officers pointedly ignored this display of emotion, and even Escamilla was too distant to provide any sort of support.

"Your grace, if I might speak." Emma leaned forward. "I saw your father in the face of the tyrant, the little duke. He was ever brave, even at the threat of torture and death. He said that Florens would never give in to the little duke, regardless of his own fate. He died, rather than be manipulated, so that he could save your life and so that you could take his seat. He had great faith in you, that you would make the right decisions and continue fighting. I see him in you, your grace."

The young duke composed himself, straightening his back, and gave her a considering look. "Who exactly are you, girl? I fancied you a servant, albeit a well-dressed one."

"She is my protege. My ward and heiress. Lady Emma Dram-Breen," said Escamilla, a touch of pride in her voice.

537

Cocks, that was news! Escamilla did not meet Emma's searching eyes, but instead focused on Malless.

With another sigh, this one much deeper, Malless went on. "Escamilla, my men are with you. We will begin the process of withdrawing with your forces, though we will need to work out some more details…"

"My lady." One of her guards—an Apple Knight—had ducked into the tent. Emma recognized him as Havert, one of the men who'd escorted them from the Plateau to Brockmore. A good man, by her estimation.

"Havert. What is so important that you interrupt a war council?" The man paled in the lantern-light, but handed Escamilla a red envelope and bowed his head.

"My apologies, my lady! We just received word from… your friend in Rostane. His messenger was near dead on his horse, so I thought this important enough to merit your immediate attention."

"Thank you, Havert. You are dismissed." His shoulders were hunched, as if he were expecting further admonition, but when none was forthcoming, he bowed to the officers and darted out of the tent.

Escamilla's fingers were on the envelope, and she began to break the seal.

"Before we were interrupted…" said Malless, "we were going to discuss the plans to retake Florens and make reparations to its people following our success in this war. I need assurances—"

"Your grace, perhaps first we should plan our withdrawal. Moving over ten thousand men, including wounded and a baggage train…" Opine began.

"Not until we discuss—"

538

"Gentleman, please. Let's start with the withdrawal and then move to future plans. Lady Dran-Breen, please call for a scribe." Escamilla rubbed her eyes and set down the red envelope from Tennyson.

A letter of warning, which lay unopened and forgotten.

It was hours before a strategy had been decided upon for an effective withdrawal, but it was done. Come first light, the army would begin an organized retreat, the cavalry providing cover. The wagons had already started heading east.

The fate of Duke Penton was still unknown, but runners had reported an inferno in Ingram. It was probably too much to hope that the disgusting man would have been caught up in the flames.

Escamilla had fallen asleep, head in her hands, immediately after the last officer had left the room, and Emma let her sleep. Morgyn still slept in the corner, her rest occasionally interrupted with a snort, whimper, or moan. Emma figured she should try to befriend the young girl. Morgyn seemed there to stay, and she had certainly been through a lot.

All of them had.

And now, Emma was Escamilla's hieress, her successor. Taking her name—Lady Dran-Breen!—and likely her fortune upon her lady's death. Her, Emma Dran, a serving girl with a crippled hand who had never made a more important decision than what tea to provide for her mistress! And, even then she'd sometimes made mistakes! And now, was she supposed to manage dozens of businesses, and negotiations with underhanded merchants and backstabbing nobles, and cater to the needs of thousands of hirelings? Not to mention the war? Emma couldn't do it. She just couldn't.

It would have been nice if Escamilla had asked her what she wanted with her life.

Out of habit, she began clearing the command table of wine cups, dumping the dregs just outside of the tent. The familiar activity was calming, and Emma started to relax. Maybe she would grab an hour of sleep tonight, after all.

A sound, just audible in the distance, made her drop her armload of cups. Her legs were suddenly jelly, and her ears strained to catch what she heard.

"Emma? Sorry, I must have fallen asleep," said Escamilla, starting at the sound of cups clattering to the ground. "What's wrong?"

"Nothing, Camilla. I thought I heard something." There'd been nothing more—just the echo of a fearful memory.

Escamilla rose stiffly, stretching her arms. "I'm getting far too old for such a late night. You were fantastic tonight, by the way. You quelled the duke's doubts while bolstering his spirit with that story of his father. He will follow us now, though I expect him to be a pain. A young royal trying to escape the substantial shadow of his father. That's how we ended up with the little duke, though I think Malless is made of better stuff."

Emma was silent for a moment, glancing over at Morgyn. The girl was finally sleeping soundly.

"Your ward? Your heiress" Emma asked, keeping her voice carefully neutral.

"Yes, my ward. I have so much yet to teach you, but I need you to have more authority among these soldiers. This is too much for me, and I fear I can no longer keep up. Seeing Empton fall today, his heart failing him… He's much younger than me. The strain of all of this could kill me at any time."

"Don't talk like that, Camilla! You are the strongest woman I know!" Truth be told, Escamilla had been looking her age more and more.

"I think not. You are more than capable of filling my shoes, you know. You are strong, stronger than you believe, Emma. Why do you think I have been pushing you all of these years?"

"All of these years? How long have you been planning this?" Emma was stunned. She thought of the questions and quizzes, the missions and errands. The huge amount of information that Escamilla expected her to keep organized in her memory. The gentle slaps when she failed, the subtle praises when she succeeded.

"From not long after your mother died. She was my friend, you know. Friend and great ally, though she perished most ignobly." Covered in shit and reeking of pungent death. "Remember when I told Penton that, upon my death, half a dozen barristers had my will and testament, naming an heir? That wasn't a bluff. It's been you for two years."

Emma's jaw was hanging open, looking as lady-like as a panting dog. She didn't know what to say.

"Escamilla, I… I don't think—" her stammering was cut off by a great screech, a thousand voices venting rage in unison.

"What in the name of Yetra was that?" asked Escamilla, her fearful expression mirroring Emma's own.

"I've no idea!" Suddenly, the late night air was full of such shrieks, splitting eardrums and loosening bowels. Soldiers were shouting and scuffling, and terrified death cries had begun to lace the night in a rising pandemonium.

There was something grimly familiar about these howls.

"We must be under attack by… something! Emma, where are my Apple Knights? We need to wake the—" Escamilla was cut off by a retching, gurgling cough. Emma rushed toward her as Escamilla tried to say something, but instead the lady hacked flecks of blood into Emma's face.

"Camilla! What is—" Morgyn was crouching just behind Escamilla in the dim lantern light, ripping her dagger from where it had been stuck into Escamilla's upper back. Emma tried to reach around Escamilla to grab at the girl, but did so with her crippled hand, catching nothing but a bit of cloth. Morgyn kicked the back of Escamilla's knee then, collapsing the pierced woman into Emma and knocking them both to the ground.

In another moment, Morgyn had dashed off into the night, with sounds of malice, battle, and death drowning out Emma's calls for help.

She finally managed to ease Escamilla to the side just as Havert, his breastplate wet with blood, rushed into the command tent.

"My lady, we… What is happening?" he called, rushing over and helping Emma with her lady. Escamilla's mouth was rimmed with crimson, and each breath was a sputtering gasp of agony. Her eyes were filled with pain, and tears mixed with the blood.

"She needs help! She needs a physician immediately! She's been stabbed!" Emma cried to him, gesturing to Captain Braston and General Opine as they rushed in. Braston was unarmored and bleeding from a horrid wound in his neck. Opine's confidence was obviously shattered.

"What? Did you do this, girl?" shouted Braston. The bearded captain stalked toward Emma, hand on his wound, but still coming strong.

Through her agony, Escamilla struggled to sit up, grabbing Emma's arm and shaking her head. Her move halted Braston, though he still gave Emma a hard look. Escamilla wanly gestured, with a shaking arm, at the tent flap. Her meaning was clear. *What is going on out there?*

"My Lady, we are under attack. These… things… came without warning. They were nearly silent at first, rushing into camp and devastating our pickets. They had infiltrated the camp before we knew it. They got many of the men while they were sleeping! They were right outside this tent before we slaughtered them. We are still fighting and have a perimeter near here. Even near dead, these fu… these creatures continue to fight us! Our losses have already been… staggering." Opine was aghast. This wasn't the war that he had prepared for. This wasn't in the storybooks.

Escamilla tried to speak, coughed up some blood, and frantically looked to Emma, her pain-filled eyes pleading. Emma gripped Escamilla's arm tightly in return, a vice, before the older woman released her and mercifully lost consciousness.

Opine and Braston stood nearby uncertainly, neither taking steps to fend off this threat, nor to plan for the future of the army. They were both dazed, stunned, unable to act. These men, these peacetime captains set adrift in a fearsome war, needed a leader. The woman who should be filling this role was currently fighting for her life, lung pierced by the knife of a traitorous little bitch.

Emma swallowed hard, feeling her own tears building up for her lady and friend, for herself. Escamilla's expectations, and her own fears, were a rising lake threatening to drown her. The still-howling creatures were mocking her submerged body.

She was a serving girl. A cripple. An oddity. She was not meant for responsibility, not meant for leadership, certainly not in a crisis.

You are strong, stronger than you believe, Emma. Escamilla's voice rang in her ears like that of a spectre. Emma took in a deep breath and blew it out slowly, exhaling the water, her fears, her inhibitions. She spoke to the captains, surprised that her voice was firm. That it did not waver.

"We must fight off this enemy. There is no other option. Rally the men, expand the perimeter, and beat off this attack. As soon as it is safe, we make a fighting retreat. We do not wait until first light. We leave immediately."

Opine simply nodded and left the tent with her words. Braston, though, shook his head as if clearing it of a fog, meeting Emma's eyes for what felt like hours. But, she did not blink, did not look away. Then, as if he'd found something that he'd been looking for, Braston gave a firm nod.

"Yes, *my lady*."

Chapter 39

The creaking supply wagons were already heading east along the road with a guard of a few hundred exhausted men, Meri among them. That lovely Emma had offered to find Merigold a tent so that she could stay near the officers, but Meri had declined. She didn't trust Escamilla, who clearly wanted to use her for her powers, use her like those greenies from Ferl's Company. Those men... they had decimated the front lines of the Rostanians. Cut through flesh as easily as a spoon cuts through a thick stew, leaving the dead heaped up in piles and causing chaos among the terrified Rostanians.

Was that what she'd done to the men back in Hunesa?

She would not be used in that way. If she were to kill men, it would be as Yetra's hand on earth, dealing death to those who deserved it—like the monsters who'd stolen her father, destroyed her village. Not to mete out wholesale destruction to soldiers and conscripts who were just following orders from powerful, pompous men and women. People just like this Lady Escamilla, who would rather expend thousands of lives than be ruled by another. Why? To save a few yets, money that the woman could obviously afford to lose?

Merigold wanted as much distance between herself and that greedy woman as possible. It also helped that, the further she was away, the better her chances were to escape this apparent prison. Though she would be penniless and friendless, have no idea where she would go, and have no way to ever find Ragen.

At some point in this night, after seeing the horrors of the battlefield, the terrors of this magic, she'd begun to truly mourn Ragen as lost, finally accepting that he was gone. She'd cried far into the night, finally releasing all the heartache that she had been pushing down so deeply inside. She would honor him, however she could, by teaching his grandson or granddaughter everything that Ragen had taught her. She touched her stomach—was it just beginning to swell? Was she truly going to be a mother?

Meri had spent the night reminiscing about her father, with both quiet laughter and quiet tears, as well as wondering what it would be like being a mother. All this in a covered wagon amidst cooking supplies.

Which was how Merigold had found herself awake when the creatures first attacked.

The howls had begun far in the distance, and Meri had initially thought they were wolves. Starving, fierce, and feral wolves, but still just something that you might expect to hear while traveling.

But, as the sounds had grown closer, it had become clear that four-legged voracious lupines would have been far preferable.

Merigold huddled in the wagon as she heard the sounds of battle begin, the soldiers fighting whatever was making such a terrible noise. She pulled her little knife from its thong, relishing the comforting grip, thanking Fenrir silently for restoring this to her. Somehow, he'd known it was important. Merigold wished that he was nearby.

The screams and sounds of combat grew closer, and something jolted her wagon. She heard her driver—usually such a quiet man—fiercely curse Yetra's name, and suddenly the wagon was out of control. Inside, Merigold held tight to her bench as pots and pans and ladles pulled free of their straps, flying around the confined area like a bottled tornado. She was struck in the face with something heavy and lost her grip on the bench, and then Meri was tossed around the wagon as it rushed forward, banging and bruising her arms and legs as she tried to protect her stomach—her child—with one arm and her head with her other.

The wagon flipped to its side and was dragged a few extra feet before skidding to a halt, the horses finally managing to break free and run. Meri tentatively checked her body and her stomach.

Nothing seemed broken, and her belly had been spared any rough blow. But dear Yetra, did her body ache!

She tentatively crawled out of the wagon, hearing the hateful, hungry calls in the distance. And one just a few feet behind her.

Merigold pounced to her feet on wobbly legs, brandishing her little knife as a pale, wiry shape, illuminated by the waxing moons, ambled toward her, dragging its leg but still moving with a jerky speed. Fueled by fear, she swung her weapon wide, aiming for the neck, but instead caught the pale thing just under its cheekbone, slicing through the thin flesh of the cheek and embedding the weapon somewhere in the meat of the mouth.

It shrieked in pain, and Merigold's limbs grew weaker as it grabbed at her despite its new wound. It bore her to the ground, tearing at her with its teeth, but struggling due to the knife still planted in its cheek and mouth. She fought to keep its face from hers, pushing back with all her strength. Despite its injuries—a hanging arm, a twisted leg, a knife in the face—it was far stronger than she.

Merigold tried to open herself to perceiving the energy at the core of this creature. The *maenen*. She had done this before when she'd most needed to. She could do it again. She had to.

She had thought, before, that she needed to seek an emptiness, a center within herself, to find the power. But, she'd been wrong. She needed to open herself up, expand her perception, allowing herself to see beyond her senses. It was a subtle line, and one that she barely understood, yet alone mastered.

But she found it now. She reached inside the creature, searching for its *maenen*.

And there was nothing there.

The nearly decayed vessel was empty, lacking even a drop of power. It had no *maenen*, no lifeforce. It lived—the blood dripping from its face was enough to prove that—but it lacked something. A soul, maybe. Even animals had *maenen*, but this creature was bereft.

Her physical strength was waning. The creature's fingers dug deeply into her shoulder, cutting off her ability to strain with that arm. She searched one last desperate time for some strength, a bit of magic. Something to fight with. Something to save her.

And found it within herself.

She harnessed the power, feeling it burn inside of her, a new white flame. It was more than she could hold. Merigold did the only thing she knew how to do; she expelled the *maenen* into the creature.

The rotting vessel overflowed with her power, the *maenen* spilling beyond its natural boundaries, crossing the threshold between ethereal and reality. The creature—the empty man— jerked back from her before its body was strained beyond capacity.

It was torn apart, blood and flesh spraying Merigold, invading her eyes and mouth as the creature exploded. Bits of gore covered her, and she retched and vomited into the bloody grass until there was nothing left. And she continued heaving, gasping for breath, her lungs burning.

Lacking the strength to rise, Merigold crawled out of the mess, shivering with weakness. Every part of her body ached and her mind was a fog. She managed to get to a tree and leaned her back against it, closing her eyes. Blotting out the sight of the ruined wagon and the scattered remains of her attacker in the early illumination of the dawn. There were still some terrible howls sounding in the distance, but Merigold was too exhausted to be afraid. Too exhausted to run.

She sat for a few minutes, gathering strength, Her belly began to roil again and she clutched at it in pain. This was not nausea, though. Her stomach began cramping, the pain building slowly but soon becoming unbearable. It was a red hot poker in her gut, concentrated brutality, and every muscle in her body tightening in response. Meri clenched her hands and toes, unable to breathe, eyes closed so tightly that it was surprising that there were tears streaming down her face. She could not even cry out.

And then, a minute of relief. Merigold desperately sucked in air, but was cut off mid-breath as another wave of agony began, tearing through her body and leaving her shivering with pain.

These waves lasted for more than an hour until Meri lay, in the early morning light, drenched in perspiration and weaker than an infant.

She felt blood running down her leg. She reached a shaking arm to pull her skirts up slightly, grimacing as she strained to sit up enough to check.

There was a lot of blood, and something more. A small, crimson lump, a few inches in diameter, lay in a pool of red. Meri thought she could make out tiny limbs…

Merigold turned away and sobbed. The power she had found to protect herself had not been her own—she had stolen it from her unborn child.

She had stolen its life.

"That was clumsily done, back in Hunesa. Such use of raw power is a certain way to get yourself killed, and make a mess doing it. And you shouldn't have run."

Cryden had found Merigold late the next afternoon, just near sunset. The oranges of the sun tore through the clouds like the sharp fingers of a vengeful goddess.

Merigold had managed to move out of sight of the wagon and her dead child. She'd thought to bury it, but couldn't bear touching the poor little thing. Instead, she'd fled despite the pain. She'd seen the shattered remains of the army march by, not three hundred yards away, but made no move or sound. She couldn't bear anyone seeing her. Especially not Ignatius, assuming he was among the survivors.

"Aren't you going to ask how I found you?"

Meri still said nothing; she just stared at him dully.

"You left a trail. You will need to learn to be more circumspect with your *miernes*," Cryden admonished.

Still no response. Cryden was probing for an ego boost, and she was not about to deliver one. She felt too empty for it. Dear Yetra. Dear, fucking Yetra. How much could one woman bear?

"My dear lady, are you alright? I apologize; I should have asked when I saw all the blood. I am so used to examining *maenen* that sometimes I forget to really look at a body. Your *maenen* is healthy, by the way. Extremely so," Cryden said consideringly, stretching a hand to help her to her feet.

"I was with the army. We were attacked," she said in a monotone, ignoring the proferred hand, not rising from where she was propped against a tree.

"I know. I ran into the remnants. A Lady Breen, I believe, told me about the attackers. We need to be moving. We must be back to Agricorinor as soon as possible. They must have word of this atrocity." Cryden was gazing to the north, his face unreadable.

Atrocity. That word couldn't even begin to describe what Meri had been through. What the entire army had been through, having been attacked, by… by... "They were people, Cryden. The creatures that attacked."

"I know." His voice was flat, and he still gazed north.

"They were empty." She remembered searching for the *maenen,* and that horrible aching gap where it should have been.

"They know only their basest instincts, primordial emotions. Anger, hunger. Hate. Pain only fuels those remaining emotions. They were called the *gwagen* by the Wasmer, the Empty. In Sestra, they were known as *paralambrash,* the soulless. Here, they simply called them the Feral." Cryden paused, scratching at the small scar about his eye. "Someone stole their *maenen.* Near all of it, over a period of time."

The Feral. They had lost what it meant to be human. Had it ripped from them.

"Why would someone do that?" Merigold asked, scared of the answer.

"Someone wanted power. The reason for that, right now, is unknown. Which is why we must get to Agricorinor. But, *someone* wanted their *maenen*, Merigold. Someone wanted their magic."

Magic. Magic had taken so much from her.

It had killed her friends, everyone she knew.

It had taken her family.

It had made her a murderer.

It had destroyed the lives of countless souls, both the unfortunate Feral who attacked, and the men and women they killed.

And, it had taken her child from her.

Merigold began struggling to her feet, taking the offered hand when it was again stretched toward her.

"Cryden, I'm sorry. I shouldn't have run. Let's go to this Agricorinor. Let me learn how to use this power," Merigold said, her body aching, but her mind solidifying with determination.

She would need to learn how to use this magic if she was to wipe it from the earth.

Epilogue

It was cold, cold as a crypt meant to preserve decaying remains.

Ragen Hinter paced the tiny, dark perimeter—three steps forward, three steps back. Two to either side. That was all that his neck shackle would allow. He paused his pacing for a moment to lean against the wall with his arms, doing inclined push-ups to keep up his strength. He needed to stay strong and limber for the infinitesimal chance that he could escape. Escape and get back to searching for his daughter.

He needed to find sweet Merigold. That poor, innocent girl. Maybe he'd overfathered her, driving her away. He knew he'd been too protective of her. But, he didn't think she'd run off with some man, like the rumors said. He'd even broken Alan's nose when the porter had the berries to say that to his face. That display of violence had some repercussions in Dunmore, but Ragen didn't care. He loved his little flower too much to allow someone to insult her honor. Now, she was all he had left, and he didn't really even have her. Just memories.

Emmet, his brother, had died during their journey in captivity. Ragen could barely remember the day it happened. Something they'd put in the slop they called porridge had kept them all docile, packed on top of each other in covered wagons, the floor slatted so they could relieve themselves without the wagon having to stop. A trail of piss and shit that anyone could follow, but no one had. Ragen had refused to eat, at first, fearing the sedative. But, eventually, the hunger had grown too strong, and he'd eaten the lumpy porridge, feeling meek and disconnected in the aftermath.

Emmet was gone, as was Farmer Denny and Maritos, the blacksmith from Yinston. Most people from Dunmore and the Duckling were dead and left behind, ignobly tossed a couple hundred yards off the path. Anyone they'd encountered on their journey had met the same fate, either made captive or killed. Ragen had vague memories of villages being torn apart, of screams and shrieks that cut through his stupor for isolated moments.

As far as he could recall, there were a few survivors he knew. Pinst, the farrier, was there when they unloaded the wagons and marched the shuffling prisoners into these damnable caves or cells or wherever they were. Lisa, one of his barmaidens, had made it too, though she seemed sick and weak. Sandra, too, had survived. The little strawberry-blonde prostitute had been crushed up against him for most of the journey, much like those times a year ago. That had been a horrible mistake. But, he had been so lonely, and thinking of Lilth…

There were screams in the distance, echoing through this damnable place. Some human, mostly male. A few female. Maybe Sandra. Many of the screams were inhuman. The howling had at first filled him with terror, but he had since adapted. The sounds of Pandemonium were just white noise now.

"A strong one, just for me."

Ragen jumped, hands in front of him. His eyes could not penetrate the blackness, but the beautiful, melodious voice of a woman could not have been more than a few steps away.

"Who are you? What am I doing here? Why—?"

Radiant laughter, so out of place in this Pandemonium. This freezing hell.

"So many questions! But we have time, sweetling. I love when they accurately select the strong." Something touched his face, and he flinched back. "They last so much longer. We will be seeing a lot of each other."

The room began glowing with a diffuse, warm light. The Duckling's common room came briefly to mind, and Ragen had to restrain sudden tears. He could see now that two other neck shackles stuck from the rough-hewn stone walls, and Ragen knew he might have neighbors.

The speaker, however, drew his full attention. She was a gorgeous woman, waist-length silvery hair flowing down her slender body, which was itself concealed by a thin, gossamer gown that would fit in in the finest ballrooms in Rostane. Her face was perfect in every dimension—nearly symmetrical aside from a small mole at the corner of her full, rose-hued lips, silver eyebrows gently peaking over her eyes. More than her perfect body and perfect face, her eyes held his attention.

Those orbs held eternity. They had seen miracle births and gruesome deaths. Grand empires built from nothing over centuries and reduced to rubble in days. Love conquering inexplicable odds, and love hideously used and betrayed.

Yetra smiled, white teeth gleaming in the gentle light, as she grabbed Ragen's bare arm and began to tear away his soul.

Acknowledgments

I've always been the sort of reader who actually *reads* the acknowledgements section. Why? I don't know any of these people, just as you, valued reader, will not know any of the names that follow. Maybe I read this section to see what is important to an author. Maybe I read it to gain a better understanding of the sheer number of people it takes to successfully create a book. Or, maybe I just automatically read whatever words pop up in front of me. If you, valued reader, have gotten this far, you are probably in the same boat as me. Ready?

Regardless, I would love to pretend that I wrote Solace Lost, the work of art that it is, in a vacuum, bereft of outside influence, tortured genius that I am. But, in reality, I had the support of some truly amazing people. Foremost, Katherine, my first and only wife so far, bizarrely supported my decision to finally take up writing… two weeks after our daughter was born. She was also my sounding board and first editor, helping me work through some bloodlettingly sharp edges in the first draft. I also am grateful to my beta reading team, each of whom are responsible for small tweaks and major changes to the book: Bill Ready, Kristina Langhammer, Dominique White, Morgan Jones, Rita Rys, and Adam Clarke. I was also amazingly lucky to have found a great editor in Jennifer Collins who caught my many, many typos, and identified inconsistencies that a blind sea cow would have noticed, and yet somehow snuck through my own editing sessions.

On the artistic front, I stumbled upon René Aiger, who created the amazing cover art for Solace Lost, and David O'Meara, who designed the cover itself and created the map of Ardia from my penciled chicken scratch on a poster board.

And lastly, and most importantly, I thank you, valued reader, for taking a chance on a first time author. It is so humbling to know that a person I don't know decided to pick up something I wrote, whether if it was from the description or the awesome cover art. I appreciate you taking that chance, and I hope you felt it was worth it. There will be more to come.

About the Author

Mike Sliter was born in the deep wilds of Cleveland, Ohio, where he fought off at least two siblings for scraps of pizza. His bedroom, growing up, was a monument to fantasy, containing a stack of worn and well-read books, a medieval Lego civilization spanning half the room, and a very real sword circa World War II. Today, he pursues his fantastical passion by writing novels to supplement his day job as a workplace consultant.

ISBN Print: 978-0-9998021-0-6

Editing by: Jennifer Collins

Cover image by: René Aiger

Book design and map design: by David O'Meara

Published by: Dragyn Press   ·

DragynPress@gmail.com

Visit http://www.authormikesliter.com/

Made in the USA
Middletown, DE
06 April 2018